THE TRIAL

C000070363

Daniel Owen (20 October 1836-22
novelist of the 19th century.

Owen was born in Mold, Flintshire, into a working class family. His father, Robert, was a coal miner, and on 10 May 1837 he and Owen's two brothers, James and Robert, were killed in a mining accident when the Argoed mine flooded. Their deaths had a profound impact on the Owen family, who were left in poverty.

Although Owen received no formal education, he acknowledged a debt to his Sunday school teachers. At the age of twelve, he was apprenticed to a tailor, Angell Jones, who was an elder with the Calvinistic Methodist Church. Owen described his apprenticeship as a 'kind of college', and began writing poetry on the encouragement of a work colleague. Owen used the tailor shop as an opportunity to discuss and argue topics with fellow workers and customers, a theme that is evident in his writing. This style of education is also reflected in Owen's novel *Rhys Lewis*, in the experiences of the character Robyn y Sowldiwr.

A further significant influence on Owen was the Reverend Roger Edwards, a minister at Bethesda Chapel, Mold, who encouraged Owen to make full use of his talent. Owen continued to write poetry, under the '*nom-de-plume*' or '*ffugenw*' Glaslwyn, entering his work into local eisteddfodau and succeeding in publishing some of it. Owen's first significant work in Welsh was a translation of the temperance novelette, *Ten Nights in a Bar-Room and What I Saw There*, by the popular nineteenth-century American author, Timothy Shay Arthur.

Owen always retained his connection with the Methodist Church, and in 1860 began to preach. He intended to become a Methodist minister and enrolled in Bala Theological College in 1865, but after two years he returned to Mold to take care of his family and was unable to complete his studies. From 1867 to 1876, Owen worked as a tailor in Mold, preaching on Sundays.

Considered one of the greatest Welsh-language novelists, Owen is also seen as the founder of the Welsh-language novel, with his Rhys Lewis being credited as the first novel written in Welsh. Owen's work has influenced many later novelists, such as Kate Roberts and T. Rowland Hughes. His published works of fiction include *Y Dreflan* (1881), *Rhys Lewis* (1885), *Enoc Huws* (1891) and *Gwen Tomos* (1894) and a collection of short stories *Straeon y Pentan* (1895).

Sources:

David Rowe, Mold & District Civic Society
and en.wikipedia.org/wiki/Daniel_Owen

THE TRIALS OF
ENOC HUWS

By

DANIEL OWEN

Based on an original 1892 translation by
Claud Vivian

Revised and updated for the modern reader by
Les Barker

BrownCow*publishers*

WELSH CLASSICS FOR ENGLISH SPEAKING READERS
—
DANIEL OWEN SIGNATURE SERIES

BrownCow*publishers*
Belgravia House, Grosvenor Street,
Mold, Flintshire CH7 1EJ
www.browncowpublishing.com

This paperback edition 2010
1

First published by Brown Cow, 2010

© Via Strategy Limited, 2010

A catalogue record for this book
is available from the British Library

ISBN: 978 0 9567031 0 1

Printed and bound in Wales by
Y Lolfa

Nid i'r doeth a'r deallus yr ysgrifennais,
ond i'r dyn cyffredin

Not for the wise and learnéd have I written,
but for the common people.

DANIEL OWEN

CONTENTS

ACKNOWLEDGMENTS

The Publishers, Mark Turner and John Mainwaring at Brown Cow, would like to thank the following for their contribution to the production of this novel:

Eirian Conlon, from Bangor University (Tŷ Pendref, Mold), for pointing John towards Daniel Owen's literature in the first place.

Nancy Vitavec, Librarian, Solano County Library in California, U.S.A., for her initial research and helpful advice.

Lawrence Rawsthorne, Head of Libraries, Culture and Heritage, Flintshire Library and Information Service, for granting us permission to use the reference copy of the Claud Vivian translation of *Enoc Huws* held at Mold Town Library.

Nia Wyn Jones, Community Librarian, Simon Gotts, Information Librarian, and all the staff at Mold Library, Museum and Gallery, for their support and assistance.

Les Barker, for his sense of humour in joining us on this venture and for completing the enormous task of revising the text with such commitment and enthusiasm.

Adam Pearce, from Bangor University, for also joining us on this adventure and for his technical input.

Huw Powell Davies, from Bethesda Chapel, Mold, and David Rowe, from Mold & District Civic Society, and any others who helped to fill in the background detail as the text developed.

Bethany Thomas and John Caleb Mainwaring, for their help inputting the source text and preparing it for revision.

en.wikipedia.org, for the use of parts of their biography of Daniel Owen, reproduced at the front of the book.

Y Lolfa, for printing the book and for all their advice.

And finally, the Welsh Books Council, for their advice, support and help getting this work out into the public domain.

Diolch i chi i gyd.

DANIEL OWEN'S FOREWORD

It seems, no doubt, inappropriate to write a foreword to a book such as 'Enoc Huws'. Yet a Welsh book would hardly be considered complete without it, any more than would a Welsh sermon without 'firstly', 'secondly', 'thirdly' and 'finally'.

The intention is in the book; and if this isn't sufficiently clear without me expressing it, then I have failed in my attempt. I'll also be surprised if some parts of our land, particularly Flintshire, don't see what was in my mind when writing it. However, I'll leave the oral history alone.

Allow me to make one observation, as this is an excellent opportunity to do so, and I haven't, as far as I recall, seen anyone call our attention to it: during the last half century, I believe, no one who knows anything about us has said that Welsh literature has revived more than a little, and has reached a higher standard than at any previous time; it is at least broader and more plentiful. With all the monthlies, bimonthlies and quarterlies, and all the books brought out constantly by the press, not to mention our newspapers, the greatest of uncircumcised and hard-faced philistines would not say that we don't yet have a literature. We are considered, if I'm not mistaken, a generation of lively, natural feeling and of strong imagination. But remarkably, nothing special or particularly good has appeared in the real Welsh mythology recently; we have to go a long way back to find that. It's true that we have scores of false fables that have appeared in our press, but as far as I can see, with a few exceptions, they are only reflections and imitations of English novels. In other countries, such as England, France and America, the greatest men gain their learning and philosophy amongst the storytellers. But in Wales, up to now, this branch of literature has been left to low grade writers like myself. How do we account for this? There is currently, as I write this, only one reason that offers itself to my mind. Wales is, from the Methodist Revival—and we should be thankful for this—a religious country, and has been steeped in its puritanical element. Our heroine is Ann Griffiths and not George Eliot. And I can easily imagine the true old non-conformist deacon, religious and godly, with Bunyan's Pilgrim open on his knee, and the tears in his eyes as he read it, and at the same time looking—quite sincerely—at the Welsh novelist as a man who tells lies to please simpletons!

I believe that period is passing. There's more than one way to educate and entertain one another. The most effective, popular and immortal story in Wales is 'The Prodigal Son', and with good reason. Amen, and may it always be so.

The history and customs of Wales, truly the Welsh life are, to date, virgin soil; and soon, I am confident, the leaders of our generation will be seen to incorporate our characteristics and our customs into this branch of literature. Until then, let Enoc Huws and the like suffice.

DANIEL OWEN

Mold, 20 October 1891

FOREWORD TO THE TRANSLATION

Since I started on the translation, people have asked me 'Why?' And although no one has asked, I'll also answer the question 'How?' Back in May, 2010, I was on a Welsh course in Mold. One of the other students was John Mainwaring. He was doing the A level Welsh exam, and for that you need to read a novel in Welsh and discuss it during the exam. Our tutor, Eirian Conlon, suggested he read 'Enoc Huws'—"her favourite book ever." John did as he was told, for Mrs Conlon is a fearsome woman and furthermore he thought, nobody makes a claim like that unless they're confident that there's some truth in it.

He was not disappointed. He was more astonished that, having lived·most of his life in and around Owen's home town, he had little clue about Owen's life or the calibre of his writing. Having stumbled on such a culturally 'rich seam' (as the miners in this book would describe it) he decided the rest of the world should learn about Owen and enjoy his work. It was at this point he invited me to work on a translation for publication.

Though I'm not sure about his choice of translator, I'm in complete agreement with his aim. I spent the first 57 years of my life in Manchester, about an hour's drive from Wales. I've travelled the world extensively, and hopefully learned something about it. Like most inhabitants of Manchester, I'd visited Wales from time to time, and as a performer I'd occasionally worked with the few Welsh language performers who managed to penetrate the border; people like Robin Huw Bowen and, years back, Siwsann George.

But I'd not heard of Daniel Owen, Islwyn Ffowc Elis, Hedd Wyn, Parry-Williams, Williams-Parry, Hywel Dda, Llewelyn Fawr, Tryweryn ... On the other side of the Dee, you don't hear about them. And when I'm listening to Radio Cymru in the car, it's always struck me how the weather, and often the news, stops at the border. I'm involved with a festival in Mold—Tegeingl— which tries to bring the two audiences and two cultures together; and I hope this book will do something similar.

Now to explain the process. I've tried to write a translation; not an adaptation, not my own novel. If Daniel wrote it, it's here. That said, word-for-word translation isn't an option; languages don't work like that. And I've tried to make it readable for today's readership, without losing the flavour of the time or its history. Throughout the process I've been aware that I have a responsibility to the Welsh community, but that I'm writing for the English speaking reader.

In the beginning, I sat here with Daniel Owen's original Welsh language version on one computer screen, and on the other, a translation by Claud Vivian dating back to Owen's time. It's a very odd translation, but has been a very useful template. I converted it, chapter by chapter, to what I thought it should be. That was the slow part of the process. About a week later, I took a second look at what I'd written, correcting mistakes and turning the English to better English. It was then sent to Adam Pearce, who's currently doing a Ph.D. in translations of Owen's work at Prifysgol Bangor; he carried out the proofreading function, and—as one who knows the subject better than most—made the occasional suggestion.

It then came back to me and I made those changes, and passed the final version to John for printing. Then I had a lie down for a very long time.

LES BARKER

Bwlchgwyn, 10 September, 2010

AN INTRODUCTION

This story was intended to be a sort of appendix to *Rhys Lewis'* *autobiography*. When publishing that work, I took the reader into my confidence about how that work came into my hands and how I was persuaded to have it printed; whether that was an appropriate step isn't of great importance now. I had enough reasons, at the time, for adopting the course I did; reasons, I must acknowledge, not appropriate on this occasion. In publishing this story. I'm conscious I'm on a much more important adventure. With the autobiography, Rhys Lewis himself was responsible for the worthiness of the work and for the detailed facts of his short life. And had it been unacceptable to the Welsh, the only significant complaint that could be made against me would be to have shown a lack of judgement. Fortunately, as far as I know, no such complaint has been made. The work was well received by young and old, and justified my hopes that the characters and circumstances described by Rhys Lewis, according to the talents given him, were neither unacceptable nor uninteresting.

But in running this story through the press, I feel rather different. I have to stand on my own two feet, as they say. I'm putting myself in a position to be criticised for not only a lack of judgement but also of ability. I'm responsible for the facts, the style, and everything about the story I'm about to tell, and my hopes are not so high for the reception it will receive from my compatriots. We all flatter ourselves that we have an opinion; that we know what's worth printing and what isn't. We're all critics, but we're not all creators. And that's the reason, perhaps, some people become judges at the Eisteddfod. We can all shout 'Boo!' or 'Encore!' according to our judgement, but most of us would cut a sad figure on the stage. This shows that the talent to perform is not as widespread as the talent to criticise. It doesn't, I think, require a higher authority to see that Wil Bryan possesses that talent. I remember well his statement (this was before he left home) to the following effect: "You know what? Although I'm only a youngster, I've dabbled, to a greater or lesser degree, as they say, with almost every art and science, up from the noble art of self-defence to writing to the press, but I know I'd cut a sorry figure dancing, although I have a little predilection to it. Although I try my best— on my own, of course, because it would be degrading going to a dancing master—although I try my best, I can't make head or tail of it. These days I don't get upset, for if a man looks soft doing anything, it's when he's dancing. Were you ever at the Ladies Club day—when there are hundreds dancing on the green—putting your fingers in your ears to avoid hearing the band, so you could see what impression the sight of them made on your mind? Try, and you'll have to take your fingers out of your ears immediately, or else believe that universal insanity's set in. I swear that if Dafydd ever looked soft, it was when he was dancing in front of the arch, and that he was thoroughly ashamed when he sobered up. But that's what I was going to say; although I'd never get anywhere with dancing, I'd never give up being a critic of the art. I know the moment someone makes a mistake or is wanting in grace. There's no need, you know, for a man to be able to do something himself to be able to judge whether other people are doing it right, or you'd have to be a cobbler's apprentice before you knew whether your shoe fitted, or whether they're up to standard."

It was an easy task in comparison to judge that Rhys Lewis' autobiography was worth printing. But it's a completely different thing whether my brain can grasp the thread of that story and follow it with consistency. I have some disadvantages Rhys Lewis did not. For one thing, Rhys Lewis had died before the autobiography reached the public, and it's human nature to be gentle with the dead. But I'm alive—at the moment, anyway—and I can't expect gentleness. And that's one of the things that separates man from animals; flaying an animal isn't expected until it's dead; but with a man (such as an author) the first question asked is 'Is he alive?' and if the answer's affirmative, 'Well, let's flay him and sell his skin to pay the reviewer'. I could name several other disadvantages, but I'll say no more, as old John Jones of Y Rhyl used to say at the end of every sermon.

I must ask the reader—if I'm honoured with such people—one favour, and I'm conscious that it's quite a thing to ask. That is, that they'll accept everything I say as undoubted fact—that is, everything that doesn't fall within the limits of their ability and experience to contradict, and indeed, lots of other things that it would be natural of them to inquire how I came to know. For example, if I, as I doubtless will, recite the thoughts of this or that mind, thoughts not expressed to any living being, it would be natural for the reader to ask, how does he know that? Dear reader, this is a great mystery; don't fret, exercise a little faith, and I give my word I'll not say anything I can't substantiate if need be.

The people of Bethel are brought to attention in this story, and though I don't intend to cover the same ground as Rhys Lewis, I will occasionally need to refer briefly to some of the characters already known to the reader, such as Thomas Bartley, Wil Bryan, etcetera. This work will not assume as religious an aspect as the Autobiography because the characters, for the most part, are not noted for their faith. I must give credit to Rhys Lewis for the correctness of his story as far as it goes, and also for his honesty, especially in the parts which uncover things about his family that don't, to say the least, reflect honour upon it; things that his friends wouldn't consider talking about. And letting pass his work detailing the evils of his father and uncle, the reader must realise the fortitude required to speak of his mother's extreme poverty. Let the reader look around ask himself how many of his acquaintances who've got on in the world speak voluntarily of their parents' poverty, of the time they lived on turnip broth?

Unless the daily struggle is to forget what's behind us? How much money would Mr. Holdyourpurse, who's succeeded in the world, earned great wealth, and through industry and talent fills high office and moves in respectable circles, give if he could cancel the story of his childhood and his neighbours' memories, and if he could be sure the old man who touches his cap doesn't remember his father was a cobbler and his wife was selling pop before he married her? As he'd be worried by meeting the old woman who now bends her knee to him, remembering several sandwiches he got from her when he had a hungry look on his face? How strange that he rejoices to hear of old people dying! Mr. Holdyourpurse now mixes with respectable people, and some of them like to talk about their family—a subject that doesn't excite his interest with some people—and poor Mr. Holdyourpurse works and sweats and has to use what talent he has to change the subject, because he can't talk about his family, unless he's doing it as a form of attack on the injustice of the Board of Guardians when they cut his mother's allowance from half a crown to eighteen pence a week. And he can't always do that, because he's now a Guardian and guilty of similar behaviour. And if every guardian behaved like Mr. Holdyourpurse there'd be less of a burden on the taxpayer, because he's told his brother, who lives in another town, not to stop living off the parish. And when his brother says he intends to visit him, Mr. Holdyourpurse sends him a ten shilling postal order with a warning to stay at home. Mrs. Holdyourpurse and the girls agree with him on this and they're afraid to meet the horrid uncle. He's a gardener by trade, and at home is respected as a good and godly man, but because he suffers severely from rheumatism he's unable to work, and is poor, and because of his poverty, his brother and sister in law and his nieces are ashamed of him. The fools! Don't they remember that the father of all of us was a gardener? And didn't he and his wife spend their best days with rags on their backs? This, doubtless, brought on their rheumatism, and from this affliction, Mr. Holdyourpurse's brother suffers terribly! But that's how the world goes; we're ashamed of the rock we were carved from and the ditch we were dug from. It's a fact that it's better for a famous father to be without a biography than have our ancestors' poverty remembered, although they know well the biographer will not reveal more than is necessary, and will temper his sentences; such as, instead of saying this: 'At this time, the parents of our subject kept a bread shop and when carrying bread round the country, they often had to go to the mountain and cut peat, and do their bit in several ways to make ends meet ...' Instead of saying that, the biographer would say: 'Although the parents of our hero were not, at this time, in an elevated and very wealthy state, they were respectable, honest, and paid their way, and possessed of other good qualities, some of which can be clearly seen in their famous son, whose story I'm now attempting to write'. They see well that in that way, the unpleasant circumstances are referred to, and that's enough. They worry that a few people know of their ancestors' poverty, and those few will become fewer every day. They live in a fool's paradise, and I gain great enjoyment from them!

It's obvious that Rhys Lewis didn't belong to that foolish-pride group. It's true he didn't become rich and didn't own an acre of his own. But he did something better; through his industry he raised himself to the respected position of a proper New Testament minister. And he didn't hesitate, when it was of service to him, to refer to the obscurity and poverty of his youth. I recall once in the seiat, talking to old Beti Williams—a little, needy, poor woman— who was known to be very ungrateful, and she found it difficult to be thankful when deprived of real necessities. And Rhys said: "True enough, Beti; it's hard to be grateful when the cupboard's bare. And you've made me remember something my mother said. When there wasn't a bit of food in the house, and no prospect of any, she said: 'Well my son, it's no achievement at all being grateful when we've got all we need. The achievement is to be thankful we put a higher price on the bread of life than on natural bread, and one thing that's necessary and so valuable is secretly hoping Mari

Lewis has chosen the good part and it isn't taken from her." Rhys Lewis didn't try to hide any of the difficulties of his youth, because, as Wil Bryan said, there was no humbug about him.

Rhys Lewis makes this observation somewhere—that he'd be happy if he'd never met Wil Bryan. With all due respect, Rhys Lewis never made a bigger mistake in his life. His connection with Wil was a great blessing. If there was a characteristic greater than all the rest put together in Rhys Lewis as a preacher, it was his naturalness, and I believe he was obliged to Wil Bryan for that. What sort of person would Rhys Lewis have been if he'd never met Wil? Well, he'd have been a big, good, innocent boy—his mother's son, because there was more sugar in his makeup, and certainly less iron; more starch and less strength; more credulity, and less faith and sharpness. But as he was, he was natural and agreeable, and he was obliged to Wil for this uncommon attribute. 'Uncommon', I said? Yes, I don't retract the word. I'm not a philistine; and I don't give best to any man living in my respect for Welsh preachers, but this can't stop me from saying that they are, as a class—there are a lot of exceptions, I know—the most unnatural speakers I know. What reason or scripture causes the preacher, more than any other public speaker, to speak inaudibly for the first quarter hour of the sermon, then start to sing, and then rave, and before the end make one fear he'll break a blood vessel. I can hardly believe that the perpetual partnership of preacher and natural authority has caused them to adopt such an unnatural style. Because this style wouldn't be so comical in other circles, it's strange that a Welsh congregation can not only not laugh, but keep straight faces while the preacher makes his arguments, tells a story, or persuades the listeners to believe the Gospel, and all of it in song! Fortunately, these days singing a sermon is busy going out of fashion and will soon have gone. But there's no doubt that Rhys Lewis would have fallen into the old style of preaching if Wil Bryan hadn't shown him it's odiousness and warned him he'd be 'humbugging' if he was guilty of such unnaturalness.

One more observation, then I'll start my story. A temptation of a preacher who's moved only among good and religious people is to look on people like Wil Bryan as wholly bad, like lepers, and avoid them, and leave them to God's care. No more heretical idea exists, and in speaking like this I don't need to tell the reader I'm not speaking of men in the theological sense. In the hearts of careless, joking and rash characters like Wil Bryan is a tender spot that can't be seen from a distance, and by the use of wisdom and the fire of God's blessing can be turned to good account. Poor indeed is the harp of a man's nature if there isn't one string that produces a lovely sound. That would be a slander on the Creator and a credit to the devil that I hope he doesn't deserve. There is honour among thieves. Often, on the belts of those who move among the ungodliest hang the greatest number of keys to the rooms of the heart. But that's enough of that. Rhys Lewis left several remarkable characters among the people of Bethel without saying anything about them, and my main task in this story will be to say a little about them, and it's time I started.

FAIR WALES

Enoc Huws was a child of the bush and the hedge, a love-child, although not of any bush or hedge in Anglesey. He was born nearer England, where the inhabitants spoke finer Welsh, and, in their opinion, were more cultivated and polished, though not more religious. Bells were not rung at his birth, and no signs of rejoicing of any sort seen or heard. Even the fact that he was a boy, and not a girl, brought not so much as a smile to the face of his relations when they heard of his arrival in the world. Indeed, some of the neighbours maintained that so little interest in him was felt, it was not known for some days to which gender he belonged, and that it was quite by accident that the matter became evident; and that by Enoc's own carelessness. The reason for all this unconcern about the new arrival was this: no one expected him or wanted to see him. I've overstated; there was one who expected him. How many sleepless nights, how much grief, anguish and mental torture, how much bitter and true repentance, of self-loathing that bordered on madness, this expectation had cost, God alone knows. I know this is a tender and sensitive matter to air. I know that it would be a more beautiful experience to listen to a fine voice singing, '*Cymru lân, gwlad y gân*'[1], to ask for more, and to receive in response: '*Hen wlad y menyg gwynion*'[2]. But the man who thought he'd the whole history of Wales in those two songs would be an idiot. I recollect, when I was a lad, that good man

---

[1] '*Cymru lân, gwlad y gân*'—'*Fair Wales, land of song*'.

[2] '*Hen wlad y menyg gwynion*'—'*old land of the white gloves*'; a reference in song to the tradition of handing white gloves to the judge when there are no trials to be held; therefore '*the old land of the white gloves*' is a land free of crime.

Abel Huws, when quite lost in the *hwyl*[3] of the chapel, used to close his eyes, especially when singing, and I got to believe that closing the eyes was a sure sign of godliness. I have changed my opinion. Closing the eyes is no sign of sanctity. And to be fair to Abel Huws, he never used to close them except in the *hwyl*. He was as keen sighted as anyone, and he called things by their right names too. No doubt, if he was alive now, he'd be considered a plain-spoken man. Certainly Abel Huws, like old fellows generally, was a little too plain in his speech; but it's to be feared that nowadays our danger is affectation and over-sensitivity; not calling things by their Welsh names, or even not calling them by any name at all. Have the things themselves ceased to exist? Or does a different light shine on them? Does such a place as hell exist in these days? Such place used to be spoken of some time ago, but you seldom hear mention of such a place now, except by the old fashioned. Is there such thing as incontinence? One hears now and then about 'disagreeable circumstances'. But no doubt the world has become more mannerly, and care must be taken of how to address it.

There was only one, as I said, who expected Enoc to come into the world, and there was not one who wanted him in the world. He was looked on as an intruder. Enoc, poor fellow, knew nothing of this; and if he had known his appearance would have created so much agitation, and occasioned so much discomfort and bitter feeling, it's likely he would have committed suicide rather than face so unwelcoming a world. But Enoc faced it, wholly innocent and defenceless. The doctor testified that Enoc was one of the finest boys he had ever seen, and that there was only one imperfection in him, which was this; that three of the toes of his left foot were stuck together, like a duck's. Whether this denoted that Enoc would be a good swimmer, the doctor did not try to determine.

---

[3] *hwyl*—literally 'fun', although the word serves a variety of purposes in Welsh; in this case, the state of ecstasy felt by believers during religious revivals, of which there were a number in Wales.

But that was neither here nor there.

Before Enoc was a month old, if he had been more aware, and if he'd not been comfortably asleep by his mother's side, he might have been eye witness to a sight he would never have forgotten. The bedroom was large and comfortable, which denoted that its owner was in better circumstances than most. It was Saturday night, or rather Sunday morning, as the clock had just struck midnight. The doctor had just left the room, intending to return soon with medicine to help Enoc's mother across the river—in other words, to die. Before leaving the house the doctor said to her father, who was a very proud man; "I'll come back in a few minutes, Mr. Davies, but I'm afraid poor Elin will not see the dawn. You'd better go and see her. Go, Mr. Davies; go, or you'll regret it later."

Mr. Davies had not seen Elin since the day Enoc was born. Elin was his only child, his only comfort, his idol. But on the day Enoc was born, Mr. Davies took an oath that he'd never speak to his daughter again. However, when the doctor said to him that Elin wouldn't see the morning, he felt a shudder inside, and it was as if his blood were freezing within him. He walked up and down the parlour half a dozen times, and the twitching of his face showed the deep torments of his proud heart. He started up the stairs, and turned back; started again, and turned back again. Yes, he had taken an oath that he would never speak to her again. But he remembered—and it was well that he remembered—that he had not said that he would not see her. He started up the stairs again, and this time did not turn back. Mr. Davies was a handsome and strong man, and had never before felt any difficulty going up the stairs. But this time he felt his legs almost giving way. There were two nurses in the room speaking quietly, and they were frightened by Mr. Davies' unexpected appearance, but neither said a word. Elin's eyes were shut and her face was as white as the pillow under her head, and her long hair, as black as her sin, was strewed loosely and carelessly about her. Mr. Davies clutched the bedpost, as of necessity, and gazed at the face of his dear daughter. What a change he saw! Was this Elin, his dear Elin? Incredible! She was but a shadow of what she had been. Yet, thought Mr. Davies, in spite of all the change, she had lost none of the beauty of which he'd always felt so proud. And, indeed, Elin was more like her mother, who he had buried about a year earlier, than he'd ever seen her. He looked fixedly at her pallid face, and his heart began to soften. But he turned his eyes and saw Enoc, with his pink face, flat nose, and bald head, and Mr. Davies' anger and wounded pride returned, and he sighed heavily. Elin opened her eyelids, revealing a pair of eyes that her father had gazed upon a thousand times with admiration. Her father was not the only person who'd admired those eyes. From the whiteness of her face, Elin's eyes seemed to her father to be blacker, brighter, and more beautiful than ever. But Elin, his dear Elin, who he'd looked upon as a model of perfection, without a flaw or a wrinkle, like the very light itself, had sinned. And in fairness to the father, it was her sin and not the disgrace—though he felt that deeply—that was like a canker gnawing at his heart; for Mr. Davies was a particular, religious, and godly man in his own way. Elin opened her eyes, and looked imploringly, though silently, into her father's eyes. After a minute of silence she said indistinctly: "Father, won't you speak to me?"

Mr. Davies said not a word, but the movements of his face and throat showed that he was suffering even more than her.

"Father," added Elin. "I've asked Jesus Christ a thousand times to forgive me. Do you think He will, father?"

Mr. Davies looked at Enoc, and clutched the bedpost still more tightly, but he did not break his oath. Elin said a second time; "If mother was alive—and she is alive—I saw her last night—and *she* has forgiven me. Won't you forgive me, dear father? I have been a bad, bad, bad daughter; but won't you forgive me, dear father?"

Mr. Davies let go of the bedpost, swayed like a drunken man, took a step forward, bent and kissed his daughter once, twice, and retreated to his former position without taking his eyes from her;

4

but never said a word. Elin smiled happily and then turned her eyes to Enoc. As though guided by instinct, one of the nurses—a mother—understood her wish, and put the baby's face to his mother's cold lips. Enoc only grunted sleepily when kissed for the last time by his mother. After doing this, Elin looked as though she was done with everyone and everything, and looked upwards endlessly. Mr. Davies didn't take his eyes off her; and even when the doctor came in, didn't appear conscious of his arrival. The doctor knew at once that poor Elin was on the point of departing this life, and didn't try to make her take the medicine. For some minutes Elin continued to gaze upwards, then said, audibly, "I'm coming now, mother; now." After one convulsive twitch, one long sigh, her spirit took wing.

"She's gone," said the doctor quietly, and at the same time took hold of Mr. Davies' arm and led him down the stairs. The doctor was relieved to reach the bottom safely, for Mr. Davies leaned heavily on him. The father's anguish was terrible, and when he fell heavily into his chair, he held his head in his hands and groaned aloud: "Oh Elin! Elin! My dear Elin!"

Suddenly he jumped agitatedly to his feet, struck the table several times till the blood spurted from his knuckles; and, as if addressing the table, said fiercely, "Enoc Huws, if you are not already in hell, may the curse of God follow you every step of your life."

He repeated the foolish words several times. The doctor stayed with him till he quieted down. Mr. Davies was comparatively young, scarcely forty years old. He was looked upon in the village as being in comfortable circumstances, and was highly respected. His daughter Elin, before the events we have touched upon, was a favourite, even with her own sex, which is saying a good deal. Her fall was a blow to scores of her friends and acquaintances, and no one, so far as I know, showed any joy at her disgrace. It is not always thus, worse luck. And of all disgraceful things, the most disgraceful is for any one to rejoice in the misfortune of his friend.

The sympathy for Mr. Davies, in his bitter trial, was deep and true, and widely shown. But he never held up his head again. The arrow had gone straight to his heart, and no one could draw it out. He sold all his goods and chattels; and the last of his old neighbours that Mr. Davies spoke to was Dafydd Jones, the man who used to carve letters on gravestones.

"Dafydd Jones," said he, "put these words on the stone that is over my wife—don't bother about the age and date:

Also
ELIN DAVIES,
'*The pitcher was broken at the well*'. "

And without so much as saying goodbye to his friends, Mr. Davies left the country.

2

THE UNION WORKHOUSE

On the death of his mother, Enoc was placed under the care of Mrs. Amos, one of the nurses referred to earlier, and it was said that Mr. Davies gave this woman a large sum of money to take Enoc "out of his sight and look after him." For some days Enoc's life was in danger, and his bulk was much reduced. It appeared that drinking the milk of different cows through an India rubber tube didn't meet his taste or agree with the constitution of his stomach. And though no one was anxious about it, it was thought the child was about to depart to the same land as his mother.

The only thing about the likelihood of Enoc's dying that caused Mrs. Amos any trouble was the fact that he had not been baptised. To die without being baptised would be a terrible disaster in Mrs. Amos' sight. And in the greatness of her hurry she went to the Methodist minister, of whose persuasion Enoc's mother was a member. He'd finished his supper and had just lit his pipe, and gave Mrs. Amos a cold and harsh reception. He refused absolutely to move out of his house, and crossed himself at the thought of touching such a mass of corruption as Enoc. He then returned to his pipe, which was nearly as black as Enoc's soul, and Mrs. Amos departed, murmuring: "If Mr. Davies hadn't gone away he wouldn't have been refused, I'll warrant." And she gave him her own blessing, in her own special way. But then Mrs. Amos knew nothing of the '*Confession of Faith*'[1] and the rules of discipline.

---

[1] '*Confession of Faith*'—A written assembly of beliefs, in the nature of God, in the truth of the scriptures, the creation, of many things. Many Christian churches, including the Calvinist Methodist Church featured most prominently in this story, have them.

After this, the nurse hastened to the house of the Wesleyan minister with the same appeal. John Wesley Thomas, too, was perfectly aware of the circumstances of the case, and very kindly, and without making any bones about it, went at once with Mrs. Amos and baptised the child, calling him by the father's name, according to Mrs. Amos' story; namely Enoc Huws. The woman felt very much obliged to Mr. Thomas for this favour, and to show her feelings, offered him a glass of whisky as a small acknowledgement for his trouble. Mr. Thomas refused her politeness, and offered a word of advice, urging her to follow baby Enoc's example, and leave the bottle alone. Mrs. Amos thanked the minister warmly for his kindness and advice, and vowed that "If ever I need to go to chapel, it will be to your chapel, Mr. Thomas; as for that other old bear, I don't know how anyone can go near him." Mr. Thomas went away laughing, and there was never a need for Mrs. Amos to go to chapel or church until she was carried to the latter place by four men.

Although it was a considerable disappointment to Mrs. Amos, it happened that the baptism, or something, brought about a remarkable change in the state of Enoc's health. Had he been baptised by the bishop the effect could not have been more miraculous. Enoc began immediately to look about him in rather an old fashioned way, and when Mrs. Amos put the India rubber pipe in his mouth, he sucked on it as eagerly and brightly as a lamb. Had he had a tail, he would have wagged it, but he made up for this deficiency by shaking his feet, and by raising his shoulders to show his enormous enjoyment. In the face of this unmistakable evidence of vitality, Mrs. Amos was thoroughly angry, and called him a "bad deceitful chap." But as the "bad deceitful chap" chose to live, that was no comfort.

Time passed, and Enoc did nothing. At least, nothing worth speaking about, except sucking the pap bottle, and as Mrs. Amos, too, was not entirely forgetful of the whisky bottle, the 'large sum of money' which Mr. Davies gave Mrs. Amos 'to keep Enoc out of his sight' soon vanished. The fact is that before Enoc was a full twelve months old, his foster mother was in severe poverty. As a consequence, she went to the relieving officer, and gave that officer to understand, in adequate Welsh, that she wasn't going to keep other people's children any longer, she couldn't afford to do it. And though she was sorry to part with the child—for, as she said, he was now a fine enough young cock—yet there was nothing else she could do. She had waited and waited to hear from Mr. Davies, and she could wait no more. If she went out washing for half a day she had to give Enoc such and such an amount of laudanum to make him sleep, and that cost money. And as for the boy's father, well he'd fled the country before Enoc was born, the wretch. After a lot of talking and a lot of delay, and appearing before the board of guardians, and a hundred other things, Mrs. Amos at last succeeded in getting Enoc off her hands and transferred safely to the care of the workhouse.

The reader's patience, I am afraid, would fail were Enoc's history followed through the workhouse, and it isn't necessary for this story. It's certain he was there until he was thirteen years old, whereupon he had to leave and earn his living, and was placed under the care of a grocer in a nearby town. It was apparent, when Enoc came out of the workhouse, that he had received a fair education in reading, writing, and 'counting', and, if his cheeks were to be believed, that he'd also had good nourishment. His body was slender and thin, and his face large and purple; he was more like an onion, roots upwards, than anything ever seen. What device do the workhouse authorities have for growing cheeks? I've been told that their usual plan is this. When the boys have eaten their bowls of skilly—porridge in a broth of consumption—they are led into the yard and placed in a row with their faces to the wall. Then they're ordered to stand on their heads as long as they can; and whoever gets most marks in the course of the year gets an extra plate of plum pudding on Christmas day—the only day pudding is made in the *tloty*[2] for the paupers. It will be seen at once that the natural effect of this is to cause the nourishment of the skilly, which nourishment, so far as quality is concerned, doctors say is the nearest there is to fresh water, run down into the cheeks and puff them out, leaving the other parts of the body to take their chances. If some of the boys have poor balance or get headaches, and are consequently unable to carry out the practise, a clout on one cheek is given today, one on the other cheek tomorrow and by a continuance of this treatment the same desirable result is brought about, viz., puffed-out cheeks, and these assure every sensible guardian that the boy is getting plenty of nourishing food. For particular reasons, this regime is not followed with the girls. Another slightly more costly method is adopted, but not widely advertised.

By whichever means, this was the appearance Enoc had when he left the poorhouse. His face was big and round, like a full moon, or like a child's first attempt to draw a man on his slate. His appearance made one think of porridge; a face of porridge, a head to hold porridge, the dejected look of porridge; in short, the local children knew at once that Enoc was a 'workhouse boy'. The workhouse had perfectly succeeded in placing its mark and its imprint on Enoc's head and face, but failed completely to change the nature of his mind. Enoc belonged to too good a stock for the workhouse to harm his brain.

Luckily for him, his new master was a sensible and kind man, and he quickly saw in Enoc the elements of an able boy. With substantial nourishment, kindness and training, Enoc soon began to lose his plump cheeks and to develop his body and legs. When he felt he was at liberty to let his hair grow long enough to put a comb to it, he began to tidy himself, and his eyes wore a more lively and observant expression. So speedy was the change in him

---

[2] *tloty*—The poorhouse, a Welsh name for the workhouse. Owen used both English and Welsh appellations, it being an English institution widely found in Wales.

that, at the end of six months, when one of the guardians came to enquire whether Enoc was being fairly treated, he scarcely knew him. His puffy cheeks had so waned, and their purple had so clearly left them, that the guardian thought Enoc had not had enough to eat, and he angrily asked his master, "Mr. Bithel, where are the boy's cheeks gone to?"

"Into his legs, sir, and other parts of his body. Since you last saw Enoc a 'redistribution of seats' has taken place. I will go indoors, sir, whilst you ask Enoc whether he has been treated fairly," said Mr. Bithel.

With the enquiry and questioning over, the guardian was fully satisfied that Enoc had not been mistreated, but he could scarcely believe that he had not the slightest *hiraeth*[3] for the workhouse; the happiest place in the world, in his opinion.

.

---

[3] *hiraeth*—a longing, esp. for the homeland, allegedly more deep in the Welsh than in the rest of mankind.

SUCCESS

As Mr. Bithel had foreseen, Enoc turned out to be an excellent boy; he picked up his business quicker than the usual run of boys. But Mr. Bithel often told him, during the last years Enoc was in his service, that he was afraid he would never make a master, as he was too modest, nervous, and credulous. This was only too true, as we'll see later. Enoc himself was not unconscious of it, and it caused him considerable vexation. He felt difficulty in contradicting anyone; and from shyness appeared often to agree with that which in truth was entirely contrary to his opinion. He always remembered, and was sometimes reminded by others, that he was a 'workhouse boy'; and perhaps this caused a great deal of his shyness. He was naturally of a gentle disposition, and when he thought of his start in life, the details of which he'd been told more than once in the workhouse, lest he should grow overly proud, his pillow was often damp with tears. The more he grew in knowledge and culture, the more painful it became to think of what he'd been told, and especially to remember that his friends also knew. Both in the '*seiat*'[1] and at chapel, Enoc often thought that people were thinking about his beginnings, whilst in reality nothing was further from their thoughts. He was liked by all, and his services were valued by his master. However, when he gained his freedom, after serving his six years as apprentice to Mr. Bithel, Enoc determined to go to another town where he

---

[1] '*seiat*'—no doubt a corruption of the English word 'society'. In the words of Dafydd Dafis who we meet in chapter 24, a '*seiat*' was '*a meeting where people could discuss things—consult and exchange thoughts*'. This was in contrast to the general gatherings of the chapel.

could keep his story to himself. And so it came about, and it was to Rhys Lewis and Wil Bryan's birthplace[2] that Enoc was led by providence.

It happened that an assistant was wanted in Siop y Groes[3]. Enoc applied for the job and got it. Siop y Groes was then kept and owned by a widow, who, since her husband's death, had been most unfortunate in her choice of assistants. For the most part, they had helped themselves rather than her. But in Enoc Huws she came across an honest, able, and industrious youth. Quickly, Enoc gave a new look to the shop, and new life to the business. This happened around the time Hugh Bryan started to go downhill. Though Rhys Lewis doesn't mention this in his autobiography, I'm sure Enoc Huws' arrival at Siop y Groes hastened the failure of 'Old Hugh', as his son called him. With the expectation of getting at 'y plwm mawr'[4], which had long been promised, Hugh Bryan had for years handed his money over to the Pwll y Gwynt mine, or, as Wil would have said, 'yn specilatio'[5]. Having spent so much money, and with Captain Trefor continuing to say they had almost found the lode, Hugh Bryan was very unwilling to give up his share in the undertaking; so much so, that having handed over all his own money, he began handing over other people's money as well. Under the circumstances, his shop suffered severely, and the result was, as Wil Bryan had prophesied before leaving home, that it was all 'U.P.' with old Hugh. Whilst he was going downhill, Enoc Huws was on his way up, and was already known as a good

---

[2] Mr. Owen has provided us with not one, but two prefaces. In the event that you have neglected to read them, I will point out that this book is a sequel to 'Rhys Lewis' and contains some of the same characters.

[3] Siop y Groes—the shop at the crossroads.

[4] 'y plwm mawr'—literally 'the big lead'; a major discovery in the lead mine. Lead mining was a major industry in Flintshire around Owen's time.

[5] 'yn specilatio'—there are times when the lazier Welsh, such as Wil Bryan, simply borrow an English word and stick 'io' at the end of it to form a verb. This is a slovenly practise, and not to be encouraged.

businessman. By now, the widow was envied for her good fortune. Wil Bryan had known for some time that Enoc was making a hole in his father's business, as well as other people's, and freely admitted it; but he was far from admiring him. Wil was too cunning to let anyone know he was envious of Enoc Huws' success, and the only unkind remark I ever heard from his lips, as far as I remember, was this; "You know, genius doesn't make a successful grocer. They're all second and third rate men. I firmly believe that; every genius of a shopkeeper I ever saw came to grief in the end. That confounded Demas, of whom Paul, or was it John, speaks in the Testament, was no more than some kind of successful provision dealer."

Wil left home, and his father went 'up the spout'; Wil would have been the last to say his father was a genius, and it wouldn't have taken him long to demonstrate that was not 'the point of his argument'. Everything, it seemed, was working in Enoc's favour, and before long he and the widow were an excellent team. She was so afraid that Enoc would be unsettled by someone offering more wages that she gave him—without his asking for it—a share in the business, and he doubled his exertions. By this means, he collected not only a little for himself, but added considerably to the widow's fortune. Months went by, and the widow cast aside the marks of widowhood; but she never did what widows usually do, viz., marry again; she died. But before doing so, she made provision in her last will and testament for Enoc to have first offer of the shop and business, and to have a reasonable time to pay the executors for the stock. Enoc jumped at this chance, and it seemed that every breeze filled the sails of his success; and widespread words of praise were heard, and still they fill and follow and tease the breeze of the '*bro*'[6].

Enoc Huws was not desirous of taking public office, and nature hadn't endowed him with the qualifications for so doing. He was, as has already been said, a little timid. But there's some human

---

[6] '*bro*'—the local area.

instinct which makes us believe that, if a man is successful in the world, he ought to cut a figure in chapel, no matter how ill-suited or how unwilling he may be. In the same way as the lord lieutenant of the county is inclined—perhaps unconsciously—to nominate a man as a magistrate because he is a squire's son, without considering for a moment his fitness to sit in judgement, some voice in the bosom of the faithful feels that when a man has got somewhere in the world, it's time that he held office. Thus it was with Enoc. Nothing, in the world or in the church, succeeds like success. Enoc's business grew rapidly. People, like sheep, will flock to the same place. On market days Enoc's shop was crammed, whilst several shopkeepers, as good men as he, and living close by, were thankful for the occasional customer. Spread a rumour that "so and so is doing well," and what a crowd he'll get to help him do better; whisper that another is struggling to make ends meet, and he'll be deserted by the crowd, and sometimes even his friends, in order to keep the ends further apart. That's how you are, human nature!

But Enoc deserved to succeed; he was an honest man, which is important, and would never spread lies either on posters or in the papers. But, as I have said, there lived in his neighbourhood men as honest as he, in the same trade as he, who couldn't pay their way. They had but a trickle of custom, and Siop y Groes a deluge, and the poor wretches strove to catch stray splashes of his success. As his business increased, so did his importance in chapel. He contributed generously. He had not, as you have heard, many of the elements of a public man; but was soon made a superintendent of the Sunday school; and few were more successful than he in finding teachers for the classes. There was something so charming about him that no one dared refuse him. Enoc was believed to be rich; and, say what you will, wealth has many advantages; not the least of which is the unlikelihood of meeting with refusal. Pitar Jones, the shoemaker, the other superintendent, although more able and of more mature judgment, would often fail to find teachers, but no one had the nerve to refuse Enoc. Pitar was often hurt deeply by the difference in people's behaviour towards him and towards his fellow superintendent. But Pitar used to forget the difference in their worldly station, and also the consciousness in the minds of all that no one knew how soon they might need Enoc's assistance.

It might have been thought Enoc wanted for nothing to make him a happy man. He had, to all appearances, succeeded in the world; he was respected by his neighbours, had been promoted in the chapel, and if he had any enemies or was the subject of envy, it was not of his own making. But how little we know the secrets of a man's heart. Enoc's opinion of himself was so modest, and his nature so unambitious, that neither position nor respect contributed greatly, if at all, to his happiness. He was a single man, and in that fact alone there are a host of griefs and trials only confessed by one '*hen lanc*'[7] to another. But Enoc did not lighten his burden even in that way. He kept his secrets entirely to himself. At the bottom of his heart he despised the idea that he belonged in any way to the Confirmed Bachelors' Club, and he hadn't the courage—the manhood—to resign. Why? Because, he thought, he'd set his heart on an unattainable object. She was the only daughter of Captain Trefor, of Tŷ'n yr Ardd[8]; and here, perhaps, I should bring the family of Tŷ'n yr Ardd to the notice of the reader.

---

[7] '*hen lanc*'—literally, an old youth. A bachelor who has been a bachelor for some time.

[8] Tŷ'n yr Ardd—the home of Captain Trefor; literally, the house in the garden.

4

CAPTAIN TREFOR

Captain Richard Trefor had been amongst us for some years, but was not a native of the village any more than was Enoc. When he first came to us, he was almost alone in being a person who never shaved, and had let his beard grow, which until it became fashionable, created a strong prejudice against him in the hearts of some good and godly people. Even that wise man, Abel Huws, rather frowned on him. It was very obvious, said those who remembered his arrival, that there wasn't much about him, and that here was a man who 'juggled for his living'. He kept moving around the mines, and very soon, though no one knew how, he had a hand in this and in that. It was generally believed that Richard Trefor was a man who lived on his wits, and certainly he was not short of them. It was said he possessed a special capability to introduce himself to everyone, and very soon he was seen talking to people to whom many of the old inhabitants had never spoken a word of Welsh[1]. Richard Trefor spoke Welsh and English with ease and fluency, and wove words endlessly when he needed to. I remember hearing Wil Bryan swear that Richard Trefor had at some stage swallowed Johnson, Webster, and Charles' dictionaries, as if swallowing three pills. Whatever the veracity of Wil's oath in respect of Johnson and Webster, it's not beyond belief that Trefor had swallowed Charles' dictionary in its entirety, for he was remarkably familiar with religious philosophy and the Scriptures were at his fingertips. In those days there was considerable discussion on religious

---

[1] There's a Welsh saying; '*Does 'na ddim Cymraeg rhyngddyn nhw*', which literally means 'There's no Welsh between them', but actually means they don't speak at all. So perhaps the Captain was speaking to people the old inhabitants had never spoken to.

subjects—'Predestination' and 'Perseverance in Grace' and the like—and Richard Trefor was reckoned one of the deepest in debate and ablest in the art of hair-splitting. At that time he was not a member of the chapel, nor was he too particular about his conduct, for it was said by some that he sometimes took a drop too much. Rhys Lewis' mother didn't think too highly of him, for I recall hearing her say: "I look on him, you see, as being very like Ifans, the road surveyor. Ifans is very particular to keep the main road fine and tidy, but seldom travels it himself. And Trefor is like that; you would consider him very careful that there is no stone or hole in the road to eternal life, but I'm afraid he himself never walks it. I heard my boy Bob say the Bible's at his fingertips, but I'd sooner hear a little of it was in his heart."

It was not long before Richard Trefor came to the Seiat, and it was obvious from the way Abel Huws questioned him that his opinion of Mr. Trefor was similar to that of Mari Lewis. I was only a boy, but I remember the evening well, and from that time onward I have never seen anyone questioned so severely before being received into the church meeting. I'm sure that if people knew beforehand they were to be questioned in such a manner, no one would become a member. I have never seen Rhys Lewis' mother—before or since—show so much pleasure. Her head on one side, the corner of her eyes fixed upon Abel, she seemed to be saying "Go on, Abel, give him a hard time." But whatever direction Abel took, Richard Trefor did not stumble; slick and smooth, he dealt with every question. I recollect that Bob Lewis and I walked back from chapel with his mother and Abel that evening, and Mari Lewis said: "Abel, you have never pleased me more than you did tonight."

"Indeed? In what way, Mari?" said Abel

"Well, in pressing that man so hard," said Mari. "But I fear the fellow's not yet had his back broken, and he has a little more work to do before he qualifies for Heaven, however slippery his tongue."

"We don't all have the same intention in coming to the *Seiat*, Mari." said Abel.

"Well, couldn't I tell, Abel, that you were hinting at something like that? Your words always have a purpose. There was not a spark of rebirth in him, was there now?" said Mari.

It is extraordinary what insight into characters the old people had, and how swift they were to separate the thief and the despoiler from those who were coming into the sheepfold. Was the concert pitch of the old people's religion higher than ours, and could they, consequently, pick out the screechers in the choir more easily? However, Richard Trefor had not been a member more than a full month before word went forth that he and Miss Prydderch—a religious and innocent young lady, reported to have a good deal of money—were going to marry. The report was soon verified—as far as the marriage was concerned; but not the money—for Miss Prydderch was just as poor as the rest of us, but happened to dress well. Richard Trefor was not above thinking about money, but if he married her for money he made a mistake. Indeed I heard him say, years after the marriage, when he had risen to a high position in the world, that he was indebted to nothing for his honourable position except his own talents and exertions, and that all he had got as a dowry with his wife was a pretty face, a heart full of admiration for him, and a box of expensive clothing. And I have no reason to doubt his veracity, for I've heard more than one of his old workmen say that he and his wife had the look of poverty about them for a while after their wedding. But success and popularity were in store for Richard Trefor. It was not possible, according to his nature of things, for so bright a light to be kept long under a bushel. As a tiger springs at its prey, so Richard Trefor one day leapt at the throat of fortune; he grasped it, and held on to it for many years.

All of Wales has heard of Pwll y Gwynt. But perhaps not everyone knows that Richard Trefor started it; that he discovered "Y plwm mawr." From the day of the discovery, his rise was evident to all. He was no longer merely Richard Trefor, but Captain Trefor, if you please. People began to look on him as some Joseph, sent by Providence to keep many people alive. A sudden change took place in people's opinions. Those who used to frown upon him soon realised that this was narrow-mindedness on their part, and lost no time in rearranging their opinions. What had been sins in Richard were merely weaknesses in Captain Trefor. Everyone has faults, and even Captain Trefor could not be expected to be perfect. The weaknesses of Captain Trefor were only natural weaknesses, weaknesses that now could be easily accounted for and be excused in a man of his position. Captain Trefor was a much better man than they used to think he was, and most certainly he was a blessing to the neighbourhood. In short, Captain Trefor was a fine example of human nature's tendency of to form an incorrect opinion of a man when he is poor, and of how he cannot hope to be justly valued until he attains some degree of worldly success. Had anyone prophesied of Captain Trefor—as Mr. Bithel had done of Enoc Huws—that he would never make a master, he would certainly have been put down as a false prophet. On Captain Trefor's shoulders lay office and authority, with grace and with propriety. It was obvious he was born to be a master. Not because he showed any lordly or oppressive arrogance. No, he was too kind and sociable for that. He had a better way, a way of saying by his behaviour to all under his authority "Look how mild I am, and how cruel I could be if I chose. Take care not to abuse my mildness. I don't ask you to touch your hat to me, but you know it would be safest if you did."

He never once officiated in the chapel service; but there was something in his appearance—on a Sunday morning, for example—which drew from every member of the congregation— very quietly—"Good morning, Captain Trefor."

5

'SUS'

As I've already remarked, Mrs. Trefor was an innocent woman; and as was entirely natural and proper, it was she of all people who admired her husband most. She never crossed him, and he, as a consequence, was extremely gentle with her. Mrs. Trefor believed that the happiness of half the human race depended on her husband, and he never undeceived her; nor did he trouble her in any sort of way with the details of his circumstances and his many cares. Indeed Mrs. Trefor had a dread of his revealing to her the mystery and importance of his social position, for fear that it would make her admire him too much, and cause her to forget her God. Mrs. Trefor knew that her husband was a man without an equal, and that the prosperity of the area depended on his word; and she also believed that in the Captain lay a glory even beyond this, about which she knew nothing, about which it would not be good for her soul to know anything, for the reason given above. She had not, for example, the slightest idea of the extent of his wealth; all she knew was that she could draw from it endlessly. Although much was taken, his wealth never lessened.

It was enough for her to know that the Captain's name was good in every shop in town. The thing that caused no little anxiety to Mrs. Trefor in the course of years was her fear that the Captain's various cares, and his painstaking study of geology, would harm his intellect by and by; for the Captain, after all, was but a man. The only way, or at least the most convenient way, thought Mrs. Trefor, in which she could be a wife worthy of Captain Trefor, and maintain her husband's dignity, was by dressing as well as she possibly could. Indeed, she had done this when her means were not equal to her wishes, but now there was no fasting for the cravings of her eyes. Yet, Mrs. Trefor was religious, and, let us hope, godly as well. No one was more regular in attending '*y moddion gras*'[1]. She was one of the aristocracy among non-conformists, one of those we admire for their loyalty, neither defecting from chapel to church, nor shifting from the Welsh language to the English.

Captain and Mrs. Trefor had a daughter; their only child, Susan Trefor, was idolised by her father, and the light of her mother's eyes. She was brought up in the full luxury of her father's success, and had every educational advantage to be had in the area in those days. I do not propose, at this point, to say what use she made of these advantages. But I remember well that, when I was a boy, Susan Trefor was looked upon as the prettiest, the most fashionable, the most learned, and the most unapproachable girl in our chapel. Miss Trefor was the model for all the young girls. She—after Abel Huws' death—was the first to be smuggled in as a full member of the chapel without questioning, and Miss Trefor's dress drew more tears from the eyes of the young women of the chapel than were drawn by all the sermons heard during that period. Few people of account were in our congregation. Consequently, Miss Trefor hardly considered the 'chapel people' suitable companions, and none of our girls were so ambitious as to aspire to such a position. But they had the privilege of seeing her on a Sunday, and they greatly valued the privilege. Very naturally, those who had the honour of speaking to Miss Trefor looked back on those occasions as the sunniest moments of their life. Miss Trefor did not attend the Sunday school, but made up for this by giving a free tea to the poor children, and on such occasions she herself would pour the tea, and it was said that, more than once, she had put her fair hand under the chin of some small curly headed boy in a very gentle way.

---

[1] '*y moddion gras*'—literally '*the means of grace*', the ways in which God works invisibly in his disciples; but to the chapel-goer, y moddion gras are the chapel meetings, where those means are debated, and where perhaps that invisible work is done.

Some slightly envious people said Miss Trefor was an empty-headed, foolish girl—aware of her good looks, and ignorant of her failings. But this could hardly have been true, and there would hardly be a better reason to say so than the fact that Wil Bryan was a great admirer of hers. Wil was not one to admire a silly flirt; and he never tired of talking of 'Susi', as he called her. Wil would let us say what we liked about Captain Trefor, and sometimes he himself was quick to speak harshly, because he had persuaded his father to 'specilatio' till he was in poverty. But not one of us dared breathe a bad word about Susi without laying himself open to the charge of being a coward, or else displaying what perfection he had managed in the noble art of self-defence. And there's another truth that should be mentioned here; that Miss Trefor herself did not despise Wil. Wil told me once, confidentially, "I understand human nature sufficiently well to assure you I am no small beer in Susi's eyes." Though, as Rhys Lewis quotes Wil in his autobiography, 'there was nothing definite between him and Susi'; but it was well known to we chapel boys that Wil had a great influence on her. We knew also that the Captain's eagle-eye had seen that Wil was not unacceptable in his daughter's eyes, and that he had shown his utter disapproval. When I once spoke to Wil about this, he said with his usual freedom of speech: "It's this way, you know. The Captain, now that my father has given all his money to Pwll y Gwynt, knows very well how things stand in our house; he knows there's not much hope of £500 a year to be had there. He thinks, you know, that he can make a better match, and in a way, I don't blame him. But if it came to a pitched battle between me and the Captain about Susi, I have a fair idea how things would turn out."

6

MISS TREFOR'S CONFESSION OF FAITH

When Wil Bryan left home, after foreseeing that it would be all 'U.P.' and "liquidation by arrangement" with Hugh Bryan, his father, the heart of one honest man was glad; that of Enoc Huws. Enoc, poor chap, was one of the most harmless and least malicious of men on earth, but he couldn't bear Wil Bryan. Wil never did him any harm, except to ignore him. And yet, if Enoc had heard that Wil had been killed or had hanged himself, I believe he could scarcely have kept from smiling, if not rejoicing. To get rid of Wil without either happening gave Enoc the opportunity to rejoice with an easy conscience. In the years he had come and gone amongst us, not twenty words had passed between him and Miss Trefor. And yet of her he thought all day and of her he dreamt all night. Though Enoc didn't see himself, in the humbleness of his spirit, as a worthy companion for Miss Trefor, and though he didn't cherish the faintest hope that the longings of his heart would ever be realised—indeed in his sensible moments he perceived that it was all a wild and foolish fancy—yet he loved to let this fancy circle and hover like a bee, constantly, over the object of his longing; and the knowledge that someone else enjoyed a closer communion filled him with jealousy and made him wretchedly miserable. At times he felt furious with himself; at other times, he laughed at his folly; but, as he said scores of times to himself, his thoughts hurt no one, and no one knew about them.

Enoc was, as has been said, very glad that Wil had left home; but he would not have made his joy known, even to his closest friend, for a hundred pounds. No longer was there a wasp between the bee and its flower; and if Enoc could have been sure no other wasp was going to turn up he could almost have been a happy man. And this comparative happiness he enjoyed for some time, letting his imagination build castles in the air of Siop y Groes. But if Enoc had known of Miss Trefor's 'castles', his own would have been scarcely higher than molehills.

Wil Bryan occupied an important place in Miss Trefor's heart. She liked his company above all things. Wil had always something to say, and that something always to the purpose. She never tired of him, and never with him found herself in the uncomfortable position of having to think what to say next, as she had to with 'the other baboons'. And even when she realised her father had reached the bottom of Hugh Bryan's pocket, it caused no dislike of Wil's company, nor any lessening of her regard for him. The Captain had more than once expressed his disapproval of her fondness for Wil, but forbidding the apple to Eve's daughter only made her want it more. Miss Trefor felt Wil's departure more than she would have wanted anyone to know, more than she admitted even to herself. For a time she lost interest in everything, and the thought of going to chapel was hateful. But this was only temporary. In spite of all the attention he'd paid her, all the kindness he had shown, and the unlimited amusement he'd afforded her for so long a time, he could not, Miss Trefor argued, have cared much about her, or he wouldn't have gone away without saying so much as a word or dropping her a line. And, like a wise and sensible girl, Miss Trefor sat down to rearrange the programme of her life and reform her principles, according to which she would shape her future. It didn't take her long to form her belief and her confession of faith. The things that used to flutter unformed, indefinite, and empty, through her mind and heart, she speedily brought into order and class, and if anyone had asked Miss Trefor by what name she called those things, I know her answer would have been 'My ideas'. The following may be mentioned as some of 'My ideas:' That she was the most beautiful girl in the country (Wil Bryan had assured her of this, and Wil was as good a judge as anyone she knew). That beauty was a talent and should attract ten other talents to itself when placed in the best market. That it was better for a young and stylish girl to live on one meal a day for three months than put on a bonnet that was out of fashion. That so far as possible she would take no notice of anyone, male or female, beneath her station, except when to do so would be looked on as a virtuous and Christian act of condescension. She would never, as far as possible, soil her hands with low and contemptible work, such as lighting the fires, washing the dishes, cleaning windows, making the beds, and the like; and if she must, no stranger's eye should see her. That she was to wait patiently and determinedly without marrying till she was twenty-five years old, if no rich gentleman came and offered himself; if such a gentleman had not come forward by then, she would no longer remain single, but would condescend to take the best tradesman she could get hold of, as long as he had money. She'd look on a preacher only as a person to be pitied, a sad and poor individual; but if she had an offer from a curate of good family, likely to have a good living, she'd consider the matter—the family and the living—and if the curate was also good looking, it would make no difference in the world how shallow and soulless he was; the more so the better, in fact, for she could then manage him as she wished. Whomsoever she married, and marry she was sure enough to do—she'd as soon be a Hottentot as an old maid— she was determined to have her own way; or, to use a common expression, she'd wear the trousers.

Those are a few of Miss Susan Trefor's 'ideas'. She had others, too, which if mentioned, would place Miss Trefor in a more pleasant light before the reader. And it's only fair to her that I should state that Miss Trefor had one 'idea' which gave colour and shape to all her 'ideas'; an immovable and constant belief that her father was rich. It took Miss Trefor a long time—several years—to foster and rear the ideas I've mentioned. I thought it proper and wise to relate this much about the Tŷ'n yr Ardd family before moving on to the next chapter.

7

DOMESTIC BLISS

It was a November night, cold and foggy, and weak-chested people kept their noses close to the hob, struggling for breath, and thinking they were the only ones in misery. A complaint such as asthma can get into the mind and circumstances of a man when he can't get his breath.

On passing Tŷ'n yr Ardd, the residence of Captain Trefor, many a poor miner short of breath envied its cosiness and the happiness of the occupants. He'd say to himself, "The Captain's eating his supper, or else he's finished his supper, is smoking his pipe and stretching out his feet, in their red slippers, towards his warm fire; and here am I, poor wretch, obliged to leave my family and work the night shift at Pwll y Gwynt. Happy is the Captain! But not every man can be a Captain; and he who was born to fourpence will never reach fivepence."

But had the miner known everything, it's doubtful he'd have changed places with him. The Captain was not eating his supper, or smoking, or stretching out his feet to the fire, but was sitting at the table, trying to write. His head inclined on his left hand, his elbow on the table and his pen idle in his right hand, he appeared to be in deep and troubled reflection. By him, on the table was a bottle of Scotch Whisky, and in the last half hour he had been to the bottle several times for help and succour. At the other end of the table sat Mrs. Trefor, busy with some sewing or other, and in an easy chair by her side, close to the fire, sat Miss Trefor, diligently engaged in some exquisite workmanship with white thread and a piece of ivory like a small fish. All three were as silent as church mice, for the wife and daughter were not allowed to talk while the Captain was writing his letters. From time to time the two looked from under their brows at him for signs of an end to his work, and the fact that his pen had been idle for ten minutes was painful to both, for both were nearly bursting with the desire to speak. The daughter gave the mother a look that said "It's taking a long time ..." and the mother's look replied, "Try to hang on a little longer." And it was only a very little longer that she had to hang on, for at the end of two minutes, the Captain threw his pen on the table, got to his feet, and walked impatiently up and down the room. Mother and daughter were afraid, for rarely had they seen him more agitated. And he said: "I can't write and I'm done with trying. I'm sick and tired, I swear it."

"Daddy," said Miss Trefor, "can I write for you?"

"*Cei*[1]," he said. He would have said '*Cewch*' if he not lost his temper. "*Cei*," he said, "if you can tell more lies than I can."

"The very idea, Daddy!" exclaimed Miss Trefor.

"The very idea?" said the Captain. "What do you two know of the trouble I have to keep things going? What have you two got to think about, except how to throw money away, and how to be the best dressed, without ever thinking too much about tomorrow? But things have come to a head and there will soon be an end to me and to all your follies; you can be sure of it."

"Oh, Richard dear," said Mrs. Trefor—for hearing the Captain talk like this was new to her—"Oh, Richard dear, I expected it would come to this. I knew you'd go out of your mind studying so much geology. Susi, fetch the doctor at once."

"Doctor be cursed," said the Captain angrily. "What's the matter with you, woman? Do you think I'm a fool? Out of my mind indeed! Well, many a man's gone out of his mind for less than this."

---

[1] '*Cei*'—"*You may*." The second person singular; used to address friends, inferiors or animals, as opposed to the more formal '*Cewch*', the second person plural, which confers more respect on a single recipient (or indicates that you're talking to several friends, inferiors or animals); precisely the same gradation applies in French, with 'tu' and 'vous'.

"You *are* out of your senses, then, Richard dear? Well, whatever shall we do now? Susi, go and fetch the doctor this minute," said Mrs. Trefor dolefully.

And to fetch the doctor she would have gone that minute, had the Captain not fixed her with a stare that pinned her, terrified, to the chair. The Captain, addressing his better half, continued: "Do you know what, woman? I knew you slept late on the day they shared out brains, but I never thought you had so few. There's not much fear of you going out of your senses for, goodness knows, you've not got any."

"Oh, no! Of course not! Of course I haven't got any sense. I'm nobody. I'm nothing. I don't understand geology. I'd like to see the woman who *does* understand geology. I remember the time when someone, who thought himself very clever, thought I had sense—and thought I had brains, and I could never get any peace from him. But I must have had no sense then or I wouldn't have listened to him. And I still have no sense; no, none at all!" said Mrs. Trefor, and she began to cry, and hid her face in her apron.

A man's heart must be as hard as a nether millstone, if his wife's tears have no effect on him. Every wife is conscious of the power of her tears, and Providence has taken care to give her an ample supply of them. How many unanswerable arguments have been shattered by a woman's tears? Even Captain Trefor was not invincible before his wife's tears, especially when Miss Trefor's tears too turned on the enemy. He was quickly routed by that tearful army, and sought terms of peace by sitting at the hearth and smoking. After which, he said, much more gently: "Sarah, forgive me. I know I'm a fool and I forgot myself. I ought to have known that you and Susi knew nothing about business. But if you only knew the trouble I'm always in, perhaps you'd forgive me. Sarah, stop crying; that's enough, that's enough. Listen to me."

"Daddy," said Susi, "I hope you're not going to talk about

business, about the Syndicate, the Board of Directors, geology, and such things, for you know that mother and I don't care for that kind of thing."

"I'm speaking to your mother, Susi. Sarah, won't you listen to me?" asked the Captain.

"Yes, if you'll talk like any other man, and not lose your temper," said Mrs. Trefor, drying her eyes and taking up her needlework once more.

"Well, I'll try," said the Captain, and by this time he'd cooled down enough to speak more or less carefully and grammatically. "You know, Sarah, that I've been connected with Pwll y Gwynt for a great many years. I was the instrument that started the work. I, and one other, formed the Company. Anyone would admit that scores of families have had their living from the mine, and that the mine has been a great help in advancing the cause of religion in these parts. Indeed, I don't know what would have become of that cause if it had not been for Pwll y Gwynt. You must admit, Sarah, that during the whole of that time you've never wanted for the comforts of life or the means of grace. We have, during this time, as a family, raised ourselves in the opinion of our neighbours, and we're looked upon with considerable respect. You do admit that, Sarah? You don't need me to remind you of our position before my connection with the mine. You know what sort of a house we had then. It wasn't a house with a stable and coach house, was it? We had no horse or trap, or servant or maid. We didn't sit in the best pew in chapel then, eh? I wasn't the man then that I am now. Richard Trefor of Williams' Court was not the same person as Captain Trefor of Tŷ'n yr Ardd. Richard Trefor, when he sat on a bench in the chapel, had a little bit of conscience. He had a little taste for the means of grace. What taste does Captain Trefor have now for the Gospel, in the pew with a cushion on it?" Have you ever thought, Sarah, how much it cost Richard Trefor to become Captain Trefor? I know I've kept all this from you for years, for fear of worrying you.

It was wrong of me. But I can't keep it from you any longer. Ruin is all that awaits us."

And the Captain began to lighten his conscience. But before he did, he took a strong dose of the Scotch Whisky.

8

HE LIGHTENS HIS CONSCIENCE

"When I started Pwll y Gwynt," said the Captain, "heaven knows I hoped it would turn out well, and the most experienced miners believed it would. There was an excellent 'look' about the mine. I had no trouble, as you know, in forming a company. With the assistance of Mr. Fox of London, I persuaded several wealthy people to join the Company; and you know, Sarah, how many of our neighbours, such as Hugh Bryan, made themselves poor buying shares in the mine, and I gave them to understand I was doing them a favour letting them have shares at any price. How lucky I was, in the eyes of other people, and in my own. How quickly those who used to call me Richard started to call me 'sir' and 'Captain'. I went to bed a common miner, slept, and woke the next morning as 'Captain' Trefor, a man of respect and influence, one whose favour was courted, one with favours to distribute wherever he wished, one who conferred a kindness by accepting the valuable gifts of others! There was scarcely a man in town would refuse anything I asked of him. You remember, Sarah, that I merely said to Mr. Nott the ironmonger that I liked his horse, and he made me a present of it the next day; for Mr. Nott knew very well that I could send many a horse his way if I chose. That gift paid Mr. Nott well. I had only to look at a gun or a silver teapot in Mr. Nott's shop, and it would be here next day 'with Mr. Nott's compliments', and many others behaved likewise. When Tŷ'n yr Ardd was empty, a number of people wanted it; but Captain Trefor got it. Sarah, can you say how much of this furniture was given to us, and why? Because I had discovered 'y plwm mawr' in Pwll y Gwynt, and because I, through my cunning, had quietly made myself Captain of the mine. I feared from the start it would turn out a false one, but I kept that to myself and hoped for the best. I'd known Mr. Fox, of London, for years. I had the measure of his conscience; and knew how well he could work the oracle. I dropped him a line and he came at once. I took him to see Pwll y Gwynt; he was close to fainting when he saw the 'look' of it, and had his heart had not been as hard as a nether millstone he would have cried like a child. He was half crazed, and shouted and leapt around like a madman. He was so pleased and happy that I swear he would have carried me on his back for ten miles. I knew exactly what sort of a man I was involved with, but he knew nothing of me. It had emerged at the hotel, before we started for Pwll y Gwynt, that I was a Methodist, and he wasn't really sure how to speak to me. At the start, he was very careful what he said. He was Mr. Fox by name and by nature. He was a great 'believer' in his own way that day; and after seeing Pwll y Gwynt, when we were having dinner, after saying grace, he enquired deeply into the history of religion in Wales and took great pains to demonstrate that Scottish Presbyterianism and Calvinist Methodism were the same thing. I knew very well that he and I were the same thing, and said to him, "Mr. Fox, that's not the point we have to deal with today; I've known about you for years, but you know nothing about me. I know that where mining is concerned, you'll not allow religion to stand in the way of success. Your experience—by that I don't mean your religious experience—is great. Our point today is how to get Pwll y Gwynt talked of, so as to form a powerful company, and get sufficient money into our hands. You know the mine has an excellent 'look'. You're the man in London, and I'm the man here; however far your conscience may stretch in London, so will mine here."

"When I'd said that, Mr. Fox shook me by the hand, called for a bottle of champagne, and from that day to this not a word of religion has passed between us. You know Mr. Fox, don't you Sarah? He's been here more than once for dinner, and he's always talked to you about religion, hasn't he? And the eye closest to you would be crying, and the other winking at me. Mr. Fox is a Scotsman, and the most infernal hypocrite—except for myself—I have ever known. Sarah, if I were to go through the whole story in detail, half of it would be as Latin to you; and the only thing you'd see clearly would be what a conscientious husband you have. But there was no Latin between Mr. Fox and I. We understood each other perfectly. We both hoped from the bottom of our hearts that Pwll y Gwynt would turn out well, and both believed from the bottom of our hearts that it would not; but like true miners, that belief was never breathed to a living soul."

"Do you follow me, Sarah? We formed, as you know, a strong company, and thousands of pounds were invested. We made a point of opening as little of the mine as possible, so its poverty would not be discovered, and took care to spend as much as we could on buildings and machinery and so on. For when people have spent a lot of money on a mine, it's more difficult for them to give it up. And in came the water to help keep the mine going, and be an excuse for every hindrance and delay. The water was a great friend to Mr. Fox and I. Several thousand pounds drowned in it. We had to replace the machinery three times to please our faithful friend Mr. Water. Every time we got new machinery, it fair emptied the pockets of the Company, and put a little more into Mr. Fox's pocket and my own; for the Company trusted our judgment as buyers, and it was only fair and just that we be paid for that judgment. It was not the Company, you understand, that paid us, but the people who made the machinery, for the books had to show that everything had been done in a straightforward manner, and that no deceit had been used. 'Commission', you know, is what the manufacturers call it, a word invented to quiet the consciences of Captains. But by now the word is in the dictionaries of candlemakers, ironmongers, timber merchants, chemists, and a thousand others."

At this point the Captain appealed to the bottle for succour.

"Do you understand me, Sarah? I know you won't have me hung.

Well, as I was saying, we took care to open the mine as slowly as possible. When we were quite certain there was a little lead in a particular part of the mine, we used to leave it there, like money in a bank, and keep it until the Company's heart was almost broken; and then, when we saw they were about to give the mine up, we went to that bank and took enough lead to throw new spirit into the Company, to carry on for a while longer. Once the Company was back in that good spirit, we'd start economising again, report this and report that, down the years; one lie this week, another lie the next, to keep things going, until now I have no new lies to tell, and it's no use going back to the old ones, for people remember them too well. The largest shareholders are utterly disgusted and enraged, and have decided they'll not go a step further. But Mr. Fox and I can say we've done our duty, and that we've done our best to keep the mine going."

"Well, Richard," said Mrs. Trefor, who'd been rendered quite dazed, and couldn't decide whether the Captain had lost his senses or had taken a drop too much; "Well, Richard, you're not saying there's no lead in Pwll y Gwynt? I've heard you tell Mr. Denman hundreds of times that there was a '*gwlad o blwm*'[1] there, and that you'd be sure to come upon it some day."

"Between you and me, Sarah," said the Captain, "I swear there's not enough lead in Pwll y Gwynt to fill my hat. But it won't help, you know, for everyone to know that. It doesn't much matter about the people in London, but I'm sorry about Denman. He's a neighbour and has severely impoverished himself. Indeed I fear Denman will be as poor as I, one of these days,"

"As poor as you, Richard? You're not saying that you're poor?" said Mrs. Trefor, with great terror.

---

[1] '*gwlad o blwm*'—literally, '*a land of lead*'. A touch of hyperbole from the Captain. You may, incidentally, have noted that '*plwm*' of earlier chapters has, for the moment, become '*blwm*'; a feature of the Welsh language known as mutation. I will not attempt to explain it; I will say only that it is an interesting and widespread phenomenon.

"As poor, Sarah, as a church mouse, with just the things you see round you. I was afraid that you and Susi—Susi, how can you sleep whilst your mother and I are talking about our circumstances?" said the Captain angrily.

"You know, father," said Susi, rubbing her eyes, "I don't like hearing anything about business."

"My girl," said the Captain, "You'll have to seek a business for yourself one of these days. Yes, Sarah, I was afraid that you and Susi were living in a fool's paradise. We are poor; understand that. A heap of money has passed through my hands, but without benefit, it has gone somewhere, and you two know where a lot of it has gone. We must look the fact in the face—*we are poor*, and it will be all over with Pwll y Gwynt before the end of the month."

"Oh, mother," cried Miss Trefor.

"Mother as much as you like," said the Captain, "and between you and me, miss, you ought to have been a mother yourself before this, instead of giving yourself such airs and graces as you do. You'll have to come down a peg or two, and take whoever you can get hold of, though he may be only a common miner."

"The idea, father!" said Miss Trefor.

"The idea be blowed! Don't you realise your position? Isn't it possible to knock anything into your empty head?" said the Captain, losing his temper a second time.

"Richard," said Mrs. Trefor, deliberately, "keep your temper. If that's our position—if we are poor, after all the years of carrying on, what are you intending to do?"

"There now, Sarah," said the Captain, "you're talking like a sensible woman. That's the question, Sarah. Well, this is my intention; to keep up appearances as long as I can, and start a new mine as soon as I'm able to."

At this point someone knocked at the door; following which Mr. Denman appeared.

9

CONFIDENTIAL

"Well, here's Mr. Denman!" said the Captain. "Speak of the devil and he's sure to appear. We were just talking about you this very minute."

"What made you talk about me?" asked Mr. Denman.

"Well," said the Captain, "I was saying … But look here, Mr. Denman, let's go to the smoking room; these women will be glad to be rid of us."

Once there, the Captain added: "Yes, this is what I was saying, Mr. Denman, before you came in, that it would be an excellent thing to see you; the only one of the neighbours who still believes in Pwll y Gwynt; an excellent thing that'll see you a rich gentleman, one day. You deserve that, Mr. Denman, I swear, if anyone ever deserved it."

"If that doesn't happen to me soon," said Mr. Denman, "I'm much more likely to end my days in the workhouse. Have you any news about Pwll y Gwynt? What sort of a 'look' has it now?"

"Well," said the Captain, "I have only the same old story to tell you, Mr. Denman, and yet not quite same old story either. There's a better 'look' there now than I've seen for some time, and yet I'm afraid to say too much lest we be disappointed. I always prefer saying too little to saying too much. But, as you know, we're having to fight the water continually; the elements are against us; and if the directors had taken my advice and had sufficiently strong machinery at the start, we'd have got the better of it long ago. But a man doesn't always get his own way, especially when he's only a servant. I will say this much—and of course I don't claim to be infallible—but so far as human knowledge can go—and by now I've gained a little experience—so far, I say, as human knowledge can go, there's a better 'look' there now than I've ever seen before. Perhaps—I don't think so, but perhaps—we'll have to be a little patient. You know yourself that the lead we've got—it wasn't much, I confess—but you know the lead we've got shows clearly that there's more of it there. The question—and the only question—is, will the Company have the patience, faith and perseverance to hold on till we come to the riches? If everyone in the Company were like you, Mr. Denman—that is, men who know something about the nature of a mine—there'd be some hope that they'd hold on. But what sort of men are they? I'll tell you; men who've made their money in a short time, merchants and the like, and so expect a mine to return a big profit in a short time—they're impatient if something doesn't pay immediately. But a mine's not like that. Sometimes you have to wait for years; and many, as you know, after spending thousands, have given up because they don't have the patience to wait. And then others come along, and with next to no expenditure, take the wealth they left behind. We have been a little unlucky in Pwll y Gwynt, and I know it's very troubling to be waiting and waiting, and be disappointed—especially when so much hard cash is being spent. I greatly hope the Company will see their way clear to carry on a little longer at least—if only for the sake of my character, to prove I spoke the truth. But, between you and me, I wouldn't be at all surprised if those Englishmen gave up, and that when we've almost reached the lead—and that would be a pity. If such a thing happened to Pwll y Gwynt, I'd swear never to work under a Board of Directors or anyone else, and insist on having my own way in working the mine."

"Do you know what, Captain," said Mr. Denman, "if those Englishmen, as you call them, were to give up the mine tomorrow, I wouldn't be sorry, in a manner of speaking. Not because I don't believe there is lead there—no, I've believed in Pwll y Gwynt from the start. But if I'd known I'd have had to spend so much money, I'd never have joined the Company. I never thought I'd have to spend more than a hundred or two, but now nearly all I have has gone;

and, whatever the Englishmen do, I'll have to give up—my pocket can't stand it."

"I hope, however," said the Captain, "you don't think I intentionally misled you. And as to your pocket, I know pretty well about that. If Captain Trefor had your pocket, he'd sleep sounder tonight. You have houses and lands, Mr. Denman, and if you give up your interest in the mine, you'll regret it for the rest of your life. It's madness to talk of giving up now when we've almost got through all our difficulties. You know I have shares in the mine, and I'll sell the shirt off my back before I give up."

"I have every faith in you, Captain," said Mr. Denman. "Indeed I'd never have thought of taking shares in the mine were it not for the fact that I know you, and that we're members of the same chapel. No, whatever happens to Pwll y Gwynt, I'll say that you are honest. But I have to give up. I may as well tell the truth. I've mortgaged my houses and lands almost to their full value—except the house I live in—and my wife knows nothing about it; if she knew, it would break her heart. She knows, by the scarcity of money around the place, that I've spent an enormous amount on Pwll y Gwynt, and she's moaning, moaning all the time; but if she knew everything, I'd have to leave."

"I'm very sorry to hear you speak like that," said the Captain, "and perhaps you'll find it hard to believe, but I've lost many a night's sleep, as Sarah knows, thinking of the great sacrifices you've made. But I hope and believe I'll see the day you tell Mrs. Denman all, and she'll praise you. But everything depends upon whether the Company has the faith and patience to go on."

"If the Company gave up the mine, what would you do, Captain? Would you live on your money?" asked Mr. Denman.

"Not entirely, Mr. Denman; I'd rather start again." said the Captain.

"Pwll y Gwynt?" asked Mr. Denman.

"Yes, Pwll y Gwynt" said the Captain, "if I had enough money. If I had the means, I'd buy Pwll y Gwynt. But as I don't have quite enough for that—indeed not nearly enough—I'd start somewhere else. My eye has been on the spot for some time, in case anything happened to Pwll y Gwynt. It's not a bad thing, Mr. Denman, to be ready for the worst. And it'll be my mine—with a few friends—and the London people won't have their fingers in this pie. It'll be a mine, on a small scale, with little expense, and will soon pay. But I'll have to gather a few friends, close to home, to take shares. One of these friends will be you, Mr. Denman. Between you and me, I have already got the Take Note,[1] and indeed I had your benefit in view as much as my own. You've spent so much, Mr. Denman, that I've been wondering how to put something your way."

"What have you got your eye on, Captain, if I may be so bold as to ask?" said Mr. Denman, greatly interested.

"Well," said the Captain, "you and I are old friends, and I know you'll not let this go any further, for the present at least. Remember that now is not the first time the place has come into my mind. No, it's been in my mind for years; I've often dreamt of it. In my mind, it's well-established—the puddling[2] is going on briskly, the engine is puffing, trollies are carrying the lead to Llanerch y Môr[3]—and yet the grass is green on the face of the soil. You understand my thoughts, Mr. Denman? In my mind the mine is old, but in reality the turf is uncut. In my mind—the Captain closed his eyes for a minute—I see it all in full production; it's old, old in my mind; but to the world it's new—indeed unknown—a perfect secret."

"Perhaps I'm too bold," said Mr. Denman, "but you've not said yet..."

"Mr. Denman," said the Captain, interrupting him; "don't use words like that. It's not possible for you to be too bold with me. As

---

[1] Take Note—a document granting the right to mine or quarry, typically in exchange for a royalty of 10 per cent to the landowner.

[2] Puddling—a process of refining lead or other metals.

[3] Llanerch y Môr—a hamlet on the Dee estuary, which in the Captain's dreams would become a thriving port.

I said, we're old friends, and I have no desire to keep anything from you; nothing, nothing. I wouldn't speak like this with anyone else. If anyone knows my secrets, it's you. I'll say more; I have never thought of the mine I speak of—I call it a mine, though it's not begun, for that's only a matter of time—I have never even thought of the venture I have my eye on, without you being—simultaneously—in my thoughts. I would say to myself—'Richard Trefor, no one else knows, but you know, there's a lot of lead in such and such a place; who'll share the treasure with you? Well, if anyone will, Mr. Denman will', I say to myself."

"I'm most obliged. Captain," said Mr. Denman, "but I'm afraid I can't risk any more. I've not another ten pounds to spend without doing wrong to my family."

"That consideration, chiefly, though not entirely," said the Captain, "obliged me to put you on the same ground as myself in this new venture. Remember there will be no English to manage us this time; you and I, up to the present time, have spent our money to please ignorant Englishmen, and as I've said, it wouldn't be a surprise if they gave up the mine and all its cost in the end; and it's time for you and I to turn our eyes to somewhere we know we can get our money back. The mine will be... wait though; I've not told you yet the name of the place I have my eye on, have I? Well the place is—it won't go any further for the present, will it, Mr. Denman? Well the name is *Coed Madog*![4] *Coed Madog*!! *Coed Madog*!!!" The Captain repeated the name in a confiding whisper, and it looked from Mr. Denman's face, as if every letter of the name was creeping down his back beneath his skin. "Yes, Coed Madog will be a mine to make money, not to throw it away on every wilderness. You and I, Mr. Denman, have *spent* enough, and it's time to start *earning*. Between

---

[4] '*Coed Madog*'—Madoc's wood. According to legend, a Prince Madoc sailed with a small fleet to Mobile, Alabama in 1170, several centuries before the time of Columbus. One hundred men disembarked to form a colony. He returned to recruit more settlers, set out, and was never heard from again. There are stories of a Welsh speaking Indian tribe; but not everything you will read here is true.

you and I, Mr. Denman, I don't have ten pounds to throw away either, but there's no need for everyone to know that. Of course, it will be necessary to spend something before the mine will pay, and that's why I said we must have a few friends with us. Now Mr. Denman, we'll look at the matter this way. You and I, in a manner of speaking, own the Coed Madog mine. We are on the same footing. Neither of us has money to throw away. Some must be spent. Therefore we need someone—or several people—to take shares. You know people better than I, and know their circumstances. If we can do good for friends of the chapel, all the better, but if we have to go to other denominations, well, it can't be helped. Who shall they be, Mr. Denman?"

"Well, Captain," said Mr. Denman, "of our own people I can think of no one more likely than Mr. Enoc Huws of Siop y Groes, and Mr. Lloyd, the lawyer."

"Wonderful," said the Captain. "How our thoughts coincide! I thought first of Mr. Huws. I know nothing of Mr. Lloyd; but Mr. Huws, it is said, is a man who's made a lot of money. He's a respectable young man, well situated as a tradesman, and, beyond doubt, religious; and if we can help him by means of the mine, we will, at the same time, be doing good for the Cause, because I myself believe that Mr. Huws is the best man we have in the chapel; that is, the best young man. The question is whether we can get him to see eye to eye with us. Mining, no doubt, is strange to him, and with such people it's not easy to put things in their proper light. Will you see him, Mr. Denman?"

"I think," said Mr. Denman, "that the best plan will be for you to send for him now."

"You have a talent for hitting the nail on the head," said the Captain; and, sitting down at the table, he wrote a courteous letter to Enoc Huws, asking him to come to Tŷ'n yr Ardd. Whilst the Captain is writing the note, and the maid subsequently taking it to the Siop y Groes, perhaps, it will be as well for me to give the reader a glimpse of Enoc's circumstances and mental state, poor fellow.

10

MARGED

Enoc Huws was only twenty-nine but already felt he was a *hen lanc*, inheriting all the discomforts of that unrestrained situation. He was a young man of tender feelings, and very careful of his reputation. In selecting his housekeeper, he took care to choose one a good deal older than himself. Her name was Marged Parri. Marged had seen the light of day at least twenty years before her master, a fact that she stressed when intricate and difficult questions arose between them, such for instance as whether potatoes ought to be peeled on Saturday night or Sunday morning, whether it would be better to boil or roast the neck of mutton, and similar momentous questions. She only mentioned her age when the correctness of her opinion was doubted. At such times she used to say "Master, I am older than you, and I should know best." Marged had never married; not, she said, because she had not had very good offers, and very often, but because she preferred the single life. But her master, Enoc Huws, thought he could see another cause for Marged's unmarried state; that cause also being her main qualification, in his view, to be his house-keeper; namely, her unlovable face. One look at Marged's face was sufficient to convince any reasonable man that she had never been kissed unless, indeed, she had at some time come across a man blind from birth. And her face was not the only likely reason for her single state; her figure was not the most beautiful, not likely to attract the admiration of any youth of good taste, nor to disturb his sleep. Marged was short and wide, as if she had at some time been made to carry an enormous load on her head, which had caused her to sink into herself somehow, shortened her neck and legs, and broadened her shoulders, waist and hips. A little work with a hammer and chisel would have made her round, and had she tumbled southwards from the top of Moel Famau, I'm told she'd have rolled to Rhuthun.

There was never a virtue without a vice, and it may be there was never a vice without virtue. In her own way Marged was not to be beaten. She would sooner have her finger broken than hear someone suggest there was the slightest untidiness in the house. Everything in her care was remarkably clean; and had anyone hinted otherwise, it would have been an unforgivable slander against Marged. Infallibility was Marged's chief virtue, and whoever doubted her was the greatest of sinners. Enoc Huws did not initially spot this infallibility. It's true he'd had excellent references before employing her, but, as has already been suggested, her chief virtue in his eyes at that time was her unearthly ugliness; so ugly that not even the most scandalous tongue would dare to make up a story that he and his house-keeper were on too-friendly terms. He had no idea of Marged's infallibility. In her first weeks in his service, Enoc Huws couldn't make head nor tail of her. If he complained about any part of her work Marged would sulk, and not speak to him for days. As a last resort, Enoc decided to praise her, to see what effect that had on her work. And one day, when Marged had prepared a dinner that no Christian of taste could possibly have eaten, he said: "Marged, it's a pity that my stomach feels so bad today, for you have given me a splendid dinner; it couldn't possibly have been better. If I had only known that you were going to give me such a good dinner, I should have invited someone; as it is, I'm afraid I'll have to go to the doctor to get something for my stomach."

"Yes," said Marged, "The dinner was good enough for any man living, but I'll make you a little wormwood tea, master, for why should you go to the doctor when I can make as good or better medicine than he?"

Enoc never again needed to complain overly about his meals. And so it was with the rest of Marged's duties. When she'd been deficient she had only to be praised, and things would be generally right the next time. The daily commendation of her master made Marged form a much higher opinion, if that were possible, of her virtues than she had to begin with, and caused her to manage all his affairs, except the shop. The shop was the only part of Enoc's empire she had not subdued. She was so completely the ruler of his house that Enoc at times feared he'd be given a month's notice. But what could he do? If he complained about anything, or if he tried to put his own plans forward, Marged would sulk, and do nothing at all—'*ni wnai na rhych na gwellt*'[1]; while, on the other hand, if he let her have her own way, things were more or less all right. To keep Marged in a good mood was equally important in Enoc's eyes, and took up almost as much of his thoughts as all his other administrative duties put together. If he wanted to introduce something to break the monotony of his bachelor life, he had to consider, for a long time, how he could do it without putting Marged out of tune. As has been said before, Marged's features were, at best, not enchanting, and Enoc dreaded seeing her angry and sulking. When she was that way, her appearance terrified him, and disturbed his sleep for nights. Though by this time he broadly understood Marged's ways, he couldn't help feeling his position was rather humiliating when he reflected that he, a successful merchant, looked up to by many of his neighbours, respected by fellow members of the chapel for his usefulness and generosity was, despite everything, required, in all his circumstances and plans, to take Marged into consideration and to carefully seek ways to '*cadw'r ddysgl yn wastad*'[2]. Had not Enoc Huws' heart—every chamber of it—been wholly possessed by Miss Trefor—though he never cherished a hope that his love would be returned—he would many a time have gone out to look for a partner in life, without

---

[1] '*ni wnai na rhych na gwellt*'—would do nothing at all; literally, would make neither furrow nor grass.

[2] '*cadw'r ddysgl yn wastad*'—to keep the peace; literally, to keep the saucer level.

caring about her worldly position, so uncomfortable did he feel. His cares were great; and as one who's given himself up to business, he had no time to make friends. Enoc was happiest when he was perfectly sure Marged was asleep. He had a small room connected to the shop, which he'd turned into a sort of office, and this was purposely filled with chests and other things so there was only room for one chair. To this room Enoc would go after supper to be alone and have a little peace. If he went to the parlour, Marged came to keep him company, fell asleep in an easy chair within two minutes, and snored like a fat pig until bedtime; and if he stopped her from doing so, Marged would be in a bad temper for three days. To prevent this disaster, Enoc regularly went to his office with the excuse that he had 'business' to do. 'Business' was the only thing Marged admitted she didn't understand. Whilst Enoc was in his office, Marged would be by the fire in the kitchen snoring like an engine, for two or sometimes three hours, for she never went to bed first, not being able to trust her master to lock the doors and turn the gas off. In truth, Enoc's position was wretched, and he was terrified that people would learn how much he lived under Marged's authority. Because of that, few friends were invited to his house, however much he might have wished it.

On the night referred to in the previous chapter, Enoc had gone to the office after having his supper. The night was cold and foggy, as I said. Enoc had been busier than usual during the day, and was extremely tired. He had not cared to go upstairs to wash and tidy himself, and he sat before the fire in clothes marked by flour; not to count the large profit he'd made that day, but to consider his lonely and uncomfortable position. If any of the young girls of the chapel had seen him that night, and known of his melancholy thoughts, no doubt several would have been ready to take pity on him. Perhaps even Miss Trefor's heart might have softened a little. His shop assistants lodged elsewhere, because Enoc didn't want them to know how much he was under Marged's governance. They had some fun now and then, but Enoc, poor wretch, as has been said, sat in front of the fire, pulled off his shoes and put on his slippers. He was too dejected to read, though the Liverpool Mercury was in his pocket. If he had gone from the kitchen to the office with the Mercury in his hand or under his arm, Marged would have known he intended to read, and would soon have followed to ask about the news. She'd done this many times, and in order to stay on good terms, he'd had to tell her something, with a cheery smile, though, if truth were told, he'd rather have urged her, in no uncertain terms, to go away and leave him in peace. Having sat still for some five minutes, Enoc appeared more agitated than usual; he wrinkled his forehead, and thrust his hands to the bottom of his trouser pockets. Then he got to his feet, reached for his pipe, filled it tightly, and smoked hard, till he blackened the ceiling of the office. Then he spat scornfully into the heart of the fire, emphasised it with his head, and underlined it by spitting twice more, as though he were making some firm decision and extinguishing someone for ever. His expression would have had a stranger believe here was a decisive and very masterly individual. But all at once, as though remembering who he was, Enoc rose cautiously to his feet, opened the door a fraction, noiselessly, and listened to see whether Marged was sleeping. After making sure such was the case, he smiled, shut the door again quietly, and on resuming his seat, said to himself, loud enough for the mice to hear; "All right, Jezebel. But living like this is ridiculous. Here I am, toiling away all day, and for what? All my staff are happier than I. Thank God no one knows what a life I have; if people got to know, I could never show my face; I'd go to America, I swear. And why must it be like this? I'm not poor. I'm doing better than most, and I think that if I were to offer myself—well I'm almost sure I could have someone—but it's no good talking; am I not the worst kind of fool? Isn't the cause of all my discomforts the fact that I dream every night, building castles in the air around Miss Trefor? True enough. But I'm going to put an end to it tonight; an end forever and ever. Why should I bother? Nothing will ever come of it, as far as I know. I'd like to have a little more courage and be more hard-faced; but be quiet; you have neither of the two. Many a man would have insisted on knowing before now whether there was any hope, and if not, would snap his fingers and turn to other fields and pastures new. But what has Enoc done? He's loved in his imagination, all alone without lifting a finger to bring things to a head. What a fool I am! What a mercy that no one knows a man's thoughts. But there is something to be said on Enoc's side; she's haughty; yes, I may as well call it by its right name; she's proud. She doesn't talk to bolder people than I, people more respectable, in the worldly meaning of the word. Though we go to the same chapel, and we've known each other for years, she'll scarcely look at me. If I was only to mention it to her, well, I can see her; it would be a small matter to give me a slap in the face. It's certain, though there's no talk of it, that she's looking for someone much higher than a grocer as a husband. Everyone knows—and she knows—that she's pretty, and that even her pride becomes her. It's a pity I'm not a gentleman. Her father, they say, is rich, and thinks a lot of her. Naturally enough. So do I. Captain Trefor, what price do you put on Susi? Well; Enoc Huws is the highest bidder! But let us consider, for the sake of argument, that this is possible, and even likely, even a fact; what would be the consequence? A revolution in my surroundings. First, I'd have to turn Marged away, and it would need two policemen to do that. Next, I'd have to refurnish the house from top to bottom, and perhaps extend it. Then all of the little money I have, and all the profit from the business, would go in maintaining our style. For how long could I hold out? A year perhaps. But still—and this is a fact—if it were possible, every farthing I have could go, if I could only live with her and call her Mrs. Huws even for only a year: if ever there was a fool, Enoc Huws is he. But stop, Enoc; you can't be a fool any longer; we'll put an end to these empty thoughts after tonight. We'll think of someone else more likely, more suitable to be a shopkeeper's wife; someone who won't cause

48

a revolution, who won't be ashamed to go behind the counter, someone who'll be a help and comfort to me. But you've *said* this many times before; yes, but I'm going to *do* it after tonight, come what may! Hello, who's there now? Hasn't the shop been open all day, I wonder? Yet some people must come and bother a man after closing time. The same people every time. It's old Mrs. Bennett, or old Murphy, I swear." Thus Enoc was talking when someone knocked loudly at the door.

11

AT CROSS-PURPOSES

As I said, someone was knocking at the door of Siop y Groes, ending Enoc's soliloquy. Within a minute, he heard Marged drag herself along the lobby, grumbling. He listened attentively, expecting to hear her lay down the law to Mrs. Bennett or old Murphy for disturbing her after closing time. Instead of which, he heard her say "Come in." Then she swung open the office door in her usual way, without knocking, and said: "Come in, my girl. Master! Oh heavens! You've been smoking unconscionably; you're bound to kill yourself one day. Here's a letter from Captain Trefor, and the girl wants an answer."

It was lucky that Enoc had a layer of flour on his face; but for that, Marged and the girl would have been bound to see he'd turned white the moment Captain Trefor's name was mentioned. With shaking hands Enoc opened the letter and read it. It contained but few words:

TŶ'N YR ARDD

DEAR SIR,—If it's not too late, and if you are not too tired after your various duties, and have not company you cannot conveniently leave, I should be much obliged if you would call round, as I'd like to talk to you on a matter of importance to you and to me. I await your reply through the messenger.

yours faithfully,
RICHARD TREFOR.

It was with some difficulty that Enoc wrote a line to send back with the girl, saying that he would come to Tŷ'n yr Ardd in half an hour's time. He had enough presence of mind to say 'half an hour', to have time to wash and dress. Enoc asked Marged for a candle.

"What does the Captain want with you, Master?" asked Marged, with her usual boldness

"Business," said Enoc quickly, a word which usually acted as a talisman on Marged. But this time it was not entirely successful, and she said: "Business, at this time of night? What business do you have to do now?"

"The Fly Wheel Company has gone beyond its latitude, and there is something the matter with the grommet" said Enoc gravely.

Marged, of course, could not comment, and the candle was fetched at once. But Enoc's mind was much disturbed, his heart beating fast, and his nerves working like a factory. After washing, he had a hard time putting on his best clothes, and when he tried to put a clean collar round his neck, he thought he never would manage it, so violently did his hands shake. He thought, more than once, he'd have to call Marged to help him. He succeeded in the end, but not before beads of sweat had appeared on his forehead. After tidying himself as best he could, he hurried downstairs, and to his surprise the first thing he saw was Marged with Captain Trefor's note in her hand; she seemed to be trying to read it, although she couldn't read. It would have been a pleasure to give her a thick ear, but he restrained himself, as he had hundreds of times before.

"I'd like to be a scholar, Master, to be able to understand business," said Marged, unconcernedly putting the note on the table and leaving the room.

"You're enough of a scholar for me, you old bag," said Enoc to himself, putting his shoes on.

Before starting out Enoc read Captain Trefor's letter a second time, and when he came to the words—which he'd not taken particular notice of before—"I want to talk to you on a matter of importance to you and to me," he blushed—'*gwridodd at ei geseiliau*'[1].What could the Captain mean? asked Enoc; was it possible that his feelings for Miss Trefor had, by some unknown means, come to the Captain's notice? Enoc was sure he'd not said a word to a living soul. And yet, he thought, the Captain must know all. Had his face or behaviour betrayed him? Or had someone read his innermost thoughts and informed the Captain? The Captain himself was a very observant man, and perhaps something of a mind-reader. Was it possible he'd been found out, and was invited to Tŷ'n yr Ardd to be rebuked for his presumption? Had he talked in his sleep? Had Marged heard him, and had she gossiped? Enoc asked himself a hundred and more questions, each more foolish than the last, and heartily regretted his promise to go to Tŷ'n yr Ardd. He thought of making an excuse to break his promise, and sending Marged with a note to that effect. But he remembered at once that she wouldn't be able to get her boots on, as her feet were in the habit of swelling in the night and didn't return to their natural size till morning. The half hour was up; he must go; or not go. He looked in the small glass he had in his office, and perceived that his face looked grey and drawn, and would make the impression on anyone who saw it that its owner was unlikely to live long. He rubbed his cheeks, summoned what courage he possessed, and set out for Tŷ'n yr Ardd. Enoc hoped that, no matter what else happened, he would not be seen that night by Miss Trefor. He felt that this was the greatest struggle he had ever made, and that his future happiness depended entirely on this visit to Tŷ'n yr Ardd. Privately, he'd often called himself a weakling, but never imagined he was one till this night, because when he knocked on the door of Tŷ'n yr Ardd, he felt his legs giving way beneath him, and had to lean against the wall to stop himself falling while waiting for someone to open the door. He was led into what Captain Trefor called the smoking room, and Enoc wasn't displeased to see

---

[1] '*gwridodd at ei geseiliau*'—literally, he blushed to his armpits. Fortunately Enoc had his shirt on by now.

no one there but the Captain and Mr. Denman. Mr. Denman was doubtless there, Enoc thought, as a witness; he felt that the matter had assumed an importance in the Captain's thoughts, and never in his life was he more glad of a chair than the one offered to him, cheerfully and hospitably, by the Captain himself.

"The Captain," reflected Enoc, "must look favourably on the matter, or perhaps he's acting the hypocrite to uncover the truth."

"I hope, Mr. Huws," said the Captain, "that you're well, though I must say—it's not complimentary, I know—that I've seen you looking better. You work too hard, I know. You people who are doing well, I am afraid, take too much out of your bodies. The body must have rest, or the price will somehow be paid, you know. You must look, as they say, after number one. Your business is large, I know, and someone must look after it. But be careful, Mr. Huws. I always say that making money isn't everything in this world, and though it is necessary ('He wants to know how much I'm worth', said Enoc to himself), we must always remember there's another world after this, ·mustn't we, Mr. Denman? While it's our duty to make the best we can of the two worlds, we must take care of the body, as I said, and not, while the sun shines on us, fall into an untimely grave. I think, Mr. Huws—forgive my boldness—that this is your danger. The world is smiling on you, ('He's trying to find out', thought Enoc), but remember that your body will only stand a certain amount of pressure, and if you put too much strain on the machinery, it's sure to break."

"I have—I have—hurried—somewhat—because I didn't—want—to keep you, Captain Trefor—waiting for me. I'm—really—out of breath—out of puff—as they say—and I'm not—some Samson of a man," said Enoc, with difficulty.

"You were foolish, Mr. Huws," said the Captain, "for half an hour's neither here nor there at this time of night. There was no need at all for you to hurry; indeed I should have come to you, Mr. Huws; for the matter about which I wish to talk has more to do with me—at my time of life—than with you. Next spring, God willing, I will be … well, at my age, a man should know a thing or two; his mind is made up, and nothing small will change it ('It's looking black for me', whispered Enoc deep inside).

"The matter I want to talk to you seriously about, Mr. Huws," added the Captain, "is one very near my heart, as Mr. Denman knows. In a manner of speaking, it's my only child, and whatever your decision may be, I will not let go ('I've had it', thought Enoc). Mr. Denman is, as you know, a father, and he must, as must I, take the future and the comfort of his family into consideration, and he is of exactly the same opinion as I about this. The matter I wish to speak to you about, Mr. Huws, is not new to me; it's not a thing of yesterday or the day before ('True enough', thought Enoc, 'but how in the world did he come to know?'). No, I've lost many a night's sleep because of it, although I've never said a word about it, even to Mrs. Trefor, to whom I ought to have spoken first of all, for she is as closely connected to it as I, so far as family comfort is concerned. But you know, Mr. Huws, though you are a '*hen lanc*'—I beg your pardon, you're not a '*hen lanc*' yet nor intend to be one, I would think—though you're unmarried, you know women don't look at things as men. Women look at things through their hearts—sentiment is all—but we men must look at things through the eye of reason. "How do I feel?" is the woman's question; but "How should it be?" is what a man asks ('I wish he'd get to the point and have done with it', said Enoc inwardly). But what I was saying is that the matter I wish to speak with you about is not a new matter to me, and Mr. Denman is the only man I've mentioned it to—is that not so, Mr. Denman?"

"Yes," said Mr. Denman, "and I must say the Captain is a very perceptive man. I could scarcely believe it at first, but the Captain is serious and determined with regard to the matter, and I urged him to send for you tonight. I thought it was better to see you on the matter, Mr. Huws, than to write a letter."

"Just so," said the Captain, "we both agreed it was better for us to come face to face so as to get a proper understanding on the matter.

Later, Mr. Huws, it will doubtless be necessary for us—even if you fall in with our project—to involve someone else, such as Mr. Lloyd the solicitor, in this business, though we'd wish to restrict it as far as possible ('He means the marriage settlement', said Enoc to his heart, which was beating more quickly). I have, with a little cunning," added the Captain, "already secured the '*virgin ground*', as they say ('Well, thank you! If she's willing, I'm going to faint', said Enoc inwardly). But the question is—will you, Mr. Huws, be willing to join in the adventure, that is, if I succeed in showing you its advantages?"

Enoc was about to say that he was sure that he was willing when the Captain continued: "I'm afraid, Mr. Huws, you're not feeling well; your complexion shows it so clearly. Come here sir, and lie on the sofa for a minute. You've overworked yourself, and your stomach, perhaps, is out of sorts. Lie down, Mr. Huws; I'll get something to revive you."

Enoc felt quite helpless and did as he was told. Though he was furious with himself for being such a weakling, he was sure he was going to faint. The Captain opened the door and shouted loudly—"Susi, bring a little brandy here at once. "No, no," said Enoc, for he'd not yet fainted, "I'll be all right directly."

"You must take something to revive yourself, Mr. Huws. You've overworked yourself," said the Captain.

Thinking that the brandy was for her father, Susi came hastily into the room with the usual quantum which, to say the least, was ample. Susi was astonished when she saw Enoc Huws lying on the sofa, his face as white as chalk; and her heart was stirred, for even Miss Trefor had a heart, and she said tenderly: "Oh, dear Mr. Huws, you're ill! Oh, I am sorry, really I am. Take this, dear Mr. Huws, do." And she put her arm round his neck to help him lift his head.

Enoc had been a Nazarite[2] from birth, but how could he refuse?

---

[2] Nazirite—Euphamism for a teetotaler. Nazirites in the Bible (e.g. Samson) took the ascetic vow described in Numbers 6:1–21 to "… *separate [themselves] from wine and similar drink*"

His hand shook so much that he couldn't hold the glass steady, and Susi took the glass in her own hand, and placed it to his lips. The drink was so fiery, and Enoc so completely unaccustomed to it, that the tears sprang into his eyes as he swallowed it.

"Don't cry, dear Mr. Huws, you'll soon be better. Come, take it all," said Susi, whether kindly or cunningly.

And take it he did; and had the contents of the glass been deadly poison, and he had known, he could not have refused it from that fair and tender hand.

"Lie down now, dear Mr. Huws, and you'll be better in a minute," said Miss Trefor.

"Thank you," said Enoc, indistinctly. Suddenly he felt extremely happy. After a few minutes he felt the urge to sing, and rather expected someone to ask him to, and he began to dredge his memory for the song he could do best, and he fixed on '*Y 'deryn ddu bigfelyn*'[3] if he was asked. No one asked, and he didn't think it correct to offer on his own account. After a while, a feeling of lethargy came over him, but he was afraid to close his eyes lest he should sleep, for he remembered that he was a snorer, and he would not, for a thousand pounds, have Susi know he belonged to that class of creatures. Once he thought he was in a fever, and then that he was dreaming. But he couldn't be dreaming, for he was certain that Susi, Captain Trefor, and Mr. Denman were looking at him. At times they seemed far away and very small, and then close—painfully close—especially the Captain and Mr. Denman. He felt eager to speak to Susi, and tell her all his thoughts, and he knew he could have done this quite fearlessly and confidently, had he not seen her father and Mr. Denman before him. He was perfectly certain in his mind that he was on good terms with every man on the face of the Earth, and that he could make an impromptu speech on any topic. How long he was like this he never found out, and he never cared to recall

---

[3] *Y 'deryn ddu bigfelyn*'—a song, concerning the yellow-beaked blackbird. The Welsh have long used birds as messengers of love, perhaps doubting the reliability of the postal service.

the occasion. He was carefully watched by the Captain, Susi, and Mr. Denman, and when they saw signs that he was coming to, the Captain said: "How do you feel now, Mr. Huws?"

"All right," said Enoc.

"I knew," said the Captain, "that a drop would do you good. Well, as it has done Mr. Huws good, Susi, wouldn't it do me good? And when you've brought it, Susi, you can leave us to finish our business—that is, if Mr. Huws feels ready to continue."

"Certainly," said Enoc, briskly. "I am ready to enter into any reasonable arrangement, and I promise you, Captain Trefor, when I come into closer association with you, if ever I do, you won't have the trouble you've had tonight. I've never felt like that before. Usually I am a strong enough man, and work as hard as practically anyone, but somehow I couldn't …"

"It's your own fault, Mr. Huws," said the Captain, before Enoc could finish the sentence. "You work *too* hard, and that's why a man like you ought to—thank you, Susi, you can go now—yes, that's why a man like you ought to have someone to share your burden and your cares, and to look after your comforts. That's your great need, Mr. Huws, and if only you'd fulfil that need you'd be a happy man. What would have become of me, sir, but for Mrs. Trefor? I'd have been in my grave long ago. Forgive my observation, Mr. Huws, but a man who has reached—well, let's say my age—ought to be a bit of a philosopher. I don't see any object or aim worthy of a man in single life. You know, Mr. Huws—for you are, like myself, one who has read a lot—when a man turns inside himself in his search for happiness he'll always fail to find it; but when he directs his endeavours towards making others happy, then he'll gain his own happiness. For example—for there's nothing better than an example—if I had made my own happiness the chief aim of my life, and if Mrs. Trefor had done the same, we should both of us have been bound to fail. But, as the great aim of Mrs. Trefor's and of my life has been for each to make the other happy, we have gained our happiness together. And this is entirely in accordance with our

Lord's teaching on self denial, no matter how loath the world is to believe such teaching. Is it not so, Mr. Denman?"

"I never heard anyone put the thing more tidily. You're very sharp, Captain," said Mr. Denman, though he'd been thinking for some time about the reception he'd get from Mrs. Denman when he went home.

"No," said the Captain, "A man doesn't have to be very sharp to discover that truth, and I'm very confident that Mr. Huws will be experienced in the matter in a few months (He's rushing the wedding; but I don't mind how soon', said Enoc to himself). But it's time for me to come to the point," added the Captain.

"Yes," said Enoc, "and I'm quite ready. The sooner we come to an understanding the better."

"Well," said the Captain, "I have been beating about the bush for rather a long time before coming to the point ('Maddeningly so', said Enoc to himself). But I would have come to it before if not for—well, there's no need to go through that again. But this is the point, Mr. Huws" (Enoc held his breath) "You know—no one knows better—except Mr. Denman and myself perhaps, that Pwll y Gwynt mine has been, and still is, a great support to the neighbourhood in which Providence thought fit to bring our lives. And perhaps …" And the Captain's discourse continued.

12

STARTING TO GRASP THE SITUATION

As I said, the Captain's discourse continued: "Perhaps, Mr. Huws, taking everything into consideration, fate has been very kind to us, and no doubt Mr. Denman can say the same. Though I have many reasons to be grateful, perhaps more than most, not the least, Mr. Huws, is that I, as a humble instrument in the hand of Providence, have had the privilege of being connected, and in no contemptible way, with a mine that has been the means—if not directly, certainly indirectly—of giving bread to some hundreds of our fellow countrymen, and helping others to prepare for a rainy day— amongst the latter of which I count you, Mr. Huws; and connected also with what has been the means, not only of providing for the body, but in a manner of speaking, in reality, and as a matter of fact, a backbone and aid to the spiritual needs of the neighbourhood, enabling us by regular and constant ministration—no matter what may be said about its quality—to provide for, or at least, to give an opportunity to provide for, the needs of the soul. And that, we must all acknowledge, is the main thing—no matter whether we think of individuals or of society as society."

('What on earth's he talking about?' Enoc asked himself).

"Perhaps," added the Captain, "I should not be far wrong if I said that Pwll y Gwynt is the backbone of this neighbourhood in a commercial sense, and perhaps would not err if I said that you, among others, have derived no small benefit from the mine. Well, sir, it is a long lane that has no turning, as the English say, and as I already explained to Mr. Denman to the best of my ability, before your arrival, it is not impossible, nor indeed improbable, that you and I will see the day, though we may hope for the best, when Pwll y Gwynt, so to speak, will come to an end—not because there's no lead there and not—though I shouldn't be the one to say so—because the mine isn't being looked after as far as that's possible for a man governed by foreigners, not only with regards language, but also where experience and practical knowledge is concerned, as Mr. Denman knows. I see by your look, Mr. Huws, that you're surprised, and that's natural enough. But remember I don't tell you this as a matter of fact. Indeed, I hope that won't happen in our lifetimes. But as I said before you came in, it would be no wonder to me if those Englishmen—and you know Mr. Huws, that all the Company are English except for Mr. Denman and myself, as bad luck would have it—Mr. Denman knows why I say, 'as bad luck would have it'—it would be no wonder to me, I say, if those Englishmen were to give the mine up before the end of the month, though to do so would be one of the greatest follies on earth, and very much against my will—not only because it would bring many families into poverty, and the neighbourhood would suffer severely, but because it would be an insult, to a greater or lesser degree, to my own character, inasmuch as I have for years, as you know, persisted in saying—and I will persist in saying—that there is lead in Pwll y Gwynt, and a lot of lead, too, if only the right way to it were taken. ("What has all this got to do with me and Susi?" Enoc asked himself.) There is no time tonight, Mr. Huws, to go into detail, and I don't need to tell you that all this is in confidence, for the present at all events. But the probability is there will soon be an end to Pwll y Gwynt, and whenever that takes place—perhaps at the end of the month, or at the end of the year—but whenever it does, the reason can be summarised thus, as Mr. Denman knows; *that I could not have my own way*, and that the Englishmen living in London think they know how to work Pwll y Gwynt better than someone who's spent half his life underground. To put it in a nutshell, Mr. Huws, it comes down to this; *I cannot have my own way in managing the mine.* My way would be to carry on with the mine, but in an entirely different way, until we find the lead, which is there as sure as you and I are here now. But the London people's way, I'm afraid, is to give the mine up, as they don't have the patience to wait. I see, Mr. Huws, that I must hurry along, though I should have liked to have gone more minutely into things. The point is this; there is nothing like being prepared for the worst." (Enoc was beginning to discover which way the wind was blowing, and had cooled down considerably.) "For fear that the worst will come; for fear that Pwll y Gwynt will come to an end, and soon; and in order, should that take place, to make some provision for the dozens of families that depend entirely on the mine, and indeed for our tradesmen and others, I have secured—not with a view to my own profit, remember, for I shall, I trust, have a little for the little that remains of my life—and everyone of my age should be above want—not for my own sake, I repeat, I have secured 'virgin ground'; in other words, a place where I can, with a little help, open a new mine—not on the same scale, it's true, as Pwll y Gwynt—but a mine which, with the expenditure of a few hundreds of pounds, will pay its way in a short time, and at the same time afford a living to scores of workers; and better than all this, in my opinion, a mine in which the people from London will have no say, and where I'll be able to manage it my own way; and Mr. Denman knows where we'd have been by now if I'd only had my own way with Pwll y Gwynt. Now, Mr. Huws, Mr. Denman and I have resolved to give you the first offer, on the '*nes penelin nag arddwrn*'[1] principle. If we confer benefit on any, we should begin with our own people. What do you say, Mr. Huws? Are you ready—for I know you have the means—are you ready, for your own sake, for the sake of the neighbourhood, and above all for the sake of our faith, to join Mr. Denman and I, and take shares in the new mine? You have, if I've not misunderstood you, already expressed your willingness if I succeeded in showing that it would be of benefit to yourself and to the neighbourhood in general. But don't promise too hastily;

---

[1] '*nes penelin nag arddwrn*'—literally, nearer elbow than wrist; closer to the heart, one might imagine; to put it another way, blood is thicker than water.

sleep on the matter; for I wouldn't wish to put any inappropriate pressure on you; indeed, I'd rather you refused, if your heart is not with us in this venture."

Whilst the Captain was ending his speech, Enoc was in somewhat of a muddle, trying to remember every word he himself had said in the course of the conversation, and whether he'd betrayed himself, and let them understand he'd been thinking of something entirely different whilst the Captain had been talking of a mine. Enoc felt sure he'd said something about being ready to enter into an arrangement regarding the Captain's proposals before he'd known what they were, and when he realised that he and the Captain were talking at cross purposes, he felt considerable difficulty in explaining his way out of the entanglement. There was an enormous difference, thought Enoc, between taking shares in a mine and taking the Captain's daughter as a wife, and he felt furious with himself for not understanding the drift of the Captain's discourse earlier. That would have saved him from half fainting; and certainly he would not have said that he was 'ready to enter into any reasonable arrangement', or spoken of 'a closer relationship', and similar foolish things, if he'd known what the Captain was talking about. When the Captain put the question directly to him, Enoc didn't see a clear way of getting out of the mess, and in order to gain time to cogitate over it, he urged the Captain to explain himself in more detail, which that gentleman did in long, verbose, rambling sentences for another quarter hour. Then Enoc said—feeling that he was breaking his usual custom, which was to tell the truth straightforwardly and honestly—"I guessed from the start, Captain, it was a mine you had in view; and, as I've said, when there is business on the table, I'm always ready to enter into any reasonable arrangement; that is to say, if something appears reasonable, and likely to be successful, I won't be backward in tackling it. But the thing must appear to be reasonable before I'll meddle with it. So far, in business, I've not made many mistakes and I've never been guilty of taking a leap in the dark. On the other hand, there must be a little darkness in every venture,"—Enoc was still thinking of Susi—"for without it there would be no venture at all—and sometimes the darkness is in the mind of the adventurer, and not in the adventure itself. The venture you speak of may be very dark to me, not perhaps because it itself is so, but because I don't possess the eyes of a Captain Trefor to see it in all its parts. Perhaps, when I come into a closer relationship with you, if it ever comes to that, as I said before, the venture will seem clear to me. Of course, the workings of a mine are foreign to me, as they have been to scores of people before me, until they became acquainted with the thing. I'll take your advice, Captain Trefor; I'll sleep on the matter, and we'll speak of it again. I'm very sorry to hear about the condition of Pwll y Gwynt, and it's important to me, and to others, that preparation for the worst be made, as you say."

"I'm pleased to hear you speak like that, Mr. Huws," said the Captain. "I'd rather hear you say you'll consider the matter, than express your readiness to take shares before understanding what you're doing. When I see a man unwilling to take a leap in the dark, as you cheerfully put it, but with his ears open to listen to reason, I feel I have a man I can deal with, with no hint of a pound of flesh, and I know then how to set about my work. What would I not give tonight, sir, if the people in London, in other words, the Pwll y Gwynt Company, were of the same spirit and way of thinking as you, Mr. Huws, that is to say, willing to listen to reason? I would give all I possess, sir—the fruit of my hard labour over many years—if they could have your temperate nature, Mr. Huws. But we'll leave things as they are for tonight."

And so they did, though the Captain talked a little more whilst Enoc was putting on his hat and preparing to leave. The Captain called Susi "to show Mr. Huws out"; and when she made her appearance, the Captain shook hands with Enoc, and went back to finish his business with Mr. Denman.

13

A CLUMSY LOVER

The night was cold and foggy, as I've said twice before, and when Miss Trefor opened the front door to let Enoc out, he felt as though the wind were taking the skin off his face.

"Take care you don't catch cold, Mr. Huws, and I hope you're feeling back to normal now," said Miss Trefor.

"As well as ever I was," said Enoc, and he thought the opportunity had arrived to say a little about his feelings toward her.

"I know where to send for a doctor in future, if I'm ill. I don't know what came over me—perhaps I hurried too much. You take care of yourself, Miss Trefor, and don't come out into the cold. I can find the gate"

"Oh," said Miss Trefor, walking along the garden path in front of Enoc, "I'm not *delicate*."

Enoc felt the sting, and said quickly, "I'm not either, as a rule; but I'd never forgive myself if you caught a cold coming to open the gate for me."

"I hope," said Susi, "you won't have cause to be so unforgiving to yourself. I may not be wearing a bonnet but I have a hard head, you know, Mr. Huws."

"I hope the same thing can't be said of your heart, Miss Trefor," said Enoc, trying to break the ice.

"My heart never wears a bonnet, Mr. Huws; that has not yet come into fashion." said Susi.

"It wasn't the bonnet I had in mind, Miss Trefor, but the hardness." said Enoc.

"That's very reasonable, Mr. Huws; it's easier to imagine hardness in the mind than a bonnet in the mind." said Susi.

"You're a rough diamond, Miss Trefor," said Enoc, no better

answer coming to mind.

"Thank you, Mr. Huws; 'rough' is what we in Flintshire call anyone who is particularly ugly, or heavily marked by smallpox—such as Marged, your housekeeper," said Susi.

"True enough, Miss Trefor," said Enoc, "but you know that some words have two meanings, and that wasn't the meaning…"

"Two meanings, Mr. Huws?" said Susi, before Enoc could finish his sentence; "Every word has half a dozen meanings for you men, for you never think what you say, nor say what you think, when your words and yourselves come face to face."

"I will say this," said Enoc, calling all the gallantry in his nature into operation; "You're an angel, Miss Trefor."

"Hah!" said Susi, "a fallen angel you mean, of course, for there are two meanings to the word. Well, had I known, Mr. Huws, you disliked me so much, you'd not have had a drop of brandy, and you could have died on the sofa, you awful man. Good night, Mr. Huws." And she ran into the house.

"Well, the clever jade! If she hadn't brightened up, I don't know how I'd have answered her," said Enoc to himself as he walked quietly home, his opinion of Miss Trefor higher than it had ever been. He thought of no one and nothing but her till he was within ten yards of the house, when Marged came into sight. Like a naughty boy who's stopped out late without his mother's permission, Enoc felt uncomfortable at the thought of facing Marged and he began to search for some sweet word to put her in a good humour.

It's not necessary to say that two hours of sleep by the fire had not softened or beautified Marged. After an hour or two's nap by the hearth, her eyelids would stick together as if secured by cobbler's wax, and she had to use her knuckles vigorously for some time before she could open her eyes. After going through this preparation, then snorting furiously for a while, Marged narrowed her eyes, wrinkled her forehead, looked at the clock and said:

"Well, in the name of sweet reason, master, where have you

been till now? If I hadn't put enough on the fire, what sort of warmth would you have had here? And I don't know what made me think of making up a good fire; I never thought you'd be out till the middle of the night like this."

"You're always very thoughtful, Marged," said Enoc. "It's a great pity indeed that you're not married. You would make a good and attentive wife."

Marged looked pleased, and Enoc supposed he'd said the right thing, but it would have been better for him to have broken a finger or to have submitted to her abuse, than utter those words. Enoc felt in the best mood he'd been in for many a year. He had, at last, succeeded in getting his foot in the door of Tŷ'n yr Ardd, and he believed that there would be no longer any estrangement between himself and Miss Trefor; and Marged's excellent humour added not a little to his happiness. He longed for Marged to go to bed, so he could enjoy and feast on his thoughts in solitude, and build brand new castles. But fair Marged didn't so much as glance towards the stairs. Rather, she sat a little closer to her master than she ever had before, and showed an unmistakable inclination for affectionate discourse. Enoc couldn't comprehend the sudden and pleasant change in Marged. He thought fate was beginning to smile on him, and that happy days awaited. He was quite ready to be without Marged's company, but she showed no sign of going to roost. Enoc soon went to bed, although Marged said it wasn't so very late after all, and that their clock was a little ahead of the town clock.

14

FOUR BEDROOMS

ROOM I. "No, she's not as unapproachable as I thought she was. It's just a way she has. Really, she's kind; I saw enough tonight to prove that. And clever too; sharp. Well, what a fool I was! I wonder if the Captain realised I was thinking of Susi while he was talking about mines. I almost said her name more than once. Lucky I didn't! What a joke that might have been. What a joke it is! What if some of the lads here got wind of the story? What a feast they'd have! Still, my mind's not quite at ease. I can't help thinking the wily old bird might have spotted I was thinking about her while he was talking about the mine, and in such a similar way! But who— '*tu yma'r haul*'[1]—could have understood what he was driving at, with his "indeed," and his "so to speak," and "as a matter of fact." Every sentence takes a year, and takes a man's breath clean away. One thing I'm really angry about: "Don't cry, dear Mr. Huws," she said. Confound her! Cry! A man of my age cry because he's ill! That's what she thought, I know; drat! But that cursed brandy brought the tears to my eyes. If I died, I couldn't have stopped them. Well, it was as hot as a glass of hellfire, I swear. And she thinking I was like some baby crying for its mother! If anything will do for me in her sight, that crying will. I must tell her. Confound it! I'd rather have lost a hundred pounds than cry like that. I swear she thinks I'm some kind of crybaby. But wait, Enoc; you're now on such terms with the family you can go back and forth, and it's as if I was dreaming. But I'll have to take shares in the new venture, or I'll be where I was before. If the venture were in Jericho I'd be

---

[1] '*tu yma'r haul*'—literally, '*this side of the sun*'; who on earth?

better pleased. Why should I throw my money away on something I know nothing at all about? Most of these mines are swindles. And yet the Captain's Susi's father, and an honest and honourable man—as far as I know. If he said it was on the moon, I'd have to take a few shares. But I'll try to be cautious at first, till I see if I have any hope with Susi. No Susi—no shares; with Susi—I'd take shares in Jupiter—may I never stir if I wouldn't."

ROOM II. "I'm twenty-five years old; and the gentleman husband hasn't arrived yet. He won't either, or he would have done before now. Perhaps they've realised, sooner than I; my father's poor. Dear God, what a shock! Seriously! Why didn't he say so earlier, instead of keeping mother and I in the dark? And letting us carry on for years! But father's always so secretive. What will people say? And what will we do? Well, you can be put away now; I won't wear you again, now we're poor, 'Humbug', as poor Wil would say, keeping up appearances with nothing but appearances to keep. And I'm not going to do it, whatever mother might say. If poor we are, poor we should appear. I'll wear a cotton frock; people won't find so much fault when our poverty becomes known. I'd like to throw this gold watch out of the window. No more of you, bracelets and gold brooch. You're not becoming to poor people. And yet you are very pretty! Here's a farewell kiss for you! Lie quiet in your cotton wool till we need to sell you to get food. Such a pretty little thing. One more kiss, then close the box over your face.

Oh, I have as my father said, given myself airs. But never again! I'll be a sensible girl now, without any of Wil's 'humbug'. But I wouldn't have 'carried on' if father had told me earlier we were poor. How will I look, I wonder, in a cotton frock? There is one somewhere about. A bit out of fashion by now, I expect, but I can alter it. Where is it? I haven't seen it since I don't know when. I'll try it on to see how I look. A sealskin? Well, you'll have to turn into cash some day, I expect. Where is that old frock? I never thought I had so many clothes. I'll be the best customer

Mr. Leviticus the pawnbroker has had for years. Heavens, can I have given it away to someone? No, here it is! Well, old frock, should old acquaintance be forgot? Father likes hearing me sing that, but no more singing for me! Do you remember me? You look very wrinkled, but tomorrow I'll put you on a chair back in front of the fire and get the wrinkles out of you. What would you think of going to chapel again? You've been deprived of *y moddion gras* for a long time, haven't you? Gracious, have I got fatter, or have you shrunk? Well, by my living on broth, and you being let out, we'll meet somehow. Gracious! There's enough room in your sleeves to live in and your waist's about a mile too long. But why don't you button? Don't I look awful? But never mind, Susi, if that mirror speaks the truth, you don't look too bad yet. Well, old frock, you beat me in one thing; when I get old, it'll be no good putting me on a chair back in front of the fire to take the wrinkles out of my face. The idea! Yes, father talks of me taking a common miner. No! no, never! No—never in a million years! Not if I were as poor as Job! What sort of baboon-like idea did Enoc have, saying I was an angel? Was he hinting at something? But I can't stand the saint, he's too pious—too strait-laced. If he'd been half a man he'd have tried to steal a kiss at the gate. But if he had, I'd have slapped him in the face. Didn't I give that old Rechabite[2] a stiff dose? He nearly choked on it! The baboon! And me saying. "Don't cry, dear Mr. Huws." Perhaps it's wrong, but I do like saying things to annoy *hen lanciau*;[3] anything, if I can, to shake them to the core. But still, he's better than a common miner. Poverty has no choice if it comes to that. He has money; a lot they say. That's one good point. But he's so old fashioned! And has it come to this, Susi? Well … well … my 'idea' always was, if I didn't marry for money, to be head over heels

---

[2] 'Rechabite'—The Independent Order of Rechabites was a Friendly Society founded in England in 1835 as part of the temperance movement to promote total abstinence from alcoholic beverages.

[3] '*hen lanciau*'—the plural. More than one 'hen lanc'.

in love with someone, fling myself out of the window into his arms at three o'clock in the morning, and run away to be married by special licence. I have no patience with people who marry quietly in chapel. I hate seeing them. And yet, perhaps, so it will be with me. With a common miner? Never ever, I'd drown myself. What, I wonder, did father want with Enoc? To suck him in, I should think, as he did with poor Hugh Bryan, and Mr. Denman. But you have to do something to keep from starving. I don't remember now whether I've said my prayers. What does it matter? The best prayer for me tonight is a good cry in bed."

ROOM III. "Are you awake, Sarah? Or—in other words—are you asleep?"

"Mm?"

"Sarah, wake up, wake up. I want to talk to you."

"What time is it, Richard?"

"Well, it's nearly midnight, or, perhaps, a little later. How time flies! Are you awake, Sarah? I am ... are you awake? Oh. Well, I'm afraid I surprised and hurt you tonight, Sarah. But I've had so much on my mind lately; the pressure has been so great, so to speak, I was afraid the boiler would burst, and I had to open a valve somewhere, and where could I do that but in my own family? To whom could I tell my troubles if not to you and Susi? But on reconsideration ... don't cry, Sarah, don't, I beseech you ... on reconsideration, as I said, perhaps I have—indeed I'm sure I have—I've exaggerated our position, and set it out, in the agitation of the moment, as worse than it is. You need not, Sarah, have rushed to your bed in depression. No, with the blessing of the Lord, we will still have a little. Indeed, perhaps, we'll be better off than ever. Even if things come to the worst, I have an eye on something, and I want you, Sarah, to warn Susi not to say a word to anyone about what I said tonight in a moment of thoughtlessness. After you went to bed, Mr. Huws of Siop y Groes came here. A very excellent young man is Mr. Huws; he's done well; and I think—indeed, I'm sure—he'll be willing to join us in the new venture. One or two more like Mr. Huws and we'll be all right. He's weak—very weak—he's overworked himself, I've no doubt. Won't you speak, Sarah?"

"Why should I speak? I've got no brains."

"That's enough, that's enough, Sarah; don't mention that again. I was afraid I'd hurt you, Sarah, and I'm sorry about that; or, in other words, I apologise, and the Gospel says: 'Let not the sun go down on your wrath'; and we ought, indeed I humbly think that you and I, up to now, have tried—so far as lay in us—to stay within the rule of the Word and even in the present circumstance—no matter how unpleasant—to me particularly—I think you can keep to that rule, inasmuch as the sun had gone down before you took offence and will not, I hope, set on your anger. Have you forgiven me, Sarah, as the Gospel would wish?"

"I have not forgiven you, Richard, for keeping me in the dark as to our standing in the world. What will people say when they know about our poverty, and how we've carried on as we have?"

"Well, you know, Sarah, that's my nature, I can't help it. It's been in me since I was a boy—that is, over-tenderness ... over-tenderness. I was never able even to kill a fly, and I remember well ... have you seen my night-cap, Sarah? Oh, here it is ... I remember well, I say, when father killed a chicken, or what was worse, a pig, I had to leave home till the cruelty was over and though I was not directly involved with the killing of the pig, I used to feel some sort of guilt for weeks, and it was only with considerable encouragement on my mother's part that I would take any of the bacon when it came to the table. You yourself know, Sarah, how I grieved when Job Jones, poor fellow, was killed in Pwll y Gwynt. It was said at the time there was some negligence, but I couldn't help that, though the whole mine was in my care, and I was, in the eyes of the law, responsible, so to speak, for poor Job's death. You know, Sarah, how I grieved. I'll tell you what I've never told you before; that I was, more than once, close to killing myself, or, in other words, committing suicide, and that was brought on by too great a grief over the young man's death. And in part, I put that intention into operation, for you know that, on that occasion, I lost more than forty pounds in weight. Where did these forty pounds, a significant part of myself, go?

Well, in a manner of speaking, it could be said I'd committed suicide with them, or in other words, I had offered them up on the altar of a sad or over-tender heart. Perhaps it will be hard for you to believe, Sarah, but it's the truth, that I have never since met Job's mother without saying to myself, "This is the mother of the boy I killed." You have, before now, Sarah, scolded me for going to the church meeting only now and then, and suggested I am degenerate in my religion; but did you know the chief cause of this is the tenderness of my heart, and because I cannot look upon Job's mother without feeling a kind of guilt, though such a thing is unreasonable in the extreme. Do you see now, Sarah, why I kept our true position from you? Over-tenderness is the reason for it all. Rather than make you unhappy, I preferred to keep all the anxiety and trouble to myself, as long as it was possible. Not because I didn't trust you, Sarah, to keep it to yourself, and not because I had forgotten the inspired guidance that we should to bear our burdens together, but in order to spare your feelings and avoid disturbing your happiness. But I can say this; I have an easy conscience, and have done my duty."

"How have you done your duty, Richard, when you knew there wasn't your hat-full of lead in Pwll y Gwynt?"

"There is duty and duty, Sarah. My duty as Captain was to work for the Company, and to give a fair and honest trial to the mine, whether there was lead there or not. Now I'm able to say there's not my hat-full of lead in Pwll y Gwynt, but, unfortunately, I didn't know that years ago. Business, Sarah, is something foreign to you, and it would be useless for me to try to explain. We'll leave it there for tonight. But I want to say a word to you about something else, though I am feeling very sleepy. You know Susi's beginning to get on in years, and the girl should have married before now. Don't you think, Sarah, that Mr. Huws would make her a very good husband? Sarah?"

"Don't bother—please!"

"Well the girl ought to have thought of someone by this time, and there is a danger of her waiting too long. If my sight has not begun to grow dull, I think that Mr. Huws would not … what I mean, Sarah, is that you might mention it to the girl … it's the mother's place to do that. What do you say Sarah? Sarah?"

"Go to sleep, and stop talking nonsense, please."

"Well, I'm sorry to weary you, and it's time perhaps we thought … perhaps of finishing … and going to sleep …"

"There, you're snoring like a fat pig. But you'll stop talking now. I suppose. Oh dear me. There's a skeleton in everybody's cupboard, as my mother said. But I never thought it would come to this. I wish in my heart I'd never married."

ROOM IV. "Well, Denman! Denman! How did you have the nerve to come home at this time of night? Ain't you ashamed of yourself, seriously, Denman, wandering round people's houses at the dead of the night? Do you see anyone else doing it?"

"A lot."

"A lot? I'd like to know who they are. Anyone of any account?"

"Yes."

I should think they're people like you. Are they people who care at all about their wives and families?"

"I haven't asked them."

"No, I thought not, I knew that without you telling me. Do you think I'm going to wait up till the middle of the night for you to come home?"

"I never asked you to."

"No, and if you did, I wouldn't do it."

"Fine."

"Fine; Haven't you got a house of your own to be in at night?"

"Eighty-two, High Street.

"Dear me; how well you remember! You never go to the wrong house?"

"I've never been that lucky."

"Lucky? Are you saying to my face, Denman, you're tired of me?"

"Tired of someone as kind as you?"

"Yes, say it plain, Denman; I know that that's what you're thinking; say it plain you don't care about me. I'm good for nothing but slaving away, and more fool me for doing it. Have you ever seen me wander round the neighbours' houses?"

"Oh, never; you've never been in Mrs. Price's house till eleven at night! Dear me, no."

"Once—once in the four seasons I go to Mrs. Price's house to have a cup of tea; you're reproaching me for that, Denman? You want me to be tied to the doorpost all year?"

"Nothing of the sort. I'd like you to go and see Mrs. Jones at her shop, half a dozen times a month, but you never do."

"You reproach me for that too, Denman? I swear I have only been in Mrs. Jones' house twice in a fortnight. If I go anywhere I get it thrown straight back in my teeth …"

"In your teeth?"

"Less of your spite, Denman! My teeth were as good as yours till lately. And what do you expect of a mother with five children? Do you expect me to stay young forever? But you have no respect for me; that's plain enough. Where have you been tonight, Denman? Where—were—you?"

"Having a drink, of course, don't you think me drunk?"

"No, I know you've not been drinking, but it would have been better if you had been drinking than being with that cursed old Captain, for I know very well that's where you've been. Weren't you, Denman?"

"Why are you asking, if you know?"

"I'll swear you were there. Tell the truth, Denman, Weren't you there?"

"To be sure, you'd never take a false oath."

"I knew as well as if I'd been with you, you were with that old devil from the mine. I've repeated it and repeated it, till my till my tongue's worn out …"

"What? Your tongue worn out?"

"Scold me as you wish, I've said enough—if so much is enough—to make you give up that cursed old venture. If other people in their silks and satins can throw their money away on ventures, there is no need for you, a man doing his best to survive, to take every penny and throw every one into Pwll y Gwynt where you'll not see so much as a farthing again. You've made us so poor we haven't even a penny to hang ourselves with. What are you thinking, Denman? When do you think you'll stop giving every penny to that cursed old Captain? And here you are going to bed without going on your knees. A true believer, to be sure."

"Look here, my good woman; if you promise to keep that tongue of yours quiet for two minutes I'll go back to saying my prayers."

"Oh, I'm allowed to say nothing! I have to be quiet and suffer everything as if I were a stone. Well, it's come to something; it has; I'm no one—no one—though I'm the mother of five children. Yes, poor children! No one cares anything about them. It's well they have a mother, or what would become of them? Some people don't need to care about them, as if they weren't related to them in any way. Well, something will come after this; it will come; it will; but I know this, I won't be here long. Strike a stone often enough and it's sure to break; and someone would care about that. Perhaps they'll see what I've lost, how ill I am! Someone knows everything, and everyone will have justice in the end. They will, they will! Some people can sleep as soon as they lie down, as if nothing troubled them. I wish I could do that. But the Great Ruler knows; yes, He knows."

15

EXPLANATION

Captain Trefor did not belong to the class of men who know not in the morning what happened the night before. There are such men; those, under the influence of the moment, or something stronger than the moment, have babbled out what has been gathering for a long time in their minds, and by the morning know next to nothing of what they said or what took place. The only thing they can claim with certainty is some confused and indefinite consciousness that they've said something they should not have said, and that something happened that should not have happened. And when an account of the previous night is related to them, there's nothing they can do but shake their heads, confess their ignorance and their sorrow, and acknowledge that they were, in some sense, not responsible. No, Captain Trefor did not belong to that class. Though at times he allowed his lips and stomach to have dealings with substantial quantities of spirits, his mind was, in a manner of speaking, a teetotaller; and kept at a respectable distance from Sir John[1]. It is not unknown for an abstainer and member of the church to keep a public house; he pays the rent, sells the liquor, but does not himself partake. There was a similar relationship between the body and the mind of Captain Trefor. His body, so to speak, made extensive use of Scotch whisky, but his brain abstained—though it didn't lecture on temperance. It would be a hard thing to get on its blind side. Even in his most joyous moments, in the company of associates who at times drank more than was beneficial for them, the Captain's brain stood sentry, as

---

[1] 'Sir John'—Sir John Barleycorn. The personification of alcohol.

it were, and was able, the day after the feast, to give a detailed account of everything that had happened.

On the morning after the night referred to, the Captain awoke quite early, with his head not only free from ache, but perfectly clear. Indeed the Captain would have called his head to account, and considered himself highly insulted, if it felt any semblance of an ache as a result of having drunk only some dozen whiskies. Headache, in the Captain's opinion, only troubled those who inherited some organic disease, and such people should stay well away from alcohol, for he'd heard that complaint—headache— was an unpleasant enough thing. And in this, the Captain disagreed with the medical profession, who said alcohol was quite unnecessary for strong people, but could do some good to the weak. The Captain believed entirely the reverse. Strong drink was intended for strong people, he said, but as to those whose legs and heads were affected by it, their duty was to stay well away from it. As a provision for this class of people, the Captain considered the '*Cymdeithas Ddirwestol*'[2] a very excellent institution, and he was a great admirer of the zeal of its promoters. Certainly, he wouldn't have hesitated, if asked, to take the chair in a temperance meeting, and he believed he wasn't alone in this position, and thought he could name more than one man similar to himself who'd occupied such a position without considering himself guilty of any inconsistency.

The Captain was on his feet early, as I said, and reviewed in his mind the revelations of the previous night with considerable satisfaction, for he had for some time perceived a darkening of his circumstances, and had more than once been on the point of preparing the minds of his wife and his daughter for this. That task was over at last; and he no longer had to assume the mask at home. He'd decided that whenever he made the revelation to

---

[2] '*Cymdeithas Ddirwestol*'—The Temperance Society.

his family, he'd set out his position in the blackest aspect possible. He thought this wiser than revealing it gradually. By painting the most hopeless portrait of his worldly position to his wife and daughter, the Captain believed he could renew his family happiness, and that things would grow better rather than grow worse. He'd also been convinced for some time that the liberty and silent encouragement he'd given his wife and daughter had created in them high and false sentiments; sentiments that were almost aristocratic. He clearly perceived that he himself had led them to cherish these sentiments, and he believed now it was his duty to undeceive them, and that not gradually, but at once; not by cutting branches, but by applying the axe directly to the trunk. He knew very well that this would cause considerable agitation and uproar in Tŷ'n yr Ardd—that there would be a little astonishment, crying, and sulking; but then it would be over in one night. 'In a manner of speaking', as he would have said, the Captain had rolled up his sleeves for the job several times, but on thinking over its effect, his courage had failed. But now the storm was over, and his wife and daughter knew the position as well as he did. Despite that, the Captain thought he'd made one mistake in the revelation, that being the truthful picture he'd given of his own deceitful life. He'd not planned to do this, and it hadn't been necessary to the object he had in view. The Captain knew very well that Mrs. Trefor looked upon him as the model of a good and honourable man; and if he happened to die suddenly, without leaving the evidence behind him, she wouldn't have hesitated, not only to place him in heaven, but to have looked upon that glorious and beautiful place as being privileged to have an extra ornament. What husband, with such knowledge as this, would not have prided himself in his wife? But now, the Captain felt he had broken the spell; and such a mistake, he confessed to himself, was not worthy of Captain Trefor. He never for a moment admitted that the whiskey had anything to do with the error—although he had got it from a different place. "No," said the Captain to himself, "I must have got a taste for making a clean breast. It was such a rare delicacy! Making the start is the thing; It's the same with a woman who's started cleaning the house, and gets the taste; she must be allowed to finish. But I made a mistake."

When the Captain came to the breakfast table that morning, he had a painful consciousness that he was a new sort of creature in Mrs. Trefor's sight; and if he hadn't been conscious of it, the fact was too apparent in her face, for it was overlaid with hopeless misery, rather than the usual glow of love and admiration. The Captain was uncomfortable, and he therefore wore the pleasantest smile that had been on his face for years, as an appropriate introduction to the right understanding between himself and Mrs. Trefor. While she was pouring coffee in solemn silence, her face like a cloud about to pour with rain, the Captain laid his two elbows on the table, his hands clasped, level with his nose, watching for an opportunity to say grace—a thing he'd not done for a very long time. And addressing the maidservant, he said: "You can go now, Kitty. We'll manage." Then, after a short silence, turning an amiable face towards Mrs. Trefor, he continued: "Sarah, I know by your look you have taken what I said last night too much to heart. We ought to remember that the best of families, and the brightest of Christians, sometimes meet with bitter times. Indeed there are examples of this, in the Holy Scripture—especially in the Old Testament—and that in an age when it was considered Providence would favour the godly, such as Jacob, Job, and David. I have been thinking, Sarah, that there may be something in ourselves that calls for this direction, and that it will in the end be to our spiritual advantage. I myself, I know, have not been half sufficiently grateful for the good and the success that Providence has thought fit to grant me for so many years, and I'm inclined to think this is a rebuke from the Lord to lead me into putting more value on spiritual than on earthly things. What do you think, Sarah?"

Mrs. Trefor burst out crying, and in the meantime the Captain helped himself again to a little bacon. Having done this, he said:

"Sarah; Sarah; don't be down-hearted. I know this is a quite a shock to you, and I'm sorry I acquainted you so suddenly with our circumstances, instead of letting you know gradually, as I myself came to know them; but that would have made you feel wretched long ago, and that wretchedness would not have improved things, but would rather have made them worse. I don't blame you at all, Sarah, for crying. You'll feel better and easier for it. Nature, worse luck, hasn't endowed me with that outlet for my feelings. I have to keep all my care within me, and it's eating me up, slowly but surely. However, Sarah, you must make an effort to compose yourself, and put your trust in God, and I too will be with you."

"You have deceived me, Richard," said Mrs. Trefor, drying her eyes.

"How so Sarah? I've spared you, I'll admit, but 'deceive' is a strong word," said the Captain.

"In this," said Mrs. Trefor, making an effort to compose herself. "You've made Susi and me think you were well off. You've let us have anything we wished for. You have taught us—not in words, I know, but in your behaviour, to look down with pity on the poor, and even on people better than ourselves, and have made us feel we were something above the common. You've encouraged us to associate with people of a higher station, and to keep away from the others. And here you are, at last, without our suspecting it, telling us we're poor, and it's all over. You've been cruel to us, Richard."

"I thought, Sarah," said the Captain, "that last night I gave you sufficient reason for my behaviour: the tenderness of my heart, and my wish to not impair your happiness in any way. Yet here you are calling it cruelty. This is my weakness, I know; my over-eagerness to make others happy, though it costs me dear. It's always been in me. But I have this comfort; that I'm not alone in this. Have I not heard you yourself say, and quite appropriately, how wise and good the Great King is, in keeping from us a foreknowledge of dark days and uncomfortable circumstances? It's strange, Sarah, that that which you consider wisdom in the Great Ruler is cruelty in His humble creature. There are things before us, such as the day of our death, unknown to us. Is it mercy or cruelty that ordained that?"

"You know quite well, Richard, that the Lord deceives no one, and if He keeps us in darkness about things to come, He has warned us to be ready for their approach. *You* didn't do that."

"No, Sarah no; for the good reason that I don't, any more than any other finite creature, know anything about the future. If I had been sure, say, a year ago, that things would end in this way, do you think I wouldn't have warned you? It's true I've long feared it would come to this; but in the course of my association with Pwll y Gwynt, how many times have I feared things would come to an end, and at the end of it all, my fears proven without foundation or cause? If I had, down the years, told you of my fears, Sarah, you would—as so different were my fears from the way things turned out—have come to believe that I was a just a nervous character, and wouldn't have believed what now is fact, that we are poor, and that Pwll y Gwynt is at an end."

"Do you know, Richard," said Mrs. Trefor, "that it's not the thought that we're poor which troubles me most, though that will be a great change to us after all our carryings on. No, our betters have come to poverty before now. A thing of that sort is a matter of Fate. What breaks my heart is what you said about yourself. I know you take a drink, though I must say I've never at any time seen signs of drink upon you. I know that you come into contact with all kinds of men; but I always believed that you were an honest, truthful, and God-fearing man, and that was the greatest comfort of my life. But after the things you said last night, I won't be able to think so now."

"I must acknowledge, Sarah," said the Captain, "that you, more than anyone else, except the Omniscient, know me best, and if I didn't know myself, I know where I'd go to get the right idea of the kind of person I am. You have, for half a lifetime, had the best opportunity of getting to know me, top to toe, as they say, and in every circumstance. And it is strange to think, Sarah, that the opinion you had of me, as I said, an opinion which took half a lifetime to form and confirm, has been demolished in an hour; indeed in half an hour, if not less than that. I am inclined, I know—I have been since I was a boy—to undervalue myself, and to set out my faults—or, if you will, my sins—in, to say the least, a rather extreme light. In other words, there's more of the publican[3] than of the Pharisee in me. And yet, Sarah, I believe you'll admit, and that freely, that the confession of sin is not an unusual thing in religious people. Indeed, I think it can be said—to put myself out of the question in this aspect—it might be said that the confession of sin is a sign and mark of godliness. Without quoting more than one—I'll have a little more bread, Sarah—thanks—without quoting more than one example from Scripture—though many come to mind—what if we were to think of David, the sweet singer of Israel. What opinion would be formed by many an irreligious man—or, as is sometimes said, a man without spiritual comprehension—about a man like David, when some—I say some—of his psalms are read? He'd believe he was the worst reprobate in the world when, in truth, David was a man after God's own heart. As I said last night, Sarah, when I look back on my own life, whilst on the whole I've tried to keep a clear conscience, I must confess I've not been perfect. And still, when one considers how many of the cauldrons of this wicked world I have of necessity—not of choice—wandered among, it's surprising how little of their soot has clung to me. You know, Sarah, next to nothing about the temptations of the world, the flesh, and the devil. You can, in private life, ponder these things

---

[3] 'publican'—Not the man behind the bar of the tavern; the Captain, as is frequently the case, is quoting the scriptures, in this case the parable of the publican and the Pharisee, 'publican' in this case denoting a public servant; to be specific, a tax collector. He was conscious of his sins; the Pharisee was not.

without sullying your soul, whilst I am obliged to move among all kinds of men, and like the apostle, am obliged to make myself all things to all men, till I feel sometimes inclined, as I did last night, on comparing your life with mine, to look on myself as a deceitful hypocrite, though I'm nothing of the kind. But who knows whether I'll be saved. We weren't all created to live a private life, and I think there is in the gospel a provision for every class of us, and that its Author takes into consideration our different circumstances."

"My heart is happy to hear you talk like that, Richard," said Mrs. Trefor, who was now considerably recovered "I hardly believed you were yourself last night. You seriously frightened me, Richard, and I thought for certain you were an irreligious man, and that you had deceived me for years."

16

MAN AND WIFE

The Captain felt very glad that he'd regained the complete trust of his wife, and said:

"I was afraid, Sarah, that you'd formed a wrong opinion of me; and that a little hurriedly. We all make mistakes. But though a man may often gain faith in a night—and I could give many instances—I have never heard, so far as I recall, of anyone having lost it in a night. Pressure of circumstances sometimes makes a man speak of himself in way he would not in quieter times. Indeed we have instances of the best of men, under the weight of the great cares, sorrows, and temptations of this wicked world, describing themselves as scoundrels, though no acquaintance would consider them so. I know myself, Sarah, of more than one really good man who felt too deeply this way, and committed suicide from self-loathing. The danger to every thoughtful man, such as myself, and to anyone conscious of his failings, is to become morbid. But what I was going to say is this, Sarah, I know that last night I spoke a little too severely about myself, though not in a scriptural sense. The heart is more deceitful than anything; wholly incorrigible.

But I trust, Sarah, that now we understand each other, and, though you, for a moment, as it were, lost me in the crowd, I expect you now realise that we are both walking the same road. But, as is too frequently the case in this life, we have neglected the really important things—spiritual matters—and fallen to considering our worldly circumstances. The tyranny of the present, as the English say, is an unpleasant enough thing, but we can't shake ourselves free of it. The fact is, Sarah, as I said last night, there will soon be an end to Pwll y Gwynt, and therefore of my income. I told Kitty not to call Susi this morning so I might be at leisure to speak with you, Sarah. Young and inexperienced people are not always wise, and though there's little danger of her doing so, I'd like you to tell Susi not to say a word about what I said last night, and to make her acquainted, in your own way, with the explanation I've given you, that is to say, about our circumstances and my conduct last night. This time yesterday the future seemed to me completely black but this morning, Sarah, I believe, I see a cloud no bigger than the palm of a man's hand, though the simile is perhaps not quite appropriate; but you understand my meaning, Sarah. The possibility of keeping a comfortable home depends entirely on whether I can start a new mine, and that possibility depends to a large degree on Mr. Enoc Huws, of Siop y Groes. If Mr. Huws joins us, and I firmly believe he will, I have still hope for a comfortable living, but if Mr. Huws refuses, I have not, for the moment, anything else in view. I have every reason to believe Mr. Huws has plenty of money, and having one person like him is better than having a hundred poor people. In a word, my hopes of extricating myself from my present circumstances depend entirely on Mr. Huws. If he turns his back, heaven only knows what will become of us. Now, Sarah, last night I said a few words to you on another matter. The question is delicate, I know, but as you know, Susi is getting older, and the girl should have been married before now and made a home for herself, for who knows what might happen to me, especially as my prospects, though not hopeless, are not so bright as they were. I think, Sarah, I know men fairly well—that is to say, no one need spell them out to me, I can read them for myself. If I'm not mistaken, and I think you will find I'm right—time will tell—I believe Mr. Huws has Susi in mind. Perhaps Mr. Huws isn't what we once had in mind for Susi; perhaps he isn't what she herself—without direction—would have in mind. But circumstances have changed, and even had they not, I, for my own part, can't see why Mr. Huws shouldn't be a good enough husband for the girl. What do you think, Sarah? Do you understand?"

"I do, Richard," said Mrs. Trefor, "I understand very well, but I don't want to *force* the girl to take anyone. And there's another thing. Perhaps, when Mr. Huws knows we're poor, he'll stop thinking about Susi."

"You know a girl's heart, Sarah," said the Captain; "No one, as far as I know, knows it better; but you don't understand a man's heart. You remember well, Sarah, that when I fell in love with you, I was under the impression you had a little money; indeed, that you were rich, but—pardon my alluding to it—I have never mentioned the matter before, so far as I remember, except once and then only slightly. You know, as I say, how few possessions came with you, but did that lessen by one iota, as they say, my love for you? Not a bit, Sarah, not a bit. Indeed now I am pleased to remember I got nothing save you yourself; and that was enough. Remember, Sarah, I mention this with the sole object of showing you that when a young man has set his mind on a young woman, learning that the object of his love is not wealthy will not change his intention towards her, nor lessen his love in any way, but rather the opposite. At least, that's been my experience, and I'm made of the same material as the generality of mankind. Besides, I fail to see why Mr. Huws—or anyone else—should be allowed to know we're poor, for the present at least."

"I'm afraid, Richard," said Mrs. Trefor, "that Susi hasn't the faintest interest in Mr. Huws. I have no complaint with the man; he's fine, as far as I know; but I'd be surprised if Susi liked him."

"The duty of parents, Sarah, as you know," said the Captain, "is to guide their children, and the duty of children is to obey, without asking questions. And as you mentioned liking, would she like, do you think, to go into service? Would she like to wash floors, with every sort of Mary Ann, and Mary Jane, and mix with their kind? You must explain to her, Sarah, in words she cannot fail to comprehend, that nothing but menial work is before her, if she's not wise and sensible at this time. Whatever happens, I must ask you and Susi, at all events, to show every respect, to be

86

welcoming, and to pay due attention to Mr. Huws when he comes here. Our livelihood, as a family, depends upon his 'yes' or 'no'. Do you understand, Sarah? But here's Susi coming down stairs, and I'm off to the mine. Remember, Sarah, I expect you to have put things straight before I come back."

"I'll do my best, Richard," said Mrs. Trefor.

"All right," said the Captain, and he was gone before Susi reached the bottom of the stairs.

17

MOTHER AND DAUGHTER

Having had years of success and plenty, after half an unworried lifetime enjoying the plentiful comforts of life, it's an unpleasant thing when those comforts gradually lessen, and when poverty, though not actually at one's side, is waiting not far away. But more heart-rending, I should think, is to believe we live in cosy abundance, that we have a fine heritage and will one day die in our own nest, and to suddenly realise we are poor and destitute. It's like a tramp dreaming he's at a sumptuous feast, amid fun and festivity, and waking suddenly to find himself starving and in misery.

Poor Susan Trefor! With the exception of the little difficulty between herself and her father about Wil Bryan, she'd known nothing of life's crises and crosswinds. She had lived for the most part on her 'ideas' and the magnificence of the future, without worry or pain. Her parents were as responsible as she, if not more so, for whatever deficiencies lay in her character. She was not by nature wanting in talent, and had she been better brought up, she would undoubtedly have been a very different girl to the one we see at this point. I think I've said before that Susi was considered a remarkably pretty girl. This was acknowledged even by those who didn't like her. What most detracted from her beauty was the obvious fact that she herself was too well aware of it. Susan neglected nothing to further beautify herself. Like the rose, Susan was as tidy and attractive first thing in the morning as she was in the evening; and, no matter how early one went to Tŷ'n yr Ardd, Susan would not be found in dishabille. She always looked ready to sit for her portrait, and I fully believe that, had there been no eye to gaze upon her, there would have been very little difference in her appearance, for she seemed to dress more to please herself than anyone else.

But on this particular morning there was a change in Susan Trefor's appearance, a change so apparent as to attract the attention of her mother the moment she saw her. She was dressed very plainly—and the old cotton frock hung on her arm. It was evident that what sleep she'd taken had been compressed into the few hours before she got up, which made her eyes swollen and sickly. When she entered the room, the following conversation took place: "What have you got there? Are you going to give it to someone?"

"No, mother; I'm going to alter it for myself."

"Indeed! What's up with you, then? Are you a fool?"

"Well, perhaps I am, mother. I know I've been enough of a fool for many years but it's not too late to change."

"What are you talking about? I don't understand you."

"Don't understand me? After what father said last night? I understand myself very well now. I know I've been a humbug for years, putting on airs, as father said. But I don't want to be a humbug any more. If I'm a poor girl, I'll dress like one."

"Don't be foolish, my dear. Your father didn't mean half of what he said last night. He was confused, you know; he's got so many things on his mind."

"If he'd told us some of the things on his mind earlier, he'd have had fewer of them. I don't believe father's been honest with us; if he's been honest with anyone."

"Susi! I must ask you not to speak of your father like that. You know nothing about business or of the trials your father has been through. Indeed, when I consider things, I'm astonished he's been able to keep his faith. He must have had help from above. And how kind he's been to keep all the trouble to himself lest we became uncomfortable."

"However, mother, we know now our true position. We know that we have been deceiving our neighbours and ourselves; we know that we are poor and will soon be poorer, and it's nothing but humbug for us to appear otherwise. I'd rather tell people we're poor than have them tell me."

"You'll do no such thing! Don't be silly, child. Haven't I told you your father didn't mean half what he said last night? He was agitated, and there's no need for you to say a word about it to anyone. You know how clever your father is. Indeed, he's too clever, and that's why people don't understand him. And if Pwll y Gwynt were to close, your father could start another mine immediately. Indeed, he is going to start one, one of these days, as you'll see, and we'll be as well off as ever we were."

"Do you know, mother? I feel very strange; I can't tell you how strange I feel. It's as if I'd been dreaming all my life, and I've just woken up and realised how things are. Thinking how I've lived, how I've behaved to people a hundred thousand times better than myself, and of my 'airs' as my father calls them, I don't know how to show my face to anyone, and I'm so ashamed I could almost die. Think what people will say! The sport they'll have with us! And I could never blame them for it. I didn't sleep a wink till seven this morning, and I believe I thought more last night—about things I should have thought about before—than I've ever thought in my whole life, and I hope I'm a little wiser than I ever was before.

"I'm glad to hear you speak like that, Susi. I was afraid you'd give way and break your heart. Truly, it's extraordinary how a man finds help, but I am afraid you've taken what your father said last night a great deal too much to heart. A man will say things in haste that he shouldn't, and the wisest of men lose their way sometimes. After your father explained to me last night and this morning, I don't see that we need, as things stand, to change our way of life in any way; for we must remember who we *still* are. And were we to change, we would harm your father and ourselves, and people would say all sorts of things about us. There's no harm in the world in being wise, as you were saying; and perhaps we should try not to be quite so extravagant, but, so far as I can see, there's no need for us to change our way of life yet."

"What light has been cast, mother, on what father said last night? And how did he explain being so cruel to you? Was it all a pack of lies?"

"No; your father's not a man to tell lies, and don't let me hear you talk like that again. You know very well I was frightened and hurt by the things he said. Circumstances sometimes change in a few hours. When your father talked last night he was seriously confused, having so much on his mind. I've often wondered how he doesn't go mad, and he must have an extraordinary mind to hold it all. Yes, as I was saying, things were looking very black to him. But Mr. Huws, of Siop y Groes, came, and he's joining your father to start a new mine. I have a very great respect for him, and I'll try to show that. I've always said Mr. Huws is a very nice man, and on thinking of it, I'm astonished we've had so little to do with him. I've often thought that Mr. Huws could be your father's best friend. Though I've heard he's the most honest shopkeeper in town, I've somehow never dealt with him, but it's there I'll deal entirely from now on, as true as I stand here. When I think of it, it is a wonder Mr. Huws isn't married, for your father said he's very rich. But he mustn't have thought of marrying, for I'm sure many a one would be glad to have him as a husband."

"I fail to see, mother, why, if a man has a lot on his mind, it should make him speak so cruelly and insultingly to anyone. Father was abominably rude to you and I last night, and I believed he was drunk or had gone mad. But he wasn't drunk, or he couldn't have gone through his life history in so much detail."

"I, confess, Susi, I've never before heard your father talk as he did, and at the time I was deeply hurt. But I forgave him all after hearing his explanation. Indeed, it would have done you good to hear him speak of his feelings this morning; he was sorry. He didn't know what to do with himself. I never heard anyone, even in the 'seiat', confess his sin more freely or sweetly. Speaking of the 'seiat', I wish your father spoke there more often, as I've told him many times. He has a gift for it, and it would be a treat to hear him, and there's a need for more of that sort of thing these days, sure enough."

"He'd have a curious sort of confession to make."

"He would indeed; that he would! He's seen so much, and mixed so much with ungodly people, and been tempted so much by the world and the flesh and the devil, as he said, and yet has had power to hold out through it all."

"What if he were to make the confession we got from him last night, mother?"

"Don't talk like an idiot, please. You know perfectly well your father wasn't himself last night, and I'm heartily vexed you didn't hear him give his reason for it all. I quite pitied him when I heard him speak so repentantly, and he had Scripture for everything. But what I was going to say is this; we must be good to Mr. Huws, for your father said everything would depend on him in starting the new mine, as Mr. Huws is so rich. But your father will take care, I know, that Mr. Huws will get all his money back with interest."

"If Enoc Huws has any money, as no doubt he has, I should advise him to take care of it himself."

"A lot you know about business. What would become of the world, as I've heard your father say, if everyone kept his money and no one speculated? And do you think your father and Mr. Huws are so foolish as to begin a new mine and spend their money, unless they're sure they'll get their money back and a good deal besides?"

"I know this, mother; that my father has not, according to his own words, any money to spend or lose, and if Enoc Huws is stupid enough to meddle with mines, he'll soon be like him, or I'll be surprised."

"What's the matter with you, eh? Haven't a lot of people become gentlemen through speculating?"

"Yes, there's Hugh Bryan and William Denman."

"No, not Hugh Bryan or William Denman; oh, you're sharp, sharp. Someone must lose, or everyone would be a gentleman.

And you've heard your father say Hugh Bryan had no business to speculate."

"Yes, after he'd spent it all."

"He was to blame for that; how was your father to know that was all he had?"

"He knew very well."

"Well, Susi, if your father heard you like that, he'd knock your head against the wall."

"There's nothing in there to damage, goodness knows."

"You know what, Susi? You're talking rubbish."

"Thank you, mother." Susi cried copiously.

"Susi, I'm sorry I said that. Stop crying and being foolish. But in truth, some extraordinary change has come over you. I've never heard you talk disrespectfully about your father before. You know there's never been a more clever or a better father, and it hurts me more than I can say to hear you talk like that. Pray for grace to see your folly, my dear. I know you've always had a mind, if you knew how, to blame your father for Hugh Bryan's fate, and I think I know why; but I thought you'd almost forgotten that folly."

"I'll never forget it, mother. And now I have a new light on it all. I know I've never taken any interest in Pwll y Gwynt. I knew nothing about it except when I happened to hear the occasional remark my father made to other people. But my heart almost broke when Hugh Bryan went to pieces after losing all his money in the mine. And I believed there was no blame on my father. But what did he say last night? Didn't he say he'd known from the beginning there was no lead in Pwll y Gwynt? And yet he was able to look on at Hugh Bryan throwing his money away till he'd lost it all, and he still keeps on letting Mr. Denman do the same. Is a thing like that honest, mother?"

"I see, my child, that you, like me, misunderstood your father, and I know it is we who misunderstood his words, and not he who worded it wrongly. Now he can say there is no lead in Pwll y Gwynt, but he didn't know this till recently. How could he know?

Set your senses to work. No matter how clever he is, there is no reason for anyone to expect even your father to know what lies in the bowels of the earth, until he has been there to look, and look carefully. Though he may have a fair idea—better than anyone else, I'm sure—where lead is to be found, even he may miss the mark sometimes."

"It's a curious thing, mother, for us both to have misunderstood father. But I'm glad to hear that was the case—if that really was the case."

"There's no 'if' about it, Susi. Didn't your father say that it was so, and how can you think otherwise? If everyone in the world was as honest as your father, the world would be a very different place, very soon; that it would. We have no right, you know—any more than anyone else—to expect to have everything we want. And in the long run it wouldn't be good for us. You can't have the sweet without the bitter, as the saying goes, and everything is for our spiritual good, as your father said. If you live to my age …"

At this point the maid came in.

18

BEATING ABOUT THE BUSH

"Yes," said Mrs. Trefor, after the maid had left, "if you live to my age, and I hope you live to be a good deal older, you'll experience many things you don't like."

"I've experienced many of them without reaching your age, mother."

"You don't know you're born yet; you'll see. Wait till you really start life—when you have the care of a house and family. And indeed, Susi, I'd like to see you settle down; married, and with a house of your own; for as nature decrees, your father and I won't be with you for ever. I've thought a lot about that lately."

"The prospect doesn't sound attractive, mother, and if that's settling down I'd rather not know I'd been born. You've never talked like this before about my settling down. You've never talked about the care of a house and family, and hardly knowing I was born, and that sort of thing. Wasn't it about not throwing myself away, not looking at anyone except my betters, remembering who I was; holding my head high, and biding my time? Wasn't that the sort of thing you always said?"

"There's some truth in what you say, Susi, but you know it was your own good I've had in view all the time, and I can only say, as your father did, that I'm not perfection in all things. And I still give you the same advice; there's no need to throw yourself away. I confess things don't look quite so what-d'you-call-it as they did, and perhaps you'll not get quite so fine a husband as we wished. But if you turn your mind to it, be wise, and, perhaps not quite so distant with some on a level with yourself—be more open with them—there are plenty of good men still out there, you know."

"Where, mother? I don't know anyone foolish enough. And what sort of wife would I be to a good man? A doll like me, not used to doing anything except idle, dress, and show myself off? If I had the offer, I wouldn't have the conscience to deceive a good man. I've changed my mind about everything since last night, mother."

"Perhaps. Indeed, I'm afraid you've got too much of your father's nature in you; thinking too little of yourself. Your father's like that, as I've often told him, and I suppose you've taken after him. And what do you mean, calling yourself a doll? You'd be very upset to hear anyone else call you one, I'm sure."

"Not at all, mother. What am I but a doll? You know very well I've never baked, or washed, or cooked, or ironed, lit the fire, or washed the dishes. I've never been taught to do such things; just to mess around with music, make slipper tops and antimacassars, and that kind of rubbish, and was always given to believe that some grand person would come and make a lady of me. And now my father says I must come down a peg or two, and take anyone I can get hold of, a common miner or anyone! Oh, mother, I'm ashamed of myself; I'm a libel on the name 'woman!' "

"Do you know what? You said you were afraid your father had gone mad. Well, I'm almost sure you've gone mad. There are hundreds of girls who have been brought up properly and don't know anything about the things you've mentioned. That's servants' work, though there's no harm in anyone knowing how to do them—in case it becomes necessary. And it's sure enough whoever you marry, you'll have a maidservant, won't you?"

"Miners don't have maidservants, mother."

"Don't talk nonsense, please; and don't keep harping on the words your father said in his despair last night. I'd feel wretched if you married a miner, that I would. But there are enough men in business who'd be glad to have you; a girl like you, who's had an education. And indeed, if I could be a young girl again, I'd rather have a man in business as a husband, rather than what they call *a gentleman*. The more I see of them, the worse they seem. But a man of business is a man of business, and there's less nonsense about them. For example now, there's Mr. Huws, of Siop y Groes; I'd much sooner marry someone like him than a lot of those who call themselves gentlemen."

"What are you driving at, mother? Why are you talking to me about Enoc Huws? Are you thinking of making a match between us? What's the man to me? What do I care about Enoc Huws—even if he were a hundred thousand times richer? He's a fine man, as far as I know, but I don't like him, and that's an end to it."

"What's up with you, then? What makes you think I'm trying to make a match between you and Mr. Huws? I just used his name as an example; don't be so conceited. It's very likely Mr. Huws wouldn't look at you. A man like him, who's well off, can have whoever he likes. Don't you deceive yourself; to be sure, wives aren't as scarce as all that. It's a strange thing I can't mention a man like Mr. Huws without you thinking I want to make a match. No such thing, my child! You be careful! There's plenty of girls as good as you who'd be glad to have Mr. Huws, so you needn't keep shrugging your shoulders. Dear me, there are. Anyone would think, the way you've been talking, you were about to wear sackcloth and ashes. But get out of the spotlight! What do we matter?"

"I've got nothing to say against Enoc Huws, mother. He's a fine man, a hundred times better than I. What I'm saying is I don't like him."

"Who cares who you like and who you don't like? And I must ask you not to call him 'Enoc' all the time. His situation, I believe, renders him worthy of respect, and he deserves to be called Mister, as much as you deserve to be called Miss."

"Much more than I, mother; you don't understand me. Enoc Huws—or Mr. Huws, as you wish me to call him—is inexpressibly better than I, but I don't like the man. And why do you talk about me marrying? I don't want to marry, and I'm not going to marry, if I have the offer, till I'm fit to marry. No common miner or businessman will have cause for eternal regret over marrying me, mother."

"Oh, indeed. What if Mr. Huws changed his mind and refused to join your father in the new venture. Would you like to go into service?"

"I would, mother, if in doing so I could learn to do something and not be a humbug. And I don't care in the least whether En— Mr. Huws—changes his mind or not. For his own sake it would be better for him to change his mind, I swear."

"What's stirred you up, eh? Have you gone completely mad? If you've got no respect for yourself, have you none for your father and myself? Susi, I've never seen you in a mood like this before. I'm afraid, my girl, that you've not found grace. Pray for it, my girl, and take care your father doesn't hear you talk like this, or it'll be all up with you. And remember—listen to what I'm saying—remember to show every respect to Mr. Huws when he comes here, and be civil to him, or your father'll make short work of giving you a roasting."

"If he did, there'd not be much fat, or loss to anyone. But don't worry, mother. From now on I'll respect everyone, and I hope neither father nor yourself will have cause to complain of my being disrespectful to any living creature. I'm going to grovel.

"You're going to do something idiotic, I'm sure. But I never thought I'd hear you talk like this, Susi. You've upset me very much, and you've almost made me believe you know nothing of the influence of religion on your heart. Many a time I've told your father he should have taken more pains to teach you its principles, and that's obvious now. I don't know what to make of you, but it's plain enough that, in spite of the many good examples you've seen, your spirit's a stranger to matters of faith, or you'd never have spoken as you did."

"You're quite right, mother. I know nothing about the influence of the Bible. If I understand the Bible, self-denial, love of God, humility and good works are religion, and my life, up to now, has been as much a stranger to such things as was the life of Lucifer. And to give you my honest opinion, mother, there's no more similarity between the religion I was taught and the religion of the Bible than there is between Beelzebub and Gabriel."

"Susi, what's up with you? Are you having hysterics, swearing and cursing and using those fearful names? Has the evil spirit possessed you?"

"I'm not cursing and swearing; and as to hysterics, I don't know what they are."

"Well, what do you think you're saying?"

"I think this; if the Lord will let me live, I'll never be a humbug again. Since last night, mother, I see everything in a new light, and I'm ashamed of myself."

"And so you should be, if I know what's what. Clever though your father may be, he never made a greater mistake than to talk of his troubles in front of you last night, for you know nothing about business, and it's not possible to get anything into your head, and once you've made up your mind to do something, nothing will change your mind. It's just as well your father hasn't heard you. You've upset me so much I don't know how in the world I'll get as far as London House, but I have to go; they said my dress would be ready for fitting this morning. And if you'd been anything like your normal self I wouldn't have minded ordering you a new dress, though it's not a month ago you last had one. Let's see what you're like when I come back. I hope you'll have come down from your high horse and I'll find a little repentance in you. I'm going now, Susi … Susi, I'm going."

"Fine, mother."

Exit Mrs. Trefor.

"Good heavens! What kind of a family are we? Either mother or myself have gone completely mad. I see nothing but poverty and disgrace before us. I must have been dreaming till today. I always hated hearing talk about 'business', 'the market', 'the Company', and such things. It was painful to think of them. They were matters for men, in my opinion. My sole object was to live, enjoy myself, dress, and talk nonsense. I knew my father was clever, and I always believed he was rich. I've lived up in a balloon and I've fallen like a stone. I never used to think—yes, that was the problem—I never *thought* about things, or thought I needed to think. My mind was asleep till this morning. But, thank God, I believe I still have a mind, like any other girl. It's a wonder I haven't lost it, not having used it for so long. Is my father an honest man? The question's never entered my mind before, and it's still not entered my mother's mind. Can it be that I misunderstood him? Is what I used to call dishonesty what others call business? I don't know what business is. I had an idea it was something upright, above board, something no one could reproach as not being honest. But it's not, or I'm an idiot. I used to think my father was perfectly honest, and I'd rather have died than find out he's not. But something's stirred me up, as my mother said; vile thoughts fill my heart. I hope I'm wrong. Did I misunderstand him? I hope so. But I got one thing wrong. I thought father and mother had been planning a match between Enoc and me. I don't know where the thought came from, if not from my vanity. O cursèd vanity! If you had a neck, I'd hang you by it, I swear. Whatever happens from now on—whatever our circumstances—there'll be no more 'humbug' in Susan Trefor. No; 'no humbug', as poor Wil used to say."

19

PWLL Y GWYNT

Of Captain Trefor's various virtues, not the least, without a doubt, was his skill in foretelling important events. And he never struck the nail more fairly on its head than with his prophesy about Pwll y Gwynt. Within a few weeks, the old mine stood idle; in the prophetic words of the Captain, Pwll y Gwynt was finished. Not only was the puddling not brisk and the trollies not carrying lead to Llanerch y Môr (and they never had), but the engine wasn't even puffing. Around Pwll y Gwynt the silence of the engine was painful to the inhabitants. Many a child had been born and reared in the sound of the Pwll y Gwynt engine, had played and gone to the day school and the chapel; parents and children were used to shouting over the sound of the engine to make themselves heard. Bob Mathews, the bird catcher, used to get sixpence a head more for every goldfinch caught in its vicinity, as it was certain the bird would sing louder and clearer than birds from elsewhere. Sundays, holidays and workdays, the thunder of the engine had been as truly a part of life in the area as would be the thunder of a river or a wild waterfall elsewhere. Now the beast was stilled, the people who were used to living near it felt as if they'd moved elsewhere; for a time, until they grew accustomed to it, it felt strange, and they were forever asking themselves what was the matter. Women looked at the clock; had it stopped? For a time, it was hard to sleep at night. The mine engine had been their cradle and when the cradle stopped its rocking, everyone opened their eyes, wide awake. But these were comparatively small, unimportant matters. The inhabitants quickly realised the true meaning of the silence. It meant that scores of men, the heads of families, were out of work; scores who had lived from hand to mouth, putting nothing aside for their futures; not only this, but the past wasn't paid for, as many a shop-keeper's book could testify. Beyond the immediate vicinity, the silence of Pwll y Gwynt was a trivial thing. The news scarcely reached the edge of the county. Perhaps, by accident, the news might reach the ears of people living ten miles away, and perhaps they'd say: "What a pity;" then never think of it again. But to the poor miners who'd depended wholly on Pwll y Gwynt for their sustenance, the idle mine was a serious and bitter matter. Their wages, goodness knows, had for years been pitifully small, scarcely fourteen shillings a week, but they were the best Captain Trefor could afford them under the circumstances. By making the foot fit the boot, they'd been able to live on this. They lived beyond the governance of the Local Board, and so, though the pigsty was often less than the necessary five yards from the house, they'd been able to keep a pig, which, when ready for the knife, would pay the rent. Thomas Bartley had preached to them for many years, especially on fair days, on the benefits to poor men of keeping pigs, and the fruits of his preaching were apparent amongst the Pwll y Gwynt miners. Though Thomas only bought two pigs, or three at the most, in the course of the year, his presence was indispensable to every fair. Seldom did his neighbours venture to buy a porker or store pig at a fair without consulting him; and if they did, they generally discovered before long they'd made a bad bargain. Thomas must have lost six clear days a year serving his neighbours without receiving a penny. Why do the judges at *Eisteddfodau* grumble about having to adjudicate for next to nothing, and that only once a year? I acknowledge that at times Thomas would realize how much time he'd lost helping others and sometimes decide he'd never go to a fair except when he really needed to buy a pig for himself. But when fair days came, his conscience began to prick him, and, anticipating the likelihood that some of his neighbours would make bad bargains, he'd say, "Barbara, I shall never in all my life be happy in my mind if I don't go to the fair," and sure enough, he did.

Thomas was talking one day about the profit to be made keeping pigs, and said: "You 'ear some folk say keepin' pigs is the stupidest thing on the face of the earth. And I've always noticed that those who talk like that are lazy people, useless at their livin'. Only yesterday, there was old Beti Williams sayin' to me: 'Thomas Bartley', says she, 'do you think as how keeping pigs pays?' And says I, 'If everybody paid as well as pigs, we'd be all right, Beti. I never saw a pig as didn't pay for itself, but I've seen many a woman as never paid'. She'd owed me two bob for mendin' a pair of boots since I don't know when, you know, but I got a chance of 'avin' a dig at the old hag, and you never seen anyone change the subject quicker. But, 'twixt you and me, and to speak partic'lar like, I don't think as 'ow keepin' pigs does pay, if you reckon up everythin', and put a price on every job as is done for 'em. To begin with, it don't pay a man who is too haughty—no offence, mind—to lay 'old of a truss of straw, and wash out the sty. And it doesn't pay a man either who ain't got the conscience to give it the proper sort of food; for, you know, a pig 'as to 'ave 'is proper sort of food or he'll never come to anythin', just like any human bein'. But what I was agoing to say—and I'll stick to it, too, as long as I breathe—a poor man, a man worth 'is day's work, will never do better than keep a pig, especially if there's a few wild carrots or nettles agrowin' near 'is house; they're champion for pigs. I look at it like this; keepin' a pig's very like a Savings Bank. You'd never say, to speak partic'lar like, as a Savings Bank pays much. Two and a half percent? It ain't worth a man's while to take a bit of money there—not for the sake of the interest—and yet no man in 'is senses'd say that it ain't a good thing to put money in a Savings Bank. To my way of thinkin'—and I, bein' a common man, 'ave raised as many pigs as any 'un in the country—keepin' a pig pays a deal better than a Savings Bank. It's this way, see. 'ere you are, thinkin' of a man as has made up his mind to be thrifty and put his coin in a Savings Bank. Very good. Say he saves a bob a week. Fine. But some weeks he'll be squeezed a bit; he may have missed a day's work or been tempted to buy somethin' he didn't really need, and the Savings Bank must pay the price, and you'll never 'ave seen less than what's in that Savings Bank by the end of the year. But if a man 'ad a pig, and the conscience to feed it well, he'd 'ave been bound to 'ave brought it food, even if he 'adn't enough for himself. I'll tell you somethin' else, too; a man don't like to go to a bank with a little bit of a trifle of coin, and if he tries to keep it in the 'ouse till it makes a tidy sum, some misfortune always comes and takes it away. Did you ever 'ear tell about Ned Jones, who tried a while back to keep 'is money in the 'ouse? No? Well this was it. Ned made up 'is mind once to give up 'is baccy and save a bit of money without his wife knowin' anythin' about it. Twelve bob 'is wages were, and Ned used to keep 'is savings 'id under the bedposts. He'd been at it fifteen weeks, and 'ad—so he said—seven and six—a 'alf-crown under three bedposts. But one day, after comin' from work, Ned suspected 'is missus 'ad been cleanin' the bedroom. She only did it about once a year, you know, and when 'is wife's back was turned, Ned rushed upstairs to see if 'is swag was safe. Well, it was like this; he put 'is shoulder under the bed—I 'eard 'im tell the story 'imself—and raised one post, 'Ah', said Ned, 'that there half-crown's gone', and he went on to another, and that 'alf-crown had skedaddled too, and so 'ad the third, and Ned never saw '*eu lliw na'u llun*'[1] again. The wife was glad eenuff to get 'old of them, I'll warrant. But there was a bit of a row, as you might imagine, and folk say they were never the same man and wife after it, and Ned smoked more than ever. It's very 'ard for a poor man to keep money in an 'ouse. 'ang on; where was I? Oh yes. A man don't like somehow to go with a trifle to a bank, for if people see 'im agoin' there all the time, they gets to say as 'ow he's worth thousands, and everyone'll go and try to borrow a bit, and if the man 'imself goes short, there ain't no sympathy for 'im. But a man who keeps a pig,

---

[1] '*eu lliw na'u llun*'—literally, their colour nor their shape. Ned never again saw hide nor hair of his half crowns.

why he takes it a sum'ut to eat three times a day, and don't notice that much, and little by little that sum'ut gets to be *somethin'* in the end, you see. They tells me as that's 'ow the Irish manage to scrape a livin', and that they'd sooner be without that there 'ome Rule than without a pig sty, and I can quite believe it. But I've noticed that there's less keepin' of pigs among poor folk than there should, especially in towns. And the reason for this, they say, ain't that the folk there are more respectable likes, but that there Local Board astops them, and because that 'merican bacon is so mighty cheap. 'em's the greatest curse that ever cum'd into this country; the Local Board and 'merican bacon; in my 'pinion. The Local Board in towns stops poor folk from keepin' pigs, so now the poor folk never think of plantin' taters in the field. For why should they plant taters if they mayn't keep a pig? And that's why they're clemmed[2] for the year, and 'ave to run off to a shop to get a penn'orth of 'merican bacon and a penn'orth of taters, instead of 'avin', as folks used to, two hogs of taters in the garden, and a pig 'angin' up in the house. I don't know 'ow on earth poor folk manage to get a bite in those towns. I've 'eard they don't look so good. And it's all acause o' the Local Board. I don't know nothin' as feeds idleness so much as that Local Board. At one time, a man, after comin' 'ome from work and washin' and 'avin' his tea, 'ud go to the tater field to give it a bit of a weedin' or forkin' over, or he'd go and clean the pig up a bit. But they all go to the pub now; and you never 'ear tell these days 'bout a tater supper. And all 'acause of that there Local Board. There never was such a thing! What did you say? To keep fevers away? Nonsense, all of it! They says if a pigsty's within five yards of the house, the fever's bound to turn up, but if it's five yards and two inches away everyone's safe! I'll

---

[2] 'clemmed'—from the Welsh verb 'clemio', to starve. But look in any book of old Lancashire folk songs and you'll find the millworkers were clemmed as well. The Brythonic language, which became Welsh, was once used across most of this island. And neither was starvation exclusive to Wales.

admit there's not so much o' small pox now than there used to be; but it's not the Local Board we 'ave a-got to thank for that, but the Great Lord and 'noculation. Do you know what? I wouldn't stand in that there Local Board's shoes for the world. They'll have a big 'count to give when the Day comes. But thank goodness I ain't in their clutches."

But I'm rambling. The fact was that almost every one of the Pwll y Gwynt miners kept a pig and planted potatoes. It's a marvel to think on how little money many Welsh labourers have been able to live and rear a sizeable family. In many a case the number of mouths to feed were nearly equal to the number of shillings earned in the week by the head of the household. They were not starving; they were not naked. Indeed they could come tidy to chapel as a family and were able to give a little to the cause. How they were able to do this, heaven only knew. One is driven to the conclusion that their needs were very small, and in these days we spend a lot of money on things we could do without. On pitifully small wages the miners of Pwll y Gwynt had been able to live, raise children, and even give them a little schooling; but how? Well, I can't imagine. It's clear not even the thriftiest of them could have put anything aside for a rainy day. Like a bird that lives from day to day, taking no heed of the morrow, so they lived from 'sist'[3] to 'sist'; and when Pwll y Gwynt stood suddenly silent, their poverty and misery lay heavy upon them. If Pwll y Gwynt had paid ten pounds a month to each miner, their grief and sorrow in that silence could scarcely have been deeper. Although the crisis came utterly unexpected to most of the miners, a few of the old hands had been not unprepared in their minds for the event. They saw clearly that no company could continually pay while getting next to nothing in return. In addition to this, Captain Trefor had his character and good name to keep up, and he'd let some of the most experienced miners into the secret some time ago. There was a

---

[3] 'sist'; an advance payment of wages.

man by the name of Sem Llwyd employed at Pwll y Gwynt, who, besides being religious and of good character, was also reckoned to be an oracle as to the best way of working mines. Sem could be very reluctant to share his opinion about anything, if he wasn't sure of his facts. When, it was determined to drive the mine in a new direction, Sem kept his opinion to himself, till success or failure had been proved, and then shared his opinion freely, and that opinion was invariably correct. Sem was never known to be mistaken. When he was pressed by Captain Trefor for an opinion on any proposed mining venture, Sem would take care to sprinkle a sufficiency of 'ifs' across his canvas, and the qualifications would be so numerous that, no matter how the venture turned out, Sem's judgement was right. Sem's judgement was *never* wrong. With regard to the way of working Pwll y Gwynt, Sem didn't hesitate to express his opinion plainly and unambiguously about one thing, and that thing, Sem well knew, was impossible for the Company to carry out. When the miners met in the tower to have a smoke, which they did often, for they didn't believe in overwork, and were all acquainted with the verse:

> "*Y mae chwech o oriau'n ddigon*
> *I bob un o'r miners mwynion,*
> *I fod rhwng y dyrus greigiau*
> *Mewn lle myglyd yn llawn maglau.*"[4]

When they met thus, Sem would wear his wisest aspect and would distribute his opinion clearly, to an audience filled with admiration for him, as to what the Pwll y Gwynt Company *ought* to have done, if they had dreams of the mine being successful.

---

[4] "*Six hours are enough,*
  For any of the gentle miners,
  To be among the confused rocks,
  In a smoky place full of snares."

Sem Llwyd was one of those whom the Captain had let into the secret, and he was not unaware of Sem's wild imaginings. When the Captain had Sem to himself, the conversation would run something like this:

"Well, Sem, what's your opinion about the old mine now?"

"Indeed Captain, it's hard to say, and be certain."

"I believe, Sem, you and I think broadly the same about Pwll y Gwynt. If I'd had my own way I should have done so and so." And then the Captain would suggest some plans which he'd been told Sem had spoken of. "But I might as well keep quiet, Sem; I've got my masters, and if the Company choose to act like this, it's their look out. But I'll tell you this much; it won't be possible to carry on like this for long."

"You never spoke a truer word, Captain, and I've said the same thing many a time, as the men know. It's a terrible thing, Captain, that a man like you, who knows how to work a mine, can't have his own way."

"However, Sem, that's how it is."

On special occasions, Sem prophesied wisely about the imminent demise of Pwll y Gwynt, and disclosed his reason; namely, the Captain couldn't have his own way. When Pwll y Gwynt closed, no one laid the blame at the Captain's door. Sem Llwyd, and others too, by this time, said the Captain had warned them, and that if the Captain had had his own way in working the mine, the engine would be puffing, the puddling going briskly, and the trollies carrying lead to Llanerch y Môr. The Company in London were the cause of all the trouble. And thus the Captain, though he'd lost his income, had succeeded in keeping his good name among his neighbours. The natives of the district believed, generally, that if the Captain had had his own way, Pwll y Gwynt would have afforded regular work for a lifetime or two at least. The Captain informed those with whom he chanced to converse on the subject, that there was a world of wealth left in the old mine, and little by little the miners themselves, some of whom had for years searched for lead and failed to find it, had come to believe the same thing; and after a while, some old miner would testify that there was a wall of lead in Pwll y Gwynt, under the water. Captain Trefor was looked upon as a martyr of the Pwll y Gwynt Company, and if the miners had not been so poor, they would have given him a testimonial. As they couldn't express their feelings in that way, they had to content themselves with cursing the Company in London, and placing their trust and hope for the future in the kindness, ability and inventiveness of Captain Trefor. But '*chwarae teg*'[5] to the Captain, he was not long in trimming the lamps of their hopes. He could scarcely go out of his house without meeting some workman or other, who would turn an anxious eye on him, waiting for some look on which to hook a hope.

The Captain would look at him with a pitying eye, take a homely hold of his lapel, and say kindly:

"Well, Benjamin my boy, things are serious, aren't they? But I knew long ago it'd come to this. What else was to be expected when I didn't get my chance to manage the mine the best way? But don't be downhearted, Benjamin, something'll turn up one of these days. Have you eaten today, Benjamin? Well, well, wait a moment; take this note to Miss Trefor." And the Captain would pull a bit of paper out of his pocket, and write on it in pencil: "*Dear Susi; give this poor devil a bite of something to eat*." Something like this happened almost daily. The Captain tried constantly to raise the afflicted spirits of the workmen, and he seldom failed to brighten the hope of men who were all but done for.

The Captain asserted that something would turn up soon to give the miners work, though not referring to anything definite. He was often asked by the tradesmen who had trusted, and were still trusting, the workmen for their sustenance:

"Captain Trefor, do you think there is any hope of Pwll y Gwynt starting again?"

---

[5] '*chwarae teg*'—'*fair play*'. An expression of approval common in Wales, in either language.

"Sir," answered the Captain, "I would not for anything create false hopes. It's not impossible that Pwll y Gwynt could start again, but very improbable. If it does, I'll have nothing to do with it, except on one condition, that I'm allowed to have my own way. You know, Mr Jones, how hard it is for a man, when he's only a servant of the Company, to get his own way, though that way be the best one. As a matter of fact, sir, if I had had my own way, Pwll y Gwynt would not only be working today, but would be paying the Company well. But between you and me—it won't go any further just for the present, Mr. Jones? Between you and me, my eyes are not on Pwll y Gwynt, but on somewhere else. You may hear something one of these days. In a neighbourhood like this, so rich in mines, Providence will soon open a door of deliverance. To me, personally, that, so to speak, would be neither here nor there. After all the trouble, anxiety, and disappointment, it's time I had a rest. But how can I rest, when I can't go out of my house without meeting scores of wretched men who are without work, and not only that, are suffering want? No sir, though I have reached that age when, so to speak, according to the order of nature, a man should have rest and leisure to think about more important matters, and prepare for the great journey which awaits us all, how can I rest? I do not forget, sir, that you and others in similar circumstances have, out of your kindness, trusted the workmen, poor fellows, with enough sustenance to keep body and soul together; I do not forget, I say, that you want your money, not because you can't do without it, but because it's only fair you should have it. No sir, with a little of the adventurous spirit on the part of those who have succeeded somewhat in the neighbourhood, and with the blessing of Providence, there will be a different slant on things in a few weeks' time, Mr Jones."

In this way, in spite of the straightened circumstances and the great poverty in the district, Captain Trefor kept the miners and the rest on their toes with the expectation that something would turn up. In the meantime, Enoc would often visit Tŷ'n yr Ardd, and the neighbours didn't shut their eyes to the fact. It was perceived that Enoc had very quickly smartened himself up. The serious man, the wealthy shopkeeper, careless in his dress, had become not a little finer, brighter and more upright. And, more wondrous still, Miss Trefor was quieter, more sober, and had thrown away all her ornaments. What other conclusion could the locals come to, other than that Enoc Huws and Miss Trefor were adapting themselves to one another. For days there was much coming and going and tea drinking amongst the neighbours, as they took the opportunity to try the case. It was generally considered that Miss Trefor was a good deal more fortunate in her choice than Enoc. It was admitted unanimously that Enoc was rich, and likely to make a good husband, whilst Miss Trefor possessed nothing in her favour except middling prettiness (which after all, was worthless so far as 'a living' was concerned)—and foolish ideas, or to put it another way, senseless pride. Some ladies were doubtful—and it's never any use telling some people to mind their own business— some ladies were doubtful whether Enoc's industry, application and business success would be able to keep up—to keep ahead would be impossible—with Miss Trefor's expectations. Many a hopeless old maid shook her head, significantly and prophetically, though she said nothing, and didn't care either, who Enoc Huws took for a wife. Now and then a mother with a houseful of unmarketable daughters made her opinion plain that she was greatly disappointed in Enoc Huws—that she'd been accustomed to look on him as a man of judgment, and certainly a religious man. But as often happened, those you thought most of would disappoint you most. It was said that some of these mothers had even changed their opinion of the tea Enoc sold, and protested that they would have to try some other shop. But it was tea that Enoc sold, not rubbish collected from under Chinese hedges. Enoc had made a name for himself for good tea, and after the mothers had 'tried some other shop', and found the tea they got there was not so productive of feminine eloquence, they one by one returned to Siop y Groes and their former faithfulness, with their self-righteousness a little diminished. Whatever truth there was in the story that Enoc and Miss Trefor were engaged, the news spread through the neighbourhood with a speed that would have brought a tinge of jealousy to the most accomplished scandal monger; but no matter how much curiosity the reader may have for knowing Enoc's real prospects, I must, for a short time, turn to other matters.

Patients – please read notes overleaf
Cleifion – a wnewch chi ddarllen y nodiadau drosodd
Page 1 of 1   Date printed: 12-Oct-2021

GRIFFITHS, Mark (Mr)

NHS Number: **496 159 6418**   EMIS Number: **501214**

School Farm, Holt Road, Cross Lanes, Wrexham, LL13 0TU

Pharmacy: Medicines Bangor Surgery

Collect Medicines from: Bangor [ ] Overton Surgery [ ]
Overton Chemist[ ] Hightown Chemist[ ]

MEDICATION REVIEWS - Our Pharmacist Jiten Mistry
will be carrying out medication reviews via a telephone
consutation. Jiten will ring you when your medication is due
to be reviewed.

Flu Vaccinations - are still available for those who are
eligible. Ring 01978 710666 to book an appointment.

Edoxaban 60mg tablets   [ ]
One To Be Taken Each Day, 28 tablet
Last Issue: 12-Oct-2021

If you need help to fill in this form please ask your pharmacist

Do you get free prescriptions ? If you are registered with a GP in Wales or have an entitlement card for free prescriptions and your prescription is dispensed in Wales you do not have to pay.

Os oes angen help arnoch i lenwi'r ffurflen hon, gofynnwch i'ch fferyllydd.

Ydych chi'n cael presgripsynau am ddim? Os ydych wedi cofrestru gyda Meddyg Teulu yng Nghymru neu o oes gennych gerdyn yn rhoi hawl i chi gael presgripsiynau am ddim, a bod eich presgripsiwn yn cael ei weinyddu yng Nghymru, nid oes rhaid i chi dalu.

If the above does not apply to you then read all the statements in **Part 1** opposite. You don't have to pay a prescription charge if any of the statements apply to you (the patient) on the day you are asked to pay. (A valid War pension exemption certificate only entitles you to free prescriptions for your accepted disablement). Put a cross in the first box that applies to you, read the declaration and complete and sign **Part 3**.

Benefits which DO NOT provide exemption. You are NOT entitled to exemption from prescription charges because you receive Pension Credit Savings Credit, Incapacity Benefit, Disability Living Allowance, Contributions based Jobseeker's Allowance or Contributions based Employment and Support Allowance. Only those benefits listed in **Part 1** provide exemption. An HC3 certificate does not entitle you to free prescriptions.

Evidence. You may be asked to provide evidence to show that you do not have to pay. You could show the relevant benefit award notice, or an exemption or pre – payment certificate. If you cannot show evidence at the time you can still get your prescription items free but your Primary Care trust will check your entitlement later i you do not show proof (see paragraph about Penalty Charges).**If you have to pay a prescription charge.** You (or your representative) should put in **Part 2** the amount you have paid and then sign and complete **Part 3**.

Need help with the cost of prescription charges ? You can get information by ringing 0845 850 1166 or by reading leaflets HC11 and HC12. You may be able to get these leaflets from your GP surgery or pharmacy. Or rin 0845 610 1112 to get one, or go to www.dh.gov.uk/helpwithhealthcosts

Not entitled to free prescriptions ? Pre – pay to reduce the cost. If you think you will have to get more than 4 items in 3 months or 14 items in 12 months it will be cheaper to buy a pre-payment certificate (PPC). Phone 0845 850 0030 to find out the cost, or order a PPC and pay by credit or debit card. You can pay for a 12 month PPC by direct debit instalment payments. Buy on-line at www.nhsbsa.nhs.uk. To pay by cheque get an application form (FP95) from your pharmacy or go to www.nhsbsa.nhs.uk/healthcosts . The FP95 tells you what to do.

Do you need a refund ? If you are unsure if you are entitled to free prescriptions you should pay for the prescription item(s) and ask for a receipt form FP57. **You** must get the FP57 form when you pay for the item(s), you cannot get the form later. If you find you didn't have to pay, you can claim your money back up to 3 month after paying. The FP57 form tells you what to do.

Patient Representative. If you are unable to collect your prescription yourself, someone can't take your completed form for you. You must complete **Part 1**. Your representative must complete **Part 2 and 3. Anyon** who collects a Schedule 2 or 3 controlled drug must sign the box in Part 3 when they collect the **item(s)** and provide proof of identity if requested.

Cynrychiolydd y Claf. Os na allwch gasglu'r presgripsiynau eich hun, gall rhywun arall fynd â'r ffurflen ar eich rhan. Rhaid i chi lenwi **Rhan 1.** Rhaid i'ch cynrychiolydd lenwi **Rhan 2 a Rhan 3. Rhaid i unrhyw un sy'n casglu cyffur a reolir o dan Atodlen 2 neu 3 lofnodi'r blwch yn Rhan 3 pan fyddant yn casglu'r eitem(au)** a dangos tystiolaeth ynghylch pwy ydynt os gofynnir am hynny.

Data Collection. Information about the prescription items on this form will be processed centrally to pay monies due to the pharmacist, doctor or appliance contractor for the items they have supplied to you. The NH will also use the information to analyse what has been prescribed and the cost. The Counter Fraud and Securit Management Service, a division of the NHS Business Services Authority, may use information from this form to prevent and detect fraud and incorrectness in the NHS.

Casglu Data. Caiff gwybodaeth am yr eitemau a ragnodwyd ar y ffurflen hon eu prosesu'n ganolog i dalu'r fferyllydd, y meddyg neu'r contractwr offer am yr eitemau a roddwyd i chi. Hefyd, bydd y GIG yn defnyddio'r wybodaeth i ddadansoddi'r hyn a ragnodwyd a'r gost. Caiff y Gwasanaeth Atal Twyll a Rheoli Diogelwch, isadran o Awdurdod Gwasanaethau Busnes y GIG, ddefnyddio'r wybodaeth ar y ffurflen hon i atal a chanfod twyll a diffyg cywirdeb yn y GIG.

Penalty Charges. If it is found that you should have paid for your prescription items, you will face penalty charges and may be prosecuted under the powers introduced by the Health Act 1999. Routine checks are carr out on exemption claims including some where proof may have been shown. You may be contacted in the co of such checks.

Using Medicines. Always use the prescribed medicines as advised. Never give your medicines to anyone else might harm them. If your medicines cause you problems or you have concerns over their effects ask your doc or pharmacist for advice. If you are not using all the medicines prescribed to you please tell your doctor or pharmacist, they will advise you and may reduce the amount of medicines you are given.

Defnyddio meddyginiaeth. Cofiwch ddefnyddio'r feddyginiaeth a ragnodwyd i chi yn unol â'r cyngor a roddwyd. Peidiwch byth â rhoi'ch meddyginiaeth i unrhyw un arall oherwydd gallai ei niweidio. Os yw'ch meddyginiaeth yn achosi problemau i chi neu os oes gennych bryderon am ei effeithiau gofynnwch i'ch me neu eich fferyllydd am gyngor. Os nad ydych yn defnyddio'r holl feddyginiaethau a ragnodwyd i chi dywed wrth eich meddyg neu eich fferyllydd. Byddant yn medru rhoi cyngor i chi ac efallai y byddant yn cwtogi a y meddyginiaethau a gewch.

Unused Medicines. If you have any unused medicines you should take them to a pharmacy for disposal

Meddyginiaethau heb eu defnyddio. Os oes gennych unrhyw feddyginiaethau heb eu defnyddio, dy fynd â nhw'n ôl i'r fferyllfa.

20

THE WISDOM OF SEM LLWYD

I believe Sem Llwyd was as good a sort of miner as I ever met. He was short and lean in body; his face was a tawny grey, and thin; his back a little bent, his chest caving in; his breath short and uncertain and he had a bad cough. He smoked a pipe, was important, knowing, wise—in his own estimation—and, in outward appearance, an old man before reaching his sixtieth year. Sem had an abundance of greyish hair, which, though not exactly trailing along the ground, one would think had never experienced the edge of a pair of scissors, but had been singed each winter, as hedges are, by the wind and the frost. His voice was harshly strong, and out of proportion, as though it wasn't his voice; as though he'd inherited it in the will of some departed relation, like the coat he wore on Sundays, which was also far too big for him. If Sem's age had not been known to a certainty, he would have been considered some ancient who'd been ignored by death, as being not worth harvesting. I remember having had an absurd idea in my mind about Sem: that he'd never die, but would crumble, bit by bit, till there was nothing left. Sem was very fond of company; not so much in order to receive as to give knowledge; and, like the rest of the human race, he enjoyed visiting families and socialising with people who most admired his wisdom. While Pwll y Gwynt was in operation, Sem had daily opportunities to lighten his bosom though, as was said in the previous chapter, he was, among his fellow workmen, very cautious as to what he said and how he said it, and always gave them to understand he knew a lot more than he divulged. The greater the hunger for knowledge, the more Sem tried to give the impression there was plenty of corn in his particular Egypt. This at times, would be very provoking, for when a greater than usual curiosity to know something became evident,

Sem would give the unmistakeable impression that he could, if he chose to, give all the information required, but would then fall into a wise silence, pulling away hard on his pipe, and turning a deaf ear to every request and question. After Pwll y Gwynt fell silent, now and then a miner would come from the fringes of the area—as the Queen of Sheba came to Solomon—to listen to Sem's wisdom; and though the miner didn't go home with the same impression as that left on the lady of Sheba, I know that Sem Llwyd's awareness of his inexhaustible store of knowledge and wisdom was not the slightest fraction less than that of Solomon.

The nearest dwelling to Sem Llwyd's house was Twmpath, the residence of an old acquaintance of the reader—Thomas Bartley—and I'm not sure that Thomas didn't experience the same feeling as that which swells the breast of many a mediocre being in Bala, knowing that he lived in the same town as a giant of the Welsh people.[1] As Sem was now idle, he not infrequently honoured the Twmpath with his presence. a man less innocent in his thoughts than Thomas Bartley might have attributed a selfish purpose to Sem's visits. Thomas was, as you'll remember, an unlearned man, free from malice, and extraordinarily conscientious and provident. At first glimpse he gave the impression that he was not all there. But there was in Thomas Bartley a sincerity and a kind of unconscious keenness, apparent to all who knew him. I think his chief characteristics were love for what was upright, just and fair, and a never-ending kindness. In short, there were in Thomas Bartley the essentials of a good neighbour. No doubt a phrenologist would have said after examining him that at his core was the 'organ of wonderment'. Whatever was in Thomas came out, and he had no great stock in reserve, as Sem Llwyd was believed to have. Indeed, seldom could two more different men have been found, as will be seen from the following conversation, which took place during

---

[1] Probably Thomas Charles; amongst many other things, a pioneer in the religious education of children, and instrumental in the foundation of the British and Foreign Bible Society.

one of the visits referred to. Thomas, when Sem came in, had just finished mending the sole of a boot, and was busy putting some black ball on it, pressing the heel against his stomach, and rubbing so vigorously that the veins of his forehead were as thick as a finger. Raising his head, shutting one eye, and holding the side of the boot between himself and the candle, Thomas said: "Well, Sem, where've you been 'idin', man? I've been 'spectin' you all day. As you're not workin', you might just as well come and squat down 'ere as nod off at 'ome. Go to the fire, Sem; I'll 'ave finished this boot in a couple of minutes, and then we can 'ave a smoke and chat."

"A man who can read, though he may be out of work, can't nod off, Thomas," said Sem.

"To be sure," said Thomas, "I'm always too much inclined to think everyone's like me. If I wasn't workin', smokin' or eatin', I'd be sleepin'; those are the only four things I do in this old world."

"It'd be a poor kind of world if everyone was like you, Thomas," said Sem.

"Quite so," said Thomas, "yet I'm quite comfortable, and I don't see those who are scholars as any great shakes. I'm just as well off as most of 'em—thank the Lord for that—for if a man's got food, drink, an' 'ealth, what else does he want?"

"You forget, Thomas," said Sem, "that a man has a mind and a soul, and you need to feed the soul as well as the body."

"To be sure; you didn't think I was as dull as that, Sem? What do we go to Chapel for, if not to get provisions for the soul? But I say, Sem, a man can't live on wisdom. Because 'ere's you and me now. I'm a dull man, and you a scholar, and though I'm a touch older, I swear I weigh twice as much, Sem, in spite of all your learnin', for you look as feeble, man, as if you lived on a pot of paste."

At this moment Sem was overtaken by a dreadful bout of coughing, and before the attack was over, Thomas had laid his work aside and sat down opposite Sem at the other side of the fire, and looking hard at him in surprise; "You know what, Sem? If I didn't know you, and didn't know you were the same ten years ago as you are now, I wouldn't give a farthin' for your life. Well, 'ow you cough, man, as if you were about to die! 'ave a smoke, Sem, and let the fit pass. Barbara, make us a cup of coffee, and let's 'ave a bit of bacon to grease Sem's inside a bit, or we'll be losin' 'im, you'll see. Sem; do you know who gave me this baccy box? Read what's on the lid."

"I see," said Sam, reading the inscription on the lid:

Presented to
Thomas Bartley, Esq.,
By his humble admirer,
W. Bryan.

"A clever lad that boy was," said Thomas, "I wonder where he is now? Sem, I've thought of asking you 'undreds of times, but I forget. Who discovered baccy? I should think you'd know, Sem?"

"Indigo Jones," said Sem.

"Oh!" said Thomas," Odd sort of a name too; as if he were 'alf Welsh. Was he Welsh, Sem?"

"Yes, likely," said Sem.

"We'll, bless him, I say! 'ave you any idea when it was, Sem?" asked Thomas.

"Any idea? I should think I have; about fifteen hundred years ago," said Sem.

"Good heavens!" said Thomas, "As long as that, Sem? You know what, there's been a fair bit of smokin' done since then."

"Yes, Thomas, there has. Yes, baccy was discovered about the time of the battle of Waterloo," said Sem.

"Wait, Sem, you're not getting mixed up now? Wasn't my father's brother in the battle of Waterloo, when they were fightin' Boney?"

"Perhaps," said Sem, "I'm talking about the battle against Polion, fifteen hundred years ago."

"Oh, is that so?" asked Thomas, "I've never 'eard of that battle. Who won, Sem?"

"We did, of course."

"Yes, I 'spect so," said Thomas. "But while we're on the subject, is the story true, Sem, that Indigo Jones' servant, the first time he saw 'is master smokin', threw a bucket of water at his 'ead?"

"Such a tradition exists, Thomas," said Sem, "but I never saw any reliable historian talk about it."

"I can easily believe that," said Thomas, "for who'd 'ave been such a fool? There's another thing I want to ask you, Sem, in which country did Indigo Jones discover baccy? I reckon it was in one of those foreign countries."

"Yes Thomas, in Bristol," said Sem.

"Oh, indeed," said Thomas, "that's why there's so much talk of Bristol baccy, but I don't care much for it. I like Chester baccy better, myself, but everyone to 'is own taste, as the man said when he kissed the mare. But that's enough of this, Sem. The worst of me is after I get definite knowledge about this sort of thing, I forget it straight away. But tell me—it just came to mind—wasn't there a very clever stonemason some time ago by the name of Indigo Jones who built the Tower of London, Llanrwst Bridge, Rhuddlan Castle, Caernarfon Castle, and a lot of things like that. I sort of remember hearin' of a man very like this Indigo Jones."

"The things you're talking about, Thomas," said Sem, "were made before Christian times—under the antediluvians—some thousands of years before Indigo Jones was born, so there's no grounds to believe the story."

"Gracious me," said Thomas, "and that's the way you 'ear people talk who aren't scholars, and don't know anythin' about 'istory. But let's get a bit nearer 'ome, Sem, because I've noticed when people start talkin' about things before the memory of man they're not at all particular about the odd thousand years or two. Tell me; is there any sign of Pwll y Gwynt startin' again?"

"None, Thomas, as far as I know, and I know as much as anyone," said Sem.

"No, I 'spect not," said Thomas, "it's a wonder it 'eld on so long. You know what, Sem, that old mine must have cost someone a devil of a lot of money; and I'll warrant a lot of them, by now, are really cursin' the miners, and are ready to chuck old Trefor down the shaft, for I'll swear he's the one who's caused 'em all the trouble."

"Caused 'em trouble, Thomas? What do you mean? If the Captain had had his own way—and my way, for that matter—Pwll y Gwynt would be paying well, for there's a heap of lead there, if they went at it the right way," said Sem.

"A heap of lead, Sem? Don't talk nonsense. If there's a heap of lead there, why didn't you bring some of it to the surface? You know what, Sem, I don't think there's many more deceitful people than miners on the face of the earth. I never saw a mine yet the miners didn't say 'ad a heap of lead in it, but they 'adn't come to it, or the water stopped them, or some such nonsense. And if the mine stops, everyone's to blame 'sept themselves. You know what; you miners will 'ave a lot to answer for one of these days. And I believe in my heart old Trefor, though he's one of our congregation, is as bad a sort as anyone I've ever seen, though he's supposed to be respectable. Tuck into the food, Sem."

"With all respect to you in your own house, Thomas," said Sem, "you don't know much about a mine. Perhaps you'll be surprised, Thomas, when I tell you that miners often know for certain there's enough lead in this place or that place, but they can't get to it; and often, though they know they could get it, they're not allowed their own way to get it from certain others who are their masters, and those others often know no more about a mine than you do. And as regards Captain Trefor, I'll say this; I never saw anyone—and I have seen a lot—who was so good a Captain of a mine. He knows exactly how to work a mine, if he had his own way; and the Captain and I are always of the same mind."

"I'd sooner," said Thomas, "you were of the same mind, than I was. Between you and me, I never liked the man. He never did anything to me, except look a bit scornful at me, but I don't like 'im, and I wouldn't mind if he 'eard me say so. I see 'im as a sort of gentleman without an estate. I've seen a few of that sort in my time; men who ride on 'orseback at the cost of the Company, and come down to clogs in the end. There's another thing, I never liked the man in chapel; he comes there as though he's doin' a favour to the Lord, and, as if the Lord would come to grief if he stayed away, I don't like that sort, Sem. We should all be the same in chapel, and everyone back in their own place when they come out. And why doesn't the man pray? A man as knowledgeable and talkative as that? But I never saw the man on 'is knees, and that's proof enough for me there's something the matter with 'is conscience, because he's not shy, everyone knows that. You'll see, Sem, if we're alive and well, we'll see that man lose his fine feathers yet."

"Thomas," said Sem, "I'm surprised at you, talking like that about a respectable man like the Captain; a man who has done so much for this area. What would become of us without men like Captain Trefor? We'd starve."

"Starve or not, Sem," said Thomas, "I firmly believe our country would be better off by 'alf without any empty thieves like 'im livin' on thievin' and deceivin' innocent folk along the years. But I'll put a stop to my talk, Sem, or we'll be 'avin' a row. Tell me, is there any truth in the yarn that the Captain's daughter and Enoc Huws are courtin'?"

"Well," said Sem, "perhaps I could throw a bit of light on that if I chose, but people very often talk when they themselves don't really know."

"There is somethin' in it, then" said Thomas.

"I didn't say that," said Sem.

"Then it's all a lie, is it?" asked Thomas.

"I didn't say that either," said Sem.

"Well, what are you sayin', man? You know what, Sem, you miners, talkin' about the simplest things, try to make them '*cyn dued a bol y fuwch ddu*'[2] and no one on earth can tell what you're drivin' at."

---

[2] '*cyn dued a bol y fuwch ddu:*' as black as a black cow's stomach. Things don't get much blacker than that.

"The things that look simple to some people are not simple to everyone, Thomas," said Sem, "and a man isn't supposed to tell all he knows, or we'd all be as wise as each other. And besides that, Thomas, there's a time for all things."

"Well, you know what, Sem; you're a wise one! I, like a fool, blurt out all I know, and I'm surprised I've not got into a pickle before now," said Thomas.

"It wouldn't pay for everyone to be like that, Thomas," said Sem, "if I were like that, one or two plans would have been killed before they'd been christened. Many a one has tried to get the story out of me, but I've been cautious, and kept it all to myself till the proper time."

"Then you think, Sem," said Thomas, "there is somethin' in the story about the Captain's daughter and Enoc Huws, but the time 'asn't come to say so?

"I didn't say any such thing, Thomas," said Sem, "but I will say this, that it's a pity when anyone tells you anything in confidence, that you've not learnt to keep it to yourself. But that can be attributed, no doubt, to a lack of education in the morning of your life."

"Likely enough, Sem, for when anyone tells me anythin', especially if they tell me not to tell anyone else, it starts to burn in my breast that very second."

"That's a great pity, Thomas," said Sem, "but with regard to the things we've hinted at, I can say this; those who know least about the matter talk most about it, and those who know everything say nothing."

"Oh," said Thomas.

"Suppose we were to put it like this, now," said Sem, "that Enoc Huws is a person who's made a lot of money, and who wants a wife. That Miss Trefor is a young woman who's 'ad a good education, and no one need be ashamed of 'er. Very well. If the two were to marry, what would anyone 'ave to say against it? Or suppose we were to put it like this; that Enoc Huws 'as never thought about

Miss Trefor, nor she about him. What would that matter to anyone else? Do you understand me, Thomas?"

"I understand precious little, Sem. Are you sayin' there's nothin' in it?" asked Thomas.

"I said no such thing, Thomas," said Sem.

"Oh," said Thomas, "then you're sayin' there is somethin' in it?"

"I said nothing of the kind, Thomas, and don't go telling anyone I did," said Sem.

"I give up, then," said Thomas, "But to tell you the truth, Sem, I always likes your conversation immensely, but I can understand everyone better than I understand you, Sem. I don't know what's the cause of it, but that's the truth; I know I'm simple."

"Well," said Sem, "suppose we were to look at it like this, then; that Enoc Huws has money—no one doubts that—and that Captain Trefor has knowledge and experience; and what if the two were consulting together with a view to some new venture?"

"Are you guessin', Sem?" asked Thomas, cautiously.

"Guessing? No, I never guess, Thomas, and I'd be pleased if some people wouldn't make guesses without any foundation in the world for what they say." said Sem.

"It's a fact, is it, that the Captain and Enoc are agoin' to start a new venture?" said Thomas.

"I never said it was a fact, Thomas," said Sem, "when something's a fact there's no need to say so; it's plain to everyone. But there are some things that none but those who can see further than the ends of their noses know of. You know, Thomas, that there's no one who knows so much about the Captain's mind as I do? Do you understand me, Thomas?"

"Well I do … if I ever did," said Thomas. "You mean, Sem, that the Captain's tryin' to suck Enoc Huws in to start a new venture?"

"Nothing of the sort, Thomas, and take care not to tell anyone that I said anything of the sort." said Sem.

"I'm glad to hear that, Sem," said Thomas, "for I've a hearty respect for Enoc Huws. I've always thought Enoc Huws is an upright and honest man. He's a lad who's come on really well, and that too in a fair way. You know what? I've bought a devil of a lot of pig food from Enoc, and I've never seen anythin' wrong about 'im. They tell me, Sem, Enoc Huws could live on 'is money when he wants to. And what's odd is he's one of the best 'uns in chapel. I don't know 'ow it is with you Dissenters over there, but with us, when a man gets on a bit in the world, you won't get more than a brief glimpse of 'im in chapel on a Sunday. But as for Enoc, it's not often he misses the services. I 'ope to goodness he's not goin' to speculate; for no matter 'ow much money he's made, old Trefor won't be long in throwing all 'is coin down a mine shaft, and he'll never see 'ead nor tail of it again; just as he did with Hugh Bryan's money, poor wretch. You know what, Sem; I remember Hugh as well off as anyone round 'ere, before he got into the Captain's clutches."

"It's a bad thing, Thomas;" said Sem, "for a man to talk about something that's not in 'is line. I don't doubt a bit, Thomas, that you're the best cobbler in the land, and as a judge of pigs, no one can beat you. But a mine is out of your line; you'll admit that, Thomas?"

"What's up with you, man?" said Thomas, raising his voice a little. "Didn't I take a little interest in the Top Mine, and didn't I spend twenty five pounds there that I never saw again, apart from what I spent on drinks. Didn't we meet in the Brown Cow every first Monday night in the month to look into things and pay over the coin, and up to the very last night, weren't the miners sayin' that there was a better 'look' to the mine than there'd ever been, and we'd all be gentlemen, and I like a fool payin' for glasses all round at the thought of 'ow rich I'd be. The usual nonsense!"

"Thomas," said Sem, standing up to leave, "didn't I tell you hundreds of times you'd get no lead in the Top Mine?"

"You didn't," said Thomas, "work in the Top Mine, nor meet

in the Brown Cow, Sem. If you'd been one of us, nobody knows what you'd have said. But don't let's have a row. You aren't goin' so soon, are you, Sem?"

"I am, Thomas, it's beginning to get late," said Sem.

"Well, 'urry back soon," said Thomas, opening the door. And having looked outside, added: "What'll it do tonight, do you think, Sem? Freeze?"

"No, not if the wind don't turn more to the north; then again, perhaps it will freeze," said Sem.

"Thomas," said Barbara, after Sem had gone—and this was the first word she had uttered since Sem had come into the house— "Thomas," she said, "What did Sem say about the talk there is about the Captain's daughter and Enoc Huws?"

"Heaven only knows," said Thomas. "He said a parcel of things on both sides, as it were, and yet I don't know what on earth he did say. I'd defy Eaton, the solicitor, to make out what Sem said for certain. But Sem 'as a wealth of words in 'is crop."

"He's got a lot of bacon in his crop tonight, anyway. But I'd as soon do without a man when you can't tell what he's been sayin'," said Barbara.

"Never mind, Barbara." said Thomas, "I 'ave a lot of fun in tryin' to guess what he's sayin'. Sem's a very learned man. "Did you see 'ow 'andy he was, givin' us the 'istory of baccy. But I've already forgotten what he said. What was the name of the man who discovered baccy, eh?"

"I don't know any more than you," said Barbara. "I think I'm sure Sem called him Bendigo Jones."

"The best thing for us to do now is rake out the fire and go to bed," said Thomas.

21

VITAL SPARK

People's love or dislike for any institution is usually derived from its originators, and from those most closely connected with it. It's difficult for most people to look at any institution or system separately from the people concerned with it. However good it may be, its existence and its success depend to a large degree on the character of those associated with it. And it must be confessed that no matter how good a principle may be, a greater importance attaches to the practice of it. One might go further, and say that many an institution, which is in itself unjust, is viewed with tolerance, and sometimes approval, because of the virtuous character of those connected with it. From a Scriptural point of view, the connection between Church and State is a grave injustice. But if all the priests, bishops, and archbishops of the Established Church were, without exception, moral, industrious, and godly-minded men, it's doubtful whether there'd be any dissent worth mentioning in Wales today. There are comparatively few people, I think, who have made themselves acquainted with the Bible, and have the success of spiritual belief close to their hearts, who disagree with the principle of a pastoral church. And what is more natural or reasonable? Whilst men need to be educated and trained, and be nourished with the sustenance of religion, a value will be set on whomsoever can satisfy that need, whether they be deacon or preacher. And what would be more reasonable than to entrust the work to the one with the greatest talent, learning, and devotion to that work? And what would be more reasonable, if a man has devoted himself to the work, than to pay him for his labour? The decrees of society ordain a salary for domestic service, and surely the Gospel is as honourable as society. Some people, alas, consider themselves too saintly to pay for religious service. "Pay a man for doing his duty?" they ask. Yes, of course; is it not for doing his duty that a man's paid—or should be paid, in every eventuality?

But what I'm referring to is this; the antagonism to the pastoral care of the church shown by some religious groups can usually be attributed to one of two things: to miserliness, or to the prejudice created by unworthy pastors. The ministry of Rhys Lewis had left a good impression on the congregation that called him to serve it. And it could do no less, for besides being a young man of powerful mind and noble heart, he had a large store of common sense; essential to a pastor, indeed to anyone who must deal with the foibles of mankind. His physical weakness made little or no difference to his influence. Perhaps his long illness disarmed those who were by nature inclined to be touchy, and won the true and warm sympathy of others. He burdened himself with as much work as his shoulders could stand; and many marvelled when they considered that he never neglected to visit the sick and the unfaithful, that he pursued the wanderers, besides being constant in his attendance at meetings, and fulfilling many other duties, that he could prepare such excellent sermons. The engine of his mind—if I may so call it—worked so powerfully and determinedly that it didn't stop even when his health failed. As the sea heaves and rolls for some time after the wind has died, or as the train still moves when the steam has been shut off, so Rhys Lewis continued his work for some time after his strength had fallen by the wayside. Thus his death appeared sudden to many people, though it was not, and though to him personally, it seemed like something that had already happened. But the end came; and when it was whispered that Rhys Lewis had died, a silent wave of sorrow moved through the hearts of acquaintances; and, like those who have seen the setting of the sun on a summer's evening, who've sat in careful contemplation of its final, fading radiance, they shook their heads in a sad happiness.

After Rhys Lewis' death, the congregation was consoled by their having a sensible and religious man to lead them in the person of Dafydd Dafis. That is to say, he was as able to '*cadw seiat*'[1] as many a preacher. No doubt the reader will remember what sort of a man he was. He was almost a man of one book. He rarely saw a newspaper, and didn't try to keep up with the times; but attended the monthly meetings and assemblies regularly. Dafydd had never been seen at a concert, or an eisteddfod; but, so far as he was able, he was at every prayer meeting and '*seiat*'. He didn't bother with politics, and at election times faithfully gave his vote to the one most generally supported by the believers. In his view, life was good for nothing but being religious; and religious in the sense he gave the word. He was wonderfully narrow in his view, and yet at the same time there was a kind of depth in him. He wasn't much of a farmer; and had he not been religious, he would have been nothing, the most pitiful of creatures. The farm, the fair, the '*seiat*', the '*sasiwn*'[2], the diary, '*y Drysorfa*'[3], the almanac, '*yr Esboniad*'[4] and the chapel—especially the last two—those were his whole world and life. He was narrow, as I said, but not surly. His religion left him fixed in gentleness. I never saw him laugh without a tear in his eye—and that in the shadow of the pulpit. All the mirth on this earth would not have made him laugh, but I know that he knew, as the son of Jesse knew, all about the happiness of those 'seated at the right hand of God'. He did not have the ability and mental cultivation of Abel Huws but had drunk deeply at the well of Abel's faith; not for nothing had he passed years in his

---

[1] '*cadw seiat*' to lead a *seiat* meeting.

[2], [3], [4] We have here a litany, a library of dissent; the *seiat*, as you already know, were the regular (or irregular) meetings of the closer membership of a chapel.

[2] The '*sasiwn*' was an open prayer meeting, which played an important role in Methodist revivals.

[3] '*y Drysorfa*', the Treasury, was a Methodist magazine

[4] and finally, '*Esboniad ar y Beibl*', '*Explanation of the Bible*', was the work of James Huws, sometimes known as Iago Trichrig.

company. His devotion to what was within him had earned more respect than admiration, especially among the young. The older members of Bethel, who'd almost finished their struggle with life, and had grown weary with their trials, regretted they'd not lived more like Dafydd Dafis; and the young, though they respected his godliness, were careful not to see him as a model to copy. In my most serious moments, as I grow old, I'm almost inclined to think a life like that of Dafydd Dafis is the only life worth living. When a man's rein has become so short it won't give when pulled, when he feels the only great event left to him in this world is to die, he isn't drawn to laughter as he was by his own follies in bygone days; the price he put on position, respect, a desk in some office, on politics, or money. When the evening of life has fallen on a man, how empty seems all the vain effort of the day; what does it matter now whether we live in a hovel or a palace? What does it matter who the Prime Minister is? The story told about the Reverend John Huws of Pont Robert is without parallel. When one of his brethren went to visit him on his deathbed, expecting to hear some word of his experiences, and asked "Well, John, how are you today?" his answer was "All right; but tell me, what's going on in Parliament nowadays?"

In my serious hours, as I said, I look at Dafydd Dafis' life with envy, but to a man with a healthy, lively mind, a life like his would perhaps appear selfish. He was a '*hen lanc*', and it may be that that selfish element unconsciously develops in the man living the single life. After all, doesn't 'self' govern every man, but wears different aspects? It's true that one of the essentials of religion is self-denial, but it's equally true that there's nothing like religion for developing a consciousness of self, and for putting a value on everything connected with self. What is there like religion for bringing a man to realise his individuality, his responsibility, and his future? These things are but different aspects of selfishness. The man who is humble, in particular, shows clearly that self has played a large part in his contemplations.

But I'm wandering. It was comforting to the church of Bethel to know that the weekly meetings, such as the '*seiat*' and prayer meeting, would not suffer much whilst Dafydd Dafis lived. The other elder, Alexander Phillips (also known as *Eos Prydain*[5]) seldom lent his presence to these meetings. In his own sphere, as leader of the choir, and as the one who cared for the church's books, Eos was excellent. But he was scarcely seen once a quarter in the '*seiat*' and prayer meeting. When the Sabbath came, he was like someone out killing snakes, or covering up a corpse, as the Welsh say. He had other things to do. He scarcely took time enough to eat, and the tuning-fork was between his teeth more often than a spoon or fork. He had a choir meeting at one o'clock in the afternoon, another at five, and one again after evening sermon, and there was more noise in his house than there were empty dishes. One of the things that gave him most joy, and quieted his conscience, was the fact that the Bethel choir had, under his leadership, sung the 'Vital Spark' most effectively after Rhys Lewis' death. If the truth were told, Eos Prydain and his choir, with praiseworthy foresight, had been practising it for some months before the minister's death; not in the chapel, of course; that would have been inappropriate, but in Eos' own rented house. As a consequence, when the sad event took place, Eos and his Choir were ready. Always after this, conscious that he and his choir were able to sing an excellent piece of music, but one only suited to a particular occasion, Eos would, while the minister preached his sermon, take stock of the congregation and check whether anyone bore the signs that the last enemy was about to claim them. If everyone seemed hale and hearty, then Eos would turn his thoughts to the tune set for the end of the service, and we could tell from his lips that he was whistling it to himself. I may as well confess; I was for some time a member of Eos' chosen choir, which is how I know these details.

---

[5] '*Eos Prydain*'—'*Britain's Nightingale*'. Alexander Phillips' '*Nom-de-plume*' for competitions such as eisteddfodau and perhaps something of an over-statement.

It was understood amongst ourselves, and amongst of course no others, that if any of the Bethel congregation were in declining health, a private practice would take place in Eos Prydain's house each Sunday night; but if all were in good health, the 'Vital Spark' would be rested for a time. We had some understood byelaws, which I won't detail here. Our chief object was to be ready at a day's notice with the 'Vital Spark'. Sometimes we held a practice when there was some possibility—such a possibility for instance as is connected with married women, though the occasion was not spoken of as such. If anyone was taken ill during the service, especially if they'd been carried out, we'd flock to Eos' house. I remember Eos in a state of great confusion once. There was among the congregation—though not a member of the chapel—a genial, crafty and clever man in his own way, by the name of Tom Jones. Tom attended very regularly, but was a noted poacher. Tom had been 'before his betters' more than once. One night he was caught poaching by the keepers on the estate. Tom didn't want to lose his catch, and a scuffle took place. He escaped their clutches; but being obliged to fight two men, he had suffered a severe knocking about, and from this poor Tom died. Now the question that troubled Eos was not whether the 'Vital Spark' should be sung, but whether it would be tolerated. However, we held a practice, and the question was laid before Dafydd Dafis. The decision was made in a moment, and Eos lamented that Tom had not died under different circumstances. Whilst I was a member of the Eos' choir, I rejoiced that Wil Bryan was gone, for I knew he would quickly discover our rehearsals, and wouldn't have refrained from revealing our 'hymbygoliaeth'[6].

I retired from the choir, and it happened thus. I was taken ill with slow fever. Eos lived next door but one to our house. About ten o'clock on the first Sunday evening of my illness, I was very ill,

---

[6] 'hymbygoliaeth'—A word of Mr. Owen's own creation, a word not in the dictionary; but I know without being told, as would any Welshman, that it means 'humbugness'.

and no one but my mother was watching me. It was a quiet night and no one walked the street. My mother was reading the Bible to herself. Suddenly I heard the sound of singing, and though I couldn't hear the words, I knew by the music that:

> *"Lend, lend your wing,*
> *I mount, I fly;*
> *Oh grave! Where is thy victory?*
> *Oh death! Where is thy sting?"*

—were the words that were being sung.

"Are any of the chapel people ill, except me?" I asked my mother.

"No, my son; why do you ask?"

"Oh nothing," said I. But that was a wretched night for me, for I saw that Eos and his choir were all for burying me at once. There were signs of recovery before the following Sunday, and though I listened diligently, I heard no more of the 'Vital Spark'. Once I was out and about again, I imagined Eos, disappointed I hadn't died, and I never again went near his choir.

22

THE PASTOR

I've been coming to this chapter for some time but, like Gwilym Hiraethog's dog, I've been running after every animal and bird that crossed my path. The work of Rhys Lewis left such a good impression on the members of Bethel that very soon after his death they grew anxious to have another pastor. And they were not long in lighting on the man. It came about very naturally. It happened that a preacher came one Sunday to occupy the pulpit at Bethel; he'd never appeared there before, or anywhere else in the county. He passed his test in excellent style. He spoke with a natural talent and a pleasant voice. The visiting preacher chanced to stay with Eos Prydain; it was his month to receive the preachers. Before retiring after their long Sunday evening's conversation, Eos asked boldly whether the visitor would be ready to accept the call if one of the county's chapels wished him to be its pastor. After a little hesitation and a little humming and hawing, the man replied that he was wholly in the hands of Providence; if it was wished that he should labour for the Lord as a pastor, he was quite ready to bring himself completely to the work; in truth, that was the chief aim of his life. Eos told the stranger that the chapel had great need of a pastor, and that they were broadly, in his opinion, ready to seek a worthy successor to Rhys Lewis, but that he had, of course, asked the question entirely on his own responsibility. At the same time Eos gave him to understand that he considered himself a pretty good judge, and knew the feeling of the chapel, and that it would be good to have foreknowledge of who was ready to be called and who was not.

Lest it should be considered that Eos had been unduly hasty in asking such a question to a man he'd never seen before and knew nothing about, I should inform the reader that the stranger had spoken most favourably of the congregation's singing, and had proved clearly, to Eos' mind, that he knew the difference between a crotchet and a demi-semi-quaver. Now this, in Eos' view, was a quality seldom found in a preacher; and he couldn't help thinking what a catch it would be to have a minister who not only appreciated music, but was a singer. And with this prospect burning in his breast, Eos was not shy of mentioning the matter to many of Bethel's members, particularly the younger ones, during the following week. By the following Sabbath, Obediah Simon—for that was his name—had been weighed and measured in the homes of the members, and not unfavourably. It was widely acknowledged that he was an excellent preacher, and Eos' testimony, that there was more excellence in Mr. Simon than had yet been seen, was accepted. And the more it was thought about, the more it appeared that he'd be the best and most worthy successor to Rhys Lewis. He was unmarried, and not unfavourable in appearance, and whispered of most approvingly by the young women of Bethel, and more privately by several of the mothers. Mr. Simon's age was a subject of much feminine debate, and it was broadly agreed that he was under thirty. The more thoughtful and observant young men were inclined to believe he was nearer forty, but freely admitted that the young women could be right, inasmuch as hard study can make a man appear older than he is, and it was obvious that Mr. Obediah Simon had been an enthusiastic student, as he wore spectacles.

But there was one among them, Thomas by name, who used to write in the press, and who was known by the '*ffugenw*'[1] Didymus; he didn't believe that Mr. Simon had studied hard, and protested

---

[1] '*ffugenw*'—literally, '*false name*', therefore '*Nom-de-plume*'. 'Eos Prydain' is another ffugenw. Writers and composers are often known by such names, and they are still used today when entering the eisteddfod competitions, to ensure that the judge cannot be swayed by knowledge of a competitor's identity.

that Obediah had cheeks like potatoes in buttermilk, that he'd never seen a hard worker with such rosy cheeks. But Didymus was quietened by the astute observation from one of the brotherhood that men's cheeks have great recuperative power, but once Latin and Greek have poked their fingers in a man's eye, "Give me back my eyesight" will be that man's cry ever after. It was a remarkable fact that the name of the Reverend Obediah Simon had been lately debated by the families of nine of every ten members of the chapel as a man likely to make an excellent pastor, though Dafydd Dafis had heard '*na siw na miw*'[2]. And it was at the monthly meeting he first heard of the rumour.

"Is it true," asked a brother elder to him, "that you're likely to call Mr. Obediah Simon to be preacher here?"

"I've not heard talk of such a thing," said Dafydd.

"Don't be so sly, Dafydd Dafis," said his friend, "for Mr. Simon himself was telling me only yesterday that his case was likely to come before the chapel very soon."

Dafydd was struck dumb, and deeply hurt. When he came home, who should be awaiting him but Didymus, who was looked upon by some of the brethren as a forthright man. When Didymus realised that the rumour was unknown to Dafydd Dafis, he told him all he knew of the matter, and Dafydd found it hard to keep from fainting. It was hard to believe there had been such widespread talk on so important a matter, and all of it, as it were, behind his back. He had been accustomed to think his service as an elder had been appreciated by the church, and though he held no high opinion of his powers, he was aware that he'd been second to none in his fidelity, and in doing his best with the powers given him. He became serious on hearing Didymus' account, and started to think he could have had no place in the opinion or love of his fellow officers, or in that of the chapel.

---

[2] '*na siw na miw*'—not the slightest whisper.

"What do the members with judgment say on the matter?" asked Dafydd.

"You know," said the doubter, "you could count those on the fingers of one hand, and you're the first I've been able to speak to about it."

"If the case were to come before the chapel, what would be your opinion of the man?" asked Dafydd.

"My opinion," said Didymus, "is, as they say at an eisteddfod, that he's not worthy of the prize, and it's best to leave it to the next competition, if you understand my meaning.[3] What's your opinion, Dafydd Dafis?"

"I'm inclined to think the same as you," said Dafydd. "But perhaps we're both doing the man an injustice. It's not right to judge a man after hearing him only once. It may be that Mr. Simon's an excellent man, and we may not find one better, but to say the least, I think that Phillips has been too hasty; far too hasty. It's not child's play to call a man to be minister to a chapel. Great discretion must be used, and one should pray more than ever for guidance. Better the evil we know than the evil we don't. The man made no special impression on my mind, but perhaps the fault was mine. I know I'm too inclined to take notice of small matters, but I didn't like to see him wearing a ring on his finger. Did you notice it?"

"Yes, I think so," said Didymus; "his best suit had been brought out, and there was a ring on his finger, and if I couldn't see for myself that the fatted calf was alive and hadn't been killed, I'd have come to the conclusion Mr. Simon was the prodigal son we hear so much about."

"I don't know if I understand you," said Dafydd, innocently. "Do you mean by saying that the fatted calf hadn't been killed that Mr. Simon didn't preach well?"

---

[3] Sometimes, in an eisteddfod, the judge will consider that none of the entries is worthy of winning. Being the best of a poor bunch is not good enough.

"Not only that," said Didymus, "but it's obvious he couldn't have preached if he had been killed, for I swear that Mr. Simon is not, and never will be, one of those of whom they say: 'though dead they still speak'."

"You're too ready to put people down, Thomas," said Dafydd. "It's very obvious that the man is well liked by the people, if the talk of him's as favourable as you say. And he's been ordained; he must have something in him, or he'd not have been."

"You know, Dafydd," said Didymus, "there's a lot of skill '*i gael Wil i'w wely*'[4]. The fact that Mr. Simon's been ordained doesn't prove he's Paul or Apollos. I know many a man with barely a soul, who's devoted years, and sacrificed everything from a sparrow to a bullock to gain the anointing oil, and when he'd got it, did nothing but depend on a silver tongue, and that's Obediah Simon: he leans on the steel of his silver tongue. But of course a man relies on his best asset. And as to being brought before the chapel, that's as good as taken place, for Eos has already sounded his praise in the ear of every member of the chapel, and gone quite mad about him, and the reason for all this enthusiasm is that Obediah Simon's a musician. If that's the sort of man we want in Bethel, well, why doesn't the man get to work on having Sims Reeves[5] as minister. Dafydd Dafis, if you don't put your foot down on this matter, I'll go and join the Latter Day Saints."

Scarcely were those words out of his mouth when Eos Prydain himself appeared. He never at any time frequented the monthly meeting, but as a dutiful Methodist and one conscious of his obligations as a deacon, it was his regular custom to visit Dafydd Dafis every month, to have an account of the monthly meeting. And doubtless it was for this purpose he'd come to the house that night. He didn't know, of course, that Didymus was already there,

---

[4] '*i gael Wil i'w wely*'—literally, to get Wil into his bed. To achieve one's objective.

[5] Sims Reeves—The foremost English tenor of the period.

or perhaps he'd have waited till the next evening. A conversation of such interest—in the writer's estimation, if not the reader's—took place, that I must devote a whole chapter to it, and a longish one too, I'm afraid.

23

DIDYMUS

It would be fair to say there wasn't a lot of brotherly love lost between Eos Prydain and Didymus. Didymus wasn't noted for civility to his superiors in office. It was generally considered that his intelligence was greater than his consideration for others, and that his talents exceeded his modesty. When an irritating, timely but anonymous letter appeared in the local press, it had usually been fathered by Didymus. Indeed, a spirit of "I don't care about anybody" pervaded his character. At the same time he was, from top to toe, a hero worshipper, and there was no greater hero in his sight than a great preacher. He also admired the 'uncommon', whether it be great or not. No one was a greater admirer of Thomas and Barbara Bartley than he. And though inwardly he'd laugh at some of Dafydd Dafis' observations he would have laid down his life for Dafydd, for he believed that Dafydd, such as he was, was 'real'. Didymus was completely unreconciled to anything he saw as humbug, but his choice of what came under that heading was sometimes questionable. As has already been suggested, Didymus didn't put much value on Eos' abilities. Eos was aware of this and on more than one occasion had suffered injury in silence, and had to pocket many a wicked word. Eos would have preferred the privacy of Didymus' room to meeting him in Dafydd Dafis' house; and yet he shook hands in a kindly way that said "I'm not frightened of you." Eos, poor fellow, tried to be on good terms with everyone, and was naturally of a sociable disposition. Dafydd Dafis didn't appear as friendly as usual and Eos didn't feel as comfortable as he would have liked. However, he tried to behave as though he were in the best of humours, and said:

"What sort of a Monthly Meeting did you have, Dafydd Dafis?"

"A very excellent one," said Dafis, drily.

"Indeed? Was there anything special there?" asked Eos.

"Yes," said Dafydd, "the spirit of wisdom and discretion marked every discussion, and the Lord looked down on our ministration."

"Oh, I'm sure," said Eos, "It's lovely to hear that. Was there any talk about the *Cymanfa Ganu*?"[1]

"No," said Dafydd, "not so far as I remember; if there was, I didn't notice it."

"So," said Eos. "It's strange how one Seiat after another goes by without any mention of something as important as the *Cymanfa Ganu*. When, I wonder, will music get the attention it deserves?"

"I've often thought, Dafydd," said Didymus, "that it wouldn't be a bad idea to have a choir drawn exclusively from the Seiat; male voices, of course. It wouldn't be impossible. It would be simple to make a rule that no one should be accepted into the Monthly Meeting without having the highest certificate for the 'Sol–Fa'. Nothing would give me greater pleasure than to see a row of old chaps like you singing alto; and I'm sure, if you formed such a choir, a lot of musical elders who never go to the Seiat would attend regularly. And perhaps you'd pick up some prize at an eisteddfod, and look how that would raise the Methodist cause in the county."

Dafydd Dafis almost laughed at the thought of a row of people like himself singing alto, and Eos said, rather bitterly:

"Thomas, you have to be sarcastic about everything. But it's no use your talking; it's impossible to get preachers to take any interest in the congregation's singing; as far as they're concerned

---

[1] *Cymanfa Ganu*—A gathering to sing hymns in four part harmony, often bringing together several local congregations, or—for example when held at the Eisteddfod Genedlaethol— the National Eisteddfod—from a wider area.

singing could have died out long ago."

"I must confess," said Didymus, "the singing of Methodist preachers has seriously deteriorated in recent years. I remember when almost all of them were able to sing, and when the congregation wouldn't have tolerated a preacher who wasn't a singer. But nowadays our ministers, as a rule, content themselves with quoting the great truths of the Gospel to us without singing them. Of course, there are honourable exceptions. A week last Sunday we had a preacher who even sang the lesson."

Eos ignored Didymus' words, and addressing Dafydd Dafis, again said: "I expect some remarks were made about our pastorate, for that's always of interest to the preachers."

"Well, no. There was no talk about the minister in public," said Dafydd.

"Why do you emphasize in public?" said Didymus.

"I'll tell you why," said Dafydd. "I was asked a question there which surprised and hurt me. A brother asked me if it was true that Mr. Simon was likely to be called as minister to the chapel; and he couldn't believe I'd never heard a word of it. But by the time I got home, and had asked around, I realised there had been a good deal of discussion about the man without my knowing anything about it."

"You are, like me, a little behind the times," said Didymus. "But in this case I was a bit ahead of you, and had known for several days that some members of Bethel had fallen in love with Mr. Simon. You know, Dafydd, that love is blind, and in this case blinder than ever, and if your sight had been a little shorter, perhaps you too would have fallen in love with the man. However, though you're a 'hen lanc', I'd have expected you, as an old friend of Bethel, to be among the first to know who she loved and who she didn't."

"I doubt there's anyone," said Eos, "who'd deny that we really need a pastor. It's time someone did something. We've heard and talked enough, and it's time we took action. And as you've hinted, there's been a lot of talk about Mr. Simon since he came here to preach; everyone liked him. Indeed I liked the man very much myself, and I never had a man more agreeable around the house. I think we could consider ourselves very lucky if we succeeded in getting Mr. Simon as our minister. That's my opinion."

"I don't wish," said Dafydd, "to suggest he's not everything we want. And nothing's more apparent than the need for a minister here. I'm tired of hearing my own voice in the '*seiat*', and you, Phillips, are only there perhaps once every two months to give a helping hand. It's time to be doing something. At the same time we need to use great caution, and to pray for the guidance of the Spirit of God. Choosing a minister is not a thing to rush at like a cow to its feed."

"No one's thinking of rushing, Dafydd," said Eos. "No one's thinking of settling the question tomorrow or the day after. But it's time to bring the matter before the chapel. Do you think we haven't, since Rhys Lewis' death, had time enough to exercise caution and pray for guidance? If we're not careful, a lifetime will go by while we talk about caution."

"Phillips," said Dafydd, "if I remember rightly, it was with you that Mr. Simon stayed when he was here. Did you give him any cause to believe his name would be brought before the chapel, and do you know anything of the man's history?"

"All I did," said Eos, "was to talk generally about our position as a church, and of the need we have for a minister. And I also happened to ask Mr. Simon if he was open to accept a call should one of the local chapels of the county think of him."

"You didn't commit yourself, or make any sort of promise then, Phillips?" asked Dafydd.

"Nothing of the sort," said Eos.

"I'm glad to hear that," said Dafydd.

"I'm glad, too," said Didymus, "for I think it's a rule, if an elder has given his word to a preacher that he'll be chosen as minister, that the chapel, as a matter of honour, is bound to uphold his word; and no harm would be done by putting the thing to the vote in the church to show the unanimity of the call. It's quite reasonable, for if the elder is entrusted with the choice of a preacher for each Sunday, and if the congregation, after hearing that preacher, hold up their hands to show their approval of the choice, why shouldn't the elder be entrusted to select the minister? The elder is the representative of the chapel, and if the chapel doesn't stand firmly behind the word of the elder, it's not worthy of the name chapel. At the same time I believe the elder should, in choosing a pastor, be in touch with the taste of the whole chapel. My own particular view is that the pastor should be a good preacher. Another person's view would be that he should manage the '*seiat*' well. But these are not everyone's views. Though I'm not myself a good musician, or care too much for music, I can't close my eyes, and more especially my ears, to the fact that music is an important point for a large part of the congregation. Now, admitting that Mr. Simon's a fluent speaker, and capable of running the '*seiat*', I don't think I'll give him my vote if he's not a fair musician."

Eos looked at Didymus' face for a moment to assure himself he wasn't joking; and as not a muscle moved to show anything other than the greatest seriousness, Eos answered happily:

"A fair musician! I can assure you that Mr. Simon is an excellent musician. I had a long talk with him about sacred music, and I never saw a minister so familiar with the subject. The singing in Bethel pleased him very much; he said it had helped him in his preaching, and gave me several hints on how to improve it. If every preacher took as much interest in music as Mr. Simon, there'd be a different aspect to the singing of our country's congregations.

"Certainly," said Didymus, "it's a pity that all our preachers are not musicians. I was a great admirer of Rhys Lewis, but he himself admitted he knew no more of music than would a crow. And though his ministration was highly successful, I couldn't help noticing it would have been a great deal more so had he been musical."

Eos beamed, for he never had heard Didymus talk so wisely.

141

"The best man, no doubt, as a minister, is the one in whom the greatest number of excellences are combined. It's better for a pastor to have a little of everything than just one great talent. In the chapel are a small number—a pity there aren't more—of young men with a little appetite for literature, and it would be well for the pastor to know a little of the subject. I wonder if Mr. Simon has any leanings toward literature?"

"I'm sure he has," said Eos, "though he didn't say as much to me. Quite by chance, he remarked that he must leave early, as he had to adjudicate on some treatise at a small eisteddfod that week."

"Mr. Simon didn't happen to mention the subject of the treatise?" asked Didymus; "That would help us to understand in what branch of literature he's considered a judge."

"Yes, certainly; if I recall," said Eos. "It was something about the flood, and on the question of whether there was an elephant in the ark or not; something like that."

"An excellent subject, and a complex one, too," said Didymus. "I've pondered a great deal over that myself. But it's a pity they didn't also ask whether there was a whale in the ark or not. There's considerable confusion about the question even now, and if it could be decided, it would throw a deal of light on the size of the ark and what is meant by a cubit. But it's clear that Mr. Simon, when at home, is considered a naturalist and an historian, if not a geologist as well. What was the prize offered for such a subject, I wonder? Mr. Simon did not happen to mention, perhaps?"

"He showed me the programme, and if I remember rightly, five shillings was the prize," said Eos.

"Another mistake," said Didymus "for a subject of that nature the prize should have been seven and six. How can we expect our best literary men to compete on such a subject when only five shillings is offered? But it's obvious that things are getting better. I'm glad to understand that Mr. Simon is literary, but we'd never have known if you hadn't mentioned it."

Dafydd Dafis was silent, and couldn't see what purpose

Didymus had in mind, talking this way, when Didymus added: "It's a great advantage to have a conversation with a man like Mr. Simon, to find out the inclinations of his mind and his personal abilities. In the pulpit a man is, as it were, at a distance, and only the preacher comes into view, and often one doesn't realise that. One has to meet and associate with a man to discover the qualities of his mind. And from what we've heard from you, I must confess that Mr. Simon is a better man than I'd have thought from hearing him preach. I'm sorry I didn't come over to talk with him."

"I'm sorry, too, and I was expecting you all the time." said Eos.

"It's no good believing first impressions," added Didymus. "Did Mr. Simon give you the idea, Phillips, that he'd moved in society? That is, did he show that he had self-respect; was he careful about his appearance and could you trust his behaviour in respectable society? For, nowadays, such things are important, and it would be of no use us considering a careless, old-fashioned, slovenly pastor; those days are over; the world has changed, and stress is now laid on behaviour and manners."

"Well," said Eos, "I almost thought Mr. Simon was far too mannerly ..."

"It's not possible for a man to be too mannerly these days," said Didymus, before Eos had finished his sentence.

"Perhaps that is indeed so," said Eos, "but what I rather feared was that Mr. Simon was too gentlemanly for us—the people of Bethel."

"There's no such thing as too gentlemanly," said Didymus.

"Well, what I mean by too gentlemanly is this; he was somehow or other too thankful. I just had to pass the mustard or help him with his coat, and he'd say 'Thank you'," said Eos.

"Quite right; a sign of good breeding." said Didymus. "You didn't notice, Phillips, whether he put anything in the maidservant's hand before he went away?"

"I didn't see him give her anything," said Eos.

"I knew that." said Didymus. "No gentleman ever lets anyone

see him give anything to the maid, but you enquire when you get home, and you'll find, I'm sure, that he gave her sixpence or a shilling."

"I wouldn't be surprised," said Eos. "And with regard to the other matter you asked about, whether he was careful about his appearance, he told me he shaved every Sunday morning, and I recollect that, when we were going to evening service, and had got as far as Start, the chemist's shop, Mr. Simon remembered he'd left his gloves on the table at home, and though we were a little late, wanted to go back for them. I was rather cross with him about it. And I remember also that he saw a deficiency in our chapel vestry; there was no glass, comb, or hair brush there."

"Dafydd," said Didymus, "make a note of that. Didn't I spot that deficiency a long time ago? But let us move on. How easy it is to misjudge a man from a distance. Mr. Simon is a much better man than I supposed. You, Phillips, having had the privilege of sharing his company, have the advantage of knowing him thoroughly. Let me to ask you another question or two about him; and keep in mind, as I said before, the various peculiarities and tendencies of the members and congregation; is Mr. Simon—in your honest opinion—fond of parties? Does he have an eye for making money? Can he play cricket? Can he play cards? Can he play billiards? In short, is he a perfect humbug?"

Eos leapt to his feet, seized his hat furiously, and looking contemptuously at Didymus, said:

"You're the biggest humbug I know, Thomas. No one knows how to take you, and when people think that you're most in earnest, that's when you're not. You treat people as good as and better than yourself as though they were children, and you think you're somebody. I swear that even if we thought of appointing the Apostle Paul as minister of Bethel, you'd make a joke of it …"

"Certainly" said Didymus.

"You talk a lot about 'humbug', but as long as I've been an elder, no one's given me as much humbug as you, and understand,

I won't stand any more of it, and if Dafydd means to back you up, well, so be it." And Eos rushed from the house, and Didymus laughed loudly.

"Thomas," said Dafydd Dafis, "I don't know what to make of you. I have a high opinion of your abilities, and I know you're much cleverer than I and that you could do much more for the cause if you chose, though you're very useful now in Sunday School. But, somehow, you play with everything; you play with the things that are most serious; and I am sure you've hurt Phillips' feelings very much tonight. You were at fault, Thomas."

"Play, Dafydd?," said Didymus, "doesn't everyone play? Isn't everything in this life a game?"

"God forbid." said Dafydd, agitated; "Not everything's a game, or what would become of us? You don't mean to say that religion is a game? That the whole world before us is a game? I'm surprised with you, Thomas, talking like that."

"I think I'm as serious as most these days," said Didymus, "but there's less hypocrisy in me. I am sick of people's humbug. I swear I'm as good a Methodist and as dutiful to the '*Hen Gorff*'[2] as anyone alive. When my mother was living and I was a young, strong lad, Henry Rees used to stay at our house on the evenings he worked, and I remember cleaning his shoes, and I put a real good polish on 'em; you could have seen your face in them. And there's nothing I'm as proud of, at this minute, as having had the privilege of cleaning Henry Rees' shoes. And, there are scores of our preachers—lesser men in every respect than Henry Rees— whose boots I should esteem it an honour to clean. Give me a preacher, no matter how small his abilities, who is honest, zealous, upright, modest, and who thinks more about the redemption of sinners than about himself, and I'll take my hat off to him, and would willingly clean his boots. But I can't stand humbug. Good

---

[2] '*Hen Gorff*'—the '*Old Body*'; the Calvinist Methodist Church.

heavens! Thirty years ago, the characteristics of a preacher were humility, zeal, godliness and a passionate desire to rescue sinners; but now the uniform is the chief characteristic; sinners recognise it and flee from those who wear it. When a thief or a murderer must be caught, they don't generally send a man in a blue uniform to do the work; they send a detective in plain clothes. You can be sure, Dafydd Dafis, we need more plain clothes officers in our pulpits these days, with a warrant and seal from the Almighty to catch men. I'm sure that Mr. Simon is one of the uniform branch, and while he's admiring his gloves, his coat and all the trimmings, sinners are escaping. What qualification for the post of pastor is a gift for music, if his soul's not permeated by the Gospel, and the urge to save sinners not the kernel of his character?"

"There's a lot of truth in what you say, but not every truth should be spoken all the time," said Dafydd.

"That's a false doctrine, Dafydd Dafis," said Didymus, "but very fashionable philosophy nowadays. The fear of telling the truth, the over-anxiety not to hurt the feelings of humbugs and little girls, raises a generation of hypocrites, makes hypocrisy respectable, and it'll soon be as difficult to find an honest man as to find a rose blooming in the spout of a kettle. Only yesterday I was talking to one of the elders of Salem about a young man who's had permission to preach there, and he said; 'Do you know what, Thomas, I'm sure God never intended that youth to be a preacher'. 'Did you say that in the 'seiat' when the young man's case was being discussed?' I asked; and he said: 'Well, no; if I had, I'd have upset people, and in fact would have caused myself trouble, for some of his family use my shop'. I call that humbug, Dafydd Dafis, and there are more of his sort than there are honest men."

"I know something about that," said Dafydd, "and I'll say something besides. No elder has a right to say what God intends. One must exercise discretion before giving a youth permission to preach, and at the same time one must be careful not to put obstacles in his way. And though it's doubtless a man's duty to speak his mind honestly and wisely, I'd prefer to fail on the side of tenderness."

"Failing on the side of tenderness is treated almost as an instruction from the Scripture now." said Didymus. "People are extraordinarily tender these days. A man is tolerated, though he's known to take a drop too much, so as not to hurt his wife's feelings; and another is allowed to play many a little prank so as not to upset his family; and in the same way, young people can do as they please. And if a John the Baptist came among us, there'd be no need for a Herod or a Herodias; the 'believers' would be the first to bring his head on a dish before the throne."

"Thomas, Thomas!" said Dafydd, "you're getting more extreme every day. I'm afraid there's too much of the violent spirit in you. To tolerate one another in love is as much our duty as speaking the truth. But we've been wandering for a while. I'm afraid from what Phillips said that he's brought the name of Mr. Simon before the church, as you told me."

"That's pretty much what took place." said Didymus.

"Well," said Dafydd, "if it comes to that, Thomas, take care to be present, and speak your mind freely, but in a humble spirit."

"I won't be around, Dafydd. Let the chapel stew in its own broth," said Didymus.

"Well, there you are;" said Dafydd. "You want people to be honest and speak the truth, but when push comes to shove, you turn your back."

"You know, Dafydd," said Didymus, "that if I went there I'd speak the plain truth. But the majority of the members wouldn't see it as the truth. I know I'm reckoned a black sheep by many of them, and if I were to speak my mind honestly, I'd be looked upon as one who was cursing Israel."

"Never mind that," said Dafydd. "Come, and speak your mind honestly, and in an appropriate spirit. And please, Thomas, don't write to the newspapers about the matter. I never see the papers myself, but they tell me you write very bitter things sometimes."

"Writing to the papers," said Didymus, "is part of my business; just as sowing turnips is a part of yours. It's the people with tender skin who say I'm abrasive; those whose skin is without blemish don't complain at all."

"That doesn't matter, Thomas." said Dafydd. "Showing up believers isn't work I'd care to do. There are already enough at that without your doing it."

"And there are plenty," said Didymus, "ready enough to throw a veil over everything. But, perhaps—I wouldn't confess my faults to just anyone—perhaps I've been rather foolish, sometimes, writing to the newspapers. I'm a little rough-natured, I know; yet I believe I feel a true interest in the cause here. I'm sure of this; that I don't get as much pleasure anywhere as I do in the chapel, and though I have my own opinion of Mr. Simon—a sort of presentiment I can't shake off—I believe at the same time that neither I, nor you, nor Eos can govern the circumstances we're now in, and that some unseen hand steers and shapes them in spite of all we may do; and that, no doubt, for some good purpose. And now, I bid you goodnight."

"It's remarkable," said Dafydd to himself, "that that man is so much disliked by the brothers. I can get on very well with him. He may be rough, and there's an itch he feels a constant need to scratch. And if the brothers learn that Thomas is against Mr. Simon, they're certain to be strongly for him. But I trust we'll be guided."

24

DAFYDD DAFIS AND THE 'SEIAT'

I'm tempted to speak further of Dafydd Dafis. After hearing Didymus report the last chapter's conversation, I thought Dafydd's feelings might be wounded, and visited him. Dafydd was not so very old, yet there was something in his appearance that brought to mind a bygone age; and when I recalled some of his observations, it seemed as if he'd been left too long in the world to be comfortable with it. He still wore '*brethyn cartref*'[1]—the wool of his own sheep—and had it not been for his niece Mary, he would have stuck with old-fashioned breeches and gaiters. After much persuasion, she'd managed to get him to wear trousers of a pepper and salt colour, and by now he felt fairly at home in them. I'm sure he'd have suffered martyrdom before he'd wear trousers the same colour and cut as mine. Until defeated by baldness, he expressed his protest against the pride of the present with hair like the eaves of a thatched roof, butting against his heavy eyebrows. On Sunday morning, on going to chapel, his niece Mary, after fastening his neckerchief, would run a comb through his hair and give it a parting, as she thought her uncle was a little absent-minded. But it was no use, for the first thing he did in chapel, after taking off his hat and sitting down, was to draw his hand over his head, from crown to forehead, and his parting would depart, and Mary's labour be wasted. But in the future his head would be, except for a narrow hem of hair, as bald as a bladder full of lard hanging from the kitchen ceiling; and indeed it looked very like one.

Though Dafydd understood next to no English, it would be a mistake to call him stupid. Perhaps his inability to speak English

---

[1] '*brethyn cartref*'—homespun cloth. Often—though in this case it's literal—used as an analogy for anything homespun, such as entertainment.

was an advantage, especially when dealing with his landlord. When Dafydd wanted to have a go at his landlord, or the man's agent, Mary would be at hand to interpret; but when Dafydd knew the man was coming with some unjustified complaint, Mary would be, as Robert Roberts of Holyhead describes solar eclipses, "invisible here." When Dafydd felt that he'd done his duty according to his conscience, he didn't care what his landlord was saying in English. "His words are water off a duck's back," he told me. I know Dafydd's English was better than the landlord's Welsh. Once—before there was any talk of a tithe war—Dafydd had threatened the parson with not paying his tithe. By doing so, he knew he'd arouse the landlord's ire, and he knew there'd be a visit within the next few days to rebuke him. Dafydd didn't want to argue or fight with him, and was looking out for him. And one morning, there was my lord, coming spurred and angry on his grey horse. Dafydd saw him coming, and said to his niece:

"Mary, go upstairs and see if anything needs doing, and don't come down till you see him turn his horse's head for home." And he went out to meet the landlord.

The landlord began by asking for Mary to interpret, and Dafydd said she'd gone upstairs, but of course the landlord couldn't understand, and poured a torrent of English on the old farmer's head. The word 'tithe' was constantly repeated, and when Dafydd got his chance, he answered in leisurely Welsh: "I know nothing, sir, about your *tai*[2], except *Tŷ Coch*[3] here, and that, as the world knows, is badly in need of repair."

The landlord understood that Dafydd was saying something about repairs, although he wished to pursue the tithe, and he scoured his brain for what Welsh as he possessed, and cried fiercely—in Welsh:

"Why no English, Dafydd?"

---

[2] '*tai*'—houses; the plural of '*tŷ*'. The Welsh language arrives at its plurals in a number of ways.

[3] '*Tŷ Coch*'. Dafydd's home, '*Red House*'.

"Why no Welsh, sir?" replied Dafydd promptly, in the same language, for why should Dafydd have more need to speak English than the landlord to speak Welsh? When the landlord saw that there was no hope, no sudden sighting of some bard to spin translations by the yard, and that it would be useless to babble in a language not understood by his tenant, he spurred his grey horse and left, and Dafydd returned, calmly, to the house. From the bottom of the stairs, he shouted "Mary, come down to the butter now, please." When Mary came down, Dafydd asked: "What was the man saying about *tai*? What do I know about his houses?

She'd been listening through a hole in the window; the windows of Ty Coch were full of holes: "It wasn't *tai* he was talking about, uncle, but *tithes*. The '*degwm*'[4] you know," said Mary.

"Oh," said Dafydd; "never mind."

I said that it would be a mistake to call Dafydd a stupid man; but the furniture of his mind was not unlike the furniture of his home. There was no *modern* furniture there. Very little had been changed over time; the old settle by the fire, the old dresser and the pewter plates on it, the old chairs, and the big table by the window, all in strong oak. After Betsy, the maid, had given them a little elbow grease, there was great charm, to my mind, in Dafydd's furniture. The only place where time had told was on the ancient eight-day clock. When it struck, its note was one of chronic bronchitis, and by then it was "in the nature of losing a little," as Dafydd said. Dafydd's mind was broadly similar; there wasn't a lot of modern thought in it. And yet he had read thoroughly the books mentioned earlier. Considering how old-fashioned he was, I often marvelled that he was so favourable to a pastorate system. But his great love was the '*seiat*'; the one who could hold a '*seiat*' well was the man for Dafydd Dafis.

As I said, I feared that Didymus had disheartened him; and so

---

[4] '*degwm*'—literally, a tenth; but in this case, the tithe. The tithe went to the Anglican church; Dafydd—and many others—did not.

I went there. It was the night of the 'seiat', and I was at Ty Coch before Dafydd had returned. I saw from his face my fears were unfounded, for he was in excellent spirits, and where could I start, save with his favourite topic?

"I see, Dafydd, you still go to the 'seiat'."

"Yes, of course; and it'd be good for you to go more than you do." said he.

"You know my circumstances," I answered; "It's extremely difficult for me, especially in summer, to leave the shop at seven o'clock and get to chapel, without doing myself harm. It's very easy for you farmers to go to the 'seiat' and the prayer meetings, but we shopkeepers would very quickly lose the race if we went regularly to the midweek meetings."

"What race are you referring to?" asked Dafydd.

"Well, the race in this world—the race in business," said I.

"Oh," said he, "Is that your race? To be first in the race in this world is your great object, is it?"

"It's the duty of everyone, Dafydd Dafis," said I "*to look after his own living.*"

"True," said Dafydd, "but there's a greater duty. A man must look after his living; but he should look more after his life. I'm afraid that living and not life is what people consider nowadays."

"You're not saying that going to the 'seiat' is indispensable to gaining eternal life?" I asked.

"No, I'm not quite that stupid. There are thousands, millions, I hope, who have gained eternal life, who were never at a 'seiat' as it's understood among Welsh non-conformist dissenters. I've heard farmers say they could do very well without going to fairs or markets, but I've noticed they don't have much grain around the place. Something very much like that, I'm afraid, is in the minds of many believers nowadays; they think they can live religiously without going to midweek services. If they can, I envy them; they must be better than we who try to attend services fairly regularly, for I know the experience of those who do attend is that they find themselves very backward, not only as to their spiritual life, but also in what they'd like to be. That's how I hear 'seiat' people talk, and that's my own experience. But the majority of believers these days are able to live a spiritual life, and perfectly self-satisfied and happy in their minds, without showing their face even once a year at a prayer meeting or 'seiat'. And some have reached such a state of perfection as to be able, without feeling harm or loss, to dispense with the Sunday morning service. And if they progress as swiftly in the future, and there's every reason to believe they will, they'll soon be able to do without any services at all, and send their contributions with Sali the maidservant. I envy them!"

"You're being sarcastic, Dafydd." said I. "I see a double meaning to your words. But wait; I'm quite sure in my mind that some of those you speak of are very sorry they can't attend services in midweek."

"Well," he said, "as you're one of them, you're more likely to know their thoughts than I."

"What? Is it possible," said I, "you're put me among the people you were describing just now? I go to the 'seiat' occasionally and I have never regretted having done so. But allow me to ask you a question, and don't think I'm suggesting anything by asking. Taking everything into consideration, changing times, the greater advantages of education, in culture and morality, how much more knowledgeable are congregations, and how much higher the worldly position of many of our chapel members, do you think the 'seiat' is relevant these days?"

Dafydd looked at me in silence, as though he were wondering whether to give up on me or not, or as if he'd have liked notice of the question. He looked at me again, and again, then filled his pipe. He did have that weakness—he was a smoker—and when he had to think hard, he turned to his pipe for assistance, as the brethren generally do. He straightened a little in his chair, and said:

"Times, as you call them, have changed greatly even in my own recollection, for the better in many things, and for the worse in others. Education has improved greatly, and nowadays small boys know more about things in general than men learned in their lifetime a while ago. But as far as I understand, no new revelation of spiritual things has been had, I've heard of no prophet having been sent from God to announce that religious meetings are unnecessary. Have you? And with regard to the '*seiat*' as an institution that has done and will continue to do great good to men's souls, I don't think there's any need to defend it, except as the Gospel itself would be defended against the attacks of the ungodly. And even if the '*seiat*' stood on the same ground as the Sunday School, without any Scriptural example or command in its favour, the reasonableness and naturalness of it would meet the approval of the heart and mind of every enlightened Christian. Have you ever heard of any movement or any strong feeling shared by many, that did not end with some form of '*seiat*', a meeting where people could discuss things—consult and exchange thoughts? There's the nationalist feeling that's recently awoken. You're one of those, I'll warrant. But you'd achieve nothing without your '*seiats*'. And you've understood that, and have, I hear, established your '*seiats*' in every corner of the land. If it's thus with the ordinary matters of life, shouldn't religion too have its '*seiat*', and shouldn't every believer to be a zealous member of it?"

"How many of those whose names are in our chapel book attend the '*seiat*?'" I asked.

"About one in three, or a little better perhaps," he answered.

"Then," said I, "how do you account for the unpopularity of the '*seiat*?'"

After thinking a little, he replied:

"If I'm not mistaken, the Methodist '*seiat*' is as old as Methodism itself. It was established when our nation was in extreme ignorance, but still aroused by men sent from God, men full of the Holy Spirit. I think the '*seiat*' originally had at least two aims; to test the reality of the convictions of the religious, and to lead them to a knowledge of things spiritual. These aims were good and of great value. As far as form is concerned, there's been very little change in our religious meetings. I think the Sunday School bears more trace of the changing times, of the advance in secular education, in culture and morality. External forces have touched the form of the '*seiat*' only slightly, and perhaps this has something to do with its unpopularity. The '*seiat profiad*', the '*seiat of experience*' it was called originally; we still ask for experience, and it is seldom to be got. I believe the word 'experience' had a meaning at the beginning that it seldom has now. At first it meant the anguish of the soul under a deep conviction of sin, or the joy of reconciliation with God. I believe also that the word has a slightly different meaning when used by the Wesleyan, rather than the Calvinistic Methodists. 'Experience' in its Wesleyan sense means how near a man has got to heaven; in its Calvinistic sense, how far away he is. The Wesleyan's experience is of how he conquered the devil; the Calvinist's experience too often is how the devil conquered him, or else that he has nothing particular on his mind. It seems to me neither is right; and yet both are right. Every man has 'experience' every day of his life; the true state of his heart with regard to things spiritual. There's room to fear that Wesley's temptation is to create a happy experience—which in fact he doesn't enjoy; and that Calvin's temptation is to put himself in the box, in front of the bench, and do so falsely, because he knows that's where he should be. One's temptation is to fly high without wings, and the other's to think he's licking the dust when he's really quite upright. The danger that threatens both is dishonesty."

"I said every man has experience, but I must withdraw those words. It's true in a sense, but not in the religious sense. If a man can live for a week without sorrow for his sins and shortcomings, without wrestling with doubt, without once thinking of the mystery and aim of his being, without fearfulness of the future disturbing his dreams, it can hardly be said the man has any experience at all in a religious sense; he belongs to the same class as the godless men of this world. But my point is this; the '*seiat*', in my opinion is a remarkably beneficial institution not only to hear religious experience, but also to create and foster it. Awareness of sin is the same now as it was a hundred and fifty years ago. The same essential difference exists now, as always, between a godly and an ungodly man. Perhaps the difference is not quite as apparent as it was. The irreligious man has come to live more like the religious; and the religious, too often, has come to live more like the irreligious. There's room to fear that, in many circumstances, a bargain has been struck between the world and the church. By now, notable conversions have become rare, and being close to being a Christian is fashionable. This, of necessity, has given a new aspect to our religious meetings. The majority of our members have been brought up religiously from childhood; and, as a rule, cannot point to any sudden revelation on their road to Damascus. And those that are brought in from the world because they were previously amongst our constant listeners, and were men of good character, have no account of experience to give, save a gradual conviction leading them to the point of offering themselves to the church. What does this teach us? Well, I think it teaches us this; that we can rarely expect troubled and fiery experiences as of old; but certainly we can expect deep and quiet experiences. Besides that, it teaches that the chief aim of our religious meetings should now be to create thoughtfulness, and meditation and daily inquiry into spiritual truth, in a way that would create interest in every class of member. We should not leave the most sacred meeting we have to chance and accident. The subject to be discussed should be known to the members before going to the meeting. There's an abundance of worthy subjects. They are old, but ever new to those worrying about their condition, such as the following: What are the true signs of conviction? In what ways are the world and the church like and unlike each other? What are the signs of spiritual growth and degeneracy? In what way can the certainty of eternal life be attained, and a host of other similar matters. I don't believe that the best way of holding a 'seiat' is to compete for the longest repetition of Sunday's sermons. If anything from the sermons is to be repeated, let the brother repeat something that went straight to his heart, something that made him move in his seat, not some long, untidy segment of the sermon. A very important question is 'Why do so few frequent the 'seiat?' One reason, doubtless, is the ever present fear in the bosom of the bashful, of being asked to say something. If they were assured they need only listen, they would, perhaps, come to the 'seiat' quite regularly. For my own part, while I would give all opportunity and encouragement to say what was on their mind, I would not press—for experience or anything else— those who wish to be silent, unless there's some special reason to call for it. Another reason, very likely, is the want of courage in us, the officers, in doing our duty towards the members. It ought to be understood that each member would be expected, so far as is possible, to attend the 'seiat' at least occasionally, if not regularly, and that those who were wilfully neglectful would not be considered members at all. But the chief reason, no doubt, that so few come to the 'seiat' is the lack of taste for religion, if not an entire lack of faith. The world, somehow, has nowadays got the upper hand. We have formed and shaped our affairs so that religion can't have fair play. A man must look after his living, as you said, but I think it's possible to arrange things better. A number of our young people are in bondage to business hours, and couldn't come to midweek services if they wanted to. It shouldn't be that way. Most Welsh shopkeepers are believers and if there was a little energy in them, everyone would be able to shut their shops by seven o'clock at the latest. But no effort worth talking about has been made. We're too worldly to say goodnight to the world at seven o'clock, and while this continues, religious meetings will not get fair play. I'm afraid that the world owns many of us; we are sheep grazing its meadows. And whoever comes here as a shepherd, whether it be Obediah Simon or someone else, if we can't escape from that, his labour will be in vain."

I offered no response to what Dafydd had said, to avoid troubling him further, and because I agreed with much he had said.

25

ENOC AND MARGED

By now, appointing a pastor to a church is such a common thing (though perhaps if it were more common it might be a good thing for many a church) and its ceremony so uniform, that I don't propose to weary the reader with a detailed narration of the event. I would suggest, for the sake of the readers of Welsh newspapers, to meet human nature's desire for variety, and to show future generations how open the human temperament is to change, and how a few years—sometimes a few months—turn men inside out, it would be of benefit to be more ceremonial in the dismissal of a pastor. With no further beating about the bush, the Reverend Obediah Simon was appointed as pastor of Bethel. After the conversation in Dafydd's house, Eos Prydain missed no opportunity of setting Mr. Simon's qualities before every member of the church he chanced to meet. By no means the least of Eos' arguments was that they wanted someone to quieten Didymus. For some reason or other Didymus too had determined to go into his shell, and be silent on the matter. On seeing that feeling was strong and general on Mr. Simon's side, Dafydd Dafis did not express his own opinion, only urging everyone to pray earnestly for guidance. At the end of three months, Mr. Simon was minister of Bethel.

Mr. Simon had scarcely moved amongst us a fortnight when the sad news spread that Pwll y Gwynt had closed down. This was an unfortunate event for him and for the chapel; and had it been known that such a misfortune was at hand, it's more than likely Mr. Simon's most zealous supporters would have hesitated before taking the step they'd taken, as many of the chapel's members depended entirely on Pwll y Gwynt; but so it was, and who can foresee such events? The step had been taken, and there was nothing to do but make the best of it. There were opponents of the pastorate system who practically hinted that the whole misfortune was a judgment on the chapel for what it had done. It was, of course, the case that other chapels, and even the Church of England, had to suffer from the judgment that fell upon the Methodist chapel.

Captain Trefor had not been present at a chapel meeting for some months, due to unavoidable circumstances; and so the chapel had been obliged to choose a pastor without the assistance of his judgment. The Captain was kept up to date with every detail of the discussions in the 'seiat' by Mrs. Trefor, who was most regular in the services. Mrs. Trefor often expressed pity that the Captain couldn't help the brethren in these discussions, but he'd answer:

"You know, Sarah, though worldly matters, so to speak, take up all my time, because the existence of many families depends on me, you know, I say, that my heart is with you; I am with you in spirit though absent in body, and I think if you are made perfect, I will be included in your perfection. And," added the Captain, "inasmuch as I agree entirely with what the chapel has done—that is, choose Mr. Simon as our minister—I can't see how the result would have been different had I been present at every meeting; for everyone knows that I favour the pastorate system, and that I have, on more than one occasion, shown, with fair and incontrovertible reasons, the unreasonableness that we—more than any other denomination—should be without a minister, one entirely free from worldly cares, to look after the spiritual welfare of the members and the neighbourhood in general."

This statement and its like satisfied Mrs. Trefor that Bethel had been kept from making a mistake, even without the Captain's counsels. To show more fully his approval of the chapel's actions, the Captain said one day: "Sarah, though our circumstances are not what they were, it wouldn't be proper to show any kind of coolness towards our minister, and it would be as well if you asked Mr. Simon to come and have a bit of supper with Mr. Huws of Siop y Groes, and Mr. Denman."

Mrs. Trefor was pleased to do so; and Mr. Simon was not loath to accept, for he'd heard that Captain Trefor was a man of influence in the neighbourhood, and was only slightly acquainted with him and his family. It's true that he'd noticed Miss Trefor, and had spoken once or twice with Mrs. Trefor.

The new venture, Coed Madog mine, was by now, not mere imagination. No, the Captain had put several men to work at sinking a shaft, and had already drawn out the plans of the office, engine house and so on, and was in correspondence about machinery. "For," as the Captain said, "it was necessary to look the matter in its face at the start. The old enemy, namely water, would be sure to pose a threat, and the Company must show that its machinery was stronger than the enemy. "Indeed," said the Captain, "wherever there's a lot of lead, there's also a lot of water. Just as it's often necessary to go through fire, in the form of gas, to get coal, it's also necessary, in almost every case, to go through water to get lead. Every treasure, sir," said the Captain, "has by nature and providence, its zealous guardian, and the guardian of lead is water. But with good fortune and fortitude, we will snatch the stronghold from the hand of the strong. With skill, patience, faith, and the heart to venture, I haven't the slightest fear or doubt but that we shall see this neighbourhood again successful, and the men prosperous from the abundance of work."

Enoc Huws was by this time a regular visitor to Tŷ'n yr Ardd, had largely overcome his shyness, and had nurtured more courage than he had once thought possible. It was heartening to see the pleasant change in him. Instead of being, as he once was, totally engrossed in the shop—the first to open and the last to close—and after closing, dragging his tired body in its floury clothes to the office to smoke his pipe and await bedtime; instead of all this, like any respectable and independent businessman, he would now order the shop to be shut the moment he heard the clock strike eight. He then went straight to his bedroom to shave and wash, came downstairs as neat as a new pin, put a rose, if he could get one, in his buttonhole, lit his cigar, picked up his silver-topped stick, and walked to Tŷ'n yr Ardd. He raised his hat with gentlemanly courtesy when he met a young woman he knew, and in return received a smile of acknowledgement, which ripened into a laugh when he'd passed by. Since Enoc first came to Siop y Groes, he'd been acknowledged by everyone to be a good young man, modest and religious, but extreme courtesy was something quite new in his character. His neighbours didn't consider the fact, which was by now well enough known, that Enoc was a partner in the new venture, sufficient reason for the sudden and complete change in him, and there was no other way of accounting for it, especially among the women, than by saying that Enoc was preparing to be a husband to Captain Trefor's daughter. Their belief was greatly strengthened in its credibility by another inescapable fact: the simultaneous change in Miss Trefor's dress and behaviour. The girl, they said, was quickly getting to know herself and beginning to be like any other girl; she put on no 'airs', didn't hold her head so high, came to chapel regularly, took notice of everyone—rich or poor—was modest in her dress, and humble in her spirit. It was evident, said her friends, that she'd given up all hope of getting a gentleman for a husband, was making herself suitable to be a shopkeeper's wife, and was setting a trap to catch Enoc Huws, poor man. It was clear, said the same authorities, that Miss Trefor's aim was to level down, and Enoc's was to level up; and that the natural consequences would soon follow; a mutual understanding, a ringing of bells, a throwing of rice and shouts of hurrah! The matter was settled by the neighbours; nothing else was possible.

On the whole Enoc felt fine, or at least appeared so; but he would have preferred to be as sure as his neighbours. Scarcely a day went by without someone or other congratulating him on his prospects. At first, this was very painful to him, especially when customers brought up the topic in front of his shop assistants. Miss Trefor's name made him feel as hot as a new loaf out of the oven. But a man can get used to almost anything; and, eventually Enoc would feel disappointed if a day went by without anyone referring to the people at Tŷ'n yr Ardd. Some of his customers, more honest than wise, dared to speak unkindly about the object of his love, and though Enoc said nothing (they were good customers), his face showed it wasn't pleasant to hear their conversations, and in his heart, hated everyone who whispered a disrespectful word about Miss Trefor. There was one plain speaking woman who came into Siop y Groes every Saturday night when they were about to close. She used to declare that Enoc and Miss Trefor were exactly like one another, and though Enoc pretended he was tired of the story, the assistants noticed that he invariably gave some sweets to her children.

Though the belief that Enoc and Miss Trefor were in love was so universal, there was one who would not suffer any talk of it, save as a foolish and senseless story, and that was Marged, Enoc's housekeeper. Marged admitted that her master visited Tŷ'n yr Ardd pretty regularly, but he had to do that, as he'd been such a fool as to invest in the new venture. But she couldn't have been in Siop y Groes for so long without knowing her master's mind, and talk of her master marrying some doll, a flighty creature like Miss Trefor, was an insult to common sense in Marged's view. Ever since the night Enoc told Marged she'd make an excellent wife, and it was a pity she wasn't married, the two had been on remarkably good terms. Marged was so kind and sociable, and so careful of his comforts in carrying out his wishes and even his suggestions, that Enoc was unable to guess the reason for the pleasant change in her behaviour, except the supposition that she'd been blessed with a brand new set of senses. Enoc put such value on this improvement, that it occurred to him one night, of his own accord, to suggest to Marged a rise in her wages. But Marged wouldn't hear such a thing; indeed, she didn't want any wages at all, save just enough to buy tidy clothes. Enoc had noticed—with pleasure—that Marged had lately smartened herself up considerably. She'd always been a bit slovenly, and it amused Enoc to notice Marged's attempts at making herself seem slender waisted and small. But though she did her best in this respect, her efforts were broadly unsuccessful, especially with regard to her waist; for after pulling and pulling, she didn't look much better than would garters tied round the middle of a sack of potatoes. And she couldn't safely add a bustle or dress improver, for the parts usually adorned by such things were already of such immoderate size that, had any addition been made, it would have been necessary to enlarge Siop y Groes. However, it was wonderful to Enoc to see this improvement in his housekeeper's appearance, for that appearance had often, in times past, been a great trial to him, and had made him fear people might believe he didn't pay her enough to buy tidy clothes. On seeing Marged so much smarter, Enoc couldn't help praising and congratulating her frequently on her appearance. Enoc was so kind and generous a man, that the fact that Marged persistently refused a rise in her wages caused him great pain. He grieved for her innocence, and his conscience wouldn't allow him to take advantage of it; Enoc could have no peace of mind without rewarding Marged somehow or other for her valuable service, her ceaseless care of him, and for making his house something like a home.

Marged was possessed of such a curious temper that her master was afraid to offer her a gift of clothes, and yet in what other way should he show his appreciation of her services? One day he fearfully offered her a brooch. Marged was greatly pleased; indeed, she was overcome and couldn't help shedding tears. On seeing her great happiness, from time to time Enoc gave her pieces of clothing equal in value to the rise in wages he'd intended to give her. Marged's joy on receipt of the presents, and their excellent effect, afforded Enoc great pleasure. One day Enoc thought a present was due to Marged, the more so as she'd firmly refused her quarter's wages, telling him to keep them for some other time. Enoc asked Marged what she'd like as a gift; he was surprised by her answer and couldn't help laughing furtively. "Well, as you're so kind, master," said Marged "I'd very much like a ring like the one you have, but not so costly."

Marged's faithfulness was so great, and her childlike innocence so apparent, that Enoc couldn't refuse her, and said: "Well, if you'd like one, go to Mr. Schwartz's shop and buy one, and tell him I'll be coming to pay for it. You'll get a decent ring for about twenty five shillings, Marged."

"You're very kind, master," said Marged, and with but little delay, off she went to Mr. Schwartz's shop. But though she tried many, Mr. Schwartz didn't own a ring big enough for Marged's finger. Had he not been an honest shopkeeper, he'd secretly have sent to the ironmonger's for a bed-curtain ring. But he didn't; he measured her finger, in order to have a ring specially made for her. When Marged told Enoc, he felt a strong desire to laugh, but didn't dare. However, the two were getting on famously, and Enoc began to wonder whether, if he successfully gained the hand and heart of Miss Trefor, married her, and brought her to Siop y Groes, perhaps it wouldn't be necessary to turn Marged away as he had feared. "Perhaps." said Enoc to himself, "she, like so many others, thinks that everything's settled between me and Miss Trefor, and is preparing for the time when Miss Trefor is Mrs. Huws; and thank goodness for that. I remember when I used to tremble at the thought of what Marged would say if I spoke of marrying. Poor Marged, the innocent and faithful old creature; I'd like to see her marry and settle down."

Though nearly all his acquaintances, in their turn, had mentioned—some playfully, others seriously—Miss Trefor's name, Enoc was surprised at times to think it had never occurred to Marged to mention her, or to say anything about the talk, so general in the neighbourhood, about his being in love. Often when he happened to have stayed late at Tŷ'n yr Ardd, Enoc expected Marged to hint broadly about what that signified. But all Marged said was, "How's the mine coming along, master?" and Enoc would say to himself, "She doesn't like to take liberties with me."

Things went on very comfortably like this in Siop y Groes for a time. Enoc had spent a good deal of money in beautifying his house, inside and out. Every new addition to the furniture was warmly welcomed by Marged, and there was but one thing wanting in Enoc's mind to make his life perfectly comfortable. But short-lived at best is the happiness of Fallen Man, and often when the cup is set to overflow and we can drink our fill, some evil spirit shatters it to atoms before our eyes. And the better the man, the more likely his misfortune, as though the heavens were too jealous to let a man enjoy this world, lest his expectations be disappointed in the next. This was all too soon proved true in the story of Enoc and Marged, as will be seen in the next chapter.

26

BREACH OF PROMISE

There was a limit to the patience and waiting around of even Enoc's housekeeper, Marged; and one night, whilst her master was staying late at Tŷ'n yr Ardd, and the night seemed long, heavy and uncomfortable to her—not to Enoc—she made up her mind to speak to her master when he came home, for she'd grown tired of living like this, and vowed she'd get a clear understanding on the matter. And when Marged had decided on something, that thing would be done with no further discussion. It's true she felt she was taking an important step, and when she heard her master ring the bell, if she'd had any nerves, she'd have felt nervous; but as she didn't have such things, the closest comparison she could make was to those days when she couldn't decide whether to cook or clean. As soon as Enoc came in, he perceived that Marged didn't look nearly as lively as usual, and he thought she must have been dozing more deeply than usual, and she wasn't fully awake. For once, to Enoc's great astonishment, Marged did not ask how the mine was going on; but, when he'd pulled off his shoes, and she'd handed him his slippers, Marged looked straight into Enoc's eyes so seriously as to remind him of her old ferocity, and said:

"Well Master, what do you mean to do?"

Enoc looked for a moment rather shy, and thought that Marged was at last going to talk about Miss Trefor. That would not be unpleasant to him, so he said, with a smile on his lips:

"What are you referring to, Marged?"

"What am I referring to? You know very well what I'm referring to. I want to know what you mean to do, for it's time you did something."

"Well," said Enoc, a little cautiously, "I think I can guess what you're referring to, and I confess it's time I did something, and I hope it won't go on like this for ever; but a man can't have his own way every time; you know that, Marged."

"What's stopping you having your own way? You've had your own way since I don't know when, and what stops you having your own way now?" said Marged?

"You don't know everything, Marged." said Enoc.

"I know that very well." said Marged. "I know I don't understand anything about business; and have you ever seen anyone who did know everything? I think I know how to keep a house as well as anyone you've ever seen, anyway."

"I've always said, as you know, Marged," said Enoc, mildly, "that no one could wish for a better housekeeper than you. Have I not said so many times, Marged?"

"What else could you say?" said Marged, more quietly than usual.

"Very true," said Enoc, "but what I was going to say is this; you've hinted that I'm a long time doing something, and so I am. But a man can't do everything he wishes. I know you feel lonely in this big old house on your own, especially since I've begun going to Tŷ'n yr Ardd and staying out late. And that's quite natural. It's not good for a man to be alone, says the Bible, and it's not good for a woman to be either. But how can I help it? I know you're tired of waiting for me to marry. But the truth about me is this—I may as well speak plainly; I've not spoken about it to anyone else—a man sometimes has to wait years before he succeeds in his attempt, and the truth is … you won't mention the thing to anyone, will you, Marged?"

"No, no, I never mentioned anything to anyone," said Marged.

"Well," said Enoc, "the truth is, I'm no nearer Miss Trefor today than I was when I started. She's a very hard girl to win. I'll admit I love her very m …"

Enoc didn't utter another word. He was terrified by Marged's appearance. He was astonished initially by her eyes, usually as unexpressive as the eyes of a fat pig, but which were now wide open and sparkling with fire like the eyes of a tigress. Enoc felt that their flames almost reached him, and unconsciously pushed his chair back. Then he saw her cheeks turn blue, and the colour spread over her whole face, but not a muscle in her body moved. Enoc was so stunned that he couldn't ask what sickness was upon her, but he believed for a certainty that Marged had gone mad, and was on the point of leaping at him and pulling him to bits, or about to have a stroke and becoming paralysed, and there was no strength left in him when Marged gave an unearthly scream, like the scream of a thousand wild cats, and fell as though dead on the floor. In a fear that was close to killing him, Enoc rushed to the front door to seek help, but before opening the door, remembered it was midnight, and that poor Marged might die while he was looking for someone. Like old King Belshazzar, his knees knocked together while he applied cold water to Marged's face; and though great was his fear, Enoc couldn't help thinking— while staring, incapable and confused, at her ugly cheeks—of the picture of Apollyon in his copy of The Pilgrim's Progress. Enoc was certain in his mind, whatever was wrong with Marged, that the beating of her heart couldn't be quicker than his own, and he had enough strength, by and by, to make the comparison, and found he was right. Suddenly, while he was taking Marged's pulse, she began to kick violently and throw her great arms about, which convinced Enoc poor Marged was having a fit. This opinion was strengthened by the fact that she was grinding her teeth furiously. Enoc had seen people in this condition before, and was therefore acquainted with the appropriate treatment. To prevent her biting her tongue, Enoc succeeded, after considerable trouble, in putting a spoon between her jaws, which, had he been sufficiently calm to enjoy the circumstance, would have added considerably to the interest of the scene, for Marged took hold of the spoon with her teeth as an old toothy smoker would grip his pipe when craving a smoke. As has already been seen, Enoc was a weakling in terms of bodily strength (I won't speak now of his mental powers) but as a true philanthropist, he was going to do all within his power to help Marged recover from her affliction, and began vigorously to beat the palms of her hands, as he had seen others do. Everyone knows how strong people are in a fit, and when Enoc began to do so, Marged—who was naturally very strong—threw out her right arm with a clenched fist, and hit Enoc on the base of his nose till he was laid out as flat as a slate on the floor, his blood flowing. Enoc leapt nimbly to his feet, full of pity for the sufferer, ignoring the blow he himself had suffered, but the blow had so weakened him, and Marged continued to kick and flail and beat until Enoc saw he had to find help somewhere. He rushed from the house, and to his joy, whom did he find—in the right place at the right time—but Jones the policeman.

"Come in at once, Mr. Jones," said Enoc.

"What's the trouble, Mr. Huws?" asked Jones slowly and calmly. "Why the shouting in your house?"

"Just Marged having a fit. Come in. Come in, at once," said Enoc.

Jones walked in, leisurely, heavy of footstep, and having come into the light, was more astonished by Enoc's bloody face than the unnatural look on Marged's face with a spoon in her mouth. Marged had become quiet, and Jones, looking into Enoc's face, said; "If seems to me, Mr. Huws, you've had the worst of the skirmish." Before Enoc could answer, Marged leapt to her feet, and looking fiercely at Enoc, said:

"You bad man ..." But seeing there was someone else in the room, she turned to the policeman and said fearlessly: "What do you want here? What's your business? Get out of here at once, or I'll make a hole in you with this poker. Are you going?"

The policeman smiled knowingly, and Enoc waved to him to go out, and followed him to the door.

"The old game, Mr. Huws, the old game," said the policeman,

leaving the house, and Enoc was too frightened to answer.

Poor man! He was nearly fainting, and his face, with the exception of the part covered in blood, was deathly white as he fell into the chair in front of Marged for a second time; on seeing his pitiful appearance, she weakened for about five seconds, and then started to speak.

"What do you want with that nuisance here? Did you think he'd take me to the gaol? I defy you! Isn't it enough for you to deceive me, and make a fool of me, without bringing a policeman here?"

"Marged," said Enoc, shaking, for at that moment he realised how things really stood. "Marged," he said, "don't shout. I beg you." Enoc believed the policeman was listening at the window.

"Don't shout? Don't shout?" said Marged at the top of her voice. "I'll shout as much as I like, and you won't stop me. Are you afraid people will hear? Yes. I know you are. But people will hear. I'll expose you to everyone, and you won't make a fool of me. I defy you!"

"How have I made a fool of you, Marged?" said Enoc, his tongue so dry it almost stuck to the roof of his mouth.

"How? How? How?" shouted Marged, "in every way! Didn't you tell me it was a pity I wasn't married, and I'd make a splendid wife? Haven't you said hundreds of times you could never want a better housekeeper?"

"Yes." said Enoc, "and I'll say so again; but how have I made a fool of you?"

"You dreadful man," said Marged, "how do you have the nerve to ask me such a question? Didn't you give me to understand you were considering me? And if you weren't, what business did you have to say such things?"

Enoc summoned all the courage he possessed, and said: "Marged, you've deceived yourself. I never gave you any cause to think such a thing, I swear; and I never thought of marrying you, any more than I'd marry a boa constrictor."

"Well, you evil accursed man!" said Marged. "What in the world did you mean by giving me all those presents, except to make a fool of me? But I've got them all, and all of them will face you yet. Don't think you can treat me like this. I'll get the best of you, and make you stick to your word. Why would I refuse a rise in my wages if you hadn't as good as said that I'd be your wife? Don't think you can turn round in your tracks like that. And as reproaching me about Boaz the conductor, that won't work, Mr. Huws. I know he had me in mind when I belonged to his choir, but I never looked at him, and I wouldn't have looked at you if I wasn't getting on in years, I've refused better men than you. But I'll make you keep your promise, sir, or you'll regret it. And to tell me to my face that you're in love with that little old worm from Tŷ'n yr Ardd! That proud, no-good flirt! I'll tell her who and what she is next time I see her, that I will. And she'll hear what sort of a person you are too, you deceitful man! And you call yourself a believer? A fine believer, deceiving a homeless orphan! I suppose you've been trying to deceive that worm at Tŷ'n yr Ardd, too? Wasn't deceiving one woman enough for you? But wait; everyone's going to know your story, and you're going to pay dearly for this! If you don't keep your word, I'll have you turned out of the 'seiat', and I'll make you as poor as Job. You won't have a shirt to put on your back; I'll do it before I've finished with you, you two-faced creature!"

To say that Enoc was by now utterly miserable would be an understatement. A thousand possible and probable disgraces appeared to him, making death there and then seem almost preferable to life. Completely careless of the consequences and with a boldness and manliness he'd never shown before, he said, with energy and feeling:

"Marged, I'd rather you planted that knife"—there was a large bread knife on the table near her—"in my heart, than hear a single disrespectful word about Miss Trefor. Say what you like about me, or hit me on the head with that poker if you want, but don't say a single word, a syllable, about Miss Trefor. She's the best, most beautiful girl in the world, I swear. Her name's too pure for your rotten breath to breathe, and cleaning her shoes would be too good for you. And saying I've made a fool of you? Look here—listen to what I am saying—If there was just you and me and an orangutan in the world, and I had to marry one of you, you'd end up an old maid! I don't care a fig for you, and I won't stand for any more of your evil tongue. You'd better pack up and leave at once."

Marged was stunned by Enoc's words and boldness. It was something completely new and out of character, and unexpectedly painful to her. Her face turned every shape, colour, and form, sometimes in a threatening, sometimes an accusing way; she opened her mouth to speak, then closed it without saying a word. After running through a series of unearthly and fiendish grimaces, Marged gave herself again to the arms of evil nature; or in other words, had a second attack of what Enoc, in his innocence, looked on as a fit, but which in truth was nothing other than hysteria, an illness which emotional and ungodly women are subject to, and an illness which had, as I've heard my mother say—and she was something of a medical authority—only one unfailing cure: to throw a bucket of cold water in the patient's face, and another down the back, and repeat the treatment till the sufferer comes to herself, which usually happens after the first two buckets. Marged fell on her back on the floor, and began to kick and scream as before. Enoc offered no help; he didn't even think of putting a spoon in Marged's mouth. Rather, he lit a candle, and went up to his bedroom.

Heaven knows Enoc was a good man, and had so tender a heart that he couldn't kill a fly or a wasp in his shop without feeling the pangs of conscience. But that night, while going upstairs to his bedroom, he hoped from the bottom of his heart, that Marged would have gnawed her tongue to pieces before the morning.

27

CONFUSION

Not until Enoc reached his bedroom did he begin to realise he was really still the same Enoc Huws. He could scarcely believe he'd been so bold with Marged—Marged, his housekeeper, for fear of whom his heart trembled! His conscience too began to reproach him for leaving her alone in such a state. He thought it his duty to go back and try to administer some sort of help. But he remembered her ferocity; he was certain that murder lurked in the corner of her eye. Life is precious, and a man should hold onto it. Enoc began to fear and tremble, and decided to lock his door. The door hadn't been locked for several years; and when Enoc set about it, he found the key had rusted in the lock, and he couldn't shift it. What could he do? He'd never been so nervous, apart from the night he first went to Tŷ'n yr Ardd. He put his box of clothes against the door and such chairs as were in the room. He added the washing stand, and something else I won't name here—for every little helps. And still he didn't feel safe from the enemy. He was perfectly conscious that all this was as nothing against Marged's Herculean strength. As a wise precaution, he opened the window in case the fortifications weren't strong enough and he needed to escape. As one end of the wooden bed stood opposite the door, Enoc put his back against the bed and his feet against the clothes box in order to strengthen the defence, and awaited the onslaught. He was heartily sorry for having spoken as he had, for who knows what vengeance his words would inspire. Enoc waited for a long time in this defensive position, and although the attack had not yet begun, pressed his legs with all his might against the box. In truth, he was on active service in the absence of the enemy—so much so that his legs were soon numb. He felt sure, with the passage of time, that Marged must have emerged from her fit, and he was gripped by the terrible thought that she'd put the poker in the fire, and was waiting for it to become white hot. His flesh crept, and he trembled at the thought of being fried on the point of the poker.

By and by, Enoc heard movement in the enemy camp, and immediately heard the stairs creak under Marged's weight. He realised she was advancing in her stockinged feet, for her footstep was soft and slow, and Enoc earnestly believed that Marged intended a surprise attack. As the door of his bedroom wouldn't shut properly, Enoc could see the light of her candle as she reached the top of the stairs, and was seized by such terror that he abandoned his defensive position and fled towards the window. He formed his mouth into the shape of an O, ready to shout 'Oh, murder!' the moment she stormed his defences. His heart beat like that of a newly captured bird, and beads of cold sweat the size of garden peas ran down his face. Marged had reached his door! But she went past, slowly and quietly, as though afraid of waking a child. Enoc was aware of every slightest sound; and when he heard her bedroom door close, he breathed a deep and deeply grateful sigh of thanks, and threw himself on the bed to try and regain a little composure, but without dropping his guard. After regaining a little strength, and reckoning that Marged ought by now to be between the sheets, he got up, went to the door, and put his ear to the crack. I think I said, at the beginning of this story, that Marged was a snorer without equal, and Enoc knew very well that if she was asleep, he'd be able to hear her groanings even from the cellar. This had often bothered him, and lest I forget to mention it at all, I'll say now that was the main, if not the only, reason for Enoc refusing to take his month of accommodating visiting preachers; though he never mentioned it. Enoc listened earnestly for the risings, swellings, and chokings of Marged's infernal apparatus, and when they reached his ears, I'm sure that not even the most harmonious music has ever aroused such well-being as that which filled Enoc's heart and mind. He felt some degree of safety, and after undressing and going to bed, he was at leisure to consider the situation.

His previous life had not been altogether a paradise, and he could call to mind many an awkward predicament and many a trying position. But all of them put together were as nothing compared to his present situation. The notion that Marged had thought he imagined making her his wife was dreadful and unwelcome to him. And yet he knew no one was to blame but himself. No one knew Marged's conceit better than he, and for the sake of sociability and peace in the house, he'd fed it for a long time. All the tender and loving words he'd used to keep her in a good temper came home like doves to their cotes, words to which he'd attached no weight, but which had been taken by Marged as the words of a lover, as he now realised. And on reflection, what would be more natural than for her to give them a particular meaning? It was as well that Marged had no witness to these expressions. But that was but a straw to a drowning man, and Enoc couldn't consider denying his words. And then there were the presents. He couldn't deny them; he himself had paid for them, and Marged wouldn't be short of witnesses to prove that. Enoc remembered the amusement he'd had on hearing Marged relate Mr. Schwartz's trouble in getting a ring to fit her. That wasn't a laughing matter now. He had also a faint recollection of hearing her call it a "migaged ring." These things, on turning them over in his mind, were hugely repugnant, and at the same time horribly serious. He went over and over the matter in his mind, and tossed and turned in his bed like a tormented animal.

As a background to his contemplation, and to magnify all these things running through his mind, stood Miss Trefor in all her beauty and unequalled charm, the only earthly object in his sight worth living for. After all, he wouldn't have worried too much about the events of the evening, had it not been for her. It was impossible that she wouldn't learn about the whole mess. Indeed, Enoc thought, it was extremely likely from Marged's threats that he and his affairs would be the talk of the neighbourhood in a few days, if not in a few hours. And no matter how hideous and improbable it might be, there were always enough people ready to believe such a story; and, when Marged showed the presents, which he could not deny, it was likely everyone would believe it. Would Miss Trefor? Whether she did or not, Enoc saw clearly that the whole business would make her despise, if not hate him, and take away the chief object of his life for ever. For the sake of gaining the respect and, if it were possible, the love of Miss Trefor, he'd already exercised great self-denial, and had spent a pile of money. In conformity with Captain Trefor's requests, he'd already spent hundreds of pounds on Coed Madog Mine, and there'd be nothing but spending for some time. Besides this he'd bought a horse and trap—and paid a hefty price for them too—and placed them at Captain Trefor's disposal to take Mrs. Trefor—who wasn't very well—out in the fresh air from time to time. He'd never have imagined putting his money into a mine, or a horse and trap, if he didn't need them, if he hadn't hoped it would all end in gaining Miss Trefor's favour, and he was ready to make greater sacrifices if he thought they'd pave the way to a place in her heart. Sometimes he thought, with inexpressible joy, that he detected some faint sign that his fidelity and thorough self-dedication to his aim was leading gradually to a happy victory. But, oh! Here was the temple he'd built tumbling down on his head; and the disaster from a direction he'd never dreamt of. The scorn of the people of Jericho could not have been more contemptuous on seeing their magnificent walls fall to merely the blowing of a ram's horn, than that of Enoc at the thought that his great expectation had been shattered by an ignorant, ugly old hag.

More than once, Enoc wondered if it was possible to buy her over. Would she accept a large sum of money to hold her tongue and go away? Enoc doubted whether it was possible, given that refusing her wages showed she put no value on money, at least as an equivalent to being his wife. At the same time, thought Enoc, perhaps fifty pounds might make her change her tune. But that would look like an admission he'd deceived her. Still, it would be a bargain if he could be certain of success. Indeed, he'd not stop at even a hundred pounds if he could but settle the matter forever. Marged wasn't literate, and even if she were, there'd have to be a witness, and that would let someone else into the secret—someone, perhaps, who'd spread the story round the neighbourhood, and Enoc would be under their thumb for the rest of his life. But what else was to be done? No other path out of the pit appeared to him. He saw clearly that it was impossible to avoid involving a third party, and in his mind was running through the list of his friends, when he remembered with dismay that Jones the policeman had already seen his situation. And what did the man mean when he said: "The old game, Mr. Huws." Was he inferring something about Enoc's character? "I'm sure he meant something like that," said Enoc, fearfully, and his spirit sank into a wretched despair of ever emerging honourably from his tribulation. Though he knew his conscience was clear, appearances were in every way against him, and he could scarcely expect even his best friends to believe his innocence. And another thing made him miserable, namely that because of the state of his nerves, he'd be sure to appear weak and guilty, though perfectly innocent, and he couldn't help asking again what evil muse was pursuing him. Enoc thought many a one in less trying circumstances might have committed suicide. Did the thought of putting an end to his life enter his mind? Yes certainly, for a moment. Enoc hid under the bedclothes; he felt himself grow hot all over, then as cold as ice the next moment. The thought came, without doubt, from hell, from whence such thoughts usually come—there's a smell of the place about them— but it was a blessing to Enoc. Up to then his thoughts had revolved round himself and his neighbours, but now God came into his mind. In the face of the circumstances, so far as his friends were concerned, he felt he'd be misunderstood and misjudged. But when the evil intention entered his head, he found himself face to face with God. That made him think in a different way, and he started to ask if there wasn't something in himself that called for punishment; for Enoc in his heart was, above all else, religious. His conscience began to reproach him for his sins. It reminded him of when, though he was so busy with his work, he'd never miss one of the midweek chapel meetings, when he read and studied the Bible and tried to do his best, in his way, for the cause of religion. Had he kept to that path? No, for months his contemplations had almost entirely revolved round Miss Trefor, Coed Madog Mine, and such things. For some time, when chapel and Tŷ'n yr Ardd had clashed, he'd sided, without exception, with Tŷ'n yr Ardd. When Miss Trefor and religion had been in question? Yes, Miss Trefor had precedence. Not only this, but he was conscious he'd lost a lot of his interest in religious matters generally; and because he'd spent a good deal on his house, Coed Madog mine, and other things, he'd reduced his contributions in the chapel and to charitable causes. He didn't derive so much enjoyment from the company of religious people as he used to, and when he came to think of it, he wasn't looked upon with the respect and liking he'd once been proud of. Some of his friends had distanced themselves from him. On Sundays, at chapel, he'd lately felt the service was too long, and if there was a meeting of the brethren, or a teaching meeting, he couldn't consider stopping for it. The fact was, Enoc admitted to himself in his bed that morning, that unless the Sabbath sermon was unusually stirring, his thoughts from beginning to end of the service would hover around Miss Trefor, and he'd set a greater price on walking home with her on a Sunday morning, though that was only an act of toleration on her part, than on the most excellent of sermons.

Enoc thought deeply about all these things, and shed tears of true repentance. "It's no wonder," said Enoc to himself "that God's angry with me, and that he is punishing me severely in his providence, by shaming me in the sight of my neighbours, and making them look at me in a way I don't deserve." But a good man can fortify himself in the omniscience of God, and though Enoc felt guilty and sinful, he found strength to rejoice a little in the fact that God knew the whole story. He wouldn't misjudge him, or set against him something he wasn't guilty of. He discovered in himself a deep debasement, a debasement he'd fallen into quite unintentionally. In loving Miss Trefor so much, he'd not intended to love God and His cause less. And now, though he felt his error deeply, an error he could only regard as a spiritual backsliding, it seemed the way to reform would be closed to him. He saw the likelihood, almost the certainty, of his being expelled from the '*seiat*'. Marged had vowed she'd do it. She would, without a doubt, make a strong case against him. All the women would believe the plain facts of her evidence, even if she had nothing else against him. But Marged could bring up other matters, which, on the face of it, would corroborate her accusation. He'd have only his own word to contradict her accusations; and granting that a few wise men might believe him, a greater number would certainly side with Marged. Some would be the more ready to believe what was laid against him, because he had lately failed in his faithfulness in attending chapel, attributing this to a guilty conscience. Enoc saw all these things in his contemplations as clearly as if they'd already taken place. He didn't know how to face the circumstances; his heart sank, and he asked: "Is there any sorrow like my sorrow?" If some intelligent, beautiful girl had accused him of breaking his promise, some small credence might be attached to it, though factual foundation be lacking; but the notion that Marged … Well, that was intolerable.

In the face of the storm before him, though he felt guilty and repentant before God for his great neglect, Enoc could find no fault within himself for falling in love with Miss Trefor. That was something he could do nothing about, in no way a matter of choice. But now, with a sigh that seemed to sweep his soul away on its wings, he bade farewell forever to his fond dream of one day making Miss Trefor, Mrs. Huws. But he declared within himself, and there was the spirit and strength of an oath in the declaration, that wheresoever his abode might be, whatsoever happened to him, he would love her to the last, and bless her with his dying breath. "Yes," said Enoc, "where will I live now? To stay in this neighbourhood's out of the question. I could never stand the disgrace! The thought of going through the whole business almost drives me mad. And what interest will I have here after losing my hope of her? None; not a speck, I swear! I'll sell every scrap I own and I'll go somewhere; I don't care where;" and Enoc turned in his bed for the hundredth time that night.

28

JONES THE POLICEMAN

Jones the policeman was an old fox, and sharper than the generality of foxes; for though he'd a long tail with a large bush, he was somehow able to hide it so even the most cunning and experienced goose couldn't tell he was a fox till its throat was in his mouth and its body thrown across his back. His father had held a very high opinion of him since he was a boy, and foreseeing that he'd some day, if he lived, be a renowned figure in the world, had given him a bit of schooling. Many a time his father had said his son wouldn't have to work, "except with his head." Though, while at school, Jones didn't wholly fulfil his father's expectations, he made his mark, in the shape of scars on the faces of several of his schoolfellows, for Jones was a strong, bony lad, and possessed a frame very suitable for putting flesh onto, when the chance came to have his share of food and drink, which didn't happen in those days in his own home. Some in the school at the same time had pleasant memories of one who never refused a present, or caused offence by offering one. Indeed, his contemporaries said that whilst at school, he voluntarily acted as treasurer to all of them, and that nothing entrusted to his hands was ever known to leave them. Jones' father was a boot-maker by trade, and, though he was convinced his son was intended for a higher calling, he was obliged by circumstances to conclude that the son must follow the trade of the father. But what harmony is there between talent and a lapstone, between excellence and an awl? All the men in his father's shop couldn't keep Jones in his seat. The only time he sat there voluntarily was when reading a newspaper. This he sometimes did for half a day. It would have been good for his father to see Jones work at his craft until something better turned up; but despite that, it was entertaining to hear him read of murders and burglaries in the newspaper. His disinclination to work strengthened his father's opinion that Jones was not intended to work "except with his head," of which belief Jones himself was fully convinced. The sympathy of his father, and Jones' antipathy to hard work were of great assistance in the broad development of his manly nature, without the slightest sign of shrivelling, and very soon he was seen as a splendid specimen of humanity. To show he wasn't disposed to be lazy, or unconscious of his strength, Jones would not refuse, on special occasions, to carry a load of coals into a gentleman's house, or to unload a waggon of flour for some of the shopkeepers, and never at any time expected more than a shilling for his trouble. And having done the work alluded to, in order to show he wasn't mercenary, Jones would go straight to the Brown Cow, to empty half pints as long as the shilling lasted, and if it happened that the Brown Cow stood in need of someone to turn a disorderly and noisy man out into the street, Jones would do that too for the small reward of three ha'pence, or rather its value in beer, for he didn't care about money. Though Jones was a shoemaker's son, there was no pride or pomposity in his character, and was often heard to declare he "was no proud chap." To prove this, he was willing to hold the head of the lowest farmer's horse, though he couldn't, in view of the depressed condition of agriculture, expect more than a penny's payment.

In this way, Jones quickly showed the virtues of a useful citizen. As he was a scholar, Jones acted as deputy and vice-regent to the town crier, when it happened that officer was away or unwell. And so excellently did he perform his duty as deputy, that he was strongly urged by a number of influential men to take up the business on his own account. At one point, Jones was so pressed to take up the post of town crier that he couldn't, after grave consideration, turn a deaf ear to the request of his fellow-townsmen without being guilty of discourtesy and of undervaluing their good opinion of him. But on reconsidering, Jones saw that the venture meant sinking such and such a sum of money in the business. He found that he'd need a bell, and that a melodious one would cost at least eight shillings. Everyone knew he'd not been mercenary, nor even particularly careful. Jones, as has been said, was a scholar, and made a written appeal to his supporters for subscriptions. His appeal was not in vain; but when he'd got seven shillings, he was smitten by his conscience. Was he going to replace his acquaintance, the town crier, a married man with several small children? Was he going to take the food from his plate? "No," said Jones, "I'm not a man to do such a thing," and went straight to the Brown Cow, put his book of subscriptions into the fire, the seven shillings into the care of commerce, and went home with an easy conscience.

Some said that Jones' custom of staying out late at night could be attributed to astronomical inclinations. This custom had become a sort of second nature to him, so he couldn't free himself of it even on dark nights when neither stars nor moon were visible. Others, who thought they knew Jones well, believed it was his anxiety for his neighbours' property that kept him out till the small hours of the morning, and that as a true benefactor of society he gave his services free and gratis, in order to try and cleanse the neighbourhood of notorious thieves, who prowled around in the darkness. Jones didn't take the credit for this, for he never at any time boasted of his voluntary service. At the same time his most wealthy neighbours could not have been unmindful of his nightly 'watchings' because, for example, Jones was never at any time short of a rabbit or a fat duck to sell at a low price to his friends; these, the good things of life, had doubtless been given him by the owner of the *Plas*[1] for the services mentioned. At election time, Jones proved to be a very useful man as a leader of the people. At that time he was a staunch Tory, and if it happened that some Radical was disturbing a public meeting, and refused to be convinced by

---

[1] '*Plas*'—The local stately home or manor house.

reasonable argument, and it was thought by the Tories that outside was the best place for the troublemaker, it was enough to give Jones a wink, and the job would be done. Jones' services to the Party, and against loutishness generally, were invaluable. These tasks, and especially the energy used to give vocal support to the speakers, very naturally created an unbearable dryness in his throat, and the Party was always mindful of this.

Jones was conscious of his undeveloped powers, and in order to avoid an erroneous step—to set out on a career where those powers might not come to light—and so as to not obstruct the intentions of Providence, Jones hesitated for some considerable time over what calling he should follow. In the meantime he placed himself at everyone's service. However, after much hesitation, Jones decided he'd definitely found the road he was intended to take. The finger of Providence was clearly present, and he hesitated no more. He took an agency for the sale of German barm, or, as he told his father: "I've decided, father, to become a yeast merchant." His father advised him to be prudent, and to weigh and consider the matter appropriately before taking on such a venture. Jones acknowledged the appropriateness and reasonableness of the advice, but he had, he said, acted upon that advice before receiving it, and had made up his mind. Jones threw himself with all his soul into the business of selling German barm. But he soon discovered it would have been better to heed his father's advice and to consider further before taking up the business. Jones had utterly neglected to consider one aspect; namely, that barm was needed in the morning, while he'd have preferred to work at night. Jones felt that he and the business didn't work harmoniously together. Although the goods he sold, under favourable circumstances, would rise, Jones had no hope that he himself would rise; not at that time of day. But this connection with business had been educational. Jones learnt that no business which involved early rising was suitable to his inclinations and his genius. He didn't care a fig about staying up all night, but getting up early was out of the question. Jones came to understand that those working for the Government rarely started early in the day, and he saw that he should in future turn his eyes toward government. To cut the story short, this consideration caused Jones, by and by, to become a policeman; and I think everyone who knew Jones would acknowledge he was cut out for the job. Apart from his father's prophecy being fulfilled—that it would never be necessary for Jones to work, except with his head—Jones himself felt entirely in his element. In the first place, he was six feet two in his stockinged feet, and as straight as a gate post. His shoulders were broad and square; like the top of a door, and his chest stuck out like a cockerel's, so much so that the first thing Jones did when he got a new coat was to pull the wadding out of the lining. Jones didn't believe in policemen made of wadding. He was so strong and powerful that he could do without carrying a staff and handcuffs. Jones despised small things like those; Jones' handcuffs were his knuckles, and his right hand was his staff, and when he was summoned to service, someone was as good as in gaol, as if the whole authority and power of the law of Great Britain and Ireland had been brought together in the tips of Jones' fingers. It was a well-known fact that he'd once taken the biggest wastrel in town to prison by the hand. When he resisted, Jones squeezed his hand till he squealed like a pig, and I heard him say afterwards he'd rather put his hand under the wheel of a waggon than in the hand of Jones the policeman.

It will be seen from these short notes that Jones was physically suited by nature to be a policeman, and, the reader will, I believe, already have made his own assessment of his mental powers. I think we should also note that, amongst his many other virtues was the ability to uncover people's history—personal, family, and social; and also a fidelity in keeping secrets when necessary. His mind was a store-house of secrets, and all under lock and key. On this account Jones was very popular, especially among those with most cause to fear him. He took no pleasure in exposing people's weaknesses. For instance, if any young man of respectable family had a tendency to particular vices, Jones would keep his eye on him till he caught him in the act, and then, after seriously threatening to complain to his parents, Jones would lower his voice, talk seriously and mysteriously, and the young man would put his hand in his pocket; but no, Jones wouldn't on any account take anything till he was forced to, and then the young man would say he was a good chap. In such cases, Jones had done his duty, and given excellent advice to the young tearaway; and if he considered he should pay for the advice, that was, after all, but an imitation of the act of a congregation who from a heartfelt wish pay preachers for their counsel. Jones was content, having shown the young man the right road, and no good would be done to anyone by making his faults known. Or, to take another example, say that a man of high position, especially one who professed to be religious, tended to take a drop too much, Jones would find him out, and if the sinner was unconscious of his fault, Jones didn't hesitate to talk to him to this effect: "There you are again, Mr. Pritchard. I'm sorry, very sorry, to see you in this state tonight. Though I don't profess to be religious myself, I have a great respect for religion, and I grieve to see those from whom we expect better things disgracing the cause. I feel it my duty to tell the minister what I know. But I'll speak with you in the morning." The first thing the transgressor would do the next morning was to send for Jones, and after much consultation, and a consequent understanding, Jones would determine, as no one knew of the fault except himself and Mrs. Pritchard, that it was wisest, for the good of the 'Cause', not to say a word about the matter. But Jones believed it was better for a man like Mr. Pritchard to be a total abstainer, and indeed, he said so more than once when they were having a glass together. In answer, Mr. Pritchard would say: "I'm too old to sign the pledge; but I'd like to be able to do as you do, Jones, and drink a belly full without my head or legs being any the worse."

"You know, Mr. Pritchard," replied Jones, "new wine should not be put in old bottles."

But for transgressors with no character to lose, no family or belongings to feel their exposure, Jones showed no mercy, but shoved them into prison, and brought them unsparingly before the justices, and he was often congratulated by the magistrates for fulfilling his duty so thoroughly and impartially. The neighbourhood under Jones' care was broadly free of the petty thefts too often heard about in other neighbourhoods, and when a theft took place at a particular hour of the night, Jones could testify honestly that he'd been there a few minutes before the theft took place, so the theft couldn't be attributed to any lack of his attention to the neighbourhood. I recollect Jones, more than once calling the public's attention to the danger of a man getting so drunk as to be 'dead drunk', because his experience, without exception, was that when he found a man in that lamentable condition, his pockets would be empty, which showed clearly that the man had been robbed by someone or other, for there's no sense in saying that every drunken man had spent every penny he had. That would be impossible, and I think Jones was right to draw attention to the fact. Jones said, and perhaps it would be profitable to those wearing the same cloth to consider his words, that a policeman shouldn't identify himself with any one church, but should show such a deep and broad catholicism that not even the wisest man would guess his creed. The policeman, said Jones, is the representative of the government of Great Britain and Ireland in every neighbourhood. The government is looked upon as the defender of all individually; as a consequence, a policeman shouldn't associate himself with any sect. But, added Jones, when a narrow-minded man has taken on the office of policeman, and feels he's too weak to refrain from joining some sect or other, it would be better to join the Church of England, for she's the mother of every sect, and in her are to be found most of the magistrates. Jones considered that every policeman should take a turn occasionally—but not too often—round the non-conformist places of worship, to see that the bad boys aren't causing a disturbance, and should take care to be at the door of the Church of England at the end of the service every Sunday morning, so the gentlefolk could see he wasn't neglecting his duty. With regard to politics, Jones' belief was this; as soon as a man takes it on himself to wear a blue coat, he should at that moment put his politics in his pocket, and not let anyone know to which party he belongs, except on particular occasions when this would be to his personal advantage.

If a man was a principled Liberal, and unable to keep from disclosing his principles, Jones' advice to him would be not to think of joining the force. But if a man was a Conservative and unable to hold his tongue, and at the same time keen to join the force, then let him; he had nothing to fear. Still, Jones' conviction was that the best policeman was the one whose political colour no one could guess. The duty of a policeman, he said, was to see to the welfare of society without leaning to one party or the other, except as circumstances might demand. In his heart, Jones inclined to the Liberal Party, but he had something against them; they were lacking in respect for the squires and old families, and he didn't see that paying in the long run. With regard to himself, the most Christian course he could take, in his own opinion, was to follow the apostle's example, and be all things to all men.

On the night Jones was called to Siop y Groes, his nocturnal duties ended at four in the morning, but as he thought that it would be fitting and beneficial to him to speak with Mr. Huws early in the day, he didn't think it worth his while to go to bed before seeing Enoc. He'd mulled over what he'd seen and heard in Siop y Groes that night, and believed that his services might be of use to the parties. Jones knew Enoc well; he knew him as one of the most innocent and purest of men he'd ever seen. He was certain Enoc was incapable of anything dishonourable, and couldn't guess the reason for what he'd seen and heard; and couldn't rest till he made himself acquainted with the whole mystery. Mystery was a thing Jones couldn't bear.

Though Enoc didn't sleep a wink that night, he stayed in his bedroom without lessening his barricade—in any way worth mentioning—till he heard Marged go downstairs. Then he dismantled the fortification as quietly as he could. Having washed, he went to the mirror to comb his hair and was terrified by the sight of his face. He was sure he looked ten years older than he had the day before. But worse than that, there was a black bruise under each eye, the effect of the blow he'd had from Marged. The anguish of Enoc's soul had been so severe through the night that he'd entirely forgotten the blow till he looked in the glass. This—for a hundredth time—brought every circumstance of the previous night to his mind. How could he show his face to anyone? His spirit sank lower than it already was, if that were possible. After pacing back and forth for a while, and pondering not a little, Enoc saw he could do nothing better than go downstairs, confess his guilt to Marged, talk nicely to her, promise everything to her—except marry her—in order to silence her, and get time for himself to collect his things, sell them, and leave the country. It was a big job, but he had to do it, and down he went. When, he reached the bottom of the stairs, his courage failed, and instead of turning into Marged's territory—the kitchen—he went into the parlour, and as he raised the window blind, the first man he saw was Jones the policeman. When a blind is drawn, the most natural thing for anyone going by is to look in that direction, and this Jones did. Enoc gave him a nod, the meaning of which was: "Good morning, Mr. Jones."

Jones misinterpreted the nod as "Come here," and hastened to the door. Enoc saw that Jones had thought he was calling him. Enoc opened the door.

"Did you call me, Mr. Huws?" asked Jones.

"No," said Enoc, "but come in."

The two went into the parlour, and Enoc shut the door.

29

MARGED BEFORE HER BETTERS

As I said, Jones and Enoc went into the parlour, and Enoc closed the door. "Forgive my error," said Jones; "I thought you were calling me, and you wanted to discuss last night's trouble."

"That was natural enough." said Enoc, in great confusion. After a short silence, he added: "Have you mentioned it to anyone, Mr. Jones?"

"No danger of that, Mr. Huws," said Jones, "it would never do for a policeman to mention everything he sees and hears here and there. No, no danger."

"Have you said anything to your wife?" asked Enoc.

"To my wife, Mr. Huws? No, I'd never say anything to any woman unless I wanted to save paying the town crier," said Jones.

"I'm glad to hear that; but I've been very unfortunate," said Enoc.

"Don't bother yourself about it, it's a common occurrence, Mr. Huws," said Jones. "You'd be surprised if I told you all I know of things the world never hears about that happen in respectable families. A policeman, sir, sees and hears more than anyone thinks; and I always say that anyone in business, especially if he has a house, shouldn't be without a wife. Human nature is human nature all over the world, sir."

Enoc looked straight into the policeman's eyes, as though trying to see the true meaning of his words, and as he could find no fulfilment, his heart sank, and he said, emotionally:

"Mr. Jones, you don't presume to suggest something about the purity of my character, do you?"

"I've known you for years, Mr. Huws." said Jones, "and I'd be sorry to suggest any such thing; I'd be very sorry to have to believe what that hulking servant said about you last night, that you're an evil accursed man; but we policemen see so much that sometimes we almost lose faith in everyone and almost believe there's not one upright person; not one. At the same time I make an effort to believe the best of every man till he's proved beyond doubt to be guilty."

Though doing his best not to tremble, Enoc felt sure that Jones was looking on him as a guilty man. As the reader knows, he was a man of weak nerves, and was overcome by his feelings; he cried copiously, feeling all the time that Jones saw his tears as tears of repentance and not of innocence. The fox saw that the goose was in his clutches, and said in an encouraging way:

"Mr. Huws, don't be foolish; you needn't fear me spreading the story any further."

Having composed himself a little, Enoc said, in rather a sorrowful tone, "Can I call you a friend? Can I trust you, Mr. Jones, if I tell you everything?"

Jones undid three buttons of his blue coat, showing a piece of old worn out waistcoat, and buttoned them up again as a sign of his ability to keep a secret, and said:

"When someone entrusts a secret to me, sir, I put it there—pointing to his heart—and keep it locked up."

Then Enoc told the whole story about Marged; the hard time he'd had with her, how much he'd had to bear; he spoke of her bad temper and his oppression, and how for the sake of peace he'd acted the hypocrite and praised her; in short he told everything—not omitting mention of Miss Trefor—and how his kindness to Marged had led to what Jones had witnessed. The only thing he omitted was barricading his bedroom door; he would have been ashamed to mention that. After finishing his story, Enoc felt a great relief. He said to Jones:

"Now what advice can you give me? I'll give you anything if you can help me out of this trouble."

During the narrative, Jones listened attentively and with great interest. He'd never heard such a story in his life, and could scarcely keep from laughing. He didn't know which to marvel most at; Enoc's stupidity or his solemnity. Jones knew from the start that Enoc was as innocent as a child, but he was no less interesting in Jones' sight on that account. He'd seen a few geese in his time, but Enoc, he thought, was the fattest he'd ever seen, and already the smell of fat was in his nostrils. Having weighed the matter seriously in his mind, and after putting his head reflectively on one side for a few moments, Jones said deliberately:

"I flatter myself, Mr. Huws, that I know when a man's speaking the truth. I've had a bit of experience in that field, and your story has the ring of truth. I'm very sorry for you, Mr. Huws, and if I can do anything to get you out of this mess I'll do so with pleasure. To an honourable man nothing's more precious in his sight than his character. In comparison with that, money is nothing. Everyone knows, at least guesses nowadays, that there's something between you and Miss Trefor; and trouble like this could damage your future, and completely upset your plans. Without mentioning your connection with the chapel—you know best about that—a thing like this can't help but affect your business and your position in town. Who knows, sir, what that miserable lump of a girl will say? I'll tell you another thing, Mr. Huws, no matter what a man's character, most people will believe the worst about him; and the worse the story, the more ready are some people to believe it. But I must say—pardon me for saying it—that you're partly to blame in this matter. There are some girls, like some horses, for whom nothing works but the whip; that's the only thing that brings them to their senses. There are some horses you shouldn't give oats to; you must keep them on hay. It's very evident to me, Mr. Huws, that you've given Marged too much oats, in a manner of speaking. If, when she first showed her bad temper, you'd shown her the door, and threatened to make a particular part of her body and your boot acquainted with one another, I've no doubt in my mind the lass would have been fine by now, and you'd have had no trouble with her at all. Instead of which, you've given her every luxury, so now nothing will do for her but to have you as a husband or harm your character. She's a woman of forty by now, I'm sure, and it's difficult, as you know, to teach old dogs new tricks. But will you trust the matter to me, Mr. Huws? I wish in my heart to be of some service to you, but will you put your case in my hands?"

"You're extremely kind, Mr. Jones," said Enoc, "and if you can help me to get out of this pickle, I'll pay generously."

"Don't mention payment, Mr. Huws," said Jones. "There are some people—I'm not suggesting you're one of them, mind; nothing of the sort—but there are some people who think pay is foremost in the mind of every policeman at all times. They're mistaken, sir. I don't say, Mr. Huws, that I don't take pay—honourable pay now and then for helping this and that person out of trouble, but I've never asked for pay; never in my life, though a policeman's wages, as you know, are small, too small by far when you think of their duties, many of which are unpleasant enough; and especially when he's a fair-sized family to keep, as I have. But there's no need for me to tell you things like this, Mr. Huws. My main object now, as a friend and neighbour, is to be of some service to you in your difficulties. I don't say I'll succeed, but I've had a bit of experience in matters like this. Will you let me go about it in my own way, Mr. Huws?"

"I'll put myself in your hands, Mr. Jones, as you're so kind," said Enoc.

"Very well," said Jones. "I have an idea. Is the girl about? Has she got up?"

"Oh yes, a while ago; she's in the kitchen," said Enoc.

"Can she read and write?" asked Jones.

"She can't read a word," said Enoc.

"Very good," said Jones. "You stay here till I call you; and if my idea succeeds, and if I call you into the kitchen, remember to look fierce and determined, if you can manage it."

Jones opened the parlour door and shut it behind him; and as he walked down the long lobby towards the kitchen, the door of which was wide open, he said, in a loud voice, so that Marged could hear, "It's no use you talking, Mr. Huws; the law must take its course."

Marged was at it, throwing things about and being noisy, and her former bad temper, which she'd kept under control for so long, was boiling up in her. She had a floor brush in her hand when Jones' words fell on her ears. She stopped suddenly, and the wild, ugly, disagreeable, and threatening look on her would have made a man less brave than Jones hesitate. But Jones didn't fear an attack, nor did he intend to make one. He walked into the kitchen, quietly but determined, locked the door, and put the key in his pocket. Then he sat at the table, and fumbled in his pockets for paper. While doing so, he pulled out a shiny pair of handcuffs—he didn't usually carry handcuffs, but today was an inspection day—and placed them casually on the table, and, in the same way, put his staff there. He did all this before uttering a word or looking at Marged, except through the corners of his eyes. He saw that his 'idea' portended well, for Marged was as though frozen to the spot, and her face was white with fear or rage. After flattening an old letter on the table, and sharpening his pencil, Jones raised his head, gazed like a lion at Marged, and said:

"Now for the law on the subject. Your name's Marged Parri, isn't it?"

"You know well enough what my name is," said Marged, trying to look unafraid.

"Very well," said Jones. "What's your age, Marged Parri?"

"What business of yours is my age?" said Marged.

"Marged Parri," said Jones; "do you know you're in the hands of the law? And that you must answer every question before appearing before the magistrate at ten o'clock this morning? What time is it now,"—looking at the clock—"Oh, there's plenty of time."

"What's the law got to do with me," asked Marged, leaning more heavily on the brush.

"What's the law got to do with you, indeed?" countered Jones. "Don't you know that you've broken the law? Specifically, the Act of Parliament for the prevention of cruelty to animals?"

"What do I know about that?" said Marged.

"I'm not, mind, going to translate for you," said Jones. You'll have a man to translate for you when you go before the Lord of the Manor. Answer me, what is your age?"

"I'm thirty five," said Marged, reluctantly.

"And the rest?" said Jones. "Tell me the truth, Marged Parri. Are you not forty five?"

Marged said not a word, and Jones said: "I know; very good," and as though speaking to himself while writing, added;"Marged ... Parri ... aged ... forty ... five ... years ... last ... birthday ... very good. Now, Marged Parri, listen to me. After having seen and heard what took place in this house last night, between eleven o'clock and midnight, it was my duty, as a policeman, to look into the matter, inasmuch as it was according to the law of Great Britain and Ireland a breach of the public peace. Now, after speaking with Mr. Huws, I'm acquainted with all the circumstances, and when I've had a few words with you, Marged Parri, we shall be ready to bring the whole case before the Lord of the Manor in the County Hall. But begin by sitting down, Marged Parri, for you'll have to stand more than enough when you get to the County Hall. I understand you have been in the service of Mr. Huws, grocer, of Siop y Groes, for some years. In the course of that period—be careful how you answer now—in the course of that period have you ever had any wrong done to you by Mr. Huws?"

"I never said I'd ever had any wrong done me by Mr. Huws," answered Marged.

"Very good. But let me put that down in writing," said Jones, making a note of something on the paper, and muttering something in English. "Then," said he, "what the devil did you mean, calling Mr. Huws in my hearing last night, an evil accursed man? Your case is settled already. You're guilty of defamation of character, a law made in the time of George the Fourth, and the punishment for breaking which is two years' imprisonment with hard labour. But that's only a small part of the complaint against you. During the time you've been in Mr. Huws' service, you've been guilty of disobedience; and not only that, but of trying to tempt your master to use words of which you could make illegal use afterwards, and you've also compelled him to purchase your proper behaviour with presents, and have even refused a rise in your wages, and indeed the wages that were due, with a special object; in plain words you have presumed to think, and not only think, but as good as say that Mr. Huws had his eye on you with a view to making you his wife. The idea! An ugly, miserable, old hag like you daring to think—daring to imagine that a gentleman like Mr. Huws, a young man who could get the most beautiful lady in the town as a wife—a rich young man, handsome, and respectable—the idea, I say, of a man like that spending even a second thinking of you. You must have gone mad—clean out of your senses, woman. And when I remember how looked like last night with a spoon in your mouth, I'm sure that you are mad, and because of that I'm inclined to pity you. Marged Parri, listen to what I say to you now. Your master knows that he can, for the misuse you've made of his kindness, put you in gaol under an Act of Parliament called the Act of Toleration for the High Court of Chancery. But fortunately for you, you have a gentle master. Mr. Huws does not wish to imprison you, and my advice to him is to put you in Denbigh asylum. But Mr. Huws is against doing that, if you promise to behave yourself in the future and sign an agreement. It appears that, at particular times—when the moon is on the wane for instance—you allow an evil spirit to possess you, and the asylum's the only place to cure such people. I have taken many there, and they know how to treat them. To begin with, they're bound hand and foot, placed in a trough, and water is pumped on them for an hour and a half. That continues every day, until they come to their senses. But Mr. Huws is a merciful man and isn't willing to see me take you to the asylum; and willing too to give you another chance. Now, Marged Parri, are you ready to promise, if Mr. Huws is merciful to you, to obey his commands, that you won't allow the evil spirit into your heart, that you'll look after his house and keep it tidy, and ask Mr. Huws' forgiveness for ever imagining him as your husband, and for calling him an evil accursed man? Remember you'll have to be in one of three places; to be a good and apologetic girl in Siop y Groes, in gaol, or in Denbigh Asylum. In which of the three places do you want to be, Marged Parri?"

Marged had been showing signs of regret and fear for some time, and she said sadly:

"I'd rather be here, and I'm sure Mr. Huws won't send me away."

"Very well," said Jones. "but there must be an agreement made." and he opened the door and called loudly for Mr. Enoc Huws. Enoc entered, feeble and trembling; trembling so much that Jones had a heartfelt wish to give him a good cursing.

30

PEACE TERMS

As I said, Enoc came feebly into the kitchen, and the policeman said:

"Now Mr. Huws, I've been explaining the law to Marged Parri—the law of Great Britain and Ireland—in connection with problems that can happen in a business establishment such as yours. Marged Parri now knows where she would be this time tomorrow morning, had you not been a merciful man; and she is repentant for her crime, and promises to sign an agreement that she will, henceforth, be obedient to your orders, tidy in the house, careful of your comforts, and acknowledge that her place is that of a servant and not the mistress, and that she will never be mistress of this house; that is, if you'll be so kind as to forgive her what has happened and give her a second chance. Do you feel, Mr. Huws, you can do that? Can you overlook what's taken place? The insult, the wrong you've suffered at the hand of one who's received so much of your kindness?"

"I think I can," said Enoc, not knowing exactly how to answer Jones.

"You're one in a thousand, sir," said Jones. "I've seen dozens put in gaol for two years for lesser crimes than the one Marged Parri is guilty of. Now, Marged Parri, as Mr. Huws is so merciful, do you repent of your sins, and ask Mr. Huws's pardon for—well, for something too dreadful to mention?"

Marged, sobbing, said nothing.

"I must have an answer, Marged Parri, or do my duty," said Jones, and he rose to his feet and picked up the handcuffs.

"Mr. Jones" said Enoc, on the point of taking Marged's side, but Jones answered quickly:

"The law must take its course, Mr. Huws. If Marged Parri is not ready to ask your forgiveness and promise to behave herself, it can be only gaol or Denbigh Asylum. What do you say, Marged Parri? One word will do it."

"Yes," said Marged, half shouting and half crying, and a tear trickled down Enoc's cheek out of pity for her.

"Very good," said Jones. "One of the most hateful things on earth to me, Mr. Huws, is to take anyone to prison, especially a woman, and I'm pleased to see Marged Parri is wise enough to repent of her error and promise to reform. I'll tell you another thing, Mr. Huws, I never yet saw a woman taken to jail that didn't die there soon after, for they treat them dreadfully; you wouldn't believe it. Now," added Jones, sitting at the table, "come here and sign this paper, for everything must be done as the law requires."

"I can't write," said Marged.

"The law permits you to put a cross," said Jones.

Marged came to the table reluctantly, and Jones put his finger on a particular part of the paper, Marged made a huge cross, practically the size of a windmill.

"Now, Mr. Huws," said Jones, "how much wages are due to Marged Parri?"

"Five pounds ten pence, I think," said Enoc.

"Bring it here, every penny," said Jones.

"What about the rise?" said Marged, more than a little recovered.

"You have forfeited the rise by misconduct, and you must regain your character before talking of the rise." said Jones.

"Perhaps ..." began Enoc.

"Mr. Huws," said Jones, for he saw Enoc was softening: "pay the money due to the servant, for we must proceed according to the law."

Enoc handed the money to Jones, and Jones presented it to Marged, and said,—

"Now, Mr. Huws, I know you're a gentle and merciful man, and I know that you wouldn't wish to harm an old homeless woman, nor spoil her character. Will you promise never to say a word to anyone about this business, on your honour now?

"I will never say a word to anyone, if ..." began Enoc.

"There must be no 'if' in the matter, Mr. Huws," said Jones. "I beseech you for the sake of an old creature like this your servant, never to mention the matter to anyone, for if the story got out, Marged Parri, poor thing, would be sport for everyone. Those black eyes won't be long mending, and you must make some excuse for them; that you knocked your head against the bedpost, or something; don't on any account, say your maidservant struck you while possessed by an evil spirit. Will you promise, Mr. Huws? Come, will you be kind? I know she doesn't deserve that, but will you promise to keep the matter quiet?"

"I will," said Enoc.

"You're one in a thousand, I say again," said Jones. "And now, Marged Parri, take care that you lead a new life, and don't tempt your master to let word of this get out, for if it once got out, you'd be sport for the whole parish, and every child in town would be shouting after you. And remember, Mr. Huws, if you have the slightest complaint against your servant, even the least of details, just tell me. I pass your house every day and I'll take care to put things to rights; because the law's the law, and I don't know what would become of us if it weren't for the law. While I remember; if you need a servant, I have a niece who's a first class housekeeper, an excellent scholar. She could come to you at a day's notice, if you should happen to need someone. Well now, I have to go, but I want to have a word with you in private, Mr. Huws, in connection with the law that governs business premises like yours."

Enoc felt hopeful again, and much lighter of heart. He saw Jones as his guardian angel. When the two had returned to the parlour. Enoc said, rubbing his hands, and smiling happily:

"Do you know what? You're a sharp one, Mr. Jones. I don't know what I'd have done if you'd not happened to come in."

"Mr. Huws," said Jones, I've had a lot of experience of this kind of thing, and I think I've put you back on safe ground. Your future comfort depends entirely on yourself; that is, on the way you behave towards your servant. She's as ignorant as a turnip, and it was on her ignorance that I worked; that was the idea. And my experience is this; I never yet saw an ignorant, bad-tempered servant who, if you turned the edge of the blade towards her, you wouldn't find was an utter coward. Now Mr. Huws, if you want peace and comfort in your house, show that you're the master. I swear, sir, that if you were to turn into a bit of a tyrant for a week, old Guinevere there would be like a lamb to you. And that's what you must do. Shout at her now and again, and make her do things there's no need to do, just to show you're the master. If you weren't religious, I'd urge you to swear at her now and again, till she danced; but there's no need to go quite that far. But I'll say this; if you don't show you're the man, if you don't raise your voice and tell her who's who you'll not be the slightest bit better off. I've driven the evil spirit out of her; and it would have been a treat for you to see her face when I was putting her to rights; but if you don't act the man, Mr. Huws, and show your authority, seven other evil spirits will go into the woman, and you'll be worse off than ever, believe me.

"You're telling the truth, Mr. Jones," said Enoc, "and I'll have to try, though it'll be difficult, to be more of the master. I've suffered more than you'd believe, and she's become very bold with me.

"I'll call in now and again," said Jones "as if to see if everything's all right, and that'll keep her under control."

As Jones said the last words, Enoc saw the maid from Tŷ'n yr Ardd crossing the street to his door with a note in her hand, and after asking Jones to excuse him for a moment, he ran to the door to receive the note, hiding his face behind his hand so Kitty wouldn't see the bruises, and returned quickly. After opening the note and reading it to himself, Enoc said:

"Well, here we go again."

"What is it now, Mr. Huws? More tribulations?" asked Jones.

"Yes," said Enoc mournfully, "an invitation from Mrs. Trefor to go there for supper tonight, to meet our minister, and how can I go with two black eyes? I'm so unlucky; nobody's ever been so unlucky!"

"You can go quite easily," said Jones; "Have you got any raw beef in the house?'

"Yes, I think so," said Enoc.

"Very good," said Jones; "I know you didn't sleep much last night, so after you've had your breakfast, cut two slices of lean beef, and go to bed; the lads in the shop can easily manage without you, put a slice on each eye, and stay in bed till after midday—yes, till two o'clock—and if you can sleep, all the better. You'll find the black bruises under your eyes will have vanished completely by one or two o'clock, and by the time you need to go to Tŷ'n yr Ardd, you'll be all right. And to avoid waste, the two slices will make an excellent dinner for the cat afterwards."

Enoc laughed at Jones' thrift, and said: "Well, indeed, you are sharp, Mr. Jones. I've never seen your like before; I'll try it, anyway."

"It's sure to serve the purpose," said Jones, "and now I must go, Mr. Huws, it's inspection day,"

"Wait; I don't know when I'll be out of your debt; take this now," said Enoc, putting a sovereign in Jones' hand. Jones looked at the sovereign in the palm of his hand, and looking amusedly at Enoc, said; "You're too generous, Mr. Huws. Do you want me to retire from the force at once? Well, I can only thank you very much, and remember; I'm at your service, Mr. Huws."

"Don't mention it; we'll talk again. Good morning," said Enoc.

31

ENOC HUWS' DREAM

Enoc ate his breakfast in silence. Marged looked sullen, tired and downhearted; exhausted, like a half-dead cat. And no wonder. The happy hope that she'd borne for so long, namely that she'd be mistress of Siop y Groes and be called Mrs. Huws, had been slain. Not only this, but she'd been threatened and treated severely by the policeman, who, henceforth, would watch her and keep her in order. Indeed, Marged considered she'd practically been taken to prison. Her face was marked with the traces of tears; she'd not cried since her mother died, and then only a little; she wouldn't have cried at all, but she thought crying was appropriate to the occasion. The loss of her mother was as nothing to her compared with losing hope of marrying her master. It was a matter of indifference to her now whether she lived or died. After the lecture she'd had from Jones the policeman, and whilst Jones and Enoc were talking in the parlour, she'd more than once thought about Boaz, the conductor. It would have been better, thought Marged, if she'd returned his glances. She now felt surer than ever, having been taunted about it, that Boaz had thought something of her when he'd looked at her so often in the practices. Poor Marged! The reason he'd turned his eyes so frequently in her direction was because she was extraordinarily discordant; and often Boaz had said to the leader of the trebles (who he married shortly after):

"Jennie, I don't know what to think of that Marged Parri, she squeals like a stuck pig, and spoils the singing. I don't want to tell her that, so I'd like some of you to make her angry if possible, and get her to leave." How open we are to misunderstanding a man's glance!

Enoc couldn't help noticing from Marged's appearance that her spirit had been broken to a large degree; but whether she'd remain in this happy state, he doubted. Enoc was perfectly conscious of the truth of what Jones the policeman had said; that he'd have to act the man if he was to keep Marged under control. If he didn't, he was quite sure that Marged would have fully regained her bad temper by the next morning. While having breakfast he pondered how he could begin the work. He had little faith in his ability to complete the task. Indeed, he couldn't be cruel to anyone, and would rather suffer a wrong than be harsh and masterful. By this time Enoc realised he needed to try showing his authority. After finishing breakfast, he went straight into the pantry, where he had not been for a long time, and felt Marged's eyes burning into his back at his accomplishing such an act of boldness. He cut two slices off the lean of the beef according to Jones' instructions and on his way upstairs, said rather nervously, "Marged, I'm going to bed, and no one's to disturb me before midday;" and lest Marged should stop him, he walked quickly upstairs to avoid hearing her reply.

Marged didn't say a word; she just looked in astonishment at the beef in his hand. She asked herself if he'd gone mad. Why in heaven's name was he taking beef up to his room? Had the policeman brought him a mastiff to keep upstairs, to keep her in order? Or did her master intend in future, rather than eat in the kitchen, to take his food upstairs, and raw, too? Or did he intend to bewitch her with the beef, as she'd heard some people bewitch warts. Marged was not a little perplexed and disturbed.

Enoc went to bed; and, in accordance with instructions, placed the beef on his eyes, with an earnest prayer for the medicine to have the desired effect. It wasn't surprising, after what he'd gone through the previous night, that he felt rather feeble upon lying on his bed. He felt his breakfast, although it had been only a small one, weighing heavily on his stomach, as if it wanted to change its quarters. He couldn't account for his sickness. The sickness grew worse, and Enoc was smitten with a frightening thought; had

Marged, he wondered, poisoned him? Nothing would have been easier, for unlike old maids in general, Marged couldn't abide cats, indeed, she'd killed about half a dozen—and as a substitute for cats, Marged used rat poison extensively. What if she'd put some of that in his breakfast thought Enoc. He felt very ill. If Marged had poisoned him, there was nothing he could do about it; he'd die; for he couldn't call for help; and taking everything into consideration, to die wouldn't be such a great misfortune. Thus was Enoc thinking when he fell into a deep sleep, so deep that he didn't wake for four hours. And who knows when he'd have woken if he hadn't had a terrible dream. He thought, in this journey of his soul, that he'd been ill and in bed for many months, and that Marged had kept his illness a secret from everyone, for neither doctor nor friend visited him in all the months of his illness. He was tortured with pain incessantly, night and day, and if he complained even a little, Marged struck him on his forehead with some instrument, which doubled his pain. Many a time, when Marged wasn't in the room, he'd have loved to be able to get up and knock on the window to anyone who happened to be passing, and to tell his friends he was ill, and he was being fearfully ill-treated; but he was too weak to get up. By some means he didn't understand, Marged had sold his shop and all his belongings, and kept the money for herself. Sometimes, to torment him, Marged put all the money on a small table in front of him, and counted it carefully many times over, and then put it away, carefully and defiantly. He was aware all the time that Marged was waiting for him to die, and that she intended burying him secretly in the garden after dark. At times, Marged struck him on the head with a big hammer until there were dents in his forehead, and then furiously grabbed his hair, raised his head from the pillow and struck him in the back of the neck with the hammer, till his forehead was knocked back into shape again. If he cried out, Marged gave him an extra blow, in front and behind. He marvelled how he could live so long under such bitter treatment, and he perceived by Marged's face that she was thoroughly tired of waiting for him to die. He was kept for weeks on end without a morsel of food. So severe was his hunger at these times that he thought, if he could have moved his head, he would have eaten the bedpost, but he couldn't even move his eyes without pain. When his hunger was at its most severe, Marged would come to the room with a dish full of the sweetest food, sit within a foot of his nose, eat the lot, and lick the dish without offering him a drop; and yet he lived. At times he tried to die, but whenever he did, death moved further away and his pain grew deeper. One day, Marged seemed to enter the room with a slender, sharp knife in her hand, and Enoc saw that she meant to kill him, and this was not entirely unwelcome, for he was tired of living. Marged hadn't spoken to him for many months, just pulled mischievous faces at him for hours on end. But now she spoke, saying she didn't intend killing him for a month or two; but her task that day was to pull his eyes out. As soon as Marged spoke, Enoc felt that, at that very moment, he'd lost the power of speech. He struggled hard, but couldn't move his tongue, which made it appear as though he agreed to Marged pulling his eyes out, which she did skillfully with the point of the knife. Enoc marvelled that putting his eyes out wasn't as painful as being hit on the forehead with the hammer. He saw—which was unexpected—he saw Marged place the eyes on the dressing table; leave them there, and then go downstairs. Enoc didn't experience a great deal of inconvenience from the loss of his eyes, but he felt a little uncomfortable seeing them looking at him all the time, and one of them, his left eye, seemed to be making fun of him: and well it might, thought Enoc, for he was aware of having deep, ugly holes on each side of his nose. At the same time, it was rather hard that one of his own eyes was making common cause with Marged against him, and he vowed within himself that, if he could come through this misfortune, he'd never forget his right eye for staying with him, like a friend, to the last. While he contemplated these matters, Marged reappeared, and told him she'd forgotten to scrape out the holes after she'd pulled his eyes out, and when she started scraping, Enoc shot upright and awoke. He realized he'd been dreaming; he tried to open his eyes, but couldn't. He began to doubt whether it had been a dream. He felt his eyes, and remembered about the beef, which explained the dream. His eyes burnt violently, but they were in his head and not on the dressing-table; and he'd never in his life felt more thankful. He jumped out of bed, washed, and discovered that Jones' medicine had done its job.

For the rest of the afternoon, Enoc tried to look alert and busy; still, it was obvious to his assistants that he was troubled and his mind was elsewhere. Enoc couldn't help congratulating himself upon the state of his affairs compared with his fears the previous night. He felt that he was indebted to Providence for sending a man of Jones' experience and ability to get him out of a mess that had seemed unavoidable a few hours earlier. His thoughts constantly turned to Tŷ'n yr Ardd, and he looked at his watch several times. He was afraid the Reverend Obediah Simon might create a favourable impression upon Miss Trefor's mind, and thereby throw him a yard or two further away from his goal. Enoc was painfully aware that Mr. Simon was more handsome than he, and although that wasn't the only thing that had prompted him to vote against when Mr. Simon's calling was being discussed in chapel, still it was part of the equation that brought Enoc to the conclusion that Mr. Simon was not the best man to have as a minister. From the little conversation he'd had with Mr. Simon, he wasn't prepared to admit that his stock of knowledge was greater than his own, but he knew that the minister was his better in conversation; more fearless and bold; or as Enoc put it, "My stock's as good as his, but he's got a better window." And Enoc worried about whether Miss Trefor would refrain from looking at the window. He'd shown his affection for her in his behaviour and indeed every way except by a definite expression of words. Indeed, in a hundred instances he'd shown he was her slave, and anxiously waited for signs that she'd appreciate and welcome his vow and his devotion, prior to a clear proclamation of his love. But so far, she'd given him very little reason to believe she understood his perseverance and his feelings towards her. The only good sign Enoc saw, and it was very precious to him, was that of late she didn't avoid his society, nor, on the whole, was she disrespectful. She hardly behaved this way when he started going to Tŷ'n yr Ardd; indeed he remembered the time she'd never miss an opportunity to hurt him if she could, though her father would frown on it. She didn't do so now, but she behaved as she would to a friend of the family. Enoc hardly thought this sufficient to tell her what was on his mind, for he thought should she turn down his proposal—if she emphatically stated there was no hope for him—well, the thought would be too much to bear, and he'd rather spend his life coming and going from Tŷ'n yr Ardd if he could thereby keep everyone else away, despite the fact he'd no hope of success. But what certainty did he have that someone wouldn't come and take away his idol while he was building his altars? None. And perhaps the Reverend Obediah Simon was the man who'd do that.

32

SEM LLWYD'S DISCOVERY

On his way to Tŷ'n yr Ardd, as I've said, Enoc Huws' heart was full of jealousy. He had an uncomfortable presentiment that the Reverend Obediah Simon would shine at the supper, put him entirely in the shade, and make his hope, which was already weak enough, weaker than ever; and if Mr. Simon had been on the moon that night, instead of at Tŷ'n yr Ardd, it would have been none the worse in Enoc's view. Enoc had thought much that afternoon, indeed more than ever before, about Mr. Simon, and whilst dressing himself in his best before leaving home, he could not for the life of him help comparing himself constantly with Mr. Simon. His opinion of the minister was not high, but Enoc was sufficiently honest to admit that his judgment was not an unprejudiced one. At the same time, whilst walking quickly to Tŷ'n yr Ardd, he more than once said to himself; "I don't know what in the world people see in the man; I never liked him."

Perhaps it was because Enoc had taken a little extra trouble with his appearance that he reached Tŷ'n yr Ardd a little after the appointed hour. When Kitty, the maid, opened the door she said:

"Well, Mr. Huws, wherever have you been till now? Miss Trefor keeps asking whether you've arrived."

Sly girl; Kitty knew very well that her remark was worth a shilling to her that night, and it would have been worth a hundred pounds in Enoc's sight, had Kitty spoken the truth. That truth was a matter between Kitty and her conscience. She opened the door of the smoking room for Enoc, where Captain Trefor, Mr. Denman, Mr. Simon, and Miss Trefor were awaiting him, and sitting by the hearth in his working clothes was Sem Lloyd. All of them, except Sem, appeared to be half drunk. On Enoc's appearance, everyone except Sem rose to their feet to shake hands with him, and Miss Trefor was the first to do so, of which Enoc took particular notice. Everyone but Sem showed a cheerfulness that Enoc couldn't comprehend. But he was not long in learning the cause of all the happiness. It would have been shamefully bold, with the Captain present, for anyone but him to have told Enoc what had put them in such a happy state. After everyone had settled down, and Enoc had taken a seat, The Captain said:

"I'm sure, Mr. Huws, you've noticed we're rather cheerful tonight, and not without reason, and I know, when you hear that reason, you too will join our rejoicing. It happens, sometimes, that we rejoice on hearing good news concerning others, but tonight we're rejoicing, not because we have good news concerning others—although it is good news for others too—but tonight we're rejoicing because we have good news concerning ourselves, and no one more than you yourself, Mr. Huws; and there's nothing wanting—to speak personally, and you will all pardon my alluding to the subject—there's nothing wanting, I say but one thing, to make my joy complete. And that is,"—and here the Captain rubbed his nose with his handkerchief—"that is—you have not, Mr. Huws—nor you, Mr. Simon—had any experience of it, but perhaps, sometime or other, you'll be in a position to understand me—that thing is that Mrs. Trefor is unable, on account of her health, to rejoice with us tonight. Mr. Denman will realise what I ..."

"Oh! Father, you're taking a long time to give Mr. Huws the news," said Miss Trefor.

"Susi," said the Captain, "I've not lived this long, I fancy, without knowing how to talk and how to behave in the company of gentlemen. But what I was going to say if it had not been for my daughter interrupting me, is that the only thing detracting a little from my joy personally, is what I've alluded to, namely, that Mrs. Trefor is unable to be with us tonight on account of illness—an illness which I hope is not dangerous. But you'll understand my feelings; a man who's been married for so many years is somehow too apt, perhaps, to fear the worst. But lest I keep you waiting too long, Mr. Huws—though I know that you, above all others, take an interest in Mrs. Trefor's health—not to keep you too long, I say, and in order to avoid being called to account again by my daughter—though I like going about things in my own way— I'll cut my story short. We have good news. Sem Llwyd has come to us with news worth hearing. They have struck the lode in Coed Madog!"

"What!" said Enoc, in great surprise, "got to the lead already?"

"That's the fact, sir, isn't it Sem?" said the Captain. Sam gave a wise nod, denoting that he had much to say, but refrained from doing so for fear they wouldn't be able to stand it.

"Hurrah! Good for us, the Coed Madog Company," said Enoc, in great joy, in which all partook except Sem.

"Excuse our folly, Mr. Simon," said the Captain, addressing the minister, "and not folly either, for nothing is more natural, sir, than for those like myself, Mr. Huws, and Mr. Denman, those who, not with selfish and worldly objects, but with a view of bringing benefit to the neighbourhood, and with a view to maintaining the cause of religion, have spent a lot of money, more than you'd believe; it's natural, I say, for such people to rejoice when they come across the hidden treasure; as natural as it was for Columbus to rejoice when he saw the leaves on the sea."

"Perfectly natural, and I rejoice with you, Captain Trefor." said Mr. Simon.

"I quite believe you," said the Captain. "it's just the thing I should have expected from a man of cultivation and learning such as you. At the same time it's possible—indeed highly natural—for those like you, who are familiar with things spiritual, and don't meddle overmuch with this world and this life—it's possible, I say, for we, these adventurers, to give you the impression we are nothing but creatures of this world and life; that is to say people only interested in making money. But that is not the case, sir;

there's another side to our nature, and I will venture to say that discoveries in the world of nature, as in the moral and spiritual world, have their charm, and that the charm lies as much in the discovery as in the thing discovered. For example …" (Miss Trefor left the room in disgust) "… think of Sir Isaac Newton; his joy would have been no less had he discovered it was something else, and not gravitation, that made the apple fall from the branch; it was the discovery itself that gave him pleasure, if I'm not mistaken. It's just the same, sir, in this case. I'm expressing my own feelings, and I believe those of Mr. Huws and Mr. Denman as well, when I say that not the only pleasure, nor the greatest, is the fact that we'll one day be possessed with a lot of wealth. I confess there is pleasure in that idea, but speaking personally, the chief pleasure is the fact that lead—be it a lot or a little—has been discovered, which verifies my prophecy, namely, that there was lead in Coed Madog. Or, to put it another way—imagine I had a choice, either that one of my relations, say—for I'm only imagining this—that one of my relations should leave me twenty thousand pounds in his will, or that I should have fifteen thousand pounds worth of lead in Coed Madog; which would I choose? The latter, sir, without a moment's thought. This may appear absurd to some people, but I believe I'm expressing the minds and sentiments of Mr. Huws and Mr. Denman, men who know something about the charm of venturing and the higher charm of discovery. Is this not how things stand, Mr. Huws?"

"Yes," said Enoc, "but let us hear about the discovery. How much have you discovered, Sem?"

"Excuse me, Mr. Huws," said the Captain. "I'll go down the mine myself in the morning, and you'll have a full report. I have no doubt that Sem ran here at top speed the very moment he caught sight of the shining treasure. He's not in a position, I know, to give you a proper idea, Mr. Huws, of the nature of the discovery; and as I said, I'll go down the mine myself in the morning, God willing. But this is certain; even if only a thimble-full had been discovered, and indeed, I don't expect by the nature of things, a large find—the fact that Sem Llwyd and his partner have discovered it—small as it may be—shows clearly there's a lot of it out of sight. Isn't that our experience as practical miners, Sem?"

"You've hit the nail on the head, Captain," said Sem.

At this point, Miss Trefor came in to announce that supper awaited them, and the company went into the parlour; but the Captain stayed to have a secret word or two with Sem Llwyd. The, conversation was but brief, as follows:

"It's not much I suppose, Sem?"

"It isn't, sir," said Sem, "hardly worth talking about, as you'll see tomorrow, but I thought it wouldn't do any harm for me to come here and say."

"You did right, Sem," said the Captain.

"The truth is, news never came at a better time; between you and me, Denman's almost given up the ghost. I'm afraid the poor fellow hasn't much money to spare, and he's obliged to stint himself to do what he's doing. But there's no doubt, Sem, that your news has raised his spirits a great deal. It's different with Mr. Huws, he's got fairly deep pockets. I hope to goodness we find something, soon, if only for Denman's sake. Between you and me, I don't expect anything there now. But we have to keep hoping, though in a manner of speaking I regret I ever started Coed Madog, and I'd never have begun it—I'd have tried to live on the little I have, if I hadn't been thinking of what would become of you, the workmen and your families."

"I don't know what would have become of us, but for Coed Madog," said Sem.

"True enough," said the Captain, "but what's your opinion, Sem, and what's the opinion of the men about the place?"

"Well, sir," said Sem, "the men—and I—are confident we'll find lead there some day."

"Pray then," said the Captain, "for your faith to become vision and your hope to be realised, for Providence has a lot to do with things like this. And another thing is that there's a bottom to the purses of we few who have to bear the cost, you know. I'll come down there tomorrow morning, Sem, if I'm alive and well. And now I must go to these friends. Don't get up, Sem; I'll tell Kitty to bring you a pint of beer, and a bit of bread and cheese."

"Thank you, sir," said Sem.

33

THE SUPPER

If I were writing for the epicurean English, I'd try to describe the feast that covered Captain Trefor's table on the night of the supper at Tŷ'n yr Ardd. But the Welsh don't care so much for descriptions of banquets; they prefer to participate. There was everything necessary for a reasonable man's stomach; and it's only fair to Miss Trefor to say that she herself had prepared the delicacies, for she had lately set out to learn cooking, and to do every kind of household work, and had become quite skilful in these matters. The Captain took care to inform his friends that Susi had been the cook; after the minister had asked a blessing, and the Captain had cast a glance down the length and breadth of the table, and at what was on it, as the chairman of a public meeting casts his eye over the programme before rising to make a speech, and he said:

"I expect you, my friends, to partake heartily of what's here just as it is, and if anything's not right, or not according to your taste, you must blame my daughter, Susi, for she's responsible for the cooking."

"Aren't you satisfied, father, with asking a blessing on the food," said Susi, "without making an apology for the one who prepared it?"

"Pardon me, Miss Trefor," said the minister, "you misinterpret Captain Trefor's words. Your father's giving us a guarantee that everything will be perfect."

"Thank you, Mr. Simon, for a revised edition of my father's words," said Susi.

('Confound the man', said Enoc to himself; 'I wish he'd choke'.)

"In any case," said the Captain, making a generous invitation to the appetites of his guests, "I hope you'll do justice to what's here.

We in Tŷ'n yr Ardd are the most insistent people in the world, Mr. Simon, and if you don't make the best of what's before you, then you yourself will be to blame, Mr. Simon."

"I'll not be guilty of that, Captain Trefor," said the minister.

('I believe you', said Enoc, to himself.)

"Very well," said the Captain. "Mr. Simon, what will you take to drink? I myself, have been accustomed to take beer; perhaps it's a fault in me, and I sometimes think when I reflect on the great evils of its misuse, that I ought, for the sake of example, to give it up, though I know doing so at my age, would be very harmful to me. Are you an abstainer, Mr. Simon?"

"I am," said Mr. Simon; "In the scriptural sense of the word. I take beer in moderation when I think it would be better for me than tea or coffee; but I wouldn't like to hurt anyone's feeling by taking it."

"That's exactly my philosophy," said the Captain, and added: "Susi, tell Kitty to bring some beer for Mr. Simon and myself, and coffee for Mr. Huws and Mr. Denman. They're both abstainers, Mr. Simon, but not prejudiced ones. So you see, counting my daughter, there are two of us against three of them."

This was scarcely what the minister had anticipated, and he said, "Everyone has a right to his opinion."

"And every opinion free to be expressed," responded the Captain.

"If every opinion's free to be expressed," said Enoc, "my own is that we who are comparatively young should, more than anyone, refrain entirely from intoxicating drink. We stand on safer ground, and have easier consciences to urge those who drink too much to abstain from the habit."

"Well, Mr. Simon," said, the Captain, "how do we answer that?"

"For my part," said Mr. Simon, "I've never been fond of disputing petty laws and human ordinances. I'd rather follow the example of the New Testament. You've observed, doubtless, Captain Trefor, that the Divine Revelation, with the exception of the Sacramental ordinance, doesn't lower itself to laying down petty rules with regard to food and drink. The kingdom of heaven is not food and drink. Essential principles are revealed to us in the Holy Word, one of which, to my thinking—and I've tried to think a little in my life—is freedom of conscience. Every man is free to read the Revelation, and has the right to understand it in his own way. If a man reads total abstinence in the Holy Scriptures, very well; that's his opinion; and if another possessing the same advantages as far as learning and mental ability are concerned, fails to find total abstinence there, he has a right to his opinion. But my personal opinion is this—and I can assure you I've not arrived at it without a lot of inquiry and reflection—that the history of human society is like the history of an individual. That's rather natural, by the way, since individuals make up human society. Every man in his boyhood is under the governance of petty rules, and at that time they're necessary and beneficial, but having been educated, and reaching the age of manhood, it would be an insult to mankind if it were bound by such rules. This is to be seen clearly in the Revelation. In its school days, human society was under ceremonial laws but under the New Testament it had reached manhood, and had thrown ceremonies to one side."

"Well, Mr. Huws," said the Captain, emptying his glass, "there's a pretty strong pill for you. What do you say in answer to that?"

"I don't profess," said Enoc, "to be an arguer, especially with a learned man like Mr. Simon. But I think I can counter the argument to my own satisfaction. If I understand the teaching of the New Testament, especially the teaching of Jesus Christ himself, there's nothing He puts more weight on than self-denial and self-sacrifice. He taught it to others, and carried it out in his own life. It wasn't what he had a right to do, or permission to do, that was the great question with Jesus Christ, but what it was his duty to do. He had a right to the greatest respect and comfort in the world. He had a right to live, if anyone ever had. And yet, for the sake of others, He went to meet adversities and lay down his life. And, thinking about it, how wonderful it is that the One who possessed the greatest freedom, a freedom no one else could possess in equal measure, should speak only once or twice of it; but spoke daily about the rules, I won't say petty rules, that He'd imposed on himself? And if the Kingdom of Heaven isn't food and drink, it is clear that the making use of intoxicating drink isn't part of it. And I think much stronger reasons could be given against ..."

"Mr. Huws," said the Captain, "pardon me. We are by now sufficiently good friends that I may take a liberty with you. It strikes me it was rather bad taste on my part to touch on the teetotal question, especially on an occasion like this, and I think the best thing I can do, after Mr. Denman has said just one word to conclude the argument, is to turn the conversation to something else. Now, Mr. Denman."

"I've noticed" said Mr. Denman, "that young ladies—that is, young ladies of the best class, are guided as it were by instinct to settle dubious questions, the questions about which men get hopelessly confused. I'll put the question in a practical form in appealing to Miss Trefor. Now, Miss Trefor; imagine there are two young men equal so far as looks, bearing, wealth and every other excellence are concerned, seeking your love, but one is an abstainer and the other takes intoxicating drink. To which of the two would you listen?"

"I wouldn't listen to either the one or the other," said Susi.

"Yes," said Mr. Denman, "but imagine that you *had* to marry either the one or the other."

"Well," said Susi, "if I *had* to marry one of them I would, of course, marry the abstainer, and that not from instinct, but from sense."

"Hear! Hear!" said Enoc, "the question's settled."

"With all due respect," said Mr. Simon, "the question's not settled, for according to Captain Trefor's evidence, Miss Trefor is an abstainer, and so is biased. If some other young lady were appealed to, perhaps she'd answer differently."

"But Mr. Denman pointed out that we were to appeal to the best class of young ladies," said Enoc.

"And there's another thing," said the Captain; "When my daughter said she wouldn't listen to either of the two, it's evident she doesn't say what she means; and if she doesn't say what she means as to the first part of her answer, there's room to believe she won't say what she means as to the second part."

"Excellent," said Mr. Simon, "perfect reasoning. It's by no means uncommon for young and pretty girls to say with determination that they'll never marry, that they'd rather be old maids, and when one day they're led to the altar, no one would be so unfeeling as to blame them for breaking their word. With a little strategy, the most strongly fortified town can be taken."

"Perhaps you're stating your own confidence and experience now, Mr. Simon," said Susi, with a little bite in her words. "But I think you'll admit that there are a few towns which haven't been taken yet, and will never be taken."

"My contention is this," said Mr. Simon, "if Jericho was taken, why can't every town be taken?"

"The fact," said Susi, "that Jericho was taken by the blowing of a ram's horn doesn't prove that even a village can be taken by the blowing of a Welsh sheep's horn, though the blower may be a priest."

"Susi," said the Captain, giving her rather a reproving look; "your danger, my girl, is to be a little too flippant, especially where there's not been a long acquaintanceship, as there has with Mr. Huws and Mr. Denman, to warrant the use of such flippancy. When you get to know my daughter better, Mr. Simon, you'll realise she's not a bad sort; but as you're a bachelor, you'll have to suffer a blow now and again. That's her failing; attacking unmarried men."

"That's the second apology for your daughter tonight, father," said Susi, "The first because I don't know how to cook, and the second because I don't know how to behave myself. You must have neglected my education, father. Did I say anything vulgar, Mr. Simon?"

"Not at all, Miss Trefor. I wouldn't give a fig for a young girl if she couldn't answer for herself," said Mr. Simon.

"Very likely," said Susi, "and I wouldn't give a fig for a man, though he could answer for himself."

"I am afraid, my girl," said the Captain, "it will be necessary for me to make a third apology for you, if you carry on that way. To talk disrespectfully of men is not one of the signs of education, and you forget that your father is a man,"

"Present company excepted, you know, father," said Susi, "and I have not, as you know, met many men; only the Pwll y Gwynt Company, the people of Bethel, and a few Methodist preachers, and my honest experience is that nine of every ten of the men I've met are windbags; creatures who ..."

"Susi, said the Captain, "everyone seems to have finished. Ring the bell for Kitty to clear the things; and I think it would be better for you to go and see how your mother is, poor thing. She has, poor woman, been left all alone tonight."

"Oh" said Susi, "I see you are going to turn me out of your 'seiat', father. Well, you'd better ask for a vote; Let everyone of the opinion that Susan Trefor should not be considered a member of this 'seiat' any longer, raise his hand."

No one raised his hand but the Captain; Susi rang the bell for Kitty and ran away laughing.

"You have a lively daughter, Captain Trefor," said Mr. Simon.

"Yes," said the Captain, "she has plenty of life in her, but I'm often afraid that she makes an unfavourable impression on the minds of strangers. Perhaps I'm guilty of letting her have too much of her own way. But I must say, and my friends here know I'm speaking the truth, that some marvellous change has come over my daughter's mind lately. A little time back, sir, she caused me a lot of pain and anxiety, for she gave me cause to think she thought of nothing but dressing herself, reading novels, and emptily dreaming her precious time away. She never soiled her hands from one end of the week to the other, and though she had a religious upbringing, so far as the teaching and example of her parents went, I had cause to fear she wasn't thinking at all about the matter of her soul, and that, as you can imagine, caused me no small pain. Since she was a child, her imagination's been lively, and by some misfortune, she continued to nourish it so that the ordinary things of life, such as household work, the labours of life, and so on, were as strange to her as if she lived on a different planet. As I've started, I may as well finish. At that time, sir, I don't think my daughter was aware there was a world of misery around her here. She personally didn't know what it was to want for anything, and she couldn't imagine at that time that anyone else could be in need, or suffering. Her heart had never been touched. Besides this, she had no idea of the value of money; a five-pound note was to her just like an old letter, and she never reflected that every pound meant such and such amount of mental effort by her father. Somehow she lived inside herself, and in spite of many attempts, it was impossible to bring her out of herself to realise the realities of life. Do I need to say that this caused me to lose many a night's sleep? But for some time past now, she has cared nothing about her dresses. She would rather, sir, go to chapel in a cotton frock than wearing a silk gown; and she's as busy as a bee with housework from early morning till night. In a word, she has gone to the opposite extreme. She'd rather wash the floor than play the piano, and though it may be difficult to believe, only yesterday, as I came home from the mine, what did I see but Susi washing the doorstep, and Kitty, the maid, looking on with dry hands. Of course something like that's ridiculous, but she insists on doing the things the maid should do. These days, the job of maid in our house is a sinecure, sir. I don't need to tell you, Mr. Simon, that such a thing as that isn't becoming to her position, but I've taken the trouble of saying so, for fear that you may come here some day and be shocked to see my daughter wearing a greasy apron, cleaning shoes, and the maid sitting by the fire reading a novel. And talking of reading, a similar change has come over her in that respect too, which has afforded great comfort to myself and her mother. She's never seen now holding a frivolous book. Her favourite book, of course, is the Bible; and you'll be surprised when I tell you I caught her last night '*dros ei phen a'i chlustiau*'[1] in Butler's 'Analogy'; but it's a fact, and if I'm not mistaken, she's borrowed several issues of the '*Traethodydd*' from my friend yonder, hasn't she, Mr. Huws? (Enoc gave an affirmative nod). If I'm not tiring you, another change I should mention is her faithfulness in attending the chapel services. You'll already have seen for yourself, Mr. Simon, that there's no one more regular in the chapel. In a word, I believe my daughter's undergone a change both of heart and disposition, and you'll pardon me, Mr. Simon, for talking so much about her. I have two reasons for doing that. The first is that I think it of advantage to you as our minister, to have the fullest possible knowledge of the true mind and heart of each member of your church, so that you can truly share with them the word of truth. And the other reason is that it will be a comfort and encouragement to you, if ever you become the head of a family, to bring up your children in the teaching and the doctrine of our Lord, as I'm sure you will. And though perhaps you'll not see the fruit of your labour at once, yet as surely as you've sown your seed in good time, so will the fruit come a hundredfold in His own good time. I'm afraid I've talked too ..."

At this point Miss Trefor returned, and said: "Mr. Huws, mother begs you not to go without seeing her."

"I'll come this minute," said Enoc, and off he went.

"It's strange," said the Captain, "the fancy Mrs. Trefor's taken to Mr. Huws. If he'd been her own son I don't think she'd like him more; and yet, when you think of it, it's not so strange, for I never

---

[1] '*dros ei phen a'i chlustiau*'—literally '*over her head and her ears*'. On this occasion, 'Completely immersed'; in more romantic circumstances, later in the book, it will mean '*head over heels*'.

met any man who was easier to like, and Mrs. Trefor and he are quite of one mind; they're naturally religious, and their thoughts run on the same lines. I always think it's no trouble in the world for some people to live religiously, and I think my wife and Mr. Huws … What, Mr. Denman, are you going home? Well, I understand your haste; you want to give Mrs. Denman the good news, don't you? I won't stop you. Good night, goodnight. He is a nice man, that Mr. Denman; you're sure to find I'm right about him. But, tell me, don't you find that beer rather bitter to the taste? It's starting to go off, I'm afraid. It's had too long a rest, having no one to drink it. Don't drink any more of it. Exchange is no robbery; I've got a little Scotch whisky, which has been here since I don't know when, as it's so seldom I look at it, and if it's like it was a month ago, you're sure to like it. Excuse me while I fetch some water; if I rang for the maid, the teetotallers upstairs would understand we were calling for more beer or mixing our drinks.

"Now, sir, I think you'll like this; say when. You take the same as I, exactly. Too much water spoils whisky. Success to the teetotal cause! Will it do, Mr. Simon?"

"First class, first class," said Mr. Simon.

"I knew you'd like it," said the Captain. "And why should a man deny himself the good things of this life? There's no sense or scripture that requires him to do so, provided we take everything thankfully. But I have to say I can't enjoy a glass of whisky in my daughter's presence, because she's lately been dreadfully prejudiced against it. Where she got her teetotal notions I don't know."

"Perhaps," said Mr. Simon. "from Mr. Huws, for though he's undoubtedly a good man, he appears to me a little ancient in his ways. It's a great pity that there is, among our best men, so much cant and narrow-mindedness, due possibly to a want of learning and of acquaintanceship with the civilized world."

"I see," said the Captain, "that you are what I thought you were, a man who's taken stock of life and characters. As you were saying, it's a pity that when a Welshman becomes a little religious he at the same time becomes narrow-minded, and I'm sure my daughter's unpleasant hostility to every kind of spirits is because she's religious, and I'm thankful for that. Now sir, permit me to say that I'm glad to have met a man who's broad in his views, and that it would be good to have your company often, when it doesn't impede your study and the labour of your ministry. In a place like Bethel, it's a rarity to have the company of a man with similar views to my own. Perhaps you'll be surprised when I say there was only a slight acquaintanceship between me and your predecessor, Rhys Lewis. As you've doubtless heard, Mr. Lewis was an excellent man, a good preacher, substantial, and very godly. But he was narrow in his views about some things. He'd not moved much in this world, and though I admired him as a preacher and respected him as a minister and servant of the Lord, I couldn't somehow feel at ease in his company. And I wouldn't be surprised if he felt the same with me; indeed, I've reason to believe that he looked rather doubtfully upon me, and feared perhaps that I didn't have the root of religion in me; and it all sprang from our different ways of thinking and of looking at things. He, sir, had moved in a small circle, and I in a big one."

"That, doubtless," said Mr. Simon, "accounted for it; and as I said before, it's a pity some of our best men are narrow-minded. Whatever else I may be, I'm not narrow-minded, thanks to my acquaintance with the world; and though I enjoy your society greatly, and hope that I'll have more of it, it's high time I headed home, when I've thanked you for your hospitality."

"Don't mention hospitality," said the Captain, "you know where I live now, and I'll be glad to see you again soon. I'd call my daughter, but you'll excuse us tonight; the next time you come here, I hope Mrs. Trefor will be well enough to welcome you."

"I'm very sorry for her illness, and remember me to her. And now goodnight, Captain Trefor," said Mr. Simon, leaving the house.

"Goodnight," said the Captain, and after closing the door, he added to himself "Goodnight, my good man. You are, I think, sir, an old stager, or you wouldn't be walking home as straight as you walked here. But perhaps you're not sorry, Mr. S., as many a time I've not been sorry, that your bed isn't far away. And that's the beauty of it. The wrong's not in the thing itself, but in being found out. Hmm; I'd better remove the traces of the feast, for what the eye doesn't see, the heart doesn't grieve. It'll be of little use though; Susi's sure to know the bottle's been honoured. She's got a nose like a retriever. But surely, aren't I master in my own house? And now I'll take a thimbleful of farewell, and go upstairs. Indeed, perhaps the old woman will say—and she is ill—that I've been neglectful of her, as I've not been up there since some time this afternoon. Now we'll go and see how matters stand," and the Captain walked upstairs without laying hold of the banisters. It always gave the Captain peace of mind if he could walk upstairs without the help of the banisters.

34

THE SICK ROOM

How various are the ways we live sometimes, at the same time and even in the same house. Whilst people in one room are enjoying laughter and happiness, in the next room—with only a few bricks between them—someone else has a sad heart, and fears for the future weighing on their soul. And thus it was in Tŷ'n yr Ardd on the night described in the last chapter. Enoc followed Miss Trefor up the stairs. Before opening the door to her mother's room, Miss Trefor said, quietly; "my mother, Mr. Huws, is a good deal worse than I thought. I thought she was having no more than a bit of a bilious attack. She's been asleep for hours and I thought she'd have come to herself when she awoke. But she's very ill; I don't somehow like how she looks."

"Wouldn't it be better to ask Mr. Simon to see her? Perhaps he could comfort her, and perhaps your mother would like him to pray with her," said Enoc.

"No," said Susi, "I have no faith in the prayers of a man who reeks of beer," and she opened the door.

"Do you feel very ill, Mrs. Trefor?" asked Enoc.

"Yes, Mr. Huws; but it's my last illness," she said.

"Good heavens, don't talk like that. I've seen you a lot worse and get better, Mrs. Trefor." said Enoc.

"No Mr. Huws, no. I feel very strange; I never felt like this, and I can't describe it. Susi thought I'd been asleep for hours, but I wasn't, for I heard her come into the room each time, and I heard you talking downstairs, especially Richard. And I wasn't awake, either. I thought I was on some great, broad river but not in a boat. There was nothing to support me, and yet there was someone or something saving me from sinking. The river ran fast, with no one but me on it. I saw that the land on each side was moving the same way, but not so quickly as the river. I passed many people on the riverbank; some I knew, but most were strangers. What surprised me was this; I didn't lose sight of those I knew, though they went further away, but I always lost sight of the strangers, and new ones took their place. I feel now, though I'm quite awake, as if I were on the river, with a feeling that I'm still moving; and I think it's death, Mr. Huws."

"Nothing of the sort, Mrs. Trefor," said Enoc, comfortingly, "it's just a little weakness. Death isn't such a beautiful thing, I'm afraid, as the feeling you describe."

"How do you know, Mr. Huws? For no one can leave the experience behind them to show what death is like, so the living might recognise it. The feeling must be new to everyone when it comes, and perhaps it's nothing like what we thought it was," said Mrs. Trefor.

"You're quite a philosopher, mother. I never heard you talk more neatly. You can be sure you're not about to die," said Miss Trefor.

"I heard your grandmother say," said Mrs Trefor, "that some people who were a bit dull in the course of their lives sharpened up wonderfully before dying, and perhaps I'm like that. Something tells me I'll not rise from this bed again. Isn't there a saying, Mr. Huws, about someone being taken away before adversity arrives?"

"Yes," said Enoc, "it's said the just are taken away before adversity. But adversity's unlikely to come to you, Mrs. Trefor. You cling to each other as a family. Providence has been good to the Captain; you have no cause to worry about your circumstances, no matter what happens round here, and you've no cause to doubt God's kindness in the future."

"We've not lived as we should, Mr. Huws," said Mrs. Trefor, "and I want to tell you something. I know you're a good and religious man. And as to circumstances; well, everyone's circumstances come to light sooner or later. It's cost me a lot of pain and grief lately, thinking that for years I've put a high price on what people call respectability; that we're better than other people; but I believe, Mr. Huws, that God has forgiven me for my folly, and I can never be thankful enough that Susi was given the grace to despise the nonsense I taught her. Oh dear, oh dear! I'm so ashamed; I don't know what to do, thinking how crazed I was. You know what? I'm afraid I used to think so much about being respectable, that if the great Saviour himself had come to the world as He did in ancient times, I'd have been too respectable to admit I belonged to Him. Yes, indeed. But I've been forgiven, I think. And Susi, the girl into whose head I pounded these ideas, was the instrument that led me to see my folly. How small are our belongings when we look at them from the edge of death!"

"We ourselves are small, every one of us, Mrs. Trefor." said Enoc, "and I always think that God looks on us with forgiving pity when we put such a high price on such small things. He remembers that we are dust."

"Yes, yes, Mr. Huws, but gold dust cost the blood of the Great Redeemer rather than that it should be lost. What will a man give in exchange for his own soul? I never saw so much value in being saved as I see today, and I'm surprised I've given so little thought to that, and I've put such a high value on fleeting things; and God spoke so plainly."

"That," said Enoc, "only proves we're all sinners. If we'd done everything we should do, we'd be angels, and not sinners. And having a clear view of our deficiencies shows that we're sinners who've been convinced; and having a true desire to be holy proves that we are sinners who've been saved. This desire doesn't come from our depraved nature; it hasn't been put in us by the world, nor by the song of the devil, and so it must come from God. And however bitter the dispensation may have been that's brought us to this state of thinking and feeling, we should be thankful for it. If earthly success and health make us forget God and the other world, we should pray for poverty and ill-health. But I've known you, Mrs. Trefor, for some years, and in all your worldly success and comfort, the matters of religion were foremost in your mind, and I often envied your spirit."

"Everyone knows their own troubles, Mr. Huws," said Mrs. Trefor. "You know nothing about my sin. But I think I can say this honestly; I don't know of any time in the last twenty years when I've not had some sort of love for Christ and His cause. But I let my mind ramble, and fell in love with things that I'd be ashamed to tell you about. But I bade farewell to them some time ago, and I think I'd like to leave this old world and go to a land without trouble where I could be comfortable and happy in a place where there's no sin and no pride; nothing but love for Christ. Perhaps I'm fooling myself, but I'm thinking like that these days."

"And what's to become of us, mother," said Susi, "That's not the highest form of religion, to my mind."

"Well, said Mrs. Trefor" "what is the highest form of religion according to your mind, Susi? Have you had some wonderful revelation lately?

"I don't believe," answered Susi "that sneaking off to heaven and leaving everybody else to take their chance is the best form of religion, if I understand what religion is."

"Well, what's religion, my girl, as you understand it? There's danger of our being mistaken, and I know you've had a great insight into religious matters lately," said Mrs. Trefor.

"No, mother," said Susi, I've had no more insight than anyone else, but until recently I'd closed my eyes to it. As you know, mother, my own self was everything to me for years; I thought only of myself. I lived to amuse myself and failed. What you call insight, mother, was that religion wasn't like that, but something quite different; something that led me to forget myself entirely. And I'm more convinced every day that self is the damnation of all, and forgetting self is the greatest blessing. I fear—perhaps I'm wrong—that there's too much self in godly people. They're forever in the 'seiat', saying they're afraid they're not saved, afraid they'll never go to heaven; and as soon as they feel ready to go there,

229

they're in a hurry to die. To do our duty without caring for the consequences is the highest form of religion, to my mind. 'What do you want me to do?' should be our question every day, without worrying at all about being saved or being lost. God will decide that, not us. I'm afraid we tend to think more about our salvation, about being safe in the end, than about doing our duty. Is not that Self dressed up as religion? Am I not right, Mr. Huws?"

"You're always right, Miss Trefor," said Enoc.

"No, not always, Mr. Huws," said Susi, "but I can't help thinking I'm right in this. Indeed you yourself made the same observation, in a different way, to Mr. Simon. And I was struck when you made the observation; wasn't the labour of Jesus Christ's soul His self-denial for the sake of others? And now, isn't the chief joy of Jesus Christ His self-denial and its consequences? I've read in some of the books I borrowed from you, Mr. Huws, that God would have been everlastingly happy in Himself if He'd never created a single creature. I wonder if I'm sinning when I say I doubt it? Is it presumption to say that even God was weary of Himself, and that was His reason for creating?"

"I'm afraid you're not right about that. Miss Trefor, and yet there's something in what you say," said Enoc.

"You must remember, Mr. Huws," said Susi, "that I've only just started to think—just begun to ponder about things. But can you tell me what made God create at all, if He was perfectly happy in Himself?"

"I can't," said Enoc. "Your question suggests there was a feeling that something was wanting in the Great Being Himself before He created. But we must remember that every perfection exists in God, and that it is useless for us to compare our knowledge with the knowledge of the Perfect One."

"Then the Perfect One created the imperfect for the sake of … what?" asked Susi.

"For His own sake, the Bible says," said Enoc.

"Here the conversation was interrupted by the appearance of

Captain Trefor, who said; "Well, what's going on? A bit of a 'seiat', I'll warrant? How are you, Sarah?"

"Weak enough, Richard; and if I didn't know you'd had company, I'd have thought you'd neglected me," said Mrs. Trefor.

"That's the only reason, Sarah. It wouldn't have been seemly to have left Mr. Simon, though my thoughts were always with you, and my heart was burning with a desire to come and tell you the good news, which you'll have heard some time ago, I know, from Susi or Mr. Huws," said the Captain.

"No father, we've not mentioned it to mother," said Susi.

"It's not possible!" said the Captain. "You've not told your mother about what filled us with happiness and rejoicing tonight?"

"What is it, Richard? Has a revival broken out?" asked Mrs. Trefor.

"No," said the Captain, "We don't have news of that nature tonight; though I must confess that there's a real need of revival, and for myself more than anyone; and, if I don't deceive myself, it would be greater in my sight, and afford me more joy to hear of a powerful revelation in a religious sense, than that raised in my mind by the glad tidings that sounded in our ears a few hours ago, for we must, if the state of the heart and the spirit is right, give precedence to spiritual and religious matters; no matter, so to speak, is …"

"Sem Llwyd said he'd found lead in Coed Madog, mother; that's the news," said Susi.

The Captain looked reprovingly at his daughter, but before saying something unpleasant, he remembered that Enoc was present, and his look softened, and Susi added, "It's getting late, father."

"Quite right," said the Captain, "that's it, Sarah; Susi's given you the good news in a word."

Mrs. Trefor had heard that lead had been found so many times in her life that the news didn't affect her much, and all she said was: "Oh."

Enoc rose to bid farewell to Mrs. Trefor, and to go home. Miss Trefor went to show Enoc out, leaving her father to expand on the good news. But this wasn't the most important thing that happened that night.

35

A REVELATION

Whilst putting a hat on his head, his coat on his back and his stick in his hand, no matter how late it may be, a man can say quite a lot of what's on his mind, if he so wishes. Enoc had vowed to himself that this night he'd tell Miss Trefor some of what was on his mind, even if it killed him. Indeed, this weighed so much on him that Sem Llwyd's news hadn't in the least lightened his mood. He said: "I don't think there's much foundation for your fears about your mother, Miss Trefor. She speaks remarkably well."

"I hope there isn't, Mr. Huws," said Susi, "but I have a dreadful feeling she won't live long. She can't cope with trials and tribulations. As you know, she's had a comfortable life, and she's used to having enough of everything, and just a little adversity knocks her down. Doubtless you've observed, Mr. Huws, that some people, especially women, expect nothing but fair weather in their lives, and like swallows, when they see the approach of winter, they begin to ready their wings for flight to some warmer land. My mother's one of those, as you saw tonight. When the world's not to her liking, she lets go as though it were a hot iron, and I know she longs to be allowed to go to heaven, and I think she'll be able to some day, for I know she loves Jesus Christ. But I think I've learnt this much now; that I'd learned nothing till I learned to suffer, and to suffer in silence."

"I never knew you'd suffered, Miss Trefor;" said Enoc: "I always thought you were fine."

"And so I am," said Miss Trefor, "but you remember Gurnal's saying; 'I know something about the sufferings of the soul'. I have suffered a little on your account, Mr. Huws."

"On my account, Miss Trefor?" said Enoc with surprise, and a thousand thoughts came into his heart.

"Yes; I know you are constantly spending money in Coed Madog Mine, and my father persuades you to do that. And though you're rich, it is very easy, in time, to spend all you have on a mine, without getting anything back, as Hugh Bryan did, poor fellow, and as Mr. Denman has nearly done. And I can't be quiet, Mr. Huws, and not make you aware. It's a terrible thing for a man, when he's worked hard and saved a little money, and earned a respected position among his neighbours, and then in the end to lose it all and become poor. I know some who are like that; and you, Mr. Huws, know them too."

"I'm afraid. Miss Trefor," said Enoc, "you're in a solemn mood tonight, and you've forgotten the news we got from Sem Llwyd."

"No," said Susi, "I've not forgotten Sem Llwyd's news; and, if it's true, I'm glad for the sake of my father and you and Mr. Denman. But don't put too much reliance on it. I've heard a lot of news like that, and nothing ever came of it; take care, Mr. Huws. Can I ask how much you've already spent on Coed Madog, if you know?"

"Oh, something like three hundred pounds, I think," said Enoc.

"Heavens! I was afraid so," said Miss Trefor.

"But I'm only one of three, Miss Trefor," said Enoc.

"Yes," said she, "the one of the three who's responsible for the money. You, Mr. Huws, are the bank."

"I don't know what you mean, Miss Trefor" said Enoc.

"What I mean is this, Mr. Huws," said she, "and I must be allowed to say it; my conscience can't be easy without saying it; that you find the money, and my father spends it, for he hasn't a pound of his own to spend."

"You're joking, Miss Trefor," said Enoc.

"I was never more serious, Mr. Huws," said Susi. "I was always afraid you believed we were rich, but the truth is we're poor, and very poor, and that, I know, is what's killing mother. For years we've lived in plenty and luxury, but since Pwll y Gwynt closed, we've been poor, and now, I'm afraid we're living on your money,

Mr. Huws. I've no idea how much Mr. Denman has spent since Coed Madog started, but I know this; my father's spent nothing, for he's had nothing to spend. I couldn't have an easy conscience without telling all this to you, Mr. Huws. And as to Sem Llwyd's good news, I only hope it's true for your sake. But I put no reliance on what Sem said. He's often said things like this, and it's always turned out to be nothing at all."

"Miss Trefor," said Enoc, utterly amazed, "you're joking. You don't mean to tell me your father's not well off?"

"My heart's too sad for jokes, Mr. Huws," said Miss Trefor. "Not only is my father not well off, but he's in debt, and if things don't change, I see no hope of his being able to pay his debts. But the fact that we're poor is no reason to make others poor. I'm almost sure my mother won't live long; she can't stand poverty. What lies ahead, I don't know; but I'm determined I won't live on deception and hypocrisy, come what may. If Coed Madog turns out well, I'll thank God for it; but if not, I don't know what will become of us. I know very well you've entrusted everything to my father, and now I've told you everything. I'd intended to weeks ago, but I couldn't go through with it. You know how things stand now, but if father knew I'd told you all this he'd practically murder me."

"You've astonished me, Miss Trefor, and yet I feel happy," said Enoc, and his face showed clearly he spoke heartfelt truth.

"Happy, Mr. Huws? Does hearing we're poor make you happy? You're not the man I thought you were." said Miss Trefor, agitated.

"Perhaps so," said Enoc, "but I hope you'll find me a better man than you thought. It might appear cruel of me to say so, but in a sense, I'm very glad to understand that you're poor, if you are in fact so."

Miss Trefor didn't answer, but with a look of contempt, went towards the door. Enoc got there before her; and shutting it and putting his back to it, said:

"Wait; let me explain myself."

"You don't need to do that," said Miss Trefor. "I see through you as I would through a window. I know you've always thought we were fairly well off. You remember well how my father used to patronise you, and how I, in my folly, used to snub you. But, now you're saying to yourself; 'the tables are turned; it's my turn now. I'll make them eat humble pie'. Well, that's only natural; it's all we deserve for our humbug; but it's mean of you, Mr. Huws, and a disappointment from a man such as you. I'd hoped, almost against hope, for your sympathy; for my object—my only object—in telling you of my father's position, was your own good; to keep you away from the same situation. If I'd been selfish, I'd have left you in the dark. But have your fling; I think I fear God, but I don't care a button for the opinion or scorn of any man on earth. Let me pass, Mr. Huws, if you please."

"Not until you're in a better temper," said Enoc. "With all your insight, and though you're so sharp, you've misunder …"

"Susi? Where are you, my girl?" shouted Captain Trefor, coming downstairs, adding, "Your mother wants you, Susi."

Though swearing was completely foreign to Enoc, something like a curse went through him when he heard the Captain's voice, and when Susi brushed past him without so much as a 'goodnight'.

"Hello Mr. Huws," said the Captain, "I thought you'd gone home long ago. But young people will always behave like young people. I remember the time, sir… Ha! ha! ha! Wait, Mr. Huws, I wouldn't mind a bit seeing you home; I need a little fresh air."

Enoc felt in very low spirits as the Captain took hold of his arm, leading him home. A keen observer would have seen it was the Captain who needed Enoc's arm, for he wasn't walking nearly as steadily as usual; but he'd have been the last to admit it, and Enoc would have been the last to notice it, especially as his thoughts were almost entirely on Miss Trefor. All the same, the Captain was in full possession of his memory, and his intellect was as clear as if he hadn't tasted a drop of whisky.

36

CAPTAIN TREFOR

When Enoc and the Captain reached the main road, the latter said: "I remember, Mr. Huws, when I was a little younger than I am now, I used to derive no small enjoyment from walking alone in the depth of night, when the noise of the world and commerce had stopped, and there was nothing, so to speak, to disturb my thoughts. To one of a contemplative nature like myself, so to speak, nothing is more pleasant to the feelings, nor indeed, more beneficial to the soul than a walk after nightfall, when a man may, as they say, divest himself of all the troubles and cares of the world, and give himself up, as it were, to communion with nature, which is, in my opinion, more impressive at night,—no Welsh word offers itself to me at the moment—more impressive. That is, I think—perhaps I'm mistaken—but I'm always open to suggestion—I think, I say, that it's easier at night, especially in a quiet night like tonight, for the spirit, as it were, to slide unconsciously into the contemplation of things spiritual and eternal. The fact is, Mr. Huws, my mind, as you know, has been taken up so fully, lately, with things earthly and transient, that I feel an inward craving, and that deeply, for respite, if only for half an hour, to fall, as I said, into contemplation of an entirely different nature, the more so because I have—as you know—just come from the sick bed of my wife, and have been, to some degree at least, made aware of the emptiness of things of this world and this life, that is to say, in comparison with things eternal. At times, Mr. Huws, I think if it wasn't that this old world has been so cruel to me, and taken up most of my time—though some people must be of this world—I think, I say, I was intended to be a philosopher. For the moment I have ten minutes' leisure from the toils of the world, my contemplations run after the big things—matters of the soul. But perhaps I'm mistaken."

"No doubt," said Enoc, for he was listening but little, and understanding less, of what the Captain was saying.

The Captain couldn't help noticing Enoc's mind was somewhere else, and in order to bring it home again, he said:

"What do you think, Mr. Huws, about Mr. Simon, our minister?"

"I think he's a fairly good musician," said Enoc.

"Yes, but what do you think of him as a minister?" asked the Captain.

"I don't know if I can give an opinion," said Enoc. "And I don't really like judging people, especially preachers. 'Speak no evil against the elders of your people' there's a saying like that somewhere. But as you ask me, I'll tell you—not my judgment, but my feeling, in confidence of course, and I wouldn't wish you to make any use of it, for I wouldn't, for anything, want to create prejudice against him. But I've felt from the start that Mr. Simon has no spiritual influence on me; nothing to elevate my thoughts on religious matters, nothing to warm my heart towards Christ. I don't feel that his sermons, his words in the 'seiat', or his social conversation, combat in any way the tendency of the world and of business to harden a man's feelings. It would be easier to forgive him that if he brought any light to my understanding, but I've never felt the slightest improvement through him. I have some idea that a minister of the Gospel should raise a man a little from this world, and make matters of faith and of the other world more pleasant in his sight. I've never felt this from Mr. Simon's preaching or company. But I'm quite ready to acknowledge that the deficiency may be in myself."

"Mr. Huws," said the Captain, "you convince me more and more every day that you've been endowed with a special talent for recognising character, and that almost instantaneously. In expressing your opinion—or as you prefer to say, your feeling— you have given expression to my feelings as well, though perhaps,

I could not have expressed them so neatly, and in so few words, for you have, so to speak, photographed Mr. Simon's character such that I can recognize the original straight away."

"I'm not sure," said Enoc, "that I've been fair to Mr. Simon, for to tell the truth, I've been prejudiced against him from the beginning. But I can say, honestly, from the bottom of my heart, that I hope I think too meanly of him, and he's a much better and more excellent man than I think.

"Sir," said the Captain, "prejudice doesn't emerge from the earth any more than sorrow; there must be some reason for your prejudice; something caused it. I believe—correct me if I'm wrong—that the reason for prejudice—in enlightened men of course—is that they are possessed, though unconsciously, of some prophetic spirit which enables them to form a true opinion of the ability and character of a man before they've had the opportunities by which ordinary men form their opinions; not everyone has this ability. No, sir, I'm afraid that you—with much modesty, I'll confess—have set out in a few words Mr. Simon's true character, and if I understand the true meaning of your words with some degree of accuracy; your opinion—or your feeling—is this; Mr. Simon has not, as old Abel Huws, all hail to his memory, used to say, Mr. Simon hasn't, I say, studied the great matters—or in other words, he's more a man of this world than of the next."

"That's my feeling, but I hope I'm wrong," said Enoc.

"I'm afraid, sir," said the Captain, "that in this, as in everything else, you've struck the nail on the head, and I'm the more convinced of it, inasmuch as Susi has more than once expressed a similar opinion. Indeed, it's as if you'd held consultations about the man, so alike are your opinions."

"As far as I remember, we've never had a conversation about Mr. Simon," said Enoc.

"That," said the Captain, "just proves you're very much alike in your way of thinking, and I can assure you, sir, that Susi doesn't go around with her eyes closed. But let me ask you; have you any reason to believe Mr. Simon has money? His appearance makes me think he's something more behind him than the small stipend he gets from us, and I think he's hinted to me more than once that he's of a good family, and Susi tells me the ring on his hand couldn't have cost less than ten pounds. My reason for asking is this; I rather thought he was taking quite an interest in Coed Madog Mine, and he'd not object if we asked him to take shares. What do you think?"

"I don't know anything about his worldly position," said Enoc, "but I'd hardly think he had money. Ministers are under a sort of obligation to dress well and appear respectable. I have occasionally seen before now a young preacher start on his journey on a Saturday, as smart as any gentleman in the land, and as bad luck would have it, without more than a penny ha'penny to his name when he'd paid for his ticket, and if it happened that the elder forgot to give him his fee, he either had to walk all the way home or borrow money. Even if I were sure Mr. Simon had money I'd hardly think it wise to ask him to take shares in Coed Madog. It would be more appropriate to encourage him to dig deeply into Biblical matters than to dig for lead like you and I. And indeed, I don't think Mr. Simon's stay in Bethel will be a long one. He already appears to me to have got through all his stock, and to have been repeating himself for some time now. But perhaps all this is my personal prejudice against the man."

"Do you know what, Mr. Huws?" said the Captain, "I'd give a lot for your power to judge character. I think it'd be impossible for any man in the world to get on the blind side of you. You're like—it's an animal, isn't it?—that the Scripture speaks of—full of eyes—and it's no wonder you've done so well. I must beg your pardon; it was only a little joke; I tried a bit of a trick on you, but I might as well not have bothered; it's impossible, as I have said, to get on your blind side. The truth is, I noticed you'd seen that Mr. Simon took a great interest in Sem Llwyd's good news, and I was heartily afraid that you, without thinking, might ask him to take shares; but I see, and I should have known, there was no need to worry. Preachers and parsons aren't the people for us, Mr. Huws. Indeed, whoever we take as partners—if we take any at all—will have to realise, now we've discovered the lead, that we're doing them a great favour; we can afford to be independent, sir, and can tell them if they're not willing to put down such and such a sum of money, now we've proved there's lead in Coed Madog, we can say, well, don't then; we can do without you, and very well too. You know what? I'm glad we've struck the lode, for the sake of Denman, poor fellow, for between you and me, I'm afraid he's spent nearly all he has."

"I'm truly sorry to hear that, but perhaps he'll get it all back some day," said Enoc.

"All of it, sir? He will, as will we, and much more besides," said the Captain. "But here we are at your palatial residence, and a noble one it is, in truth. Taking the house and the shop together, there are few better, if any, in the town, in my opinion. But what I was going to say, had it not been for my eyes falling on your beautiful house—what I was going to say is this; that I'm going to ask you a favour, which, as you know, is not usual in me. Indeed, I've asked so few favours that I feel most ill-suited to the task. But what I was going to say is this; you know we've spent a good deal on Coed Madog, though not a penny's been wasted. Perhaps I should have let you into my family secrets before now, Mr. Huws, but I've always been accustomed to be rather close; indeed my family know very little about my circumstances. It's my own fault, I know. But the fact is that the little money I've amassed in the years of my labour—and it's been no small labour, as you know— has been sunk in a safe place, for I always have tried to remember my family. Don't open the door, Mr. Huws, till I finish my story. I've always tried to remember my family and provide for them, in case Providence thought it wise to take me away suddenly, so they wouldn't be dependent on parish or parson. I now rather fear I've been too careful about the future, but at the same time, I don't feel anxious about what I've done. Well, the consequence, as you may have gathered, is that I don't have a lot of money handy at the moment, and I'd consider it a favour—a very great favour—if you could, without causing yourself any inconvenience, lend me a hundred pounds—not to carry on the mine, understand, but to me personally, for I have a little set aside to carry on the mine, but I ask this as a favour, so that I may have—as I said—without disturbing other things—a little money in the house; for I'm afraid they think I'm poor, and their spirits are low. I'll give you my I.O.U., and you'll get it back with interest at the end of one, two, three, four months, or a year, just according to the way I decide to call things in. I wouldn't dare to ask for this favour—indeed I'd decided to call a few things in—if it hadn't been for the good news we had from Sem Llwyd tonight."

"You can have it by all means, and welcome; come in, sir," said Enoc, and in they went. "Good heavens, there's nothing but the darkness of Egypt here!" added Enoc, after opening the door, and he was hardly exaggerating, for Marged had put the gas out, and let the fire get low in the grate, and to all appearances, had gone to bed some time ago.

"I'm sorry to bring you to such an uncomfortable place," said Enoc, lighting the gas, "but you see what sort of a life a bachelor has."

"Just so," said the Captain, "but who's responsible? It appears to me, Mr. Huws, that you like your misery as much as Diogenes liked his tub, for I know—I don't think, I know,—that you could, with such a home, and with such a situation as yours, charm the best and prettiest girl in the parish to warm and cheer your residence, merely by lifting your little finger. Yours is self-imposed misery, Mr. Huws."

"I know a little about that," said Enoc, "but I'll make out the cheque for you now, Captain Trefor."

"If it's the same to you, Mr. Huws," said the Captain, "I'd prefer having it in gold or notes, but don't cause yourself any inconvenience. You know, Mr. Huws, just as little pigs have big ears, so small bankers have big eyes; but whatever's most convenient to you."

"I think I can give it you in notes," said Enoc.

"Very good," said the Captain; "but wait; are you sure you're not causing yourself any inconvenience by doing so?"

"Not at all," said Enoc, going to the office to fetch the notes; and while he was there, the Captain looked contentedly at the fire, such as it was, softly whistling the old tune 'Innocence'.

Enoc came back with the notes, and placed them one by one on the table. The Captain took them up gracefully, and putting them carefully in his pocket book, said:

"Thank you, sir. If you'll be so kind as to give me a piece of paper, and pen and ink, I'll give you my acknowledgement for them, Mr. Huws."

"Don't bother," said Enoc.

"No, sir; business is business," said the Captain, "though, it must be confessed, such a thing is only necessary as protection for an honest man against the tricks of a dishonest one, and is not essential, so to speak, between people of character. At the same time ... well, I'll remember it tomorrow. And now, Mr. Huws, on looking at that clock, the old saying comes to my mind—'*tempus fugit*'—and in order to maintain propriety, I must be off home, though I'd have liked to have stayed in your company."

"May I accompany you home, sir?" asked Enoc.

"No, Mr. Huws," said the Captain, "not because I wouldn't be glad of your company, but you know, under our present circumstances, if you did come, we'd slip into conversation about the world and its affairs, and I, as I suggested earlier, would like a few minutes of solitude, to think and to contemplate higher things. But thank you, Mr. Huws, all the same."

After shaking hands warmly, the Captain went away, completely content with the success of his mission.

37

CASTLES IN THE AIR

When he was alone, Enoc pulled his chair up to the morsel of fire left in the grate; he filled and lit his pipe, and put himself in the most advantageous corporeal position to review the whole situation.

Captain Trefor had merely added one more proof to his already immeasurable knowledge of human nature when he said, on seeing Mr. Denman going home so early after supper that night, that he was in a hurry to tell Mrs. Denman the good news. That was the fact. This was the happiest night Mr. Denman had known for a long time. Poor wretch! In unbounded faith in the ability, foresight, and honesty of Captain Trefor, he'd forfeited all he owned, and this, as it were, unknown to his wife; for though she guessed he'd spent an abundance on mines, she never imagined it had all gone 'down a mine shaft', as Thomas Bartley used to say. Between Pwll y Gwynt and Coed Madog, Mr. Denman had had a very miserable world of it for some time. The Captain had an enchanter's influence over him. Mr. Denman remembered the time he'd had a few houses, some land, and a little money, and when he'd looked upon himself as being fairly comfortable. But now, nearly all had gone through the Captain's hands and was buried in the bowels of the earth, without hope of resurrection. And the more he spent, the harder it was to stop speculating, for no one had ever found the 'mother lode' without speculating, and in hope of 'luck' Mr. Denman's property had dwindled away like ice on a slate roof in the heat of the sun. Besides this, Mr. Denman had suffered for years the daily croakings of his wife, who deafened and pained him with reproaches for the folly that carried his money to 'that cursed old Captain'. This had destroyed his home comforts, and for a long time before the end of Pwll y Gwynt, Mr. Denman had not taken his wife into his confidence, and had lived in daily fear that she'd realise how much he'd spent, and how little he had he could call his own. If he'd seen his way clear to getting out of trouble, and disclosing his position to Mrs. Denman, he'd have been quite delighted to throw the whole thing up and start life afresh. He pondered day and night how to broach the subject, and tell his wife the worst; and the matter came to weigh daily heavier on him, for he saw clearly it must end soon. Keeping all this in his breast worried him, and was gradually eating him away, and his neighbours said he was ageing severely. Little did they know of his anxieties and his fears.

But it's a long lane that has no turning, and on this night having heard Sem Llwyd's good news, there was a contented smile on Mr. Denman's face and a rejuvenated spirit within him. Hardly anyone would have recognised his step as he hastened homeward. He walked like a young man. And no wonder, for, like Bunyan's pilgrim, the load that had almost overwhelmed him had fallen to the ground. Mr. Denman remembered the prophetic words of the Captain on the night he agreed to join the Coed Madog venture. "Mr. Denman," the Captain had said, "I see the time when you'll tell all to Mrs. Denman, and she'll praise you." Mr. Denman was astonished at the Captain's power of foresight. "And what luck," said he to himself, "that I didn't lose heart! What a blessing! Hundreds would have lost heart and given it all up long ago. But I always believed the Captain was somewhere near it. Who else would have spent all he had, I wonder? But I'll get it all back now, a hundredfold. And I'm thankful I can go home and show a happy face and tell my wife all! I'll get a bit of home comfort now, I expect, something I've not had for years. 'The Lord has given'." and with the words of Job on his lips, Mr. Denman went home happy.

By nature, Mrs. Denman wasn't ill-tempered; but frequent evenings waiting for her husband to come home—till ten, eleven, and sometimes midnight, together with the fact, by now sufficiently apparent, that they were getting poorer each day, had lent a sad aspect to her face and a tone of complaint to her voice. The children had just gone to bed, and Mrs. Denman had put herself in a chair by the fire, to doze until her husband's return. She was surprised when she saw him come in, lively and bright, before she'd closed her eyes for the first time. She realised from his look that something out of the ordinary had happened, and she said, a little ironically: "Dear me! What's up?"

"I'll tell you, Mary dear, as soon as I've taken my shoes off," he said. And having done this, he pulled his chair to the fire, put his feet on the hob, looked contentedly at his wife, and said:

"At last! At last, Mary!"

"At last what, Denman?" asked Mrs. Denman.

"We've—found—the lead! Found—the lead—Mary; struck the lode, Mary; at last! And I'm as happy as a lark! I'm reborn! I know I've caused you a lot of anxiety, investing and investing for so many years, and spending so much, and you'd have been more anxious by half, had you known all. But I always knew; something told me we'd find lead soon, and now we have, and thank heaven for it, for it was nearly all up with me; I was just about losing heart, and almost thought I'd die a poor man. But thank heaven, I say again."

"Tell me more plainly, Denman, I don't understand you," said Mrs. Denman.

"I will, Mary dear, as plain as the midday sun. I know I've kept you in the dark, Mary, and you don't know much about mines. I was at fault, and now I can ask you to forgive me and I know you'll forgive me when I tell you all I've spent on mines, Mary— more than you've ever dreamt. Well, I may as well admit the truth now. I've spent all I had; the houses and the land and everything are gone, except the little stock in the shop, and tonight, I'm not sorry; indeed, I'm thankful that I stuck to it; for had I given up only a week ago, I'd have lost the lot. But I'll get it all back now, and a lot more besides. I could never work myself up enough to tell you till tonight, Mary; but everything's all right now. Many a time you've called Captain Trefor 'an old cursed Captain', eh, Mary? But you'll never call him that again. The Captain's a good man. But to come to the point, and to speak plainly, Sem Llwyd has struck the lode in Coed Madog, Mary—that is, you know, he's found lead—and no one knows how rich we'll be, for the Captain and I and Mr. Huws of Siop y Groes own the whole mine. No, no one knows how rich we'll be, Mary."

"But is it true, Denman? What if the whole thing's a lie, and you've spent all you have. Oh dear! I feel quite ill; is it true, Denman?"

"True, my dear wife? Do you think that Sem doesn't know the difference between lead and dirt? True? It's as true as you're sitting in that chair. I know the news is so good it's hard to credit it, but it's quite true; we're made for life, Mary, and thank God for that! And do you know what, Mary, I was just thinking you and I are beginning to get on in years, and that the best thing for us now would be to give up this business in a few weeks, for it's nothing but trouble and strife. Why should we bother with business when we've got enough to live respectably? It'd be madness. I'll buy a pony and trap just to run to the mine and knock around a bit, and take you out sometimes on a nice day. We must think about this too: giving a good education to these kids—the little dears. I think Bobi'd make a preacher or a lawyer; he's so sharp; and after he's been to a good school, I'll send him to the College in Bala. And as for Lusi, we must teach her music, for it's plain to everyone it's in her. We'll talk again about the other children," said Mr. Denman.

"Oh, Denman, it's like a dream hearing you talk like this."

"Yes, it is; but it's true enough all the same, Mary. The way of Providence is wonderful; it's wonderful. But tell me, Mary, is there anything in the house we could have for a tasty bit of supper? To tell you the truth, though there was a first class supper at Tŷ'n yr Ardd, I couldn't for the life of me be bothered with it, somehow, after learning we'd found lead in Coed Madog; and I'd like to have a tasty supper with you now, if we could?"

"There's a few steaks, Denman, but I was keeping them for tomorrow's dinner," said Mrs. Denman.

"Never mind tomorrow, Mary, let's have them. We don't need to save anymore; we'll have enough of everything and more. Oh, let's have a comfortable supper together, and talk things over; what we'll do and so on, because I know I won't sleep tonight; my mind's too excited."

Mrs. Denman would scarcely believe that it was her husband talking to her, so gentle and friendly were his words, and so different his spirit. For a long time she'd had nothing from him but short and ill-tempered answers and a sour and touchy temper. She felt as though she'd been thrown back to the first six months of their marriage, and she was agreeably surprised. She'd never, at any time, had much belief that any good would come of his 'venturing', but there was something so new in his temper, and his conversation that night was so destitute of "if" and "but for," which was so utterly rare to her, that she almost believed a season of joy and happiness had dawned on them. And yet she couldn't completely believe it, and couldn't, though she tried, give way to joy as Mr. Denman did. She felt a thousand hopes awaken in her breast; and at the same time, doubt she couldn't account for held that hope on a rope, on a short rein. While Mrs. Denman, poor soul, was looking for the 'tasty bit' of supper according to the wish of her husband, the architect of innumerable imaginary castles, it would have been difficult to divine her real feelings. For as her face was lit by a smile of gladness, there followed immediately a deep sigh. She was hopeful and fearful; happy and sad in turn, and more than once asked:

"But Denman, do you believe it's really true?" And when Denman declared that it was as true as the Lord's prayer, well, she couldn't but believe him, and Mrs. Denman at last felt that she'd also been re-created. Indeed, so fully was she possessed by the same good spirits as her husband, that at some amusing remark of his, her laugh rang through the house. She'd not laughed for years, and this laughter was so loud and strident it woke Sami, their youngest son. This occurred just as Mrs. Denman had put the onions in the frying pan with the steaks. After waking, the lad listened attentively, and heard his father's loud and joyful voice in the kitchen. Then the sweet smell of the onions and the steaks reached his nostrils. He slipped quietly out of bed and downstairs. As Denman was in mid-speech, and the noise of the frying pan at its highest, Sammy stood, to the great amazement of his parents, in the middle of the kitchen in his nightshirt, and said:

"Can I have some meat, daddy?"

If Sammy had got up in this fashion the night before, he'd have had a hiding he'd not have forgotten. But the circumstances were different; his father had found lead, and said hospitably:

"You shall, my dear chap; come here to your daddy's knee, my little bit of gold. Can you have some meat? You can have as much as you like for as long as you live. And you can have everything else your dear heart can imagine, can't he, Mary?"

And so Mr. and Mrs. Denman passed the happy time till it grew morning, planning a thousand things they'd do after reaching the mother lode. And it was not until the Cochin China cock had crowed on his roost in the back yard that Mr. Denman said:

"Well, Mary, we must go to bed—just as a matter of convention—but as to sleeping, that's out of the question."

I must now return to the subject of my story, who I left meditating before the remnants of his fire.

38

A NEW LOVER

While Enoc meditated before his small fire, which had by now nearly gone out, was it Sem Llwyd's good news of discovering lead in Coed Madog that filled his thoughts? I very much doubt it. Before now men have forgotten their necessary sustenance, defied the advice and forfeited the love of their parents, scorned their inheritance and made little of their own lives, and all because of some element or principle or feeling in their heart called love. The fact is ridiculous enough, but a fact it is in spite of that. And when we recall that it's not only the fools of this world who've been overcome, but sometimes the best and foremost of our race, it's necessary and correct that we bachelors doff our hats to it and acknowledge that there is some much greater mystery to it than we can discern or fathom. In someone like Enoc Huws who was, if he was anything, a businessman, and as quick sighted as any man when it came to making money, it might have been thought that what he'd learned tonight, namely that they'd struck lead in Coed Madog, would have been enough to fill his thoughts for a fortnight at least. But, strange to say, while he was ruminating in front of the fire, Sem Llwyd's good news never once crossed his mind. There wasn't room in his heart for it. He had only one great thought—diverging, it's true, into different directions—and that thought, to his right, to his left, behind and in front of him, was *Susan Trefor*. By now, she was everything to him, and apart from her, there was no worth to anything in his sight. And the more he saw of her, the more he spoke with her, the fairer, more beautiful, and more precious she became in his mind. At one time he looked on her as a treasure too precious for him to ever hope to own. But circumstances had changed a good deal since then. He himself was richer than he'd ever been, and his business continued to grow. His discussions with Captain Trefor had brought him into closer connection with his idol, and familiarity had not, as often happens, lessened her charm in the least, but, on the contrary, had intensified it. To earn the love and heart of Miss Trefor was, in his view, now within the bounds of possibility, if not probability. He saw that he wasn't unworthy of respect in her sight; they generally agreed in their views, and at times Enoc thought she admired some things in him. He had from the beginning sought the approval of her mother, and had exceeded his expectations, for he knew he'd a warm place in Mrs Trefor's heart. If Captain Trefor's courteous behaviour was any omen neither was Enoc despicable in his sight. Enoc felt sure he controlled the outer defences, and had fully armed himself that night for his energetic endeavour to conquer the castle. But no sooner, as the reader will remember, had he begun the attack than he was contemptuously repulsed, and this entirely by mishap. To speak clearly, free from allegory, Enoc thought that he'd never had a better opportunity than he'd had that night of making his true feelings known to Miss Trefor. Her story about her father's straitened circumstances had seemed to him an excellent opportunity to show the magnanimity of his nature and the sincerity of his admiration for her as a person, independent of her property and position. But his words had hurt and seriously angered her, and before he'd had time to explain their meaning, the Captain—a plague on him!—had made his appearance.

"The best news I've had since I don't know when," said Enoc to himself, "was hearing her say they're poor. Now, I think, she's more likely to listen to my proposal. Now, security and protection from need won't be worthless in her sight, and under the circumstances, my love for her is bound to appear more disinterested. And that's what I was going to say, if I'd had time. But there was the old Captain coming downstairs. Confound it! Two minutes would have done the trick. No one's ever been so unlucky, I swear. And she misunderstood my words. I hurt her, poor thing, and now I heartily wish I hadn't said a word. Little does she know I'd rather cut off a finger than cause her the slightest pain. She's angry with me tonight, I know. And what would be the best thing to do? I've a good mind to write her a letter to explain myself and tell all. But that'd be ridiculous when I see her so often. I'll go there tomorrow, for things must come to a head now. I must explain why I said I was glad to hear they were poor. But the worst of it is, they're not poor. It was easy to understand that from the Captain's words tonight. He's deceived them; he's kept his affairs from them, the old fox. I knew it was impossible. And yet I'd have been happier if they'd really been poor, for if they had, there might perhaps be room to hope she'd be more ready to accept my proposal, and; heaven knows I'd be glad to put all I have in the world at her disposal, and to keep the old people too if need be. But I wonder if she was trying me? It's not possible she doesn't know I think of her, and perhaps she was testing me. Who knows? But something will have to happen soon, for I can't go on living like …"

Someone knocked lightly at the window. Enoc looked in fear in that direction, and noticed for the first time that Marged hadn't pulled down the blind. Beyond the glass, Enoc saw a shining helmet, and under it the beaming face of Jones, the policeman. Enoc opened the door, and Jones said:

"You were deep in thought, Mr. Huws! I was just calling your attention to the blind not being pulled down."

"Thank you," said Enoc, "I hadn't noticed. How did Marged forget it, I wonder? Come in, Mr. Jones."

"Just for a minute, sir, for I have to go about my business," said Jones. "How did you get on at Tŷ'n yr Ardd? Did you enjoy yourself? Now I think of it, how are the eyes? Oh, I see, they're fine. I knew the beef would mend them."

"You're an excellent doctor, Mr. Jones," said Enoc. "No one noticed anything wrong with them, as far as I know. Well, we had a very happy night, and good news too. I'm glad to say, Mr. Jones, and you'll be glad to hear it, that we've found lead in Coed Madog."

"Is that a fact, Mr. Huws?" asked Jones.

"A fact it is. Sem Llwyd struck the lode tonight," said Enoc.

"Sem Llwyd, eh?" said Jones. "Sem wouldn't be at all bothered about taking a bit of lead down the shaft in his pocket. Sem's an old stager, Mr. Huws. Did you ever hear about Elis, the Baptist, some time ago? No? Well this was it. Elis and one or two others were searching for lead somewhere over near Penyboncyn, and working alternate shifts. They'd been at it for months, and Elis had almost lost heart, and they had real trouble getting him to work his shift. One day, what did one of the partners do—knowing Elis was on the next shift—but take a lump of lead as big as his fist and hide it in the place Elis was going to. On the way home after finishing his shift, he called at Elis' house, and said: 'Are you going, Elis? You know what, there's a better look there than I've ever seen, Elis'.

'Is there?' said Elis. 'Why do you say that?'

'Well', said the partner, 'I can't say exactly, but you go and judge for yourself'.

'Well, I suppose I'd better go once more, though I've just about lost all hope', said Elis. And away he went in his woollen jacket and hard hat. But he hadn't been down more than ten minutes when he rushed up the ladders—he doesn't know how to this day—and down into town with his hat in one hand and the lead in the other, half breathless, shouting: 'The Lord hath given, and the Lord hath taken away'. And that was all the lead Elis ever found in Penyboncyn. But this was the funny part; just after that trick on Elis, a preacher came to the Baptist chapel, and his text was 'The Lord hath given', and there was everybody turning their eyes on Elis, and he slipped out of the chapel in disgust. If I were you, Mr. Huws, I'd go and look for myself; go down the mine tomorrow."

"What? Me? Down the shaft, Mr. Jones? I wouldn't go for a thousand pounds," said Enoc.

"Ha ha!" said Jones, "A fine one you are to venture, Mr. Huws. How do you know the miners are telling you the truth? I'd never believe a miner."

"If they told me lies all my life," said Enoc, "I'd never go down the shaft, for I know I'd go dizzy, and I'd be at the bottom, dead as a doornail, before you could count two; and what good would lead or anything else be to me then?

"None," said Jones; "but you'd have a good chance to lie in a lead coffin like a gentleman. But tell me, wasn't it strange for the Captain to be out so late tonight?"

"Oh! You saw the Captain?" asked Enoc.

"Yes," said Jones, "I've just come from Tŷ'n yr Ardd. I was gleaning after your feast, and I got something there that you teetotalers didn't; I got a glass of whisky with the old man."

"Where did you bump into the Captain?" asked Enoc.

"Oddly," said Jones. "I was just coming to the corner of the high street and I heard a knocking, and what did I see but someone knocking at Lloyd the lawyer's door. Lloyd was going to bed, for there was a light in the upstairs window. I couldn't see who was knocking, but he went in, and I thought I'd like to know who it was. He wasn't more than five minutes, and who was it but the Captain. He was right pleased to see me, and I went to see him home. The old man's ailing; he was very unsteady on his feet tonight. But what he'd be wanting with old Lloyd at that time of night, I don't know."

"Likely some business," said Enoc thoughtfully.

"So he said," said Jones, and seeing that Enoc looked rather surprised, added: "Haven't you any idea, Mr. Huws?"

"None at all," said Enoc, thinking that Jones, when their acquaintanceship was so slight, was a little barefaced and inquisitive.

"Hmm," said Jones and—after a short silence—continued, "you know what, Mr. Huws, I don't think the Captain is as well off as people believe."

"What makes you think that?" asked Enoc.

"Well," said Jones, "I can't tell you exactly, somehow, but what do you think about it, Mr. Huws?"

"Well, the impudence!" said Enoc to himself, adding audibly; "Captain Trefor's worldly position is quite unknown to me, and it doesn't matter a great deal to me what his position is; whether he's rich or poor."

"Ah," said Jones, "it looks very much like rain. I can scarcely believe you, Mr. Huws."

"Why?" asked Enoc.

"Because," said Jones, "people are wiser now than they were a while ago. I married when I was twenty three, and I married a poor girl. If I'd been patient, it wouldn't have been any more trouble to marry a girl with two or three thousand pounds; the parson would have taken the same time over the service, and I'd not need to wear this uniform. But now men take time to look around, and take care that the wife brings something to the house besides a sharp tongue. Quite right, too. And though I must confess there's beauty, learning, and sense there without a doubt, I don't think someone I know would be so attentive at Tŷ'n yr Ardd if he didn't believe there was something else there too."

"The one you refer to, Mr. Jones, is not so worldly and mercenary as that, and if there was anything more than friendship between himself and Miss Trefor, and he found that her father was not well off, or even that he was poor, it wouldn't cause the slightest change in his intentions towards her," said Enoc.

"You are a wonderful man, Mr. Huws; you are quite an exception in this kind of thing," said Jones.

"I don't know about that," said Enoc, "but I do know this; I wouldn't consider love to be love at all if circumstances changed it in the least."

"I see, Mr. Huws, that you have old-fashioned notions about love," said Jones; "the love these novels talk about. But when it comes to real life, you see very little trust placed in it, even among those who thought they had it. And you remember the proverb; 'When poverty comes in through the door, love flies out of the window'."

"No proverb was ever more false in my opinion," said Enoc. "No doubt poverty coming in through the door has served to show many a time that there never was any true love in the house. When a man has fallen '*dros ei ben a'i glustiau*'[1] in love with beauty and worth and has been struck deaf and dumb, as though by lightning, he can never shake that off, no matter how much may come to light, if it doesn't directly reflect on the one he has fallen in love with, it can't change him at all, to my mind; poverty is a misfortune and not an evil, and wealth is an accident, and neither the one nor the other can detract much from or add to the true value of a beautiful and virtuous girl. That's my view, Mr. Jones."

"You *are* getting beyond me now, Mr. Huws," said Jones. "I don't know much about things like that. But would you be surprised if I told you the Captain was hard up?"

"I would, of course," said Enoc.

"What would you say if I told you the Captain had been served with a writ for twenty five pounds?" asked Jones.

"I'd say someone had told you a lie," said Enoc.

"What if I said I know it's a fact?" asked Jones.

"I'd say," said Enoc, "that I know that the Captain isn't short of two or three times twenty five pounds. There's some mistake, Mr. Jones."

"There isn't a mistake, sir. And if the Captain had twice twenty five pounds, I know he's parted with half of it tonight," said Jones.

Enoc smiled, and said to himself, "They are poor after all, thank heavens."

"I thought it my duty as a friend to tell you this, Mr. Huws ," said Jones, "for it would be unfortunate if you took a false step, and if I were in your place I should make myself conspicuous by my absence at Tŷ'n yr Ardd. I don't doubt they'll do their best to trap you into marrying their daughter, but it'll be a bad look out for you, Mr. Huws."

---

[1] '*dros ei ben a'i glustiau*'—well, here we are again, over his head and his ears. This time it means '*head over heels*'.

"The fact," said Enoc, "if fact it is, that the Captain's been served with a writ doesn't prove he's poor. The Captain's an odd sort of man, and perhaps he'd made up his mind not to pay till he himself chose to. But how did you learn this, Mr. Jones?"

"I can't answer that question, Mr. Huws, without betraying a confidence. Policemen know a thousand things that they can't tell how they came to know them. But it's true enough, believe me; and I could tell you more, but I see from your face you don't believe me," said Jones.

Enoc couldn't conceal his joy, and Jones rose to leave, saying: "Time will tell, Mr. Huws, but take care and keep your eyes open, and you're sure to find that I ... What was that noise? Do you have cats here?"

"No," said Enoc, "there are more mice than cats here. Marged kills every cat that comes in. But there was a noise, wasn't there? What was it, I wonder?"

"It was in the back room. Let's go and look in case there are thieves about," said Jones.

Enoc lit a candle, and not without fear, after the mention of thieves, he went towards the back room, but brave too as Jones was right behind him. Enoc opened the door, holding the candle at arm's length and keeping his body as far back as possible. As soon as the candle came into the room, someone behind the door tried to blow it out, and Enoc leapt back in terror, striking Jones in the stomach. Jones snatched the candle from his hand and pushed Enoc unwillingly before him into the room, and in the scuffle they heard someone say, quietly: "It's me, master."

"Yes, and who else?" asked Jones, moving the candle around the room. The light disclosed a most harmless sight, too harmless to merit such a fright as Enoc had had, for he'd been horribly frightened; he was trembling like a leaf, his face as white as death. In the room there was a bench, about two yards long, which was used by Marged on washing days for holding the bowls. When Jones and Enoc entered Marged was sitting at one end of this bench, with her chin against her bosom, and her finger in her mouth, looking shyly and guiltily at the floor. Behind the door stood, or rather, crouched, as if in the act of rising from his seat, a well-known character called Tom Solet. Tom wore corduroy trousers, which were too short at top and bottom. At the bottom they were high above his ankles, and bound by a cord under his knees, and at top they had fallen to his hips and were secured by a strap and buckle, and a plain shirt drooped untidily over them. Tom's shirt had always been plain; of a colour that didn't show dirt, with a huge collar like that of a coat, so as not to need a neckerchief. To avoid the usual waistcoat, Tom wore a waistcoat with sleeves, and though it was double breasted with big buttons, it was always open, summer and winter. This was Tom's attire to come courting. It wasn't the first time he'd been at the task, for he'd buried three wives, and he'd not seen the need to wear anything different on this occasion. Still, Tom was an honest man, and had worked for years under the Local Board, and had wheeled a barrow so much he could never stand up straight; as I said, he was always halfway between sitting and standing. When caught in the back room by Enoc and Jones the policeman, Tom didn't show anything like Marged's confusion, and there was more of fun to be found in his face than fright. Jones asked him: "Well, Tom, what's your business in a house like this at this time of night?"

Tom smiled, and pointed with a nod and a wink toward Marged, meaning 'My business is with her'.

"What?" said Jones, "did you come to court Marged?"

Tom gave an affirmative nod, and hitched his trousers.

"Oh," said Jones, "how long's this business been going on, Tom?"

Tom gave a double nod toward Marged, which meant: 'Ask her'.

"How long, Marged?" asked Jones.

"He's wanted to talk to me for a long time, but he's never come in till tonight," said Marged.

"So," said Jones. "But stop, Tom. You buried your last wife ages ago; about three months, isn't it, Tom?"

Tom gave a triple nod, the translation being: 'Yes, poor thing'.

"I rather thought so," said Jones. "And you're thinking of settling with Marged and making a wife of her, Tom?"

Tom gave a conditional nod, as if to say: 'If she's willing'.

"Well, Marged, what do you say about Tom's offer? Tom's an honest man, sober, in steady work, gets fifteen shillings a week, and has a house and furniture. Are you agreeable, Marged?"

"I don't really know; but perhaps I couldn't do much better," said Marged.

"I believe," said Jones, "you'd be doing very well. You won't get an offer like this every day. And you, Tom, can consider yourself extremely lucky if you get Marged for a wife, for she's a tidy woman, healthy, able and hard-working, besides having a bit of money (Tom's face brightened at hearing this) and it'd be foolish to waste time; the sooner you come together the better. What do you say, Tom?"

Tom gave a nod of entire consent.

"What do you say, Marged?" asked Jones.

"Just as he wishes," said Marged.

"Well," said Jones, "if Mr. Huws is willing to let Marged leave without giving notice, the best thing, Tom, would be for you to put the banns up next Sunday.

Tom looked enquiringly at Mr. Huws' face, and Enoc said: "If Marged wishes that, I won't prevent her. Indeed, I'll be pleased to see her make a home for herself, though I'll be sorry to lose her," said Enoc, telling a small lie.

"You've stopped too soon, Mr. Huws," said Jones. "I was rather expecting to hear you say you'd give the wedding breakfast."

"Well, I will, and perhaps I'll give her a little present too, for Marged's been a good and honest servant." said Enoc.

"I knew," said Jones, "you'd act like a gentleman."

"Thank you sir," said Marged, and Tom touched his forelock as an acknowledgment of the kindness.

"Now," said Jones, "I'll leave you, and get yourself home,

Tom, in ten minutes or so, and remember, we won't be hearing anything about a breach of promise, for there are two witnesses here, remember.

Tom gave a nod with the left side of his head, as much as to say: "No fear."

And thus Enoc and Jones left the lovers. Once out of earshot, the latter said: "That's a big job done, isn't it Mr. Huws?"

"I think so, indeed," said Enoc, "and just fancy, not a single word came out of his head the whole time."

"He spoke a lot with his head though," said Jones. "That man's nod, sir, is as good as his word. And now you're getting rid of the old buzzard forever. You know what, Mr. Huws, it's raining favours on you today."

"It's no use me denying it," said Enoc; "I'll be heartily glad to get rid of Marged, and Tom Solet's taken a weight off my mind."

"I believe you," said Jones. "And now I must go about my business. But I have a favour to ask you, Mr. Huws; I noticed yesterday that you have some enormous fine home cured hams in your shop; will you trust me with one till next pay day? I'm a bit hard up at the moment, but I'll pay you for sure next pay day."

"You'll do nothing of the sort, Mr. Jones," said Enoc. "But I'll send you a ham free and gratis tomorrow, and thanks for your kindness. It'll be in your house by midday."

"You're too generous, Mr. Huws, and I can only thank you from the bottom of my heart and say goodnight." said Jones.

39

AT LAST

The definite signs that Marged was going to be married, and soon, afforded Enoc a good deal of peace of mind, for the greater part of his fears and anxieties for the future revolved around her, and he could do no less than be surprised and marvel at the easy way in which Tom Solet had reached his goal, whilst he himself had been in turmoil for years, and was, as far as he could see, no nearer his goal now than at the beginning. This led Enoc's contemplations down their natural channel, that is, toward Miss Trefor, as they went at all times and from everywhere. He scarcely slept that night. He'd resolved to make his love known to Miss Trefor, but the preface had been unhappy, and had wounded her severely. Enoc looked to the sermon to explain the preface, rather contrary to the usual rule; and it's a big thing to break with tradition. He never got to deliver the sermon, as we've seen, and so the preface remained dark. At the same time, after hearing what Jones the policeman had said, Enoc considered the preface had been good, and the misfortune was not having the opportunity to preach. In other words, after the conversation with Jones, Enoc couldn't see that he was mistaken in declaring his joy when Miss Trefor said her father was poor, as by doing so he'd proved the rightness and constancy of his affection. After the mishap, he couldn't rest till he'd explained himself; and therefore, as early as was decent, he went to Tŷ'n yr Ardd with the excuse of enquiring after Mrs. Trefor's health. On asking Kitty, the maid, he found Mrs. Trefor was a good deal worse, that they'd had to call the doctor, that he'd ordered complete peace, and that the Captain had gone to the mine to look into Sem Llwyd's discovery. Enoc wasn't willing to turn back at this, and told Kitty to inform Mrs. Trefor that he was asking about them, which she did, and returned in a minute with word that Mrs. Trefor was too ill to see anyone. Enoc went back in low spirits, and intent on returning later. Although he was very sorry about Mrs. Trefor's illness, what grieved him most was not having an opportunity to explain himself to Miss Trefor. As he was on the point of starting for Tŷ'n yr Ardd in the evening, hoping for some opportunity, if only for two minutes, to talk to Miss Trefor, the Captain came in, and said: "There's never sweet without bitter, Mr. Huws, and I never felt till today how true that proverb is. I'd intended to call earlier to report on my visit to the mine, and I would have done had not family problems, namely Mrs. Trefor's illness prevented me; she is, as I understand you know, considerably worse today than last night. And she's truly very ill, though the doctor assures us there's no present danger. I know, Mr. Huws, that you understand my feelings and sympathise with me in my trouble, for though I expect that with your prayers and those of others, she'll be restored, I say that if wise Providence sees fit to take her away, my pilgrimage will be at an end with regard to this world and things worldly; for—so to speak—I'd have nothing left in the world worth living for. But what I was going to refer to—and I must be brief—I can't stay long in the present circumstances—I was going to refer to this—that I would have called earlier in the day, if it hadn't been for what I've mentioned—to give you a report on the true worth of what Sem Llwyd described to us last night. It comes to this, Mr. Huws, and I'll put it to you in simple terms; it is, as I said last night, like the leaves on the water, and shows that the mainland is near. In itself, it's not large; indeed it's small, except as a sure sign of greater things. Under ordinary circumstances, sir, this would be a matter of great joy to me; but when one has become, that is, one of my age, and with the anxiety I have today for the life of my wife—it's neither here nor there, for if she's taken away (and here the Captain blew his nose hard), I'll be left alone; completely alone, sir."

"You forget, Captain Trefor," said Enoc, "even if you lost

Mrs. Trefor, and I hope and believe you won't for a long time to come, you'll still have a most excellent daughter with you."

"No," said the Captain, "I don't forget that, Mr. Huws; but what certainty do I have that someone—that you, or someone like you—won't take her from me? Indeed, that's the probability; that's the way of the world, that's the way of Providence."

It was pleasant for Enoc to hear the Captain speak thus, and the question flashed into his mind of whether he should mention his love for the Captain's daughter, and his intense desire to make her his wife. But before he could put the thought into words, the Captain said: "And now, Mr. Huws, I must say goodnight, and till there's a change at home I'm afraid I won't be able to give much attention to Coed Madog, and under the circumstances, I know you'll excuse me," and away he went.

Once again, Enoc had missed his chance; he was always missing it, and he began to think some evil fate followed him, and that he'd been born under an unlucky star. Enoc believed a little in fate, and that night he recited sadly to himself more than once the '*hen bennill*'[1] he'd seen in some song or other:

> *Ni wiw mo'r tynu yn erbyn tynged,*
> *Mae'n rhaid i'r blaened gael ei ffors,*
> *Rwyf wedi'm tyngu er's pymthengnydd*
> *I wasanaethu'r Brenin Siors.*[2]

---

[1] '*hen bennill*'—literally, an old verse. Traditional folk songs are known as '*hen benillion*'— *penillion* being the plural, and the '*p*' mutating to '*b*' because of the adjective '*hen*' before the noun. As I think I've said before, it's an interesting language.

[2] It may be that this is not a real '*hen bennill*'. It may be that Mr. Owen wrote it; as authors sometimes do. It translates as:

> "*Ni wiw mo'r tynu yn erbyn tynged,*
> *Mae'n rhaid i'r blaened gael ei ffors,*
> *Rwyf wedi'm tyngu er's pymthengnydd*
> *I wasanaethu'r Brenin Siors.*"

> "It's no use resisting fate,
> The planet must have its force.
> I swore a fortnight ago
> To serve King George."

But he could draw little comfort from the verse, and though he called frequently at Tŷ'n yr Ardd during the following days, he never had chance to talk to Miss Trefor and explain himself. Mrs. Trefor's serious and prolonged illness prevented him daily from even glimpsing the one he loved so much. A fortnight went by without any sign of improvement in Mrs. Trefor's health; a fortnight that felt like a year, inasmuch as he was utterly deprived of the company of his *Morfydd*[3]. He could have suffered this had not been for the consciousness within him every hour of the day and night that Susi cherished unkind feelings towards him, arising entirely from a misunderstanding.

Although Marged was remarkably sociable and good-tempered at the prospect of her marriage, which was to take place in a few days, Enoc couldn't eat or sleep. Marged saw that something important was worrying her master but she couldn't imagine anything accounting for this, except the fact that she was leaving, and she'd often say, on seeing him unable to eat, "Don't fret, master, you'll get as good a servant as me from somewhere."

"I don't know," was Enoc's only answer. His misery was so great he could bear it no longer, so he wrote to Miss Trefor begging her for a few minutes conversation on an important matter. Though she'd pretended to be very angry with him, Miss Trefor thought when she received Enoc's note that her father was in some trouble, and it would be madness to do him an injury by appearing obstinate to Enoc. She fixed a time for his visit, namely the next afternoon. Having gained her permission, Enoc did nothing but compose in his mind a full explanation of what he'd said to her a fortnight back. He composed a clear, compact, and effective exposition of his feelings towards her and went over it hundreds

---

[3] *Morfydd*—Owen is referring either to Morfydd, lover of the Welsh poet Dafydd ap Gwilym, for whom he wrote many of the finest love poems in the language; or the daughter of Urien from Welsh legend, born in Llanferres, not too far from Mr. Owen's home. There was an enduring love between Morfydd and Cynon, one of King Arthur's warriors.

of times, till he knew it better than his prayers. But when the time came, and he came face to face with Miss Trefor in the parlour of Tŷ'n yr Ardd after the long fast of a fortnight, without sight of her friendly face, he felt like a man too long without food who's been led to a banquet. Enoc instantly saw that Miss Trefor looked thinner and paler, but he'd never seen her look more charming. His tongue stuck to the roof of his mouth, and every word he'd composed went clean out of his head. Miss Trefor shook his hand, coolly and formally, and asked him to sit down, and having waited a minute in silence, said: "Well, Mr. Huws, what is it you want to say to me?"

After considerable coughing and clearing of his throat, Enoc said, half choking: "I have a lot of things I want to say to you, if I knew how; The thing that troubles me most is that I fear I hurt you by saying I was glad to hear your father was poor, and you know I didn't have time or opportunity to explain what I meant in saying so. I know it was a strange thing to say …"

"Go on, Mr. Huws, for I don't have a lot of time," said Miss Trefor.

"Well," said Enoc, and he began to feel that he was being helped, and 'there's wonderful help to be got', as Mrs. Trefor had said in another context. "Well," said Enoc, "in a sense I'm saying the same thing again; and I beg you not to run away till I've finished my story. The common opinion of your neighbours, Miss Trefor, is that your father is fairly well off, and that was my opinion, till recently. But now I must believe your father isn't at all wealthy. In one sense, I'm very sorry; and in another sense I'm very happy to know that that's how he stands, as I said the other evening. I know when I said this a fortnight ago, that I hurt you deeply, and perhaps, I'll make you angry again when I tell you why I said so, and still say so. And I'm not without fear, Miss Trefor, when I tell you why, that you'll be angry with me for ever …"

"Go on, Mr. Huws; there's no one with mother except Kitty; and she'll be calling for me soon," said Miss Trefor.

"Well," said Enoc, "it's hard to believe you don't know my feelings before I tell you. It's impossible for you not to have understood from my behaviour for a long time back that I cherish a feeling towards you for which friendship isn't the appropriate word. I know it's presumptuous of me, but I can't help it. I love you, Miss Trefor, and love you so much I can't imagine it possible to love anyone more …"

Enoc stopped for a moment, expecting her to say something, but she didn't say a word; she just looked him calmly and composedly in the face. Enoc continued, with a little more confidence: "That was my only reason for saying I was glad to hear of your father's situation. If you'd been rich—and thank heavens you're not—you might have thought I had selfish motives; but, indeed, it is you yourself that I love, and not what's around you. I'm sorry to be speaking of a thing like this when your mother is so ill; but forgive me, I can't stand it any longer. Give me one word, just one word of encouragement, and I'll be perfectly happy. But if you refuse me, well, I'm afraid I'll go mad."

"Mr. Huws," said Susi, and Enoc wondered how she could speak with such self-possession, "I'm so very sorry to hear your story, believe me. I'm so sorry to hear you speak like that. I remember the time, when I was a silly, senseless flirt, when in my heart I'd despise and mock you. Forgive me that stupidity; I didn't know you then. When I knew you better, and saw your honesty, your honour, your endless kindness, I learned to respect you, and respect you greatly. I knew long ago that every word you say is true; or I should say that you always try to tell the truth. You always carry your heart on your sleeve; it's impossible not to see that. I'm indebted to you for a thousand things, and more. You've put a lot into my empty head, indeed you have. You've made me believe there is such a thing as an honest, upright, and good man. I see only one weakness in you, that you've been so unwise as to give your love to a foolish flirt like me. And let me try to be like you in one respect, Mr. Huws, to be honest and not hypocritical. I've known for a long time that you've thought something of me. I'd have been as blind as a bat not to have seen it. And I gave you the chance, dozens of times, to speak your mind. And why? So I could tell you, Mr. Huws, that it's no use you thinking about me in that way; no use at all."

"Miss Trefor," said Enoc, his heart in his mouth, "you're not serious?"

"As serious," said she, "as if I were on trial, and I'm very sorry to have to say it, Mr. Huws; for I know—it'd be hypocritical to say otherwise – that this is very painful to you. But to consider your request, Mr. Huws, is impossible; impossible."

"Why? Give me a reason why," said Enoc sadly.

"I can't tell you why, Mr. Huws," said Susi, "And remember the pain's not all on your side. Knowing—and it was impossible to not know—that you'd set your heart on me pained me severely. Not, remember, that I don't consider it a great compliment. For a girl to be liked, to be loved by any man, however mean he may be—is a compliment to her, and she should value it. But when someone like me—yes, like me—you know me well—is loved by one like you, Mr. Huws—a man, as I said, for whom I have the greatest respect, well, she should feel proud; and I do feel proud; and remember that no ear will ever—never ever—hear that Susan Trefor refused Enoc Huws."

"They won't, I hope, because Susan Trefor will, I trust, some day accept his offer, and then people wouldn't believe it had happened," said Enoc.

"Never, Mr. Huws. And I beg you, put the thought aside, wholly and forever, and don't mention it again. Come here every day; there's no one I like to see as much as you. My mother thinks the world of you, and father, I'm afraid, lives off you; but dear Mr. Huws, don't ever say anything like this again.

"Why? Tell me the reason why," said Enoc again.

"Well," said Susi after some hesitation; "We're too alike. We've talked so much, exchanged ideas and done that for so long, that sometimes it frightens me, trying to work out whether I'm Susan

Trefor or Enoc Huws. We're too much alike to be husband and wife. That's not my idea of a husband and wife. My idea is they should be entirely opposite to one other, for I know if I had a husband like myself, I'd quickly come to hate him as I often hate myself."

Enoc smiled joyfully and said: "I'm glad to learn, Miss Trefor, that you don't hate me now, and I'll be quite content to be hated someday as a part of yourself. I'll take the risk.

"It's more of a risk than you imagine, Mr. Huws; you'd have reason to repent it all your life. Now I must go; and don't waste a minute thinking of it again, Mr. Huws, I beg you," she said.

"Then," said Enoc, gravely, "I must cease to live. Not to think of you, Miss Trefor, would be like not existing. Before you go—I'm sorry to keep you so long—say you'll take a week, a fortnight, even a month, to consider the matter, and don't say it's impossible."

"I considered, the matter carefully, Mr. Huws, before you brought it forward. I'm not playing with you just to torment you. I've got too much respect for you to do that. I'm speaking my mind honestly, and nothing will make me change my mind. You'll see one day it's best for you and me. I hope we'll always be friends—great friends—but anything more than that ... well, you understand my thinking, Mr. Huws. I want to cause you as little pain as possible; for anything that pains you is sure to pain me."

"Well," said. Enoc, "if that's your decision, you can be sure you'll be in pain as long as you live, or rather as long as I live; for I know that henceforth I'll have no peace, day or night."

"You're mistaken, Mr. Huws," said Susi, "when we understand each other, this—like everything else—will pass; the love and the hate of the best of us is but a lodger for the night; something else will come in its turn to occupy our thoughts, and so on, and so on, till we ourselves are forgotten."

"You wouldn't talk like that, Miss Trefor," said Enoc very sadly, "if you knew how I love you. God knows you're my everything, and I put no value on anything on earth except you. But will you answer me one question before you go?"

"I don't really know, Mr. Huws, for I ask myself a lot of questions that I can't answer,"

"But you'll be able to answer the question I want to ask," said Enoc.

"There are some questions it's not wise to answer, and shouldn't be answered," she said.

"You can judge that for yourself," said Enoc. "Let me ask you; Have you given your love to someone else?"

For a moment, and for the first time in the course of the conversation, Susi appeared confused, and as though she'd lost a little of her self-assurance, but she said at once: "To whom, Mr. Huws, could I have given my love? You know that no man comes near Tŷ'n yr Ardd but you."

"You've not answered my question, Miss Trefor," said Enoc.

"Well," she said, measuring her words carefully; "I've not met a man I admire more than you for some years, Mr. Huws. Will that satisfy you?"

"It won't," said Enoc. "I'm very bold, I admit, but you've not answered my question."

"I've answered it as best I can," she said.

"And you've got nothing better and nothing more comforting to tell me before you go?" asked Enoc, getting to his feet; and his eyes filled with tears despite of his best efforts.

"Nothing, dear Mr. Huws," and her eyes were not especially dry. She added, extending her hand in farewell, "Hurry back; when mother's a little better, it would do her heart good to see you."

And so she left him, going towards her mother's room. At the top of the stairs she stopped suddenly, turned into her own room, and looked in the mirror; the first thing any pretty girl does on going to her bedroom. Then she threw herself into a chair and wept. After a couple of minutes she leapt to her feet, bathed her face, not forgetting to tidy her hair. If anyone had been beside her, they'd have heard her whisper: "Poor fellow; I knew very well he felt that way. He's a good man—very good—and better still as you come to know him; I must confess I like him more every day. He's an upright and honourable man, and there's no humbug about him. If I were sure—quite sure—that *he* wouldn't come, well, I'd put my arms round his neck and kiss him, for I must admit the truth; I'm very fond of him. No, I couldn't! The idea! Never, never ever! Although I don't know what's going to become of me. I'll have to earn my living somehow. But I'll keep my oath and take my chance. And yet perhaps I'm making a rod for my own back; it's all sentiment. Many would have been proud of the compliment. Oh, good heavens, what problems we have in this world! And we're not here long. How's mother now, I wonder, poor dear?"

And into her mother's room she went, happy as a lark, as if nothing had happened.

40

ENOC HUWS' OATH

Never had Enoc Huws been so miserable; of course the last sorrow is best remembered. In all his troubles he had, for some time now, been able to have some degree of happiness by dreaming of himself and Miss Trefor as man and wife. Indeed, the dream had been so vivid to him at times, and had extended so far into the future, that he'd seen himself, with his hair turning to grey, a father of four children, two boys and two girls, with whose names and looks he was well acquainted; and he was especially fond of the youngest. But now his dream had vanished like mist in the morning. Not quite, perhaps, for he confessed to himself he'd cut a most sorry figure in making his proposal to Miss Trefor, and he thought sometimes, that had he been sufficiently self-possessed to speak in the way he'd prepared, the result might have been different. And yet he couldn't forget how definite she was in refusing his proposal. At the same time, Enoc recollected how good natured and kind she'd been, even in that refusal. Indeed, she'd acknowledged that she'd respected him more and more as she grew more acquainted with him, and who knew whether, as she came to know him better still, she'd come to love him deeply? Thoughts like these filled his heart, poor fellow, and indeed his stomach too, for he ate next to nothing, and Marged often said it was a waste of time preparing his meals, and a robin couldn't live on what Enoc ate. Little did she know that the bread of angels was his sustenance in those days.

Enoc wasn't conceited or proud, nor in any way one who entertained high ideas about himself; his tendency was the other way, to a fault. But his failure with Miss Trefor disturbed the very roots of his nature. This was natural enough, for nothing makes a man feel as if he's been skinned alive so much as being refused by a girl. Mercifully such a thing seldom happens, for men are wise as a rule and, like the good man who composed '*Rhodd Mam*'[1], he knows what the answer will be before asking the question; and that was Enoc's mistake; he should have known the answer before he asked the question. There's a little self-respect in the humblest and meekest of men, and you've only to tread on his corns to find this out; doing so makes him instantly clench his fist. I imagine few men think less of themselves, or about themselves, than did Enoc, but Miss Trefor's refusal caused him to spend some little time measuring and weighing himself. After doing this, he decided he was a better man than he'd thought he was. Enoc came to a conscious conclusion that he wasn't a fool, that he wasn't, as far as appearance went, to be despised, that he was, in a worldly sense, quite comfortably off; as to his position in the town, fairly respected, and that Miss Trefor wouldn't have been lowering herself by accepting his proposal. He decided—and the decision was an important one to him—to fall back on his honour; and inwardly vowed he'd not go to Tŷ'n yr Ardd again unless he was asked. The oath didn't mean, for he took great care to have a complete understanding between himself and his conscience, that he wouldn't propose again to Miss Trefor at some future date; indeed, he wasn't without hope of a successful proposal in the near future. The oath was but a sort of tribute due to his wounded dignity. And in executing the oath, he felt it occasioned a great sacrifice on his part, and someone else also felt something, but he didn't know that. Enoc kept his oath for … well, we'll see how long. It must be admitted that although Enoc now seldom crossed the threshold of his house, his spirit was more than ever in Tŷ'n yr Ardd. He fell naturally into his former practise of going to his office after supper, pretending to Marged that he had business to do. There he

---

[1] '*Rhodd Mam*'—Mother's Gift. A catechism for children used by the Methodist Church in Wales; being a catechism, the answers were obviously known in advance. John Parry was the good man who wrote it.

stayed for hours every night, and the only business he did was to smoke unceasingly, nod his head significantly, and as before, spit emphatically into the heart of the fire. If every conversation he'd shared with himself on those evenings had been written down, they'd make a weighty volume.

To break a little into the monotony of his meditations, the wedding of Marged and Tom Solet came unexpectedly upon Enoc. It's true that Marged had mentioned the approaching event more than once, such as by reminding him he'd promised to give the breakfast, and then by asking what she should prepare for the breakfast, and who and how many people she should invite to come and partake of the feast. Enoc gave her 'carte blanche' to do as she liked, and to invite whoever she wished, and thought no more about the matter. So absent-minded was he, that he didn't fully realise that Marged was going to leave him till she, on the afternoon before the wedding, invited him into the back kitchen to see the preparations with his own eyes. There was a couple of fowl, a home cured ham, a tongue of beef, and a large cold piece of roast beef; the fowl dressed with parsley, and the neck of the ham neatly adorned with pink and white paper. Enoc hadn't imagined that Marged would have taken advantage of his permission by indulging in things like these. But though he knew it was all at his expense, his heart didn't begrudge it, for Enoc believed that what was worth doing was worth doing well. When Enoc saw the delicacies, he smiled—the first smile seen on his face for some days, and said: "Who cooked for you, Marged?"

"I did, of course," said Marged.

And Enoc said to himself, "Where there's a will there's a way, I never saw her turn out things like this before"; and he added, intending the remark to be a little biting: "You've forgotten one important thing, Marged; where's the wedding cake?"

"No I didn't forget it, master, but I didn't like to be so bold as to order too much, and I suppose it's too late now," said Marged.

"It probably is; we'll have to try and manage without one," said

Enoc, adding: "Who's coming to eat all this, Marged?"

"Well," said Marged, "there's me, and Tom, and you and Betsi Pwel, and Robert Jones, and you, and the men in the shop, I suppose, and me. Oh, there'll be a lot of us, and there's Tom, too."

"You should," said Enoc, "on any account invite Mr. Brown, the parson, and Hugh, the sexton; he's buried a lot in his time, and Jones the policeman, and especially Didymus, the reporter, or you'll not get the wedding reported in the newspaper."

"I'd really like it to be in the newspaper, but I've never spoken to Didymus" said Marged.

"Well," said Enoc, "I'll ask Didymus and Jones the policeman, and you ask the others, and if it hadn't been too late, I'd have invited the Chairman of the Local Board and the Lord Lieutenant of the County. Lord Mostyn and Sir Watkin are abroad, or I'd have asked them, too."

"That's a pity," said Marged.

"It can't be helped," said Enoc with a sad face. He had no difficulty wearing a sad face nowadays.

"You understand, master," said Marged, as Enoc was leaving, "that you have to give me away?"

"What are you saying, Marged?" said Enoc, and his face was genuinely sad now.

"You have to give me away."

"I don't understand you."

"Well," said Marged, "Mr. Brown, the parson, said I need someone to give me away, and I couldn't think of anyone except you, master, and Mr. Brown said you'd do fine; I couldn't wish for anyone better."

"I don't know anything about such things, and I'd rather someone else did the job, Marged," said Enoc.

"It's too late to ask anyone else, master," said Marged.

"What time tomorrow does the wedding take place?" asked Enoc.

"When the clock strikes eight," said Marged.

Enoc hesitated for a minute and then, thinking no one would be about at that time of day, said: "Well, it looks as if I'll have to try to do the job, but remember to call me early enough, Marged."

"You can trust me to do that," said Marged.

As Enoc had never seen a wedding in the Church of England, he didn't know what duties were connected with 'giving away', though he had some idea that 'giving in marriage' was a Scriptural quotation. He began to feel afraid and uncomfortable. And to avoid making a fool of himself, he thought the best thing, after shutting up the shop, would be to run down to Mr. Brown, the parson, and find out the nature of the duties; and this he did. Enoc and the kind old parson were on excellent terms, and he got a hearty welcome, and a weight off his mind, when Mr. Brown explained that he wasn't expected to do anything except say "I do" when asked who was giving the bride away.

"And now, Mr. Huws," said the old parson, full in body and jovial in appearance—he had, by this time, completely forgotten the sharp lecture he'd had from Rhys Lewis' mother, and his Welsh not one bit better—"now, Mr. Huws," said he, "You don't come here often; will you take a glass of wine?"

"No thank you, Mr. Brown. I'm not used to such things; I'm an abstainer," said Enoc.

"Do you know what, Mr. Huws, you Calvinists are a funny lot; you're worse than Catholics. You think yourselves too godly to take the good things the Great King's given to his humble creatures, and think you'll go to heaven before other people because of it. But believe me, Mr. Huws, you won't. You won't get there a step quicker for not taking God's creations; you'll see. And you've always, as I said many a time to Abel Huws—he was a good Christian—got your heads hidden in your feathers like a hen moulting. It's soon enough to moult when we have to leave this place. It's an odd sin too, not to take the best things you can have in life, and pulling a long face as if your nose was on a grindstone all the time. It shows an ungrateful and sinful spirit, and you'll see someday Mr. Huws, that I'm right."

"I almost believe you're right already, Mr. Brown," said Enoc," for my nose has been on a grindstone long enough, goodness knows."

"I know that," said Mr. Brown, "but let me see … but I'd better hold my tongue. I know Mr. Simon will marry you, but that doesn't matter. When will it take place, Mr. Huws? Miss Trefor's a very proper sort of girl, and likely to make a good wife. When is it to be, Mr. Huws?"

"Heaven only knows," said Enoc, rising to leave.

"There you are, Mr. Huws," said Mr. Brown, on shaking hands with Enoc; "aren't you ashamed of yourself? I've married Tom Solet three times, and tomorrow will be the fourth. Shame on you. Remember, Mr. Huws, if Mr. Simon won't marry you, I will, and for nothing; I'd count it an honour, and I'd tie you up safe enough."

Nothing is better for a man troubled and depressed in spirit than mixing with other people. Enoc felt, after worrying alone for days and nights, lighter and brighter of spirit after he'd been to the Rectory and spoken to Mr. Brown. Though Enoc was so without hope, Mr. Brown's reference to Miss Trefor as his future wife was without doubt, balm to his wounds. ('Why would everyone talk like this, if the thing's not to be?' said Enoc to himself.) By now, he was starting to feel some interest in Marged's wedding, and wasn't sorry he'd have to take some part in it; This would give him a little experience for when his turn came. He directed his steps towards Didymus' dwelling, to invite him to the breakfast, but was saved the journey, for on his way he chanced on Jones the policeman. Jones, unlike his brethren, turned up—in some way Enoc couldn't account for—whenever he was needed, and though Enoc wasn't particularly fond of him, he felt he was under so much obligation to him, and Jones had so much to do with his fate, he could do no less than admire and respect him.

"Hello," said Jones, "you're a stranger, aren't you? I haven't seen for I don't know how long, Mr. Huws. Tell me, have you stopped going to Tŷ'n yr Ardd?"

"I've not been there for some days," said Enoc.

"Ah," said Jones, "I knew that's how it would be. Wasn't I right? I'm glad you understand it all now. But the old woman's very sick, I heard?"

"Have you heard anything today?" asked Enoc.

"Yes, Mr. Huws. She's a lot worse. There'll be a crisis there some day; but I'm glad you understand how things are," said Jones.

"Will you be free in the morning? Will you come to Marged's wedding breakfast? She's prepared plenty of food, and it'd be a pity if it wasn't eaten. Can you come? asked Enoc.

"I can, and I'll be glad of the chance," said Jones. "And so the old Mary Magdalene's leaving you? What a deliverance!"

"It is," said Enoc, "and I wish it was all over. But tell me, have you seen Didymus tonight? I'd like him to be there, too."

"Leave that to me, Mr. Huws. I'll see him shortly," said Jones.

"Thank you, and remember to be there in time," said Enoc, filled with worry as to whether he himself would be able to get up early enough to give Marged away.

41

MARRY THEY WILL

Enoc couldn't for the life of him get to sleep the night before Marged's wedding—indeed, he wasn't able to sleep—except fitfully—since the afternoon he was last at Tŷ'n yr Ardd. He would toss and turn in his bed until it was almost time to get up, and then when Marged knocked on his bedroom door at seven—just as she did every morning throughout the year—Enoc would feel half-dead from lack of sleep. The night before Marged's wedding, Enoc had heard the clock strike one, two, three, four, five, and he hadn't slept a wink; and then he slept like a log. At quarter to six, Marged knocked hard on his bedroom door. Enoc answered in his sleep, but in fact he knew no more about her having knocked than if she'd knocked on the side of the moon. Marged waited for the clock to strike six, then went to his door and asked politely: "Are you getting up, master?" No answer. Marged knocked again, but there was no response. She was seriously alarmed, and thought he'd died, and she set off to seek help; but she turned back, and put her ear to the crack of the door. How curious; not so long before, Enoc had listened anxiously at the same crack for Marged's snoring; and here she was now, listening just as anxiously for Enoc's snores. What importance there is in snoring; and what a relief it was to hear Enoc snoring heavily and regularly, and what power it lent to her arm to knock on the door till it was almost off its hinges; if she'd knocked so hard on the lid of a coffin, she'd have awakened the dead.

"Hello! What's the matter?" said Enoc, jumping out of bed and thinking the house was coming down around his head.

"If you don't mind, master … you're going to be late," said Marged.

"All right, Marged," said Enoc, and started to realise where he was, and what was to happen that morning. He looked at his watch; five past six; there was plenty of time. He sat on the side of the bed; just for a minute, before he began to dress himself. He closed his eyes, just for a minute, then it seemed as though he was trying to hit something with the left side of his head, and after failing, he tried with the right side, but to no purpose. He changed his tactics, and like a billy goat, tried to hit the something with his forehead, and came close to falling, which made him open his eyes, to shut them again, and to go through the same process many times, till he heard Marged coming noisily up the stairs and saying: "Well in the name of all that's righteous ..." but Enoc coughed loudly, as though half choking, and Marged turned back.

He was, by this time, quite awake, and in order to convince Marged of this, he made as much noise as he could, by for instance, lifting the lid of his clothes box and letting it fall suddenly, and banging the water jug against the sink, as if he were selling crockery. He looked at his watch; ten past seven! Where in the world had he been since five past six? He could hardly believe his eyes. He must have been asleep, for it felt as if he'd just been sitting on the side of the bed for a couple of minutes. Enoc sympathised greatly with Marged now, for he realised he must have caused her a good deal of anxiety; and in order to convince her fully that he was really awake and almost ready to come down, Enoc, completely out of character, sang out loud, though his heart wasn't in it. In a few minutes, he was down in the kitchen and smartly dressed, and this put an end to Marged's worries. She, along with Betsi Pwel, had been ready to go to church for some time. Marged said: "Well, master, I was just thinking you'd never get up, and here it is, twenty past seven."

"There's plenty of time; and I suspect you never got to bed at all, Marged, having prepared a breakfast like this, and then being ready so soon," said Enoc.

"Yes I did," said Marged, "but, oh dear, I've been up since four by the clock in the bedroom, and that was half an hour too early, and everything was ready before Betsi came; and when did you come, Betsi?"

"Half past five by the town clock," said Betsi.

"You're rare ones; I'd like to be as wide-awake in the morning," said Enoc.

"I'll warrant you'll be wide-awake enough on the morning you and Miss Trefor get married, won't he, Betsi?" said Marged.

"Can I have a cup of tea, please, Marged, for I feel very what d'you call it," said Enoc.

"Well, there's been a cup waiting for you for an hour, master. But remember, don't have more than a slice or two of bread and butter with it, or you'll not be able to enjoy your breakfast when we come back from the church," said Marged, all sweetness and light. "And now," she said, after pouring Enoc's tea, "as Betsi lives near the church, we'll go there, and you'll be in church when the clock strikes eight, won't you, master?"

"Of course I will," said Enoc; and Marged and Betsi departed. Enoc drank the cup of tea without touching the bread and butter. Then he filled his pipe, because there was plenty of time to have a smoke before going to church, and he sat down in a comfortable chair in front of the fire. He felt extremely sleepy, and well he might, for, as I've pointed out, he'd hardly slept for weeks, and there was no use him going to the church too soon. Enoc began to smoke and think, and let his pipe go out. He lit his pipe again and again, his chin fell on his chest, his pipe fell from his hand, and then … then he slept heavily. He was awakened by a hammering on the door. Enoc leapt to his feet, looked at the clock; quarter past eight! He flung his hat on his head and rushed to the door. Jones the policeman was there, having come to fetch him, protesting that Marged had almost had a fit, and Mr. Brown was swearing he wouldn't go on with the service if Enoc didn't come to give Marged away. Jones and Enoc rushed to the church. Jones went to the vestry to alert Mr. Brown to Enoc's arrival, and

Enoc went ahead of him up to the altar. In a single glance, Enoc saw more than he'd bargained for. There were between a hundred and fifty and two hundred people who'd come to see the ceremony in the old church, everyone smiling from ear to ear, and grinning derisively. But more obvious than the rest, near the altar, and anxiously awaiting his arrival, Enoc saw Marged's face, looking like a full moon, and as red as a cock's comb. Enoc didn't know where to hide his shame; he was dripping with sweat; and when he'd sat down by the altar, and run his hand through his hair, it was as damp as a dishcloth. Mr. Brown immediately came forward in his clerical robes. By now eighty years old, he looked plump and kindly, but with harmless mischief in his look that morning. Mr. Brown took the trouble to organise the company, and, out of pity for Enoc, put him with his back to the congregation, for which Enoc was very thankful. Though Enoc was so flustered, he couldn't help noticing the great variety in the attire of the wedding party. Marged and Betsi Pwel were dressed in brand new green gowns the colour of grass, and bonnets the same colour, heavily trimmed with red; a red so bright as to give Enoc a headache looking at it. Robert Jones, the best man, who also worked under the Local Board, was in a coat and waistcoat of home-made stuff woven in Caerwys which had seen a few winters, and yellow trousers which were starting to darken about the knees, clear proof that Robert wore them to chapel on Sundays and to the midweek prayer meetings. But the bridegroom, Tom Solet, gained most of his attention; Tom was considered a bit of a miser, and Enoc well knew this. But Enoc saw that Tom, no doubt after hearing Jones the policeman say Marged had money, had invested in a new pair of corduroy trousers, with a large fly and big white horn buttons; they were too long by three inches, and turned up to that extent at the bottom. To be fair to Tom, he'd not worn them till this morning, so how could he have had them altered? On his back was a coat of blue superfine West of England cloth and a canary coloured waistcoat with brass buttons, and whatever were their deficiencies—and there were—the tailor who'd designed and made them had gone to render up his account many years ago. These had been Tom's wedding coat and waistcoat when he'd married his first wife, and they were now hearing the wedding service for the fourth time, and no doubt knew it well as did Mr. Brown himself. Enoc was struck, too, by the different appearances of those before him. Marged and Betsi—especially Marged—had happy faces as red as furnaces. Robert Jones was pale and serious, as if he were on trial, and Tom was clearly relishing his portion, with his face toward the ground, looking from under his brows like a pig eating peas. Enoc felt the absurdity of his position, and wondered what had induced him to place himself in such company. Though Mr. Brown hurried through the service, it seemed terribly long to Enoc. And yet the service was not without comfort and pleasure to him. Enoc was, as the reader knows, a generous man, and had given away much in the course of his life, but never had his heart been more willing to give than when he gave away Marged, and he'd have happily given her away sooner, had he been asked. Mr. Brown didn't waste time on these occasions, and Enoc was glad to get into the vestry, out of the sight of the congregation, to finish the business, and to be a witness to the cross of the one and of the other. Mr. Brown handed the certificate to Tom Solet, and Tom pulled his purse from his breast pocket to pay for the marriage, but Mr. Brown stopped him, saying: "Never mind, Tom, I won't charge you this time. I'll treat it as a discount on the others, but remember, Tom, I'll charge you next time."

At this, Marged looked at him indignantly, and didn't invite him to the breakfast, and the sexton had to suffer the same fate.

Enoc slipped home along one of the back streets, and didn't see the shower of rice poured on the happy couple's heads, though it was his rice, for he learned later that Marged had supplied the neighbours with rice the previous evening to honour her wedding.

My chapter's already too long to find room for describing the breakfast; suffice to say that the conversation between Jones the policeman and Didymus was as good as a sermon, and that in their company Enoc forgot his troubles for three quarters of an hour. On her wedding day Marged only got one present, and that from her master, namely a lovely set of crockery, which caused the taciturn bridegroom to remark—his only words in the course of the breakfast: "Those things'll look nice in our corner cupboard."

But in the long and detailed account sent by Didymus to the *County Chronicle*, it was said 'the presents were too numerous to mention'. And that was no doubt true; for it's pretty certain Didymus didn't count every cup, saucer, plate, bowl, and teapot in the set. After the breakfast, the world called on Jones the policeman and Didymus to depart, and after about an hour Enoc bade farewell to Marged and Tom, who went off to spend their '*mis mêl*'[1], or rather their honey day, at the Coach and Horses, a public house about a mile from town. Here, Tom had celebrated all his weddings, and generally invited friends and well-wishers to celebrate with him there, notably Isaac the harpist. On this occasion, they stayed in the Coach and Horses till midnight and it was in a handcart—so it was reported to Enoc, though he didn't enquire into the truth of it—in a handcart, that Tom was brought home that night, Robert Jones in the shafts, pulling, and Marged pushing from behind. Enoc's dealings with Marged did not entirely end on this day, for a few days later she had problems, and it was to Enoc she went with her troubles; but that's the last, as far as I know, the reader will hear of Marged. Perhaps I should add that Marged survived Tom Solet; he'd at last met his match.

It's hardly necessary to say that Enoc, after the breakfast and merriment of the morning, wasn't in a mood to go to the shop, and when he looked at the table and saw the abundance of uneaten food, he—in accordance with his good nature—sent one

---

[1] '*mis mêl*'—literally '*honey month*', which is no doubt where the word '*honeymoon*' comes from, a month being roughly one 'moon' or lunar cycle.

of his lads to invite the old and needy men and women of the neighbourhood to his house, and there he fed them, and made them tea and coffee himself, till nothing but crumbs and bare bones remained. At last he was left by himself in the midst of the mess, and for the first time, realised he was without a maidservant, and hadn't thought of seeking one. He didn't know which way to turn and was ashamed to think how inept he'd been. After putting some coal on the fire, which had nearly gone out, Enoc went to the parlour, away from the dirty dishes and the mess, hoping to see Jones the policeman—his succour in all misfortune—passing by. He believed Jones would be able to find him a maidservant immediately. He looked through the window for hours, expecting to see Jones, but Jones might have gone by unnoticed many times, for Enoc had long forgotten who he was looking for, and his thoughts were entirely possessed by Miss Trefor. Afternoon was on its way when there before his window stood a young, smart, and attractive girl. She looked at the window and at the door, up and down, as though she doubted whether this was the house she wanted.

"Who in the world is that lady?" said Enoc to himself. Then the lady knocked at the door, and Enoc went to open it.

"Are you Mr. Huws, sir?" asked she.

"Yes, that's my name," said Enoc.

"May I speak with you?"

"Yes, Oh yes; come in," said Enoc.

Enoc put a chair for her near the window, so as to get a good look at her, for he'd noticed she was worth looking at. After sitting down, the lady said with a smile, disclosing a set of teeth (her own) as alike as peas in a pod: "I've called, Mr. Huws, to ask if you want a housekeeper."

"Just the thing I do want," said Enoc, "but I'm afraid my place wouldn't suit you; there's no one here but myself, I don't have a maidservant, and my housekeeper has to do all that needs to be done in the house."

"I know that, and it makes no difference to me, for I'm used to work, and I know how to keep a house." said the young girl; Enoc was surprised at hearing her say so, for her attire, in his opinion, was smart and expensive.

"Very good," said Enoc. "What wages are you asking?"

"Twenty pounds; I've been getting more," she said.

"That's five pounds more than I've been paying," said Enoc.

"I hope," said the young woman, "that you'll see the difference in the service, for I've been in good places, and I've learned a good deal."

"Well," said Enoc, "I don't mind paying twenty pounds if you suit me," for he believed her appearance, when compared with Marged, was worth five pounds, and he added, "When could you start?"

"Whenever you like," she said.

"Well," said Enoc, I'd like you to start at once, for to tell the truth, there's no one here now, and the house is in a mess. Could you come in the morning?"

"I'll come tonight at nine o'clock, if I may," said the young woman.

"Excellent. What's your name?" asked Enoc.

"I'm Miss Bifan," she said.

"Very well, Miss Bifan, you'll be here by nine then," said Enoc. And thus the discussions ended, and as Enoc opened the door for Miss Bifan to leave, he saw Kitty, the maidservant from Tŷ'n yr Ardd, coming towards him with a note. Had some spirit whispered in Miss Trefor's ear that she now had a rival?

42

GONE

Enoc read the note:

"Tŷ'n yr Ardd,

Dear Mr. Huws,

You have become a great stranger. As far as I remember, I said nothing when we last spoke that would be sufficient reason for this estrangement, and if I did, I apologise. There is something said in a certain Book about visiting the sins of the fathers on the children, but I don't believe the Book mentioned visiting the sins of the daughters on the parents. Perhaps it did and I've forgotten. However, you know you're valued by my father, and dear to my mother, and it is scarcely just or worthy of you to punish them for their daughter's sin. My father is low and weary of spirit. I know he believes I've offended you. Poor me! I try to do my duty, according to my lights, but in spite of all, I offend everyone around me. My mother, I'm sorry to say, gets worse each day. I've done my best for her, God knows, and my heart is almost breaking. She can't understand why you don't come to see her. Will you come? She won't be here long. Mr. Simon has been here at times, but she doesn't seem to care very much for him. Will you come to see her? If seeing me is any hindrance, I'll promise to go down to the cellar while you're here.

Yours truly,
S. TREFOR.

P.S. Excuse my Welsh, you know I'm not used to writing in Welsh.—S.T.

"Tell Miss Trefor I'll be there at once," said Enoc to Kitty.

"She badly wants to see you, Mr. Huws," said Kitty.

"Who does?" asked Enoc.

"Miss Trefor," said Kitty, who knew how to please Enoc.

"How do you know that, Kitty?"

"Because I know," said Kitty, "because she doesn't look the same since you stopped coming; it's as if she were in a dream. Did you quarrel, Mr. Huws?"

"Your mistress is very ill, Kitty, and Miss Trefor has enough troubles without thinking about me," said Enoc.

"She has, heaven knows," said Kitty, "more than you know about. She hasn't taken off her things for I don't know how long, and I don't know how she manages. And I'm afraid the mistress will never get better; she's behaving very strangely, as if she had something on her mind. And master is—you won't tell that I told you, Mr. Huws? He's not acting right."

"Well, what's he doing, Kitty?" asked Enoc.

"You won't say I told you Mr. Huws?—he's drinking constantly day and night, till he is quite stupid, and that vexes Miss Trefor. It's a curious house, I can tell you. She's often asked when I last saw you, and she wonders why you don't go there. I know she badly wants to see you, sir."

"Take care not to tell anyone your master's drinking, Kitty," said Enoc . "Under stress, a man does many things he shouldn't do, and wouldn't do at other times, and your mistress' illness has doubtless greatly affected him. Mind, Kitty; don't say anything to anyone."

"Me? I wouldn't take my weight in gold to tell anyone; except you, because you're like one of the family, Mr. Huws," said Kitty.

"All right, Kitty, go back now and tell Miss Trefor I'll come soon," said Enoc.

"She *will* be glad to see you," said Kitty.

Getting to hear something from Miss Trefor, and especially getting an invitation to Tŷ'n yr Ardd, was like a salve to Enoc's wound. At the same time he determined to not appear to hurry.

He judged that to rush there immediately, would be '*infra dig*'. Though he was burning with desire to go, he waited for over an hour before starting, and when he went, he walked in a leisurely and self-respectful manner. On his way he pondered how Susi would look at him, and what she'd say to him. He swore he'd not say a syllable about what took place when they had last spoke, unless she mentioned it first. And Enoc kept his word, because he found something else to think about. Though it wasn't yet dark, the curtains were closed at every window of Tŷ'n yr Ardd, and as Enoc neared the house he felt there was a strange, alien look to it, and he couldn't make out what it was. His mind was too absorbed to realise that the closed curtains were the cause. Enoc knocked at the door, and Kitty came to open it. Kitty's eyes were wide and pale and she said quietly,

"She's gone, Mr. Huws."

"Who?" asked Enoc.

"The mistress." said Kitty.

"Gone where?" asked Enoc.

"She's dead," said Kitty.

"Dead," said Enoc, as though he'd been shot by the news, and he could scarcely move. Kitty gave a nod of confirmation, closed the door carefully, and led Enoc into the parlour, where the Captain and Miss Trefor were sitting silently with heads downcast. As he entered the room, Miss Trefor rose to her feet, and without saying a word, shook Enoc's hand, gripping it tightly and nervously, sending a tremor through his whole body. The Captain did the same. Enoc fell into a chair, overcome by his feelings, for he'd loved Mrs. Trefor greatly, for her own sake, as well for being Susi's mother, and he hadn't imagined her death was at hand. Though Enoc was generally not too perceptive, he couldn't help seeing that the Captain was heavy with drink. He looked listlessly into the fire, with tears rolling down his cheeks.

Drunkenness makes a man incautious, and in some circumstances is the means of bringing out what little good is left in his nature.

I know a man who was never seen to pray except when he was drunk; and I have known one or two men from whom it was not possible to get a gift or charity except when they were in their cups. Even Captain Trefor, who'd lived for years in deceit and hypocrisy was not wholly bereft of some sort of feeling. There was a remnant left of human nature in him. Enoc's *true* feelings touched what feelings the Captain still had, and he wept. Miss Trefor's feelings had for weeks been stretched to their limits, and refused now to give way, and her face was composed and unfurrowed, but deathly white, as though she'd lost every drop of her blood. She was not displeased to see Enoc show such feelings; he and her mother had been great friends, and she somehow felt that Enoc's face was an interpreter of whatever language had died in her own face. The Captain, as usual, was first to speak, and said: "This is a heavy blow, Mr. Huws, especially to me, and so to speak, a deadly blow, for when a man has reached... that is to say, has lost his life partner, and that too without having thought the thing was near, is to one at my age, the same thing, in a manner of speaking, as losing his own life, for she was my life and my everything, and I can almost say—and I will say—that I'd wish to go into the grave with her."

"If you and I, father," said Susi, "were as ready as mother was, that would be the best thing for us, to go together, but I'm afraid we're not. Mother loved Jesus Christ; can we say that? Death is a terrible thing, father, if we can't say we love Jesus Christ."

"That's true enough, my girl, and let's hope we'll be able to say that when the time comes," said the Captain, who, no matter how serious were the circumstances, could be hypocritical, and no matter how drunk he was, his mind was crystal clear.

"The time," said Susi, wishing to make the best of the occasion— for her father's way of living had pained her much; and Enoc marvelled how she could be so self-possessed; "the time, as you know, father, cannot be predicted, as it could not with mother."

"The Holy Scriptures teach us that, and several quotations come fresh into my mind at this moment," said the Captain.

"Did your mother go quickly at the end, Miss Trefor?" asked Enoc.

"Most quickly and unexpectedly, Mr. Huws," said Susi.

"Yes, most quickly; but you and I did our best for her," said the Captain.

"I didn't do my best for her, father, and I'll never forgive myself for my carelessness. I thought she was no worse than she'd been for days and I left her for ten minutes to write a letter; and by the time I came back she was dead, without my having been able to do anything for her; not so much as to hold her dear hand to ease her dying. Oh, it seems so cruel for her to have died alone; it's eating me inside."

"It was the will of the Lord, my girl," said the Captain, "to take His servant Moses to Himself without any eye to see it; and so it was with your mother."

"Yes," said Susi, with a sting in her words, "Moses was taken in that way while the people sinned, and perhaps it was the same here."

"It is a great grief to me, Miss Trefor," said Enoc, "that I didn't get to see your mother before she died."

"How was that, Mr. Huws? What was the reason for your long absence?" asked the Captain.

"None of us thought," said Susi, to conceal Enoc's difficulty in answering, "that mother was so near death. Scarcely anyone here has seen her except Mr. Simon and the doctor. I'm very glad you've come here tonight, Mr. Huws, for I know nothing about the arrangements that must be seen to on such an occasion; but I know you'll help us, Mr. Huws. We haven't the means to go to great expense."

"Not the means?" said the Captain. "What do you mean, Susi? Not the means? Your mother shall be buried like a princess, if my eyes are open to see it. But it's not fitting for us to walk here and there, and Mr. Huws will do all that for us, in accordance with his usual kindness."

"Leave it all to me, I'll make all the necessary arrangements," said Enoc.

At that moment Kitty came to the door, and beckoned to Miss Trefor, who left the room.

Enoc said: "Captain Trefor, I'm going to ask you a favour, and I hope you won't refuse me. You know that Mrs. Trefor and I were great friends. I looked upon her as a mother to me. Will you allow me—don't be angry with me for asking such a thing—to make all the arrangements for the funeral and bear the whole cost? I'd be happy to do that if you'll let me."

"Thank you, Mr. Huws," said the Captain, "but it's impossible, for that would take away my last privilege. I couldn't think of anyone doing such a thing, at least not without asking my daughter, and I know she'd be equally opposed to it; indeed more so."

"I'd meant to ask you," said Enoc, "if you'd consent to it, not to say a word to Miss Trefor or anyone else about the matter, and I'd consider it a privilege to be allowed to do this for Mrs. Trefor. I hope I've not offended you, but I wish to be able to do this."

"Well," said the Captain, and he stopped a minute as if to consider, "if anyone else, yes, even Sir Watkin himself, had offered to do such a thing, I'd have said, 'No, thank you'. But when I recall what friendship there was between you and Mrs. Trefor, and indeed my personal obligations to you, I can't say 'No' to you, Mr. Huws; on condition that no one is to know about it."

"Many thanks," said Enoc; "and now I'll go about the arrangements, and don't you worry about anything."

The Captain tried to stand to shake hands with Enoc, but fell back into his chair. He realised that his drunkenness was obvious, and said: "Mr. Huws, pardon me; in my bitter tribulation I have taken two, ('and twenty', he might almost have added) glasses of whisky, and through not being very used to it, it has affected me. I know you'll forgive me at this time; my troubles are great."

"They are," said Enoc, "and I'm sorry for you, but allow me to be bold with you. Keep from intoxicating drink—for a few days, anyway; decorum requires it."

"Quite right, I will; goodnight, dear Mr. Huws," said the Captain.

After saying goodnight to Miss Trefor, Enoc left; and by this time he had enough on his mind; the new maid coming to the house by nine o'clock and carrying out all the arrangements for Mrs. Trefor's funeral.

"Susi," said the Captain, "put your mind at rest; Mr. Huws will look after all the arrangements. And now go to bed, my girl. I can't think about bed tonight; I'll just throw myself on the sofa. Good night, my dear girl."

Susi left the room with a sigh, and the Captain threw himself on the sofa, and slept heavily. After the laying out woman had completed certain strange procedures—which persist today in such circumstances—upon the body, and had gone away, Susi went to bed, taking Kitty with her, for she thought she couldn't be alone that night. After ten minutes, Kitty was sleeping quietly and peacefully. But Miss Trefor couldn't sleep. She knew her father was snoring on the sofa, though she couldn't hear him. All was silence and the silence lay heavy on her. She felt lonely and frightened, and said, "Kit, Kit, are you asleep, Kit?"

Kitty did not answer, she'd given way to slumber, which, after all the running around, and coming and going, she'd well earned. Miss Trefor went close up to her and whispered, "Yes, sleep, Kit, you've had no more rest than I for weeks, and you deserve peace tonight. But how is it I can't sleep? Oh, this silence keeps me awake. How strange and alien it all is; How different it was this time last night! The running up and down the stairs, and poor mother with us, alive though ill; how quiet it is tonight. How far she's gone. Oh, heavens, this very minute I thought I heard her say 'Give me a drink, my dear child'. Did I imagine it? I'm almost sure I heard her. I'll be listening more carefully next time. I'm weak—and fanciful. How hard it is to believe she'll never speak another word. She was here earlier; this afternoon. Where is she now? Yes, she; because there's only her body in the next room. Where is *she*? In the great eternal world! Where is that great eternal world? Is it far away? Has she arrived? Has someone come to fetch her, to show her the way? Or has her spirit wandered and got lost in space? Will she wander around, I wonder, for thousands of years before finding the everlasting world? Oh why didn't I stay with her till the end, instead of going to write to Enoc Huws? Perhaps she'd have told me Jesus Christ was with her. The night before last, she repeated the verse, 'When you pass through the waters I will be with you'. He didn't forget her, did He? He didn't need to be with someone else at just that moment? How foolishly I'm talking! Am I losing my senses? Kit, are you asleep? Oh, how lonely I am—and I will be! We have no friends; I never felt any great need for friends before. But we have no special ones. Yes, we have; Enoc Huws is a true friend, the only friend we have. How stupid I was to refuse him. There's no better man in the county, and I know we've been entirely dependent on him for a while. I think I love him very much, and yet I can't reconcile myself to the thought of marrying him. If he were to propose again, I wouldn't refuse him. No, I don't think I'll get another proposal from him; I'll stick with my father. I wish father was godly; but he isn't; it's no use flattering him. He's a slave to drink and pretends to be otherwise, as if even I didn't know. My duty, I think, is to stick with him to the end. Oh God, bless this occasion for his salvation's sake. How awkward everything will be without a mother; what will become of me with such a father? I'll try to do my duty, and trust in God. Oh, how we all have deserted my dearest mother, and how soon! To leave her in that dark room with no one to keep her company, as though we don't belong to her! Oh, it's cruel; how soon! I'm mad—no, I'm not—I'm sure that it's harsh and cruel, to leave her all alone, and I'll go and keep her company; I can't stay here."

Day dawned; Kit awoke after ten hours of sweet sleep, which was rare for her, and sat up in bed. She recalled all that had happened the previous day. She looked for Miss Trefor; she must have got up earlier, and that wasn't unusual. She dressed hurriedly. She went down to the kitchen, which was cold and without a fire in the grate, and went towards the parlour, the door of which was ajar. She opened it quietly. The Captain was sleeping heavily on the sofa, but Miss Trefor wasn't there. She closed the door carefully. "She must have gone out," thought Kit. She inspected the doors; they were locked, just as she'd left them before going to bed the previous night. Even Kit began to worry. She couldn't think of lighting a fire and making any sort of noise without first learning where Miss Trefor was. She took off her slippers so as not to make a sound, and went upstairs and to her own bedroom. No; no one was there. She searched the other rooms with the same result. There was only one other place to look. Had she dared, by herself, go into the room where her mother lay? The door of that room was half open, and Kitty felt a shiver like water run down her back as she opened it a little wider and peeped in. Yes, there she was. Half dressed, with a shawl over her shoulders, Susan lay alongside her mother's body on the bed, with her right arm around her, and her head against her head on the pillow! It seems incredible, but it was a fact. And there was little difference between them: the two faces were as white as snow, the two bodies perfectly still, one in a deep sleep and *breathing*, and the other in a deep sleep, and *not breathing*.

43

CAPTAIN TREFOR'S SOLILOQUY

Miss Bifan had taken her place as housekeeper in Siop y Groes before Enoc remembered he'd not asked about her character, or even inquired to whom she was related or where she'd last been in service. And now it was too late to ask. "What does it matter to whom she's related or where she was last," said Enoc, "as long as she serves her purpose?" Besides, Enoc had enough to think about, without spending time thinking about his new housekeeper. He'd undertaken to make the arrangements for Mrs. Trefor's funeral, and this he did, sparing neither expense nor trouble. For the funeral, the service in the house was read by Mr. Simon, and at the church and graveyard by Mr. Brown, and Captain Trefor declared that everything had passed off 'most happily'. After a day or two, in accordance with the Captain's wishes, all the bills were sent to him and—in Miss Trefor's absence—Enoc added up the total cost, and presented the money to the Captain. Then the Captain went round and paid everybody. On settling each bill, the Captain said he was surprised at it being so small; that he'd expected it to have been as much again, and indeed—so to speak—had it been three times as much, he wouldn't have grumbled. He spoke like this to everyone when paying them, and it made the recipients, especially the man who made the coffin, lament he'd not charged more; and the latter said, after the Captain had turned his back, "No matter what people say, the Captain's got plenty of money."

After a while everyone, with two or three exceptions, forgot that such a person as Mrs. Trefor had ever existed. And so, dear reader, will you and I be forgotten one of these days. When we die, our neighbours will ask two questions. The first: How old were we? And the older the better; those who are younger will flatter themselves that they might attain our age. The second: How much were we worth? In other words, how much property do we leave behind us? If it's a lot, the living person will comfort himself by thinking he might acquire so much before he dies; and if it's little or nothing, they'll comfort themselves by thinking that if they die poor, they won't be the first. After gaining this knowledge, and putting the shutters up as our corpse goes by on its way to the churchyard, and pulling them down again when everything's passed, that will be the end of it. The next day, everything will go on just as if we hadn't been a part of this wondrous old world. Mr. Simon preached a sufficiently dry funeral sermon, and Eos Prydain and his choir sang 'The Vital Spark', and then there was only one who truly felt that everywhere was empty without Mrs. Trefor. I almost forgot to mention that one of the Coed Madog miners, who was a bard, and was known by the euphonious '*ffugenw*' of 'Roaring Lion', sent two '*englynion*'[1] to the *County Chronicle* on Mrs. Trefor's death; but I must say that they were no more like *englynion* than a cow is like a haystack. It's true they were the best the Roarer could produce, for he spent three nights writing them, and they gave great satisfaction to his fellow-workmen, and even to the Captain, for when he next saw the 'Lion' he gave him a two shilling piece.

Thus Mrs. Trefor ended her days; and before many hours had passed, the Captain had cast off his cares. Now he had time to give full attention to Coed Madog mine. But there was one thing that troubled him, and troubled him greatly. His position was something like this; he was poor. He believed by this time—no matter what he'd believed before—that there wasn't a shred of

---

[1] '*englynion*'—the plural of '*englyn*'. Poetry is a complex matter in Wales. Here, there are two types of poetry; poetry with rules and poetry without rules. Poetry with rules comes in twenty-four different metres, and the englyn is one of those twenty-four. Four lines of ten, six, seven and seven syllables. To explain the rules would require another book, and that book has already been written.

a hope of lead in Coed Madog. And yet Coed Madog was his only hope; and if that died, he'd not have a shilling to his name. His conscience, if he had one, knew it was Enoc Huws' money that was carrying on the mine; Mr. Denman had for some time failed to answer the calls, though he was still in name a co-owner. The Captain, too, thought he was sufficiently sharp to perceive that the only reason Enoc continued to spend so much on the mine was his love for Miss Trefor—his daughter—and the minute that came to an end, he and Coed Madog would go to the dogs. Indeed he'd feared, when Enoc had for a time ceased to visit Tŷ'n yr Ardd, that the misfortune had come to pass, and that was why he'd fallen into drinking more than usual. But now he comforted himself that his daughter and Enoc appeared to be on most friendly terms. But … (Away with 'but', here I am, using it in two consecutive sentences! I remember Dr. Edwards of Bala mocking the Welshman's use of the word 'but' when it serves no purpose. But I think 'but' is necessary here; and as every preacher, having listed the main points of the sermon, begins again with "But firstly"—a purposeless 'but' if I ever heard one—surely I may use it where there's real need) … but, thought the Captain, if his daughter and Enoc Huws were likely to marry, he would, by carrying on the mine, impoverish his son-in-law, and thus 'so to speak', make himself poor, and throw away money he might some day need to keep body and soul together. At that time the Captain would have given a lot for definite information about Enoc and his daughter's relationship. The Captain devoted great diligence and watchfulness to discerning whether Susi and Enoc were in love. He lowered himself so much as to listen at the keyhole when they were in a room by themselves, and even hid in the garden when Enoc was leaving. And on more than one occasion, while doing so, he'd talk to himself, along these lines: "Well, Mr. Huws, it's about the time you normally go home; and you are, as a rule, quite punctual. And Susi's sure to come and open the gate and say goodnight. And if I saw you give my daughter a kiss, sir—and it would be wonderful to see it—tomorrow I'd speak to you after this fashion: 'Mr. Huws, my hopes have turned out to be hollow. I am but a fallible being, and I've been disappointed. I'm afraid there's no hope of our finding lead in Coed Madog, and it would be folly for you and I to spend more money. I feel honesty requires I tell you this. At the same time, if you're keen to carry on, I'll take my chance with you, though I must confess my purse is not as full as yours, and the bottom's already in sight. If you take my advice, I honestly think it best to give up'."

Soon, Enoc would come out, and Susi with him. They'd talk about the weather, shake hands in a friendly manner, say goodnight, and that would be it; and the Captain would curse the day he was born. If there was no more than friendship between Enoc and his daughter, the Captain felt it his duty to carry on the mine as long as he could. But, for the life of him, he couldn't help believing there was some understanding between the young people, and if so, it would be a shame for Enoc to spend his money uselessly, and perhaps bring himself to a position where he couldn't afford to marry. After some mental turmoil, and not a little pondering, the Captain determined to put the question directly to his daughter. And one night, when he and she were in the parlour, and he'd anointed his resolve with a fair dose of whisky, the Captain said: "Susi, something's been weighing heavily on my mind for some time, and causing me a little anxiety, indeed, making me live between hope and fear, and, in a manner of speaking, making me unfit, to some degree, to give due attention to my duties; duties, my girl, that as you know, require my full attention."

"What's that, father?" said Susi.

"Well," said the Captain, "it's a delicate matter, I know, but your mother, bless her, has left us, and because of that, you and I should confide more in one another, my child. The question is this—and I know you'll answer it honestly and openly; is there anything between you and Enoc Huws? Don't be afraid to answer, Susi, for I know, however things stand, you'll have done right."

"Anything between Mr. Huws and me in what way, father?" asked Susi.

"Well," said the Captain, "I expected you to understand my question without my having to spell it out; but what I want to ask—and as a father, I consider I have a right to ask, is this: are you engaged to Mr. Huws?"

"Engaged in what, father?" asked Miss Trefor.

"Engaged to be married, of course; you understand very well what I mean, Susi, but you want to torment me," said the Captain, a little peevishly.

"Good gracious! I've never been engaged to Mr. Huws or anyone else," said Susi, emphatically.

"And there's no quiet understanding between you two that it will come to that one of these days?" asked the Captain, adding, "Remember I've nothing to say against it."

"None at all, father, nor any likelihood of such a thing ever taking place. What made you think of such a thing?" said Susi.

"Well," said the Captain, disappointed, "I didn't think the thing was impossible, or indeed improbable, but if things are as you say, all right; I know it's no use my ordering you to do this or that, and that you'll do what you like."

"I'll try my best to do what's right, father, and my intention is to stick with you to the bitter end," said Susi.

"Bitter it'll be, I'm afraid, my girl," said the Captain, thoughtfully. There the conversation ended, and Susi was thankful her father hadn't asked whether Enoc had proposed, for she'd have had to tell the truth, and she knew her father would have been furious if he'd heard the truth. The Captain pondered a great deal that night. He'd always flattered himself that he understood human nature tolerably well, but he had to admit his daughter was a mystery to him. He could have sworn there was something between her and Enoc Huws, but he'd been mistaken. And yet he felt sure in his mind that Enoc had intentions toward Susi; still at the same time it was fairly obvious—for Susi never lied—that he hadn't made his intentions known. What was the man thinking? If he'd set his mind on Susi, why didn't he say so, and have done with it? "For," said the Captain to himself, "she wouldn't be such a fool as to refuse him. If she did, I'd kill her. Have I deceived myself, for so long, as to Mr. Huws' intentions? It's possible. Perhaps, after all, understanding a '*hen lanc*' is out of my line, though I always think I understand almost everything. And what am I to do? I'd be sorry to despoil Mr. Huws of all his money, and yet if I gave up Coed Madog, I'd be lost. And it's pretty clear that Enoc will lose heart and give it all up; he can't keep on; it's impossible that he'd keep on, always paying out, with no prospect of profit. And from where will that come? I thought Mr. Huws would have proposed to Susi before now; indeed they would have been married, and spared me all this trouble, for I'd have found comfort in their care. But now I see I must try to form some sort of a company to work Coed Madog; it's not possible for one man to bear the whole cost, and for me to get my wages. Getting machinery and the like are out of the question—all Mr. Huws' money would go—every farthing—in getting what's needed, and I can't bear to ask him to do that, even if he were such a fool as to do what I ask. And none of it would do any good in the end. But I need to do something to get my living. As to Denman, poor man, he's likely to be up the spout like me any day now. There's nothing else for it but try to form a company, and swear there's as much lead in Coed Madog as the world would ever want, but money's needed to get at it. If I had ten or a dozen fairly rich people. I could carry on for a while yet, and who knows what might turn up in the meantime; that is, somewhere else, for there's no more lead in Coed Madog than there is in my waistcoat pocket. If I could form a company, that would lighten Mr. Huws' burden, for I'm sorry to be robbing him of so much, whether he marries Susi or not. I must set Sem Llwyd to work preaching the prospects of Coed Madog Mine, and so on and so forth. Now Sem knows I'm a bit hard up, and I can't grease his hand the way I used to, he's become more independent, but he must act according to my instructions. I know he knows my secret, the stupid fool. But Sem's under my thumb, and he knows that very well. I saved his neck when Job Jones, poor fellow, was killed in Pwll y Gwynt. I don't know what made Sem take such a dislike to that clever lad. But as I said to Sem, he'll remember that night as long as he lives; it'd be so easy for me to prove him responsible for … well, as sure as my name is … yes, but who knows that except Sem? We're quits! But I must think of forming some sort of Company, *pro. tem.*, as they say, to get me over this particular stile."

44

THE REVEREND OBEDIAH SIMON

Mr. Obediah Simon, the preacher, and Eos Prydain were bosom friends. Mr. Simon had never seen a more faithful or single-minded man than Eos, and Eos had never seen a preacher who understood half as much about sol-ffa[1] as Mr. Simon. And Eos wasn't backward in making this known. After repeatedly hearing Eos praise Mr. Simon for his knowledge of sol-ffa, Thomas Bartley said he utterly failed to see what such knowledge had to do with preaching the Gospel, and he believed that Dafydd Dafis, a farmer by trade, probably knew a good deal more than Mr. Simon about '*sofl-ffa*'[2]. "And as for preachin'," added Thomas, "Mr. Simon's sermons are much too deep for my sort, and for Barbara, and we'd a thousand times sooner be listenin' to old John Dafis from Nercwys. There's a man who knows well the ways of 'is neighbours, in my opinion. You know what, I don't 'ave much taste for Mr. Simon's sermons till he gets near the end of 'em. I know it's my fault, and the man's good enough in 'is way. 'ave I ever told you what sort of a preacher I like? No? Well, this is my idea of a preacher—perhaps I'm wrong, but this is the sort I like—a preacher who speaks 'is text loud enough for us all to 'ear 'im. Now, since I've started to get old, and my 'earin's not quite as sharp as it was, I don't 'ear 'alf what they're asayin' in the text, and if a man loses the text, he's like a dog lost in a fair. There's

---

[1] 'sol-ffa'—Tonic 'sol-fa' is a pedagogical technique for teaching sight-singing, invented by Sarah Ann Glover (1785–1867) of Norwich, England and popularised by John Curwen. By the end of the nineteenth century, this notation was very widespread in Britain.

[2] '*sofl-ffa*'—A play on words which falls rather flat when translated. '*sofl*' means '*stubble*', and '*ffa*' means '*beans*', which in English, alas, means nothing whatsoever.

another thing I like in a preacher, I like 'em to be sprightly and not mumblin' to 'emselves all the time. I've got no time for these slow, 'eavy preachers, they always make me feel miserable. And that's where I say the Wesleyans beat us Methodists. Do you know what, I went to a Wesleyan meetin' a bit ago, and a roaring good meetin' it was too, and there wasn't a single preacher mutterin' to 'imself; they were all ready for action, and aputtin' their hearts in it. But there was a preacher in our chapel about a month ago, a fine and very tidy sort of man he was too, and he looked smart, but he preached so down-'arted and slow that I said to Barbara on the way 'ome from the mornin' service, 'You know what, Barbara, that man said some very good things, but I'm sure he's lost 'is wife, and very recently too; it was obvious, and I'm very sorry for 'im'. But when I asked Dafydd Dafis, I found out, and I was right glad to 'ear it, that 'is wife and kids were alive and well, and the man was worth thousands. But I'd never 'ave thought so from listenin' to 'im. There's another thing I like in a preacher, that he gives us a bit of a story now and then, like that man from '*Sir Drefaldwyn*'[3], or somewhere down south. What's 'is name? ...'ang on ... Oh yes, Joseph Tomos. You know what, he's the neatest preacher these ears of mine 'ave ever 'eard. I could listen to 'im for ever ... he's got as many stories as you like, and all of 'em just right, and he 'as so many of 'em in every sermon, and, each of 'em fits so tidy I've wondered sometimes whether he didn't imagine some of 'em; they'd be no worse for that, you know. Tell me why that man 'asn't been made a Doctor of Divinity? 'aven't the 'mericans 'eard of 'im? There's some mistake somewhere, I'm sure. And I 'eard Didymus say—and he knows almost everythin'—there's some with the title of Doctor Divine who got it by mistake. But there'd be no mistake givin' it to old Joseph, because wiser people than me say he's one of the best. But this is what I was sayin', I'd like a preacher like 'im,

---

[3] '*Sir Drefaldwyn*'—Montgomeryshire.

and I'd walk four miles tonight to hear 'im. Another thing I like in a preacher is for 'im to always get better towards the end. You 'ear some preachers who are the same at the end as they were at the beginnin'; to my mind, that's not right. Everythin' should be better at the end than the beginnin', or what's the use of beginnin' at all? 'ere I am now, beginnin'; but in case you get tired of me the last thing I'll say I'd like in a preacher is that he talks enough about Jesus Christ. I don't know what in the world is a good sermon, if it doesn't talk about Jesus Christ, and Dafydd Dafis is of the same mind as me on this, and if anyone knows what a sermon is, he knows. And yet these days I've 'eard sermons '*heb sinc na sôn*'[4] of Jesus Christ, except a bit in the prayers. But what I started with is this, that Mr. Simon's preachin' is a great deal too deep for the likes of me."

Thomas Bartley's description of Mr. Simon as a preacher was hardly correct, for his style wasn't particularly deep. Possibly the way Mr. Simon had preached of late was too deep for Thomas, because it was a fact that our minister had for some time now gone beyond singing the sermon, and—addressing his remarks principally to the young people, lectured a great deal on evolution and negativism, and had spoken a little about agnosticism, with the laudable object of preparing and strengthening the minds of Bethel's youth against the destructive floods soon to engulf the faithful of Wales. He had also put before them—and with some force—the arguments of unbelievers, and broke them into tiny fragments. Sometimes Mr. Simon arranged a sort of debating society, by bringing an unbeliever—one of the strongest—into the ring; and after giving him every advantage, giving him the high ground, and putting his back to the sun, would bring Saint Paul into the arena as his opponent, taking it upon himself to see fair play, and acting as a referee or umpire. Mr. Simon did his best

---

[4] '*heb sinc na sôn*'—'without a tinkle or a mention'; without a trace.

to appear unbiased, yet at the end of every round, it was easy to see he was giving Saint Paul rest to keep him strong, was patting him the back; and, as seemed appropriate, taking every care that he won in the end. No doubt this was this kind of '*endin*' Thomas Bartley liked. It's doubtful whether it was wise of Mr. Simon to speak so much to the people of Bethel about the counter arguments of non-believers, for not one in fifty of them had previously realised such arguments existed. But having heard Mr. Simon discuss them, some of the youths began, after the corrupt fashion of the human heart, to cherish them. It was amusing enough now and then to hear some stupid idler, who wouldn't have read a hundred pages in his life, pretending to be something of an atheist, and using words and phrases of whose meaning he knew next to nothing. Doubtless with the best intentions, Mr. Simon had used all his talents to persuade the Bethel youths not to read this or that particular book. They'd not previously heard of the book, but two or three of them immediately asked for it. Didymus protested that Mr. Simon's advice and counsel to the young were the most effective means imaginable of bringing about the precisely opposite consequence to that desired, and that Mr. Simon reminded him of a schoolmaster who, before letting the children out of school one afternoon, said, 'Children, I want to give you some advice and I hope you'll listen to it and obey it; take care, on your way home not to put small stones in the ears of donkeys by the side of the road. That's cruel, very cruel; make sure I don't hear of any of you being guilty of such a mean act'.

The children had never before heard of it, and to their great amusement, filled the ears of the first donkey they saw with small stones. When the commandment came, sin revived. Which king was it that forbade his subjects to smoke? The number of smokers rose sharply that year! Mr. Simon's intentions, like that of the schoolmaster, were praiseworthy, but forbidden fruit is always desirable to the eye. To be honest, it must be said that

Mr. Simon's ministry didn't really suit the Bethel congregation, and though every kindness was shown him, and even Didymus, who was naturally so bitter-natured, proved no great stumbling block to him, Mr. Simon quickly began to feel uncomfortable. He saw there was insufficient intelligence in Bethel to appreciate his talents. And that was not his greatest disappointment. It was not an uncommon thing, Mr. Simon said to himself, for a man's worth to go unrecognised by a congregation of illiterate workmen; but he would have expected the monthly meeting, where the cream of the county's faithful collected, to have put a true value on his scholarship. But even the '*seiat*', after a warm welcome on his first visit, had almost completely ignored him. This was not comforting to a man conscious that he possessed talent and intellectual ability beyond the common, for it's humbug to say that others should judge the merits of a man, and what place he should have in society. Who can know a man so well as he himself? Who knows the length, breadth, height and depth of his abilities as well as he?

During his stay at Bethel, Mr. Simon had kept his reputation intact, and he could, to some degree, thank Eos Prydain for this. When he learned Mr. Simon was visiting Tŷ'n yr Ardd rather frequently, Eos gave him a hint to be careful the Captain didn't ruin him. This caused Mr. Simon to think things over, and he saw the suggestion was not without merit, because once the Captain had realised Mr. Simon wasn't an abstainer, he always offered him spirits when he went there, and Mr. Simon was soon convinced that he did this hoping to one day stain his name, and render him powerless to give advice or to discipline anyone who drank to excess. Fortunately, Mr. Simon saw this in time, and though he greatly valued freedom, and used to look on teetotallers as the most immoderate people in the world, he believed that his duty as a minister of the Gospel was to take the pledge. But as I've already suggested, Mr. Simon didn't see enough scope for himself in Bethel, or indeed in Wales, and resolved to go to America. When he made his decision known to the church, the usual credit was given to his wisdom, and considerable grief was shown (by Eos Prydain and his choir). Eos consoled himself and his friends by saying Mr. Simon would, in the great land to the west, be made a Doctor of Music, if not also a Doctor of Divinity. Eos also took the trouble to tell Mr. Simon he'd have had a testimonial, had it not been that the state of trade in the neighbourhood was so dreadfully depressed, and so many were out of work. Mr. Simon could do nothing but to take the will for the deed.

Somewhere in the body of this story, I said—I can't remember where—that whenever a member of the Chapel had departed—the word used to describe one who's died—Eos and his choir would sing the 'Vital Spark' in the chapel. In Mr. Simon's farewell meeting, before he set off to America, Eos thought—inasmuch as Mr. Simon was departing—that it wouldn't be inappropriate to sing the 'Vital Spark'; and this was agreed to. But Eos strenuously refused Didymus' variation, which went as follows:

> "*Lend, lend me your wing*
> *I sail! I fly!*
> *Oh wind! Where is thy victory?*
> *Oh sea, where is thy sting?*"

Eos acknowledged its appropriateness, but was afraid, as the choir hadn't practised, they'd be confused, and they therefore stuck to the original. A meeting was held to bid a very warm farewell to Mr. Simon. Dafydd Dafis spoke very effectively, and expressed the heartfelt hope that Mr. Simon would be able to make his home in America. Amongst many other good things, Eos said that Mr. Simon's service with the sol-ffa class was such that no price could ever be put on it, and he was confident that, having reached America, he would not neglect the sol-ffa. I happened to be sitting next to Thomas Bartley, and when Eos made this observation,

Thomas said in my ear: "What's the man on about, eh? Don't they grow Indian corn in 'merica? I never 'eard they do much with '*ffa*'[5]. You know what, Eos is as daft as I am, except he can sing a bit."

Eos went to Liverpool to gaze his last on Mr. Simon and stayed until the final moment on the boat that would carry him to the west; and he solemnly declared, on his return to Bethel with tears in his eyes, that the last words he heard from Mr. Simon's lips were 'sol-ffa'.

Thus ended Mr. Simon's ministry in Bethel. When I began to write this story, I proposed saying a good deal about his ministration and about the course of religion in its different aspects during his connection with Bethel, but somehow I've slipped into writing of lesser matters. I dislike at all times judging of the lives of public men, especially preachers, afraid of erring through ignorance. Because of that, I'll give the reader the summary of a conversation that took place between two who've spoken together already in this story; two much more able than I to report on the life and labour of Mr. Simon.

---

[5] '*ffa*'—it still means 'beans' in Welsh. As for Americans not doing much with them. B. C. Unseld and Theodore F. Seward, with Biglow and Main publishers, imported Curwen's tonic 'sol-fa' to the United States, but the method was never widely received, the Americans choosing to develop their own system, and probably their own beans as well.

45

THE REPORTER

On particular occasions—occasions of some importance—Didymus used to pay a visit to Dafydd Dafis. And these visits were beneficial to both, for Dafydd required a spur, and Didymus sometimes restraint. Didymus derived more from Dafydd than Dafydd from Didymus. As a newspaper reporter—for that was his main occupation—Didymus was inclined, like the generality of his brethren, to go to extremes—to exaggerate, to decide complex matters over which a thoughtful man would hesitate—and to state his thoughts in a rather oracular and authoritative manner. Many a time when he was about to write an account of some meeting or event, with his mind full of incisive and half-formed sentences, and when he was thinking of how to put it to this or that person, a conversation with Dafydd Dafis had been an effective way to smooth and make the whole proportionate, and sometimes of causing him to throw it all overboard, just as was Jonah into the sea.

Mr. Simon's farewell meeting was an event in Bethel, and an excellent opportunity, thought Didymus, to throw light on his stay in our midst; and as well as filling three columns of the *County Chronicle*, for which he would receive a fair payment, this would also be an opportunity to speak his mind on preaching and preachers, thoughts on both of which had been gathering within him for some time. But before pouring them onto paper, it was no doubt wise that Didymus paid a visit to Dafydd Dafis.

"I rather expected you here tonight, Thomas," Dafydd said, "and I'm glad you've come. I've been thinking a lot today of what you'd say in the paper about last night's meeting, for I know you'll be expected, by reason of your calling, to say something. And I was hoping, and praying too I think, that wisdom would guide you."

"Well," said Didymus, "I want to give a report—verbatim and literatim—of your speech, Dafydd."

"What do you mean by that, Thomas?"

"To put every word you said in the paper, for there was nothing else worth listening to," said Didymus.

"Nonsense," said Dafydd. "No, but seriously, what are you going to say about the meeting? You must remember, Thomas, that it's not just the people of Bethel who read the paper, and I'd like you to be careful."

"What would you say if you were in my place, Dafydd?"

"I don't know, I'm sure," said Dafydd. I rather think I wouldn't say anything."

"How will I earn a crust, saying nothing?" asked Didymus. "It's a matter of necessity for me to write this and that in *the Chronicle* every week, to be able to live. And you never saw such trouble as I sometimes have making a major story from next to nothing. A reporter in a small place like this has to be at it inventing all the time. And you'd be surprised how many speeches I'm always having to make up that were never made. Every month I send reports to *the Chronicle* of the speeches of the Local Board; do you think half of them took place? No fear! There aren't three members of the board that can assemble two sentences grammatically. Indeed, before now I've awarded an epic oration to a man who'd done no more than nod his head in approval."

"You're a smart lad, Thomas, but do you think you're doing right?" asked Dafydd.

"Quite right," said Didymus, "and it's just the same at the Board of Guardians, you know. There's old Llwyd, of Wern Oleu. I remember him once trying to make a speech and he started like this; 'Mistir cheerman, I did remember when I am a boy …' It wouldn't do to report it like that in the paper, you know, so I wrote; 'Mr. Chairman, the subject now under discussion forcibly reminds me of my boyhood …' and I gave him a sharp speech he never made. I swear at the last Board the only thing old Llwyd said was 'I beg to second resolution'; and he sweated buckets saying that; but I gave him a tidy little speech in *the Chronicle*, because I knew he'd be pleased. And for the life of me, I couldn't help smiling when I met him at the fair. He said—swaggering insufferably—You know what, Thomas, you sent in a very neat report of the Board of Guardians' last meeting. You wrote practically word for word what I said. When will you come for a bite of supper, eh?' I had quite a job keeping a straight face while I was telling him I couldn't go to Wern Oleu that week. And as sure as you're sitting in that chair, I got one of Wern Oleu's ducks the next morning."

"Well, I never heard such a thing," said Dafydd. "But tell me, what do the other members say when they read in the paper about old Llwyd giving speeches?"

"Nothing at all! For they all know that if I reported the speeches of the best of them as they're spoken, they'd paint a pitiful picture. There's some sort of freemasonry about them; don't tell them I've told you anything about it. Indeed I've never heard the chairman complain when I've added a big chunk to his speech."

"You know, I wouldn't care for that sort of thing; it doesn't seem upright and honest, somehow," said Dafydd.

"Each to his own; '*pob taleidiaeth rhag tylodi*'[1], Dafydd. The work of a reporter is to invent what's in a man's mind, and how he'd have expressed his thoughts if he'd been able to; and if I succeed in speaking those unspoken thoughts, all is well," said Didymus.

"But what sort of a report will you give of Mr. Simon's farewell meeting?" asked Dafydd.

---

[1] '*pob taleidiaeth rhag tylodi*'—every payment for fear of poverty. A rather archaic phrase, containing an element of cynghanedd—proverbs often do—which I believe I mentioned earlier. If you split the line in two, the syllables bearing the stress in each half would be '*leid*' and '*lod*'. Both those syllables are preceded by the consonants '*t*' and '*l*' and immediately followed by '*d*', creating a balance. The phrase would form a line of cynghanedd draws, were it not for the irritating presence of 'pob', which would really need a balancing '*p*' and '*b*' before the '*t*' and '*l*' in the second half. Should you have the urge to write poetry in accordance with these strange rules, there is, as I said, a book available; but it might be better to stay indoors until the urge has passed.

"I haven't got a clue," said Didymus. "I must cobble something together, and I'd like to say a lot of what's on my mind, and report a little on the time Mr. Simon has come and gone amongst us. But there's one thing makes me hesitate, and that's why I came here tonight. I don't want anything I've ever seen to injure the pastorate in the county. There's enough prejudice against them already, and I know if I spoke my mind in the paper, it would create more prejudice. But honestly now, Dafydd, did Mr. Simon's ministry serve a single good purpose while he was here?"

"Yes, without doubt," said Dafydd, "It convinced nearly everyone, I believe, of the folly of jumping at a man about whom no one knows anything, and will be the means, I hope, of securing a good man next time."

"I hope you're right," said Didymus. "Men of Mr. Simon's stamp—and there are many of them—degrade and damn the pastorate of our land, and lessen the love of the people towards those who are true ministers. I'm as zealous about the pastorate of the church as Edward Morgan of Dyffryn, but I'm afraid, not that there's too much guidance for congregations to find ministers, but too little guidance about what sort of men they should be. The problem, I'm afraid, is at the very beginning. To begin with, a young man falls into a fancy for the post of preacher. He sees it's a position of honour, and that no one's so dear to and respected by the Welsh as a preacher. In his folly, the young man thinks it's an easy job, free of labour except for some four hours on the Sabbath, and the pay's quite reasonable. He falls into that fancy as I said, and then starts wearing a long black coat, a hat with a broad brim, and a waistcoat buttoned to the top on Sundays. His next step will be to be tired of his trade, and saunter around on weekdays in his long coat; the preacher's livery. And as no one thinks he'd make a preacher, he himself will some day say to his friends that his mind's set on being a minister. Everyone's surprised. But having thought, everyone admits he looks like a preacher as far as his clothes are concerned. And so on and so on, without me following him till he comes out of college, and through luck is called to be a pastor. Then he begins to look askance at the old godly preachers (who are not pastors) who have guided many a sinner into the way of life. I strongly believe that no youth should be allowed to start preaching if he's not head and shoulders above the others of his own age in ability, knowledge, and culture, and if he's not become notable as a successful teacher in the Sunday school, the children's meetings, the prayer meetings, and every area within reach in which to make himself useful, and to show the honesty of his zeal by doing good. I don't believe in allowing a young man to jump from obscurity into the pulpit, for once he's climbed the pulpit steps, it's very hard to tell him not to go there again. And I don't believe the request to be allowed to preach should come from the young man. It should come as a request or command from others to him; from those who've noticed him, and seen suitability in him."

"I agree with much of what you say, Thomas," said Dafydd, "but you know very well that had some we recognize as true preachers waited till the church asked them to preach, they'd still not have begun. Sometimes there's a church without enough sense to see the elements of a preacher in a youth intended by God to be a preacher."

"That's an exception," said Didymus. "There's a saying that a poet is born and not made. And it's quite true. How many bards that were born bards are there in Wales today? You can count them on your fingers. But the ones who spin rhymes and wear pseudonyms are without number. In the same way a preacher must be born a preacher, or he'll be a rhymester forever. There's no point at all apprenticing a man to be a preacher; that's making a parson, not making a preacher."

"Do you mean to say, Thomas, you could count the true Welsh preachers on your fingers?" asked Dafydd.

"Nothing of the sort," said Didymus, "mercifully they're a great host. Wales has more need for preachers than for bards, and God has created more of them. But, perhaps the proportion of the

313

rhymesters among both classes is broadly similar. Don't you think, Dafydd, that we get too much preaching?"

"Too much preaching? There's no such thing as too much preaching. I could listen to the gospel being preached every day of my life," said Dafydd.

"Well," said Didymus, "I'm afraid we get too much by half of the sort of preaching there is. When there were only about a dozen preachers in Wales, and they were all top quality, there used to be more taste for the Gospel, and half as many again were saved, but when anybody has the chance to drag out a story, to make it cold and dull, it serves no purpose except to accustom the listeners to the facts, and deprive them of their novelty, to induce a mood of disinterest by the time someone does come to tell the story in all its charm and force. Do you think that if Saint Paul had sent half a hundred mediocrities ahead of him to recite the tale he'd tell in his turn, he'd have filled the world with the gospel of Christ? I'm afraid he'd have failed in his work."

"What would become of all our meetings, especially our small rural meetings, if you were to succeed in putting a stop to all the preachers who don't convince us they were born, or were intended to be preachers, and if Wales had to depend entirely on preachers who, according to the testimony of everyone's conscience, had been sent?" asked Dafydd.

"What's becoming of them now?" asked Didymus. "Are they being added to from the outside world? Are not the descendants of the congregations themselves all that keeps them from decreasing? Besides that, the over-anxiety to fill the pulpit in every mountain and vale with anybody keeps the congregations from falling back on their own resources, and breeds apathy and spiritual laziness. By having someone in the pulpit every Sabbath, though he be but a man of wood, the congregation feels it's done its duty, whereas had it been left to itself, as with the Sunday school, it would have gone to work and would have done something."

"You're not thinking of doing away with preaching, are

you Thomas?" asked Dafydd.

"Good gracious! Not on any account!" said Didymus. "Preaching the Gospel is the means God has ordained to save the world; and Wales, more than any country under the sun, is more indebted to its preachers than to anyone or anything else. But if I could, I'd do away with the most negligent preaching; that is, I'd do away with every preacher not gifted with the spirit of ministration, the sort who fill gaps, and saves having prayer meetings."

"But who'll decide who are the true preachers, and who are the ones who fill the gaps?" asked Dafydd.

"The congregations, of course, by ballot," said Didymus, "for the congregations know very well the difference between a real preacher and the imitation filling the pulpit. These days, almost every congregation considers they should have two sermons on the Sabbath, and rather than have an 'empty Sunday' the elders go hunting for any Tom, Dick or Harry. To my mind, it'd be much better for us to stew in our own juice, even for a month, till it was our turn to have the preacher, rather than keep a small shop open every Sunday as is done now. And perhaps that would raise an appetite for the Gospel as there was long ago, when crowds travelled miles to listen to the preacher, and came home with enough to live on for weeks."

"A fine life that would be for us," said Dafydd; "and our own juice wouldn't last long, I'm afraid. You always have wild and impossible notions, Thomas. But let's talk sense. What are you going to say in the paper about last night's meeting?"

"I've a mind to follow your suggestion and say nothing," said Didymus, "that is, to write a short, harmless paragraph. For the best I could say about Mr. Simon would be that he was a man of the livery. I never saw a more clerical clergyman. I swear if his coat had been one sixteenth of an inch too short he'd never have looked at it, let alone worn it; and if his waistcoat had hidden or shown one thousandth part of a thread more or less of his white collar than it should, it would have given him typhoid fever and deprived him of what gospel there was in him. Oh yes, don't forget the collar; that's indispensable to a minister these days; that's to say, a minister of the livery. And not a white handkerchief twice round the neck like the old giants of old. What would it have taken for John Jones of Talysarn to wear one of these Jesuitical collars? He'd have reckoned himself worthy of hell fire if he'd put one round his neck."

"Good gracious! Be quiet, Thomas, you're getting more presumptuous every day," cried Dafydd.

"What I'm saying is true and serious, Dafydd," said Didymus. "What in the name of reason requires a preacher to dress differently to other people, and make you think, looking at his throat, that he intends to commit suicide in a tidy manner? Why does a minister need to look more unnatural than any other creature on earth? Who was it, forty years ago, that mocked the Welsh curates for their priest's clothes? Wasn't it the Dissenting ministers? But today the curate, poor fellow, can't compare with some of the Methodist preachers and Independent ministers in their place in the world, as far as coat, collar and hat are concerned; compared with the priest, they're archbishops, I swear it! Remember I'm all for a preacher dressing well and respectably and I hate seeing a preacher dressed slovenly, but this over-clerical dressing makes me sick and raises my bile. And the least talented and least eager to save sinners are the most clerical of the lot. Do you know what, I was listening to one of Wales's greatest preachers last week, and though he preached excellently, I got as great a blessing from looking at his black necktie and the naturalness of the man as I did from his sermon. One like he has no need of a livery, Dafydd."

"Well, well, Thomas my boy," said Dafydd; "you keep stumbling over very small things, and if you were as blind as Bartimaeus, you'd get more out of the services."

"I shouldn't wonder. But I can see, and seeing things like this makes me weak, and less of a Methodist every day. And I'm not alone; this clerical dressing brings a tear to the eyes of thousands.

There's none of the prestige of the '*Hen Gorff*' in it. But the sum of what's been said is this; Mr. Simon was a man of the livery, one apprenticed to be a preacher, without having been born a preacher. I'd like to say a little about him in the paper, but I'll take your advice for fear I'll say something I shouldn't. I must try to come across some enormous potato or prolific sow somewhere to make up the news of the week. Goodbye, and be good."

46

VARIOUS

Many weeks passed by, and though Sem Llwyd told as many rose-tinted lies as he could about the prospects of Coed Madog Mine, and the Captain strained every muscle to attract his moneyed neighbours, their efforts were not crowned with success. The future looked black; and to deepen the Captain's grief, Mr. Denman—after fighting hard, and having given him as much money as he was able, to keep an interest in Coed Madog—had, despite his best efforts, gone bankrupt and had sold up, moved to a small house, paying rent of half a crown a week, and had taken work as an assistant for eighteen shillings a week, in order to survive. My powers would fail me if I tried to describe all the reproaches the poor creature had suffered from his wife; and indeed, on thinking of the comfortable position he'd enjoyed when he owned houses and land and a good stock in his shop, it was no wonder that Mrs. Denman grumbled daily, and reminded him frequently of how he'd carried all he owned to 'that cursed old Captain'. Mr. Denman, poor man, was now forced to suffer in silence, but what pained him most was his inability to pay his debts. He had no future hope of peace and quiet, except in the grave, a haven he was fast approaching. But through it all, Mr. Denman continued to go to chapel, and seemed to derive more pleasure than ever from the services; and as Dafydd Dafis said, though Mr. Denman, after years of great sacrifice and struggle, had failed to find lead, it was very evident he'd found the 'precious pearl'.

The Captain could not do less than wonder that Enoc Huws continued to spend money on Coed Madog, and that heartily and cheerfully, and he frequently said to himself, "Mr. Huws must be doing remarkable business to keep spending so much. It's cruel to let him go on like this. But what would become of me if he put a stop to it?" And Enoc *was* doing remarkable business, and didn't care a lot about money. The Captain couldn't help noticing that Enoc seemed happier and livelier than he'd been for years.

"No doubt," said the Captain, "Mr. Huws has more home comfort with his new housekeeper. I don't know what made him keep that old sack of a Marged so long. But this Miss Bifan seems a superior sort of woman. I only hope Mr. Huws doesn't marry her. Those good-looking girls make dangerous housekeepers for '*hen lanciau*'. I wouldn't be at all surprised if it ended that way. Indeed there is something attractive about her. If I were a young man myself, well …"

The reader will remember that Enoc had engaged Miss Bifan without enquiring about her character, or asking where she'd last been in service. When Jones the policeman heard the story, he laughed from the depths of his heart, and couldn't help admiring his old friend Enoc's credulous innocence. But Jones didn't rest till he had her whole history—so he thought—and when he'd got it, didn't delay in informing Enoc. According to Jones, Miss Bifan's story went something like this: She was the only daughter of a respectable farmer living about four miles from Bethel. She'd been brought up religiously, had a little education, and while still young, had won prizes for singing, reading and answering questions in competitive meetings, and was reckoned much more talented than others her own age. Though still quite young, she'd been looked on as the prettiest girl in the district, which made her female friends envious, and the lads quarrel. By now, Miss Bifan had been in service with respectable families in various places, and the only complaints brought against her by those respectable families were: firstly, that she dressed too well; secondly, that she made their daughters look common, ugly and unsightly; thirdly, that she always had a lover and was always a favourite with the sons of the respectable families; and lastly, that she was light fingered. When the policeman narrated all this to Enoc, he believed the evidence for all but the last of the complaints, and said zealously: "Of course the girl dresses well, and what's that to anyone else? It's no business of the master or mistress to tell a girl how and what to wear, if she pays for her own clothing. And the girl's pretty too, there's no doubt about it, but she can't help that, and I can easily believe the girls in the family look common next to her, and the boys like the way she looks. What's more natural? But there's no reason to blame her for that; it's nothing but envy, mean envy. You know what; there are some families who think a maidservant's got no business to be nice-looking, and if they could, they'd give her smallpox, if not a hare lip. It wouldn't be remarkable if she has a lover; and if she hasn't one—and she says she hasn't—it shows the lads are as blind as gateposts. Very often, Mr. Jones, a girl like Miss Bifan will have half a dozen sweethearts, while the girls in the family are longing for one, and no one'll look at them. Haven't I got to do all I know to watch the lads in the shop? Every day, they're making excuses to come into the house, and I know their sole object is to get a look at, and a word with Miss Bifan. And what's more natural? Wouldn't I do the same, were it not for someone you know about? But as to her being light fingered, I'll never believe that. Hundreds of poor maidservants are dreadfully wronged. When the sprig of a son has pawned his gold studs to get drink—oh the maid's stolen them, of course! When the daughter's lost her brooch or cuff-links whilst gallivanting, and doesn't dare tell her mother about it, the wretched maid has taken them! The maid's the family scapegoat. The humbugs! Miss Bifan's a splendid girl, Mr. Jones, and this house is like heaven compared to how it was when Marged was here."

The policeman listened to Enoc in silence, admiring his faith and trust; but anyone looking deeply into his eyes would have read his thoughts as: 'Where ignorance is bliss, 'tis folly to be wise'.

No doubt the happiness of his home contributed to Enoc's cheerfulness. But if happiness was in his home alone, he'd hardly have stayed away from it till eleven o'clock on four or five nights each week. Enoc must have found as much amusement at Tŷ'n yr Ardd, as he was there so often. And Enoc didn't need to consult Captain Trefor several times a week about Coed Madog, where only a few men were now employed. And even if he had considered that necessary, the Captain hadn't recently been available at Tŷ'n yr Ardd every night of the week. Soon after Mrs. Trefor's death, the Captain had begun going to the Brown Cow on midweek evenings. Some thought that after the death of Mrs. Trefor he felt lonely, and that a little help from company might heal his *hiraeth*. And perhaps he had another object; by leaving Miss Trefor the more lonely, she'd have more leisure to consider her position and realise her loss, for young people are not, as a rule, given to reflection. Perhaps solitude would be good for her. But Miss Trefor didn't take that view of things, and she felt her father's behaviour—so soon after burying her mother—leaving her alone in the house till the middle of the night, was most unkind, and if Enoc Huws had not been so thoughtful and good-natured as to visit her so often, her solitude would have been almost unbearable.

For quite a time before her mother's death, Miss Trefor had felt that there was a gulf between her and her father, and that this gulf was daily widening. This caused her great sorrow. She remembered a time when she looked on her father with innocent admiration, and considered him higher and better than men generally. This was long, long ago and she looked on that time with a regretful heart. She made many energetic attempts to rekindle the flame, but the old feelings wouldn't return. At times, she thought she'd formed ideas—she knew not from where they came—about rectitude, truth, and honour, that no man—not only not her father, but no man—could stand being measured and weighed by, and then she'd remember Enoc Huws; she could find no fault in him. Many a time she was frightened and felt guilty, thinking of the ideas she'd cherished about her father. But in spite of her efforts, she felt that the chasm between them was growing wider. But she never for a moment forgot two things, that he was her father, and that she'd taken an oath to stay with him while he lived. The former only added to her sorrows, seeing his constant deterioration after her mother died; and the latter only made her realise the extent of the wretchedness ahead. Still, she remembered she had a friend, a friend to the hilt, and she could no longer, without being guilty of the most heartless ingratitude, and the greatest treachery to her own best feelings, refrain from rewarding his constancy. Duty had been her life's watchword for many years, and she believed, in view of the change in her intentions, that it was her duty to inform her father of this. For some time now, she'd been watching for an opportunity to do this, but the Captain, when at home, was usually in a bad temper, and when he returned late from the Brown Cow, he was too dull and drowsy for her to think of raising the matter. At last the opportunity came, and Susi told her father of her relationship with Enoc Huws, as will be narrated hereafter.

47

THE BROWN COW

The fact is, as was suggested in the last chapter, that Enoc had finally succeeded in his endeavours. Miss Trefor had promised to be his wife. And if anyone ever deserved to succeed, Enoc did, for his fidelity had been unfailing and his sacrifice clearly priceless. How this was brought about, I don't intend to say, for in such circumstances, and they're all much alike, there's so much folly and so much tittle tattle that every man who's been married six months is heartily ashamed to remember he went through such a laughable episode, and he doesn't like to hear about it. For that reason I won't mention it, for if I did it would give pleasure to no one but a few boys; and I'm not writing this story for boys, but for sensible men. It's sufficient to say that Miss Trefor had promised to marry Enoc Huws, which had transported him immediately to the seventh heaven, and had caused Miss Trefor, as I said earlier, to consider it her duty to inform her father.

I've mentioned the Brown Cow more than once in this story. The Brown Cow was a very old-fashioned public house on the edge of town. The house by now has undergone alterations, but I'm speaking of it as it was some time ago. No one alive remembers it ever being anything other than a public house. It was a large house and very well suited for the business, and in the old days, the drovers would stay there the night before a fair. It was said there was no cellar in the country as good as the Brown Cow's for keeping beer, and in those days the family used to brew their own. Above the door was a board, and on it a picture of a cow painted by someone—no one knew who—which was saved from decay by being varnished every year. It was obvious from the picture the cow would have won nothing at an agricultural show in our day, for her hips seemed to be almost coming through her skin, and her legs were so stiff everyone knew she suffered from rheumatism. Besides that, there was a mass of curls on her forehead, which made her look more like a bull than a cow. And yet this cow must have had some charm, for there's a story of a man who once kept the Brown Cow taking it into his head to pull down the cow and replace it with a White Horse. After a fortnight he'd lost all his trade, and he had to put the old cow back over the door, whereupon the customers returned, and the house is successful to this day. There were two rooms at the front, and two at the back. On the left side as you went in was the spirit room, or the bar. On the right was the large kitchen; on one side of this room was a big oak dresser. No one knew its age, and on it were valuable bright pewter plates which added an air of dignity on winter nights when there was a big fire in the adjacent grate. On the opposite side a wide bench ran along the wall, and on the third side, close to the fire, there was a high settle, which seated four or five. With the exception of a big strong table in the middle of the floor, there was no other furniture in the room. True, there was a double barrelled gun on one of the beams, and usually some sides of bacon, and a ham or two on another beam; considering that so much smoking went on in the room, it could have been called smoked bacon. But those things could scarcely be called furniture. Oh, on one of the walls was a picture of old Sir Watkin[1], and a picture of a fox hunt, in which one of the riders had fallen on his back while jumping a gate, and the horse had gone some distance riderless, and looked very wild. The common customers of the Brown Cow, such as the miners, cobblers, millers, tailors and the like, assembled in the big kitchen. In the good old days, before a Welsh newspaper existed,

---

[1] Sir Watkin—Sir Watkin Williams Wynn; he's been mentioned once or twice before. There's been a long line of them; baronets all, and often members of parliament too. I know not which one hung on the wall of the Brown Cow. Lord Mostyn also cropped up a while ago. He built Llandudno, though probably not unaided.

and before there was talk of teetotalism, the old codgers of Bethel used to go to the big kitchen after dark; not so much for the sake of the harmless home-brew as for the innocent conversation, and to get what news they could from some travelling pedlar or poet staying the night. At least that's what my grandparents told me. And with what eagerness the old codgers, open mouthed, used to receive the pedlar's news, though it be two months old. In the pedlar's absence, many a good story was told in the big kitchen of the Brown Cow. That, alas, is not the way of a public house today. Beardless, empty headed lads frequent them now, like animals, to drink Kelstryn and to go home in a worse state than animals.

As I said, there were also two rooms at the back; the family lived in one and the other was kept as a kind of parlour for the best class of customers such as shopkeepers, and a few religious people who liked to have a pint without being seen. In this room, too, would sit any respectable lodger who chanced to stay the night, unless he preferred company in the big kitchen. To cut a long story short, it was to this room that Captain Trefor was conducted by the landlady, Mrs. Prys, when he first visited the Brown Cow. It should be said that Mrs. Prys considered her house had been honoured in no small way when the Captain crossed its threshold, for she knew well the Black Lion was the only house to which the Captain had previously paid homage. Great was the fuss she made welcoming the Captain, and great her joy that there was respectable company—three shopkeepers—on the occasion of his first visit. The Captain enjoyed himself so much that be said, on bidding farewell to Mrs. Prys, that he'd go no more to the Lion, and this would not be his last visit—*Deo Volente*—to the Brown Cow. Mrs. Prys was a hospitable and good natured old woman, and in her own kind way she dragged the Captain by his hand to the bar, and made him drink her good health in a glass of mountain dew, to have his opinion. The Captain praised the whisky, and as he liked it, Mrs. Prys begged him to take another glass "just for her sake." The Captain obeyed, for he never liked to refuse a lady.

The Captain was as good as his word—he was always that—and from that night on he visited the Brown Cow three, sometimes four times a week. As he was a first rate conversationalist, and was fairly well acquainted with what went on in the world, his visits to the Brown Cow caused the company in the parlour to grow to five, and eventually to half a dozen, and at times to more than that. The company made much of his society, and Mrs. Prys enjoyed his visits more than anyone. The Captain saw this quite clearly, and it's natural for every man to value those who rightly value his society. He felt, without flattering himself, he was head and shoulders higher in ability, gifts, knowledge, and especially in telling stories, than all the rest put together, and he knew that the company concurred. In truth, had he not been too much of a gentleman to so lower himself, he need not have spent anything on drink, for the company almost fought for the honour of paying his 'shot'. So great was the attention paid to what he said, so great was the value put on his views, and so great was the pleasure all this gave him, that the company of the Brown Cow became necessary each night of the week. The Captain quieted his conscience with the thought that there was no longer any pleasure for him at home, now that he had lost his dear wife. It was true he had a daughter, but what society is there between young and old, between summer and winter? Before he began frequenting the public house, the Captain had been a heavy and regular drinker at home, and though he'd never get drunk—that is, so drunk he couldn't walk straight, or that he'd keep falling, or, indeed, that he'd lose his head—the effect of his long drinking became obvious in his appearance. For some time, he'd not been as neat and tidy in his dress, his shoulders had dropped, his legs more shaky every day, and his face, which had originally been a very handsome one, was fast becoming all of one colour, with no difference between his lips and his cheeks, and every part of his face seemed to be striving to be the same colour as his nose, which had been the first to change colour to one like no other in the world. The closest I can imagine would be the liver of a calf newly struck by lightning. I'm sure that none of the companions of his youth would have recognised him. The Captain gave a scientific reason for this extraordinary colouring by attributing it to certain subterraneous gases which he, as Captain of the mine, had come in contact with, and some affinity in his skin had caused a chemical process to which other miners were not subject. But the truth is, when he began to frequent the Brown Cow, little more was needed to finish him off. Miss Trefor saw this clearly, and it was more evident to her every day. What grief of mind, what anguish of heart, all this occasioned, none but she knew. She was afraid of talking to him about it, and she knew that doing so would be futile. She saw clearly her father could not keep on walking the road he walked, and perhaps this made her more ready to listen to Enoc's offer, and to finally become engaged. However, she considered it her duty to inform her father. For a long time, she'd waited for him to be in a good temper, for she didn't know how he'd take it. She believed it would be agreeable to him, but she was afraid he'd be angry because he'd not been consulted prior to so important a promise, for the Captain thought highly of his dignity. In the mornings and afternoons, when he was sober, his mood was perverse and troubled, and the least thing would transport him to utter fury; and after returning from the Brown Cow, he would be sullen and sleepy; and Miss Trefor didn't think it right to mention the matter on the Sabbath. And thus, weeks went by before she got chance to tell him. More than once, Enoc offered to speak to the Captain, but Miss Trefor refused, for inasmuch as she'd promised to marry Enoc before consulting her father, and was determined to fulfil that promise no matter what he said, it was her duty to inform him of the fact, and once she believed something was her duty, nothing would deflect her.

But at last the opportunity came, and in this way. One night, when the Captain went to the Brown Cow, there was a stranger among the company; or rather, he was not among the company;

for he sat writing, as travellers often do, at a small table down the other end of the room, and the Captain would have thought he was a traveller had he not seen at once he was an old man, his head as white as snow. Having glanced at him, he thought no more about him. Everything carried on as usual; the company were there till closing time, and they left the gentleman still writing. He was there the next night at his table, reading on this occasion, his face half turned towards the company, but without appearing to understand anything the Captain and his friends were saying, or taking any interest in them. Before leaving that evening, the Captain went to the bar and asked Mrs. Prys who the old gentleman was. Mrs. Prys could give no information other than that he was English, arrived from America, by all appearances very rich; intended to stay for a day or two, drank no intoxicating drink, said nothing to anyone unless it was necessary, and was always reading or writing. Mrs. Prys added she was sure the stranger was a real gentleman, for his pockets were full of gold.

"Just the man for me," said the Captain on his way home, "but he's too old to speculate, and only here for two or three days, and he's a teetotaller. I never saw any good from these teetotallers except Enoc Huws. They're too cautious to speculate; and so goodbye, Yankee, you're not worth another thought."

Next day the Captain saw the old gentleman in the street, talking with Jones the policeman, as if asking about this and that; and after taking a look at him, he agreed with Mrs. Prys that he looked like a gentleman. He stood straight and seemed strong, though doubtless a man of seventy-five or more. He dressed well, and he'd shaved his cheeks, but had left a moustache on his upper lip and a beard on his chin, and wore a slouch hat. "A real American," said the Captain. The old gentleman stayed at the Brown Cow for several days; regularly in his corner, reading either a newspaper or a book. Inasmuch as he was an English-speaking American, and the Captain and his friends spoke Welsh, the company didn't feel his presence was any hindrance to their freedom. Inasmuch too as the stranger appeared to come from a higher circle of society than they, and was particularly reserved, none of them felt eager to approach him, and everything went on as usual. But if any of them had been sharp enough, they'd have seen the stranger was not so wholly disinterested in the company as they thought. For whenever the Captain spoke, the gentleman might have been seen to close his eyes; not to think but to listen carefully. At other times, he'd look at the Captain over the top of the book or paper he was reading. He'd do this whenever the Captain spoke, but no one noticed. He'd been at the Brown Cow for eight days. Between times he'd walked here and there in the neighbourhood. He'd made friends with no one, and never been seen to speak to anyone but Jones the policeman. It's true he'd gone to Siop y Groes almost every day to buy cigars, for he smoked incessantly. But Jones appeared to be the only one on friendly terms with him, and had supplied him with such information he possessed about the neighbourhood and its people. But even Jones didn't know the stranger's business here in Bethel, and Mrs. Prys didn't even know his name.

One night—it was a Monday night—the Captain had been rather late in joining the company in the Brown Cow. While he apologised and explained the reason for his lateness, namely the sheer bulk of his correspondence, he happened to look in the American's direction, and saw that the latter was gazing earnestly at him over top of the book he was reading. The stranger lowered his eyes. The Captain was struck by something, for he hesitated in mid-sentence and lost his track, which was very strange for him. Seeing the Captain look in the stranger's direction, and then hesitate, the whole company looked in the same direction, but saw only the stranger, lost in his book. The Captain was not himself that night; he was quieter, and it was as if something weighed on his mind. And so it did; his mind was more troubled than anyone imagined. After a few minutes he said quietly to his friends that they must excuse him that night; something had come over him; he didn't feel well. He added that he must have caught a chill, or he'd worked too hard that day; "for," he said, "so to speak, I feel quite faintish." One of his friends offered to see him home, but the Captain didn't wish it. As he left the room, he looked at the stranger from the corner of his eye, but his departure didn't seem to concern the old man; his eyes were fixed on his book. Mrs. Prys was surprised that the Captain was going home so early, and when he said he wasn't feeling well, the old woman thrust a pint bottle of mountain dew into his pocket in spite of his protests, charging him to take "a warm drop before going to bed."

"I'm a fool, a complete fool! It's all imagination! It's impossible! My mind's playing tricks with me tonight. And I couldn't help it, although it's complete nonsense. What can a guilty conscience invent? I've a good mind to go back; no, I can't go there again tonight, even though it's all pure nonsense."

The Captain spoke to himself in such a manner on the way home. By the time he reached Tŷ'n yr Ardd his mind had quietened itself, and he was firmly convinced his imagination had played tricks on him; and yet he wanted someone to talk to, for he'd be bad company for himself that night. Enoc Huws was not at Tŷ'n yr Ardd that evening, but Susi was there, and the Captain was thankful for it; he'd never been so glad of her company. Miss Trefor was surprised to see him home so early and still more surprised to find him so kind and friendly, and anxious for her to stay and talk with him, and perfectly sober too. The chance had come to tell her story; she'd never have a better chance; and she told him, as you'll see ...

48

A GUILTY CONSCIENCE

To see her father home between nine and ten at night, without a sign of drink on him, and to find him kind and loving, and as if he were afraid of her leaving him for two minutes, was something Miss Trefor could scarcely believe, and at times she thought she was dreaming. Her mind went back to when she was a girl, when she thought her father was the best man in the world, and when she loved him with all her heart. He was still the same person, she thought, but the cursed drink had made him seem different, and she felt guilty—terribly guilty—for ever having felt differently about him, and for feeling cold towards him; for that night he was exactly as he'd been long ago; pleasant, loving and sociable; and it must have been the drink that made him otherwise. What had made him come home early and sober that night? What had made him like his old self? She knew not; but all her love for him was reawakened and she longed to put her arms round him and kiss him, something she hadn't done, and wouldn't have dared to do, for many, many years. Little did she know—and the fact was astonishing in itself—that the disturbance in his mind, the storm in his conscience, had brought him home early and sober and given him his old sweetness. All this was nothing but a deep desire for the sympathy of someone he knew to be true and to have something to drive his thoughts away from himself. In truth, the Captain had never known such a craving to drown himself in strong drink; it was like a ravening lion in him that night. But he felt a stern necessity demanded that he kept his head and his heart clear till he was completely certain his fears were without foundation and he'd been deceived by his imagination. Miss Trefor, however, was remarkably happy that night, and thought her prayers were beginning to be answered, and her father could, after all, die a good and godly man. But something else had weighed on her mind for weeks, as I've said, namely her engagement to Enoc Huws; and now her father was in such a mood that she could venture to tell him. On seeing him so tender and fatherly she almost regretted not having asked him before giving her promise to Enoc Huws. But that couldn't be helped, and she said, shyly and fearfully: "Father. I want to tell you something; you won't be angry, will you?"

"Angry with you, my dear child? What should I be angry with you about? I know nobody cares about me now but you, and I know you've done nothing wrong," said the Captain.

"I hope I've done nothing wrong," said Susi, "and to avoid beating about the bush—I've promised to marry Enoc Huws."

The Captain looked at her astonished, as though he couldn't believe his ears, and after staring at her in silence for half a minute, he said: "God bless you both! When did you give him your promise, Susi?"

"Several weeks, if not months, ago now," she said.

"Hmm," said the Captain. "I've got nothing to say against it. I have no serious objection to your marrying Mr. Huws. But, so to speak, Susi, I'd have liked you to have consulted your father before entering into such a serious arrangement. But never mind that."

"It was my fault, father," said she, "and I'm sorry I didn't speak to you first. But it's done, and I hope you'll forgive me, and you have no objection."

"I can only say, my child, as I said before;" said the Captain, "God bless you both. But so to speak, I knew a time, yes I knew a time when I'd have been upset if anyone—no matter who—had received a promise of marriage from the daughter—the only daughter—of Captain Trefor, without first pleading, then pleading again, with her father. But Captain Trefor's not Captain Trefor any more; everyone knows that, alas, and his own daughter's no exception and has behaved accordingly. But Mr. Huws is fortunate, I must say that to your face, Susi; he's very fortunate, and I can only live on my memories; lovely memories, it's true, but still just memories; and

332

try to content myself with what they call 'fallen greatness'. I'm not the first to fall from the mountain top into the mud. No; but the old lion's not dead yet, and there is more mettle in him than many imagine; he's not a hundred years old, and perhaps he may, with the blessing of the One who granted him success in bygone days, still be looked on as someone worth consulting."

Susi hadn't expected such biting remarks and said—the words almost sticking in her throat: "Father, I didn't mean to hurt you by not asking you, and your words hurt me. And even now, if you'll always be as you are tonight—sober, kind and gentle—I'll withdraw my promise, if you tell me to."

"What?" said the Captain, "the daughter of Captain Trefor break her promise? No, my dear child; had you given your promise to the poorest half-starving miner at Coed Madog I'd make you fulfil it, if it was in my power. 'Breaking a promise' isn't in Captain Trefor's dictionary, and not worthy of the prestige of his family. But I must say again that Mr. Huws is a lucky man, and under the circumstances perhaps you couldn't do better. Put your mind at rest, my dear child; I, so to speak, greatly approve of what you've done; indeed I'm happy to think you have a living, whatever my situation might be, and no matter what may become of me. I'll make the sacrifice; the parish and the workhouse are open to all."

"I don't intend to leave you, father; that's understood between Mr. Huws and I. You shall have the same home as I, and I know you can depend on Mr. Huws' kindness. Indeed, I consider it's I, not Mr. Huws, who's lucky," said Susi.

"I think, Susi," said the Captain, "if things turn out as I expect I won't need to depend on the kindness of anyone whatever. At the same time, don't think I don't appreciate your fidelity and your kind intentions towards me. Perhaps I'll be glad of them; who knows? As to Mr. Huws, I know him pretty well, and I'll not be sorry he's my son-in-law. Why isn't Mr. Huws here tonight, Susi? After our conversation, I feel, so to speak, a kind of *hiraeth* to see him."

"He said something needed him, and he couldn't come tonight," said Susi.

"Well," said the Captain, "though my soul is sad, I can only repeat God bless you."

And thus ended, harmlessly enough, what Miss Trefor had greatly feared and worried about so much. The truth was, this was the best news the Captain could have had; this was what he'd wanted for many years, and he and Mrs. Trefor had done all they could to attain this object. After Mrs. Trefor's death, the Captain had watched them often, seeking signs of love, and having failed in that, as I said, he'd been so anxious that his daughter should secure Enoc as a husband, that he could no longer suffer the uncertainty, and had asked his daughter the question straight out. Deep was his disappointment when he heard there was no more than friendship between them, nor any likelihood of anything more, and so there was nothing else to do but continue to bleed poor Enoc. Lately, he'd been expecting daily to hear Enoc say he'd not spend a penny more on Coed Madog; and then what would become of him—the Captain? At times, this weighed so heavily on his mind that he longed to go to the Brown Cow and drown his worries in whisky. But what his heart had craved for so long had come to pass. The Captain knew that if Enoc Huws had promised to marry his daughter, he would do so, and this gave him so much joy that he couldn't describe it even to himself. The Captain now considered it his duty, as an honest man—and who would doubt his honesty?—to tell Enoc it would be pointless for him, and indeed for the Captain himself, to spend more on Coed Madog.

"I'll tell him tomorrow," thought the Captain. "It's my duty as an honest man to tell him, for he and I have spent too much already, and there's no more sign of lead there than in this clock case here. I'm heartily glad things have ended so well. But this is just one more proof that I know men fairly well. I knew for years that Mr. Huws had his mind on Susi; and thank God she's been so lucky. I was starting to worry about what would become of her, poor girl."

Thus the Captain conversed with himself after Susi had gone

to bed. If the conversation between the two had occurred the previous night, the Captain would count himself content. But he wasn't happy; something, true or imaginary, was gnawing at his conscience. He looked at the clock; it was just quarter past ten. He paced up and down the parlour for a further quarter of an hour, then stopped to listen. Susi and Kitty had been sleeping a while, he thought. He pulled off his slippers and put on his shoes, put on his top coat, and a cap he wore around the house, and went out as quietly as possible. He walked quickly and furtively towards Sem Llwyd's house. Sem had gone to bed, and when he heard someone knock on the door he opened the window and stuck his head out, complete with a huge woollen nightcap tied under his chin. When he realised it was the Captain, he came straight downstairs. Sem, like many a bachelor, kept the fire smouldering all night through the year, and so as not to keep the Captain waiting he came down without putting on more than his drawers and slippers. They talked for half an hour, Sem bent double on a low stool, and the Captain in a chair, one on each side of the fire. A photograph of the two would have been amusing; yet the two were serious. They talked in a low tone, as if they were afraid of anyone hearing them, and indeed, they were; though even if they'd shouted, there was no need to worry at that time of night. Though the two were intent on conversation, Sem couldn't help realising the Captain could see that the candles lighting his abode were from Coed Madog. On this occasion, that was neither here or there. After the discussion, the Captain gave Sem definite and detailed instructions, then left, and Sem smoked his pipe, huddled up in his woollen drawers, to consider the matter. Never in his life had there been a wiser look on the old sage than there was that night.

The Captain returned quickly to Tŷ'n yr Ardd, and it would have been almost impossible to hear him open and close the door and go to the parlour. When he got there, his first thought was to get the bottle of whisky from the cupboard. But though he'd been a slave to drink, the old Captain had an incredibly strong will, and said to himself: "No, not tonight; I must keep my head clear, for a while anyway. Not a drop till I'm absolutely certain in my mind. I'll listen to what Sem says tomorrow; he'll settle the question. I'll go to bed—to not sleep a wink, I know. I hope to God there's no cause for my fears. But he's terribly alike! Still I'm almost certain it's all foolish imagination. After all, a guilty conscience is a terrible thing! But I'll see what Sem says. I've got cause to be thankful. And if everything's all right, I don't have to worry any more about Susi; she's safe, thank God."

The Captain didn't sleep a wink that night. Foreseeing this, he'd taken his pipe and tobacco to his bedroom, and he smoked a great deal, but never touched a drop of intoxicating drink, though there was plenty in the house; he needed his head clear and his mind alert, as he said. He was possessed by two feelings: endless happiness at the prospect of having Enoc as his son-in-law, and great fear that what had crossed his mind that night might turn out to be true. His state of mind was such that he himself, though gifted with such great descriptive powers, could not have accurately described it. But he comforted himself by thinking he'd not have to suffer this uncertainty for long. Sem Llwyd would settle it one way or the other.

Sem didn't go to work at Coed Madog the next morning. He dressed in his Sunday clothes, and he was seen early in the morning, sauntering round town, and hanging about near the Brown Cow. Indeed, though Sem pretended to be teetotal, he slipped into the Brown Cow more than once for two penn'orth when there were no Dissenters about. As Captain Trefor's lieutenant, Sem got a hearty welcome at the Brown Cow, and Mrs. Prys inquired kindly after the Captain's health. Sem shook his head wisely and suggested that the Captain's health wasn't what he or any of the miners would have wished, and Mrs. Prys gave a sigh, free of charge, that was worth twopence to Sem. Sem's report was ready before midday, and he hastened to Tŷ'n yr Ardd.

49

THE CAPTAIN AND ENOC

The Captain couldn't touch a morsel of breakfast, and Miss Trefor thought her father was grieving at the prospect of Enoc taking her away, or that he was in a state of repentance. She believed the latter was more likely, inasmuch as this morning she'd seen no sign that he'd been drinking after she'd gone to bed the previous night; unlike, almost without exception, every other night of the year. She thought he'd changed at last, and her heart was filled with gratitude. And though she pretended she was sorry he couldn't eat, her heart leapt with joy at the thought that something had happened to make him see the sinfulness of his life. Little did she know what was spoiling his appetite. After breakfast, the Captain told his daughter he had a lot of writing to do that morning, which was a hint that he wanted the parlour to himself. He didn't write a word. He paced the room for hours, often looking anxiously out of the window for Sem Llwyd. It was nearly dinner time before he saw Sem in the distance, walking hurriedly towards Tŷ'n yr Ardd. His heart beat fast as Sem approached. He feared, and longed, to hear what Sem had to say. Before Sem had opened the garden gate, the Captain had opened the front door and was trying to guess from Sem's face what his report would be. Sem looked joyful, and the Captain read that as a good sign. When the two had gone into the parlour and closed the door, the Captain asked, full of anxiety:

"Well, Sem, what do you think?"

"All nonsense," said Sem, "he's not a bit like him, and yet there is a sort of likeness in him. But it's not him, I swear."

"Are you quite sure, Sem?"

"As sure as I'm alive," said Sem. "That man's not much more than seventy, and you know that wouldn't be his age. No chance; don't be afraid, put your mind at rest. It's impossible; just think how old he'd be now."

"True," said the Captain "but are you quite sure, Sem?"

"Perfectly sure, Captain; no one can fool me. It was just a wild fancy that came into your head," said Sem.

"No doubt, Sem," said the Captain "and thank God for that. I've had enough trouble without this. You've taken a great load off my mind, Sem, and if I weren't afraid my daughter would know something had happened, I'd ask you to stay for dinner. Here; take this five shilling piece and go to work this afternoon. I've got something to tell you one day, Sem."

Sem went away, pensively, for he wasn't nearly as sure as he'd pretended to be. When he'd seen how anxious and troubled the Captain was, he'd done his best to drive away his disquiet and give him peace, and Sem thought there'd be trouble for him the day misfortune found his old master and contemporary; and indeed, Sem thought honestly that, though it wasn't an impossibility, the Captain's fear was without reason; it'd be a most improbable event. At the same time Sem couldn't help thinking a lot that day, and the Captain's visit the previous night had revived memories he'd long had buried in his bosom; and their burying had been a great advantage to Sem in connection with the Captain.

The Captain was a different man after hearing Sem Llwyd's account. Sem had, as the Captain had said, taken a heavy load from his mind, and he thought he could now safely take a shot of whisky. He took the bottle from the cupboard, and rather than call for water, which would have alerted Susi, he decided he'd take it neat—no great feat for the Captain. However, when he'd filled the glass, and was on the point of swallowing, Susi came suddenly into the room to ask him what time he wanted his dinner. The Captain looked guilty and troubled, and his daughter surprised and sad to see him return to his cursed habit so early in the day, when she'd thought a change had come over him, and he'd turned over a new leaf. Her heart sank when she saw the bottle on the table and the full

338

glass; and the Captain, seeing what ran through her mind, said: "I'm not bothered about dinner at all, my girl, for I don't somehow feel at all well. And that's the reason I'm taking a drop of whisky now to see if I feel any better for it. Indeed, I'd decided last night, though I didn't tell you, not to touch it at all. But the best doctors agree it's dangerous for someone who's used to taking a drop each day to give it up too suddenly. And now I believe that, for I'm sure that's what's caused my illness. And as for dinner, I think you'd better make me a cup of coffee; my stomach's too bad to take anything else. You might fry a bit of ham and an egg or two; or something else, my girl."

Saying "Very well." Miss Trefor departed, sad and disappointed, and totally convinced that the 'great change' in her father hadn't happened yet. And her conviction was entirely correct. At dinner, Miss Trefor asked her father the reason for Sem Llwyd's early visit, and the Captain replied, readily enough: "Sem, poor chap, came with bad news. The truth is, Susi, that Sem and I are by now quite convinced we won't find lead in Coed Madog. In the way of time and the nature of things, we should have found it by now if we were going to find it at all. Now, despite our best efforts, we've given up all hope. That's the conclusion Sem and I came to this morning. How to break the news to Mr. Huws, I don't know, and it's almost driving me mad; but it has to be done, and at once. I know Mr. Huws will be unwilling, for I've never seen anyone with such a spirit for venturing. But I must use all my influence to persuade him to give the place up, for my conscience tells me that's my duty. And indeed, I can't afford to spend any more. It's starting to strain my resources. It'd do no harm if you said a word or two to the same effect, Susi."

Susi saw things a great deal better than her father thought. She knew at once that what she'd told him the previous night, that she'd promised to marry Enoc, was the reason for giving up Coed Madog. She was glad to hear it, for she'd believed for a long time they'd never find lead in Coed Madog. And when she thought she and Enoc would be husband and wife in a few weeks' time, she found her father's decision to give up the mine very acceptable, for she knew Enoc had been spending a pile of money on the mine each month. She agreed with her father's decision and he praised her ability to see the nature of things.

It became clear there was little disturbance in the Captain's stomach, but he didn't leave the house that day, for he had no inclination to visit the Brown Cow for particular reasons, and also because he wished to speak with Enoc, who was sure to pay a visit to Tŷ'n yr Ardd that evening. Enoc faithfully fulfilled his appointment, and he was quite surprised when Miss Trefor told him her father was at home and wished to speak with him about the mine; for of late, he'd seldom found the Captain at home after nightfall. When Enoc entered the parlour, the Captain assumed a look of solemnity, and said: "I've been wanting to see you, Mr. Huws, for some two weeks, and I've been thoroughly afraid of seeing you; but I've decided to go through with it tonight."

Enoc laughed, for he was in an excellent humour these days and said: "Why in the world would you be afraid to see me?"

"I'll tell you," said the Captain, "whatever the consequences might be. I hope, Mr. Huws, that after I've told you that of which my conscience cannot be easy without the telling, I hope, I say, you won't look on me as a dishonest or deceitful man, for I am neither the one nor the other. It is possible for the most upright man to fail in his endeavours and his judgment and though, so to speak, I can—if you'll permit me—congratulate myself on not being specially remarkable for failing in endeavours or in judgment, yet I do not maintain that I am entirely free and pure of the defects mentioned heretofore. Indeed, such men are few and far between, and I don't claim to be one of the few, though, in a manner of speaking, I flatter myself that if I'm not one of them, I am, if I don't deceive myself, one who's rather close to that brotherhood. I think you know me sufficiently well to believe that if I made a mistake I wouldn't have done it intentionally, and neither would the mistake be attributable, speaking generally, to a want of scientific knowledge, so far as that goes. But perhaps, in my innocence, I might take too much for granted. Such a thing is possible, I know. But rather than keep you too long in expectation, and be torturing my heart more than I ought; and allow me to tell you that what I'm going to tell you is the greatest sorrow I've ever known, and you know that I know something about great sorrows; but this is the greatest sorrow, believe me; in order to not keep you too long in ignorance, as I said, it comes to this, Mr. Huws; You won't be so angry as to never forgive me when I've told you, will you?"

"Go on, Captain Trefor," said Enoc, seriously enough, for he'd begun to believe, by this time, that the Captain was going to say he didn't approve of his taking Miss Trefor as his wife.

"But I'd like you to promise, thinking of what friends we've been, that you'll not be so angry as to never forgive me. But, I must confess that if you were, it would be no more than I deserve, though not what I deserve either, for I swear that I have, in the course of our transactions, been perfectly honest so far as my conscience goes. But this is it, Mr. Huws, and it almost makes me mad, but a feeling of duty and the call of a clear conscience compel me to tell you the tale. I've given up all future hope of finding lead in Coed Madog, and on thinking of all the anxiety and worry, and of how sure I was that we'd find lead there, and on thinking of all the money you and I have spent, though I have to say it's not what I spent but what you've spent that troubles me; on thinking of all this, I say, I'm almost driven mad, and I'm compelled to confess that I've made a mistake—the only mistake in a lifetime of mining—but I must admit it. And now, Mr. Huws, I am, in spite of everything, forced to come to the conclusion it would be futile to spend another farthing on the mine, and I'd like to be able to persuade you to make the same decision. But are you angry with me? Do you loathe and hate me with a complete and everlasting hatred, Mr. Huws?"

"I have trusted you from the beginning, as you know, Captain Trefor," said Enoc, "and if you believe it would be best to give the whole thing up, all right. The best of us make mistakes, and the man who speculates must sometimes look on losses and disappointments. It can't be helped, if that's the way things stand, and I don't care a single farthing about giving up the mine if there's no hope of lead there."

"You kill me with your kindness, Mr. Huws," said the Captain, putting his head in his hands, as if trying to cry, "but the money! You've spent a pile of it, dear Mr. Huws."

"It can't be helped," said Enoc "and don't worry about it, I haven't spent everything yet."

"Thank God for that," said the Captain, without removing his head from his hands. "Destroying poor Denman was enough, without destroying you too. But I've always been honest, God knows!"

"No one doubts it," said Enoc, "for you've lost too, and the disappointment's as great for you as it is for me. We're not the first to fail, and there's no point crying over spilt milk.

The Captain had achieved his object, and after saying a great deal more in the same vein, going over and over his grief that fate had gone against him till he'd won Enoc's full sympathy, he said, when Enoc was on the point of starting homeward:

"Mr. Huws, Susi's told me something that's like so much oil on the wound of my disappointment over the mine, which, briefly, so as not to keep you, is that you've fallen in love with one another, and that's not a thing to be wondered at, and that it will end some day, as such things usually do, by your coming together in marriage. And no matter what becomes of me in my old age, when I've been left alone, I must say the news has cheered me to no small degree; for it's too late in the day for me to follow my own interest, and seeing my only daughter in the care of a sober, good, kind man, quite capable of keeping her from want, will be, to say the least, a help to me when the time comes; and of necessity, that time can't be far away; to quote the Scriptures, if you will allow me so to do; 'Now lettest thou thy servant depart in peace'. I'll be happy to think of you as my son-in-law, and think my daughter's been so lucky; but remember

I'll consider you too just as lucky."

"Thank you for your good opinions of me," said Enoc, "and I'll do my best to be worthy of them. I know you couldn't praise Miss Trefor too highly; she's the best girl in the world, to my mind. And as to leaving you alone, that's out of the question. If it's agreeable to you, Captain Trefor, you can spend the rest of your days with me, and I'll do all in my power to make you happy."

"You kill me with your kindness, I say, Mr. Huws. But perhaps I'll not need so much care and kindness from anyone. Man proposes, God disposes, but we'll speak of that again."

Was the Captain, like Saul, among the prophets? After spending a little time in Miss Trefor's company, Enoc went home a happy man, so happy he didn't know how to be sufficiently thankful for his happiness.

50

THE LAST VENTURE

Next morning the Captain sent word to Sem Llwyd, telling him to inform the workmen of Coed Madog that, for particular reasons, work at the mine would cease at the end of the week, and that their services wouldn't be required till further notice. "But remember," said the Captain as a postscript, "that you, Sem, will not be in want while I have a penny." It was bad news for the workmen; but it was what they'd been expecting for some time, and they were surprised their work had continued for so long.

The Captain did nothing, 'so to speak', for a couple of days, except to contemplate and plan his daughter's marriage. He had so much faith in his organisational ability that he was determined to have his own way in making the arrangements in a style appropriate to the bride's situation and to give honour to the event in the sight of his neighbours. He spared neither expense nor trouble. His own position required that dignity be given to the event, and Mr. Huws had sufficient means to pay the bill. He was remarkably happy, particularly kind to his daughter, and treated himself to frequent glasses of whisky; this was, in his opinion appropriate to the circumstances. He'd have loved to have gone to his old companions in the Brown Cow and given them a subtle hint about the great event taking place very soon. But he was waiting for the stranger to leave, for he was obliged to admit to himself that the man's face reminded him of something he'd rather not think about. At considerable sacrifice, he stayed at home for two days and two nights. On the third night, such *hiraeth* came over him for the company in the Brown Cow that he was unable to resist. "And it's a certainty," said the Captain to himself "the old man will have gone by now." And to the

Brown Cow he went, where he had a warm welcome, and many were the inquiries about his health. To his great disappointment, however, the white-headed old gentleman was still in his corner, and appeared quite unconscious of the Captain's coming into the room; as usual, he was lost in his book. Having had Sem Llwyd's testimony, and indeed, after he had himself had a second look, he didn't seem so alike as the Captain had thought the first time he'd seen him. Yet the stranger reminded him of someone else, and made him feel uncomfortable. That night the Captain didn't stay late in the Brown Cow, and when he came home, Miss Trefor noticed he looked serious and worried; quite different from how he'd been for two days. When she asked him why, he said: "Haven't you heard the news, Susi?"

"What news?"

"Poor old Hugh Bryan's dead," said the Captain.

"What? Old Mr. Bryan, Oh dear! Oh dear!" said Susi, and a thousand things rushed into her mind. But Wil Bryan was the first of them. Where was he? Would he come home to bury his father? What sort of a man was he now? Was he as handsome? How could she face him? While these things ran through her mind, someone knocked at the door, and she went to open it. It was a bright; moonlit night, and when she opened the door, Susi saw a respectable white-headed gentleman. The stranger wanted to see the Captain. Susi led him into the parlour to her father. She was glad someone had come to visit him, to give her time to run and look after old Mrs. Bryan, for Susi couldn't forget the old times. And it was as well for her that she thought so, for otherwise she'd have been bound to see that when the old gentleman went into the parlour, her father's face went as white as chalk, and that his legs could scarcely support him as he rose to receive his visitor.

Susi snatched up a cloak and threw it round her head, so no one would recognize her, and ran to see Mrs. Bryan in her hour of need. She was there a long time—nearly an hour—and before she ran back, she'd heard enough from the old woman to make her uneasy. But she'd given Enoc her promise, and she wouldn't break that promise, come what may. On turning the corner of the street when hurrying home, she stopped suddenly; she saw her father and the gentleman, coming towards her. The two stood opposite Siop y Groes, and after a long discussion, she saw her father turn home without so much as shaking hands with the gentleman, and the latter knocking at Enoc's door. This explained the note she'd had from Enoc in the course of the day, saying he had an appointment with a gentleman that evening. Miss Trefor hurried off another way, so as to be home before her father. This was not difficult, for the old Captain walked slowly, with his hands behind his back and his eyes fixed on the ground, as if his soul had been stolen from him. Susi met him innocently in the lobby and asked if he needed anything from her before she went to bed.

"No, my girl." said the Captain, and his words sounded as though they came from the grave, but she didn't notice their tone; she had her own thoughts to trouble her. With such turmoil within her, Miss Trefor didn't sleep for some hours, and though she listened attentively, she didn't hear her father come to bed. At times she imagined she'd heard him pace up and down the parlour, but thought later it was all imagination. The next morning she rose early as usual; indeed she was downstairs before Kit. She went straight to the parlour, and was greatly alarmed by what she saw there. Her father lay on the sofa, seemingly in a deep sleep. On the table by his side were two empty whisky bottles. She saw too, the moment she entered the room, a letter addressed to her on the mantelpiece. She put it in her pocket and swept the empty bottles from sight, for she didn't like even Kit to know her father had been drinking heavily during the night. Having done so, she didn't really know whether she should leave her father to sleep off his drunkenness or wake him. But what if he slept himself to death? She decided to wake him. She went to him. He was sleeping soundly, and she hesitated to disturb him. She placed her hand lightly on his, and found it as cold as a lump of ice. She put her ear to his mouth. He wasn't breathing; the old Captain was, 'so to speak', as dead as a doornail.

As a general rule, Miss Trefor's self-possession was unequalled, and many times in the past, under the most painful circumstances, she'd shown a force of mind and such mastery of her feelings as to make Kit think her hard, when it wasn't hardness at all, but strength of mind. But the moment she realised her father was dead, her scream echoed round the whole house and she fell to the floor in a faint. This brought Kit, half dressed, to the room in a second, and seeing the unexpected, and thinking that the Captain and Miss Trefor—both of them—were stone dead, she cried out with all her strength, as women do, and rushed outside, still screaming. This brought several people to the house within a few minutes, and someone ran for the doctor. Before the doctor arrived—and as it happened, he was close by—it was discovered that Miss Trefor had fainted, but that the Captain had gone to join the Majority. When the doctor appeared, the room was, as is usual under such circumstances, full of people desirous of doing anything in their power, but with no power to do anything but consume the fresh air. After clearing out all but a couple, the doctor turned his attention to the most serious matter, namely the Captain, and while he was thus occupied, Miss Trefor began to revive, and soon came to herself. The doctor said what everyone knew—that the Captain was undoubtedly dead, and added what everyone didn't know, that the cause of death was heart disease, brought on by excessive mental labour. And after asking Miss Trefor a little about the circumstances and getting no reply, save that she'd found her father just as he'd found him, the doctor went away. Soon, the neighbours went away, and Miss Trefor and Kitty were left alone for a while. In her great trial, Miss Trefor thought of Enoc Huws, and asked Kit to go and fetch him and if he'd not already heard, to break the terrible news as gently as she could so as not to frighten him. Whilst Kit was on her way, Miss Trefor remembered the letter, opened it in fear and trembling, and read:

"My dear Susi,

I write these words to you from fear I won't see the morning, and indeed, so to speak, I don't care whether I see it or not, for life is now a heavy burden to me. My dear daughter, I love you dearly, but I know what you'll think of your father in a few days' time, and I'm most anxious to be taken away before I have to face you and face my neighbours; I feel sure I can't, and would rather die than do so. It's all over for me. My iniquity has been great and odious, and you'll be surprised I could hide it for so long. But I can hide it no longer; all will come out, and soon. God pursues me and I cannot flee; it's hard, and I can barely think. I've tried to pray but I can't, and it'll make no difference to my situation whether I'm here or in the other world by morning. What a mercy that your mother's gone before me! Oh, why was it not possible for you also to go before me, before all this came to light? I could never expect you to forgive me; it would be a miracle if you did. My dear daughter, I'm filled with remorse for having brought everlasting disgrace on your pure name. My life has been a life of deceit and hypocrisy, and I can only express surprise that the world was so easily deceived. And I have deceived, yes, even you, my dear daughter. The only good left in me, for years past, has been my love for you, my dear Susi; and for your sake I wish I could shed tears of fire, but I cannot; and that little good left in me has become my greatest sorrow. But for it I might feel some of the daring of a ... Well, I won't write the word. I won't torment your feelings, or cause you unnecessary pain by describing what I've been or what I am now. Indeed, I doubt whether I should have said as much as I have. This, I hope, is the end, but I can't leave without saying something. What breaks my heart most—if there can be a sorrow greater than the rest—is that Mr. Huws cannot, under the circumstances that will come to light, marry you; it's impossible, and the thought of what might become of you, my dear Susi, sets my soul on fire. Still I hope he'll be kind to you; he can't help it. God bless him and you too.

Of course if I am alive in the morning, and in my senses, you won't see this letter; but if I'm dead—and I hope you find me so—read it to yourself, keep its contents to yourself, and burn it. And now, my dear Susi, farewell forever, I hope.

Your wicked and unworthy father,

Richard Trefor.

P.S. If it's in your power at any time to do a favour for Sem Llwyd, do it; He was very faithful to me—R.T."

Miss Trefor's eyes had grown dull before she finished reading the letter, and as though unconsciously, she threw it in the fire. The letter was in flames when Kitty returned to find Miss Trefor prostrate, and whispering sadly: "Oh! Mr. Huws! Where's Mr. Huws, dear Kit?"

"Mr. Huws is very ill in bed, and a gentleman and the doctor have been with him all night," said Kit, crying. Another blow to poor Susi, and though she was normally so self-possessed, a mist passed over her eyes and she knew no more till she woke late that afternoon in her bed, and Kit and a neighbour watched over her.

That was a sad day in Bethel, as I well remember Didymus ably reporting in *the County Chronicle* the following week. In one house lay the body of old Hugh Bryan, a man who was once a respected and successful tradesman, but by venturing for lead had spent all his money and a good deal of other people's money too, and who later, by hard work and the help of his loving son, had paid every farthing of his debts and, happy and contented, had lived on little. In another house lay the mortal remains of the renowned Captain Trefor, a man noted for his uprightness, kindness and influence, one who had done a great deal for the neighbourhood by promoting speculation and providing employment, a man for whom respect in certain circles was unbounded. The hopes of a multitude would have hung on him for years to come, but now he'd taken his leave to receive his reward. And how beautiful it was, said some of his admirers, that he'd been taken away in his sleep. Sudden death, sudden glory! And it was no wonder—as it was so sudden—that his lovely daughter had been, so to speak, struck down. And no wonder either that the person who—had he lived but a few weeks more—the Captain would have welcomed as his son in law, had also been laid low. The grief of the district and the surrounding countryside was great and deep. But such calamities happen; they can't be prevented.

The next day, someone would arrive by train, having travelled a considerable distance; not to undo what had happened—that was impossible; but to pour a little oil on troubled waters.

51

THE AMERICAN

Now, in order to explain the last chapter, and indeed, to throw a little light on the whole story—a story it's time I brought to an end—I must tell what took place between Enoc Huws and the American on the night Captain Trefor died. During his stay in the Brown Cow, the stranger had, as I said earlier, called almost daily at Siop y Groes to buy cigars, for he was a constant smoker; and he and Enoc had had many an interesting conversation. It was clear to Enoc that here was a man who'd seen a lot of the world, and he'd learnt something from him every time they spoke. But the chief topic of conversation was always America, and no matter where they began, the old gentleman took care they ended up in the big Continent in the west. He'd said so much about the country, and was so full of its praises, that Enoc was almost eager to go there, and had it not been for certain circumstances, no doubt he'd have decided to go. Early in the day he was due to visit Captain Trefor, the old gentleman said he'd like to discuss a business matter with Enoc for an hour after the shop was shut. Enoc considered this quite an honour, and had invited the stranger to supper, and the invitation had been gratefully accepted. Following Enoc's orders, Miss Bifan prepared as good a supper as anyone could wish, for she was an able girl, much appreciated by Enoc. As I've said, the old gentleman went straight from Tŷ'n yr Ardd to Siop y Groes, and in the course of the supper, he and Enoc chatted amiably about this and that. After supper, they lit their cigars, and the gentleman spoke in Welsh—and they were the first words of Welsh Enoc had heard from him—and Enoc's eyes opened wide with surprise.

"I said to you this morning, Mr. Huws, that I wanted a word with you privately. I'm a Welshman as you see, and considering how little Welsh I've heard over the years, I hope you'll agree I've not become too much of a '*Dic Sion Dafydd*'[1]. I left Wales many years ago, more years than you can remember. I was driven from this country by trying circumstances. I wasn't poor; indeed, I think I was considered quite wealthy. I had, before I left, buried my parents, my only brother and my two sisters. I'd been married for many years, and had one daughter, and I believe I can say there wasn't a prettier or more virtuous girl around …" (here the old man's eyes moistened, and something caught his throat, and for a moment or two he couldn't go on). By and by, he continued; "Excuse me, Mr. Huws; the time comes vividly back to mind. After a short illness my wife died. That was a terrible blow to me. I felt more and more alone every day, and that my friends, my true friends, were in another world, and sometimes I longed to be allowed to join them. But I still had my daughter with me, and she was, at that time, worth more than all the world to me. As I've already said, so dear was she in my sight, I thought she had no equal. My business was quite large, and I had a young man—well, some fifteen years younger than I—clever and able—looking after things when difficulties prevented me paying attention to it. I entrusted everything to him; he lived in my house, and was looked on as one of us. For some time, I was in low spirits, and didn't care for the affairs of this world. In a while—mercifully, time restores us—I came to myself, and started to look at my books. I saw at once that things were not in order, and the young man realised I knew this. He didn't come to the office next morning, and when I made enquiries, I found he'd left the country. This created a doubt in my mind, and I devoted myself day and night to examining my affairs. I quickly discovered the young man I'd thought so much of had defrauded me of three hundred pounds. It was late at night when I returned home after making the discovery, and I

---

[1] '*Dic Sion Dafydd*'—someone who has forsaken the Welsh language in favour of English, generally for personal advancement or for the sake of fashion.

was, as you can imagine, horrified and angry, and intended to put the matter in the hands of the police at once. I told my daughter everything; for she was the only one I could talk to at the time. She was very frightened and put her arms round my neck and, weeping copiously, begged me not to say a word to anyone about it; three hundred pounds wasn't a lot to me and she wanted me to think of all his work and his fidelity. I listened to her, but little I knew then of the reason for her pleadings. I closed my eyes to it, and no one's heard a word of it from that day till this, for I could never refuse my daughter; she was my everything in those days. But my cup of sorrow was not yet full. The greatest and most bitter trial, more unbearable than all the rest together, awaited me. I won't go into detail. But try to imagine my feelings when I one day realised it hadn't been enough for the young man to steal three hundred pounds, but that he had also deceived and debased my daughter. A grandson was born to me before I knew or suspected anything. I almost went out of my mind, and thousands of times I've been thankful that the cause of all my misfortune was beyond my reach, for I'm sure I'd have strangled him, though I knew I'd be hanged the next day. I didn't look at or speak to my daughter for a month. I know I was mad; and God alone knows what anguish this caused us both later. Indeed, for I must tell you everything, I never again spoke to her. I saw her a few minutes before she died; and how lovely she was, even in the clutches of death (At this point the old gentleman broke down once more, and Enoc was in no better state), she begged me to forgive her, and said other things I still can't relate, though thirty-three years have passed. I was a stubborn fool! But I kissed her twice, and I've thanked God a thousand times for having done that. It's my only consolation. My daughter took this as a sign I'd forgiven her, a heavenly smile spread over her dear face, and her spirit took flight. For some time I was like a madman, and in my madness I sold all I owned. After putting the child into the care of an old woman and, giving her something for her trouble—not nearly enough—I went to America. But I couldn't leave my sorrows behind me in Wales; they were with me there just the same. I saw that the only medicine for me was to give myself entirely up to business. I was used to doing that, and after a time it brought salvation from sorrow; except that, now and again down the years it returned like a shower of rain. I took a fair amount of money to America, and made a lot more there. About nine months ago, my age demanded I give up the business—I felt I wasn't what I used to be—with the intention of living happily on my fortune. But I couldn't; I tried everything, but I wasn't happy. I had more time to think about the old times. In the end I decided to return to Wales to inquire about my grandson, if he was alive. I thought it was the only amends I could make for my folly. I determined that no one should know who I was till I found my grandson, and if he was worth acknowledging, I'd make him my heir. Now, Mr. Huws, I've put this plan into action, and I'm pleased to tell you that, after two months' discreet searching, I found my grandson a few weeks ago, and found him to be a man respected among his neighbours, a man I won't be ashamed of when we sail to America, a companion in my old age, and the heir to my wealth."

"Thank God," said Enoc from the bottom of his heart. "But tell me, sir; how did you find him?"

"I'll tell you some other time, Mr. Huws. You are my grandson; I am your grandfather," said the old gentleman, laying his face between his hands on the table.

It's not necessary to say Enoc was amazed, and when the reader recalls what he well knows—how weak were Enoc's nerves—it's also unnecessary to say the occasion was more than he could stand. In time, his grandfather continued: "But I've only told half the story. When I came back to Wales, I didn't imagine—or wish—to meet your father. I thought the devil would have parcelled him up long ago, for I'd handed him over to that gentleman before I left home. But he's a long time taking him. Your father is the man—if he's worthy of the name 'man'—who calls himself Captain Trefor.

That wasn't his baptismal name. His real name is Enoc Huws; and old Mrs. Amos gave you his name. I recognised him the first night I went to the Brown Cow. But to be sure, I took time to ask around and make discreet enquiries, and to look at him in more detail. He is your father, I'm sorry to say, one of the worst scoundrels on earth, as I told him tonight in his own house. And if it weren't for you and his pretty daughter, I'd have done away with him by tomorrow night. Do not the toes of one of your feet stick together? So do his, if you care to look. I know this is a terrible blow to you, though I, on the other hand, look on it as providential that I arrived in time to stop you marrying your sister. But don't give way; show you're a man; this was bound to come to light, and you should be thankful. Hold up your head, dear boy; don't give way to your feelings."

It was very easy to say, 'don't give way', but Enoc felt he'd been stabbed in the heart, and did give way. Mr. Davies didn't know his grandson, or how sensitive he was, or he'd have made the disclosure more gently. Enoc had to lie down on the sofa, and looked so ill as to slightly alarm his grandfather. He rang for Miss Bifan, and asked her to fetch a doctor at once, which she did. Enoc was carried to his bed, and his grandfather, Miss Bifan and the doctor attended him through the night.

52

THE LAST LOOK

Next morning, Enoc felt a little better and doubtless would have been able to leave his bed if Miss Bifan hadn't come suddenly into the room and told him that Captain Trefor had been found dead on the sofa. This was a second shock to his feelings, but Mr. Davies, his grandfather, received the news with surprise and a smile, saying quietly, as if to himself, "I knew he'd die in his clothes." Enoc thought constantly of Susi, and though the nature of his love had changed after learning she was his sister, it was not one iota less. His heart was close to breaking in his sympathy with her troubles, and several times in the course of that day he sent Miss Bifan to Tŷ'n yr Ardd, to enquire about her. What tormented Enoc was how he could tell Miss Trefor about their relationship, and about what he'd learned. His grandfather understood his difficulty and said: "Leave that to me, my boy. I know you're very anxious, but when we've buried Captain Trefor, we'll set about the matter. Everything's sure to end well, for all this is just the way of Providence and of God for bringing things to light, and into their right place. I feel happier this minute than I have for thirty three years."

Enoc, poor fellow, could not feel as his grandfather felt; he looked on him with mixed feelings; he'd brought a bitter experience upon Enoc; and yet he couldn't help thinking how providential had been his coming to Bethel; and if he'd waited a month or two more before making his appearance, what a great disaster would have happened. Enoc's mind was considerably eased when his grandfather said: "No one alive knows the story I've told you, my boy, and the Captain, as they call him here, has been silenced forever; and for your sake and the sake of his daughter, we must keep it to ourselves. Of course, we must offer some sort of sensible explanation to Miss Huws—I mean Miss Trefor—and we must make some arrangements for her, because of the understanding you had. I'm glad to hear she's a sensible girl, and will know how to behave when she learns everything, if indeed her father hasn't already told her, for I was there last night."

Enoc did his best to recover in order to go and console Miss Trefor, and his grandfather too did what he could, for the old man was now staying at Siop y Groes. Enoc wasn't strong enough to go out till the day of the Captain's funeral. But Susi hadn't been left alone. There had been another young man taking every care of her for the last two days, and though he'd come home to painful circumstances of his own, he'd given her a great deal of comfort. Was Susi unfaithful to Enoc? Impossible. Her word was as strong as any statute. But Wil was so kind, and so handsome, and had so much to say, and so on, and so on ...

It had been intended to bury the Captain and Hugh Bryan on the same day, but as the former was swelling, they had to bury him a day early. Leaving his grandfather in the parlour of Siop y Groes with a box of cigars by his side, Enoc made his way, with difficulty, to Tỳ'n yr Ardd in time for the funeral. Of course, it was with new and strange feelings that he set out to see Miss Trefor, and he was never more surprised in his life than when he found her sitting on the sofa in the little parlour, like an picture, with her hand in that of Wil Bryan. When Enoc appeared, Susi pulled her hand free, and looked him straight in the face, as if to say: "Don't doubt me, Mr. Huws; I'm still faithful to you." She squeezed his hand, broke out in tears, and said, half choking: "Wil, here's the best man in the world."

Enoc and Wil exchanged a friendly handshake, for by now Enoc felt not a shred of envy towards Wil, and Wil too, was enough of a gentleman, having heard from his mother that Susi and Enoc were engaged, to feel kindly and warmly disposed towards him. But before they had chance to talk came the confusion and noise of the coffin being carried downstairs, and of someone fetching chairs; and Mr. Brown the parson was at the door with his book. Wil and Enoc walked together in the funeral procession, and the latter felt how weak and insignificant he was next to Wil, and how much better a match Wil would be for Susi. Wil thought about the old Captain they were carrying to his distant home. What a change it would be for him to have to be silent; and unless he'd changed, Wil was sure the first thing old Trefor would do—wherever he'd ended up—would be to try and persuade someone to speculate. Wil honestly considered his gaffer—that is, his father, who'd be buried the next day—would have a better chance of advancement. Of course he didn't say so, but such were his thoughts at the funeral.

As they stood round the grave and Mr. Brown told of the certain hope of everlasting life for his dear brother, Wil happened to raise his head, and who should he see nearby, smartly dressed, but Thomas Bartley. Thomas, believing the neighbourhood had had a happy deliverance that day, had come out in his best suit for the funeral, the suit he'd worn when he went to Bala to see Rhys Lewis. The black dress coat was not one iota more worn, and the big white collar as stiff as ever. When Wil spotted him, Thomas was holding his big beaver hat to his right ear, as though listening to what it had to say, and he looked oddly devotional. The sight of him was the biggest treat Wil had had for years, and a thousand amusing memories crowded his mind, and he had to hide his face lest people thought he was joking at so solemn an event. Thomas had also seen Wil, and the moment the service ended, he strode over and, shaking hands heartily, said: "Well, old friend; you've turned up at last, then? Where've you been, then?"

"In Birmingham lately, Thomas," said Wil.

"I thought so: I knew you'd be abroad somewhere, or we'd 'ave 'eard about you afore now. You know what, you've turned into a strapping lad. Are you thinking of stayin' a while?"

"I'll be here for a bit, anyway. How's Barbara, Thomas?" asked Wil.

"She's always acomplaining of 'er limbs, you see, very bad. You'll come over, won't you? You'll 'ave a lot to tell us, I'm sure. There's food in the house, remember. Don't be a stranger."

"I won't, Thomas. I'll be over as soon as this business is over," said Wil.

"Yes, and a big business it is, too, and we're lucky it only 'appens once a lifetime, or I don't know 'ow we'd cope," said Thomas.

Two days later, on the day after Hugh Bryan's funeral, Enoc and his grandfather went to Tŷ'n yr Ardd. The grandfather took on the unpleasant task of telling Miss Trefor of her relationship to Enoc. Before setting out, Enoc and his grandfather had decided, in order to spare Miss Trefor's feelings, not to mention her father's dishonesty while in Mr. Davies' service. The meeting lasted several hours, but nothing would be gained by giving an account, for there were tears and lamentations, and there's no pleasure in hearing such things. Enoc did one thing he'd never done before, strange to say; he kissed Miss Trefor. And all's well that ends well.

A few days later, Miss Trefor sold all the furniture from Tŷ'n yr Ardd and everything that had belonged to her father, and went to live at Siop y Groes, taking Kit with her. Mr. Davies continued to live with Enoc, and Wil Bryan divided his time between consoling his widowed mother, and amusing the family—for they were a family—at Siop y Groes. After a few months, Mr. Davies became restless to return to America, but was unwilling to do so till all had been brought to a safe and secure conclusion. The pace of life quickened; one morning, without the neighbours knowing, Wil and Susi were made husband and wife in the old parish church. Enoc acted as best man and Miss Bifan as bridesmaid, and Enoc's grandfather gave away the bride.

When the ceremony was over, Wil and Susi started to leave, but Mr. Brown and Mr. Davies called out together: "Stop; we haven't finished yet," and Enoc said: "One good turn deserves another." Wil became best man and Susi the bridesmaid; and Enoc and Miss Bifan were married then and there. It had been a secret between Mr. Brown, Mr. Davies, Enoc, and his new love. The company, Mr. Brown included, returned to Siop y Groes to enjoy an excellent breakfast. Only one thing was wanting in the arrangements, according to Mr. Brown:

"You should have given us a little wine, Mr. Huws, on such an occasion. You Calvinists never know how to do things properly."

Enoc himself felt there was something wanting, but scarcely believed the want lay in that direction. The two married couples, along with Kitty and Mr. Davies, left on the midday train. After a week, Wil and his wife returned to Siop y Groes but neither Enoc nor his wife, nor Mr. Davies, nor Kit, were seen again in Bethel.

Wil was now the owner of Siop y Groes. How the shop became his, no one has the right to know, and I'm not going to say. He took his old mother to live there, and Susi was very kind to her as long as she lived. Like his predecessor, Wil Bryan was a successful tradesman, and soon became a man of influence in the town. In his first winter back in his old home, he gave a series of lectures in the Methodist schoolroom, which made his name. The subject of the lectures was 'The Nature of Man'. Wil used that title rather than 'Human Nature' so as to meet the literary tastes of the different denominations. The schoolroom was crowded every night, though the tickets cost sixpence. Thomas Bartley took two tickets for each lecture, one for himself and one for Barbara, though poor Barbara could not surmount the door step, due to 'pain in her limbs'. Thomas' fidelity in attending the lectures was so great that Wil insisted he act as chairman for the last of the lectures, and the old brother of Twmpath thought it a great honour, and it created an undying envy in Sem Llwyd's breast towards him. The night Thomas Bartley was chairman was a night like no other. Seven hundred tickets were bought, though the schoolroom only held two hundred. Wil's lectures, written in shorthand, are somewhere among my papers, if I can only find them. But as the trials of Enoc Huws are the subject of my story, and he now lives the life of a gentleman in Chicago, where he's greatly respected, it would be as well to end the story here as anywhere else, and perhaps some would say I should have ended it long ago.

THE END